Emmanuel Guib Marc Boutavant

ARIOL

Top Dog

PAPERCUTZ™
New York

ARiOL Graphic Novels available from PAPERCUTZ™

ARIOL graphic novels are also available digitally wherever e-books are sold.

ARiOL
Just a Donkey Like You and Me
PAPERCUTZ

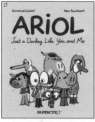

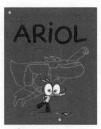

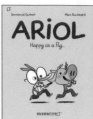

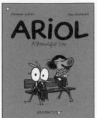

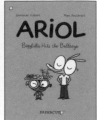

Graphic Novel #1
"Just a Donkey Like You and Me"

ARiOL

Graphic Novel #2
"Thunder Horse"

ARiOL
Happy as a Pig...
PAPERCUTZ

Graphic Novel #3
"Happy as a Pig..."

ARiOL
A Beautiful Cow

Graphic Novel #4
"A Beautiful Cow"

ARiOL
Bizzbilla Hits the Bullseye
PAPERCUTZ

Graphic Novel #5
"Bizzbilla Hits the Bullseye"

ARiOL

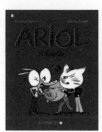

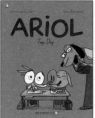

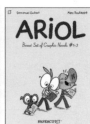

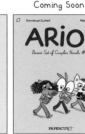

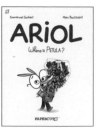

Graphic Novel #6
"A Nasty Cat"

ARiOL
Top Dog
PAPERCUTZ

Graphic Novel #7
"Top Dog"

ARiOL
Boxed Set of Graphic Novels #1-3
PAPERCUTZ

Boxed Set of Graphic Novels #1-3

Coming Soon

ARiOL
Boxed Set of Graphic Novels #4-6
PAPERCUTZ

Boxed Set of Graphic Novels #4-6

ARiOL
Where's PETULA?
PAPERCUTZ

"Where's Petula?" Graphic Novel

ARIOL graphic novels are available for $12.99 only in paperback, except for "Where's Petula?" which is $9.99. The ARIOL Boxed Sets are $38.99 each. Available from booksellers everywhere. You can also order online from papercutz.com. Or call 1-800-886-1223, Monday through Friday, 9 – 5 EST. MC, Visa, and AmEx accepted. To order by mail, please add $4.00 for postage and handling for first book ordered, $1.00 for each additional book and make check payable to NBM Publishing. Send to: Papercutz, 160 Broadway, Suite 700, East Wing, New York, NY 10038.

papercutz.com

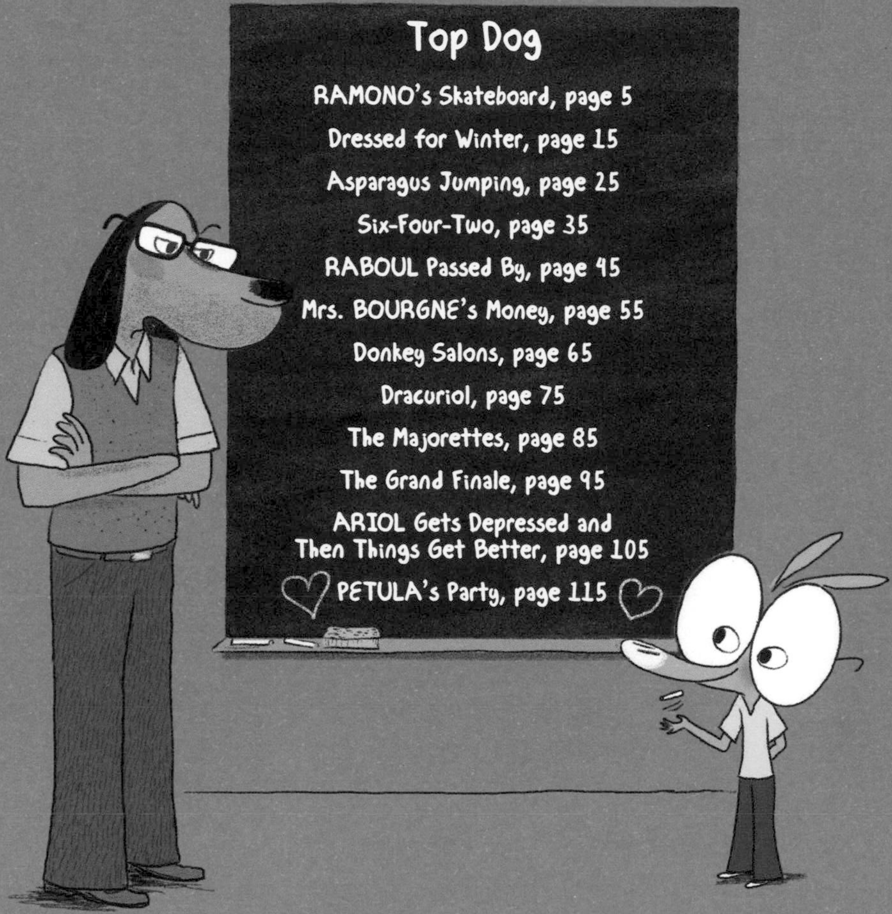
Top Dog
RAMONO's Skateboard, page 5
Dressed for Winter, page 15
Asparagus Jumping, page 25
Six-Four-Two, page 35
RABOUL Passed By, page 45
Mrs. BOURGNE's Money, page 55
Donkey Salons, page 65
Dracuriol, page 75
The Majorettes, page 85
The Grand Finale, page 95
ARIOL Gets Depressed and Then Things Get Better, page 105
PETULA's Party, page 115

To Miss Miermon,
— Emmanuel Guibert

L
j gn
ARIOL
V.07

ARIOL

#7 "Top Dog"

Emmanuel Guibert — Writer
Marc Boutavant — Artist
Rémi Chaurand — Colorist
Joe Johnson — Translation
Bryan Senka — Letterer
Jeff Whitman — Production Coordinator
Bethany Bryan — Associate Editor

Jim Salicrup
Editor-in-Chief

Volume 7: Le maître chien © Bayard Editions, 2012

ISBN: 978-1-62991-280-6

Printed in China
Manufactured by Regent Publishing Services, Hong Kong,
Printed December 2015 in Shenzhen, Guangdong, China

Papercutz books may be purchased for business or promotional use. For information on bulk purchases
please contact Macmillan Corporate and Premium Sales Department at (800) 221-7945 x5442.

Distributed by Macmillan
First Papercutz Printing

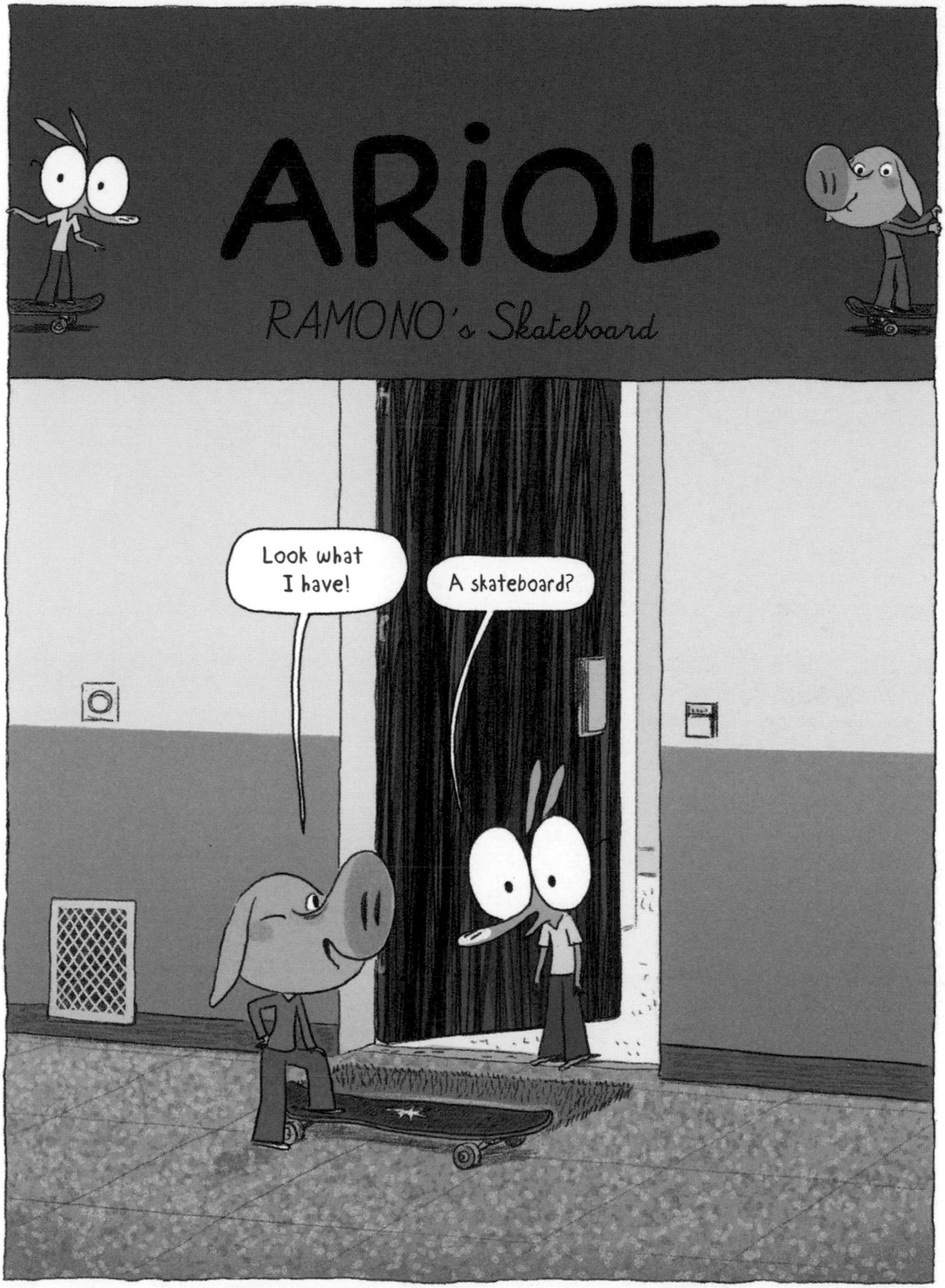
ARiOL
RAMONO's Skateboard
Look what I have!
A skateboard?

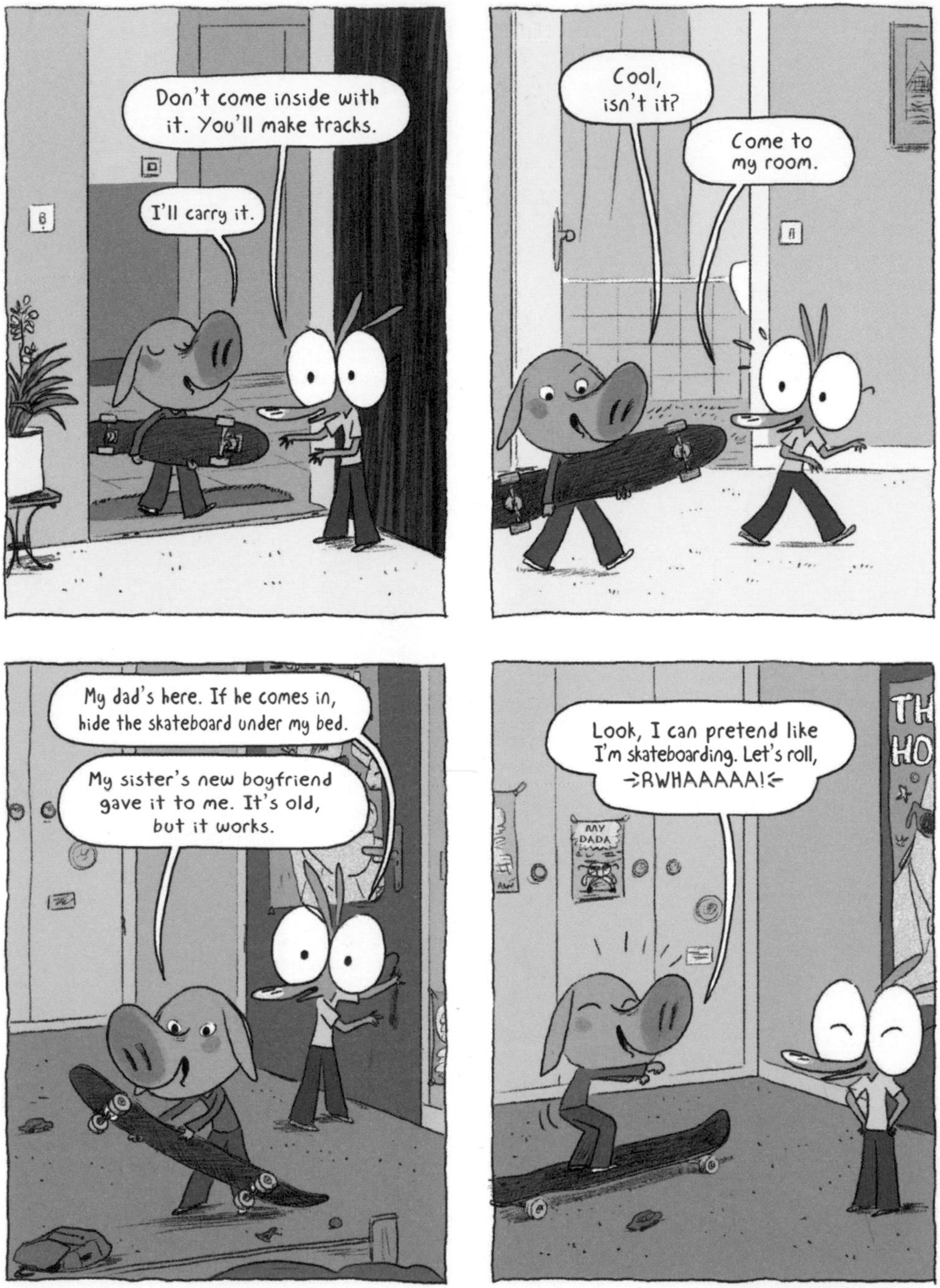
Don't come inside with it. You'll make tracks.
I'll carry it.
Cool, isn't it?
Come to my room.
My dad's here. If he comes in, hide the skateboard under my bed.
My sister's new boyfriend gave it to me. It's old, but it works.
Look, I can pretend like I'm skateboarding. Let's roll, ⇒RWHAAAAA!⇐
MY DADA

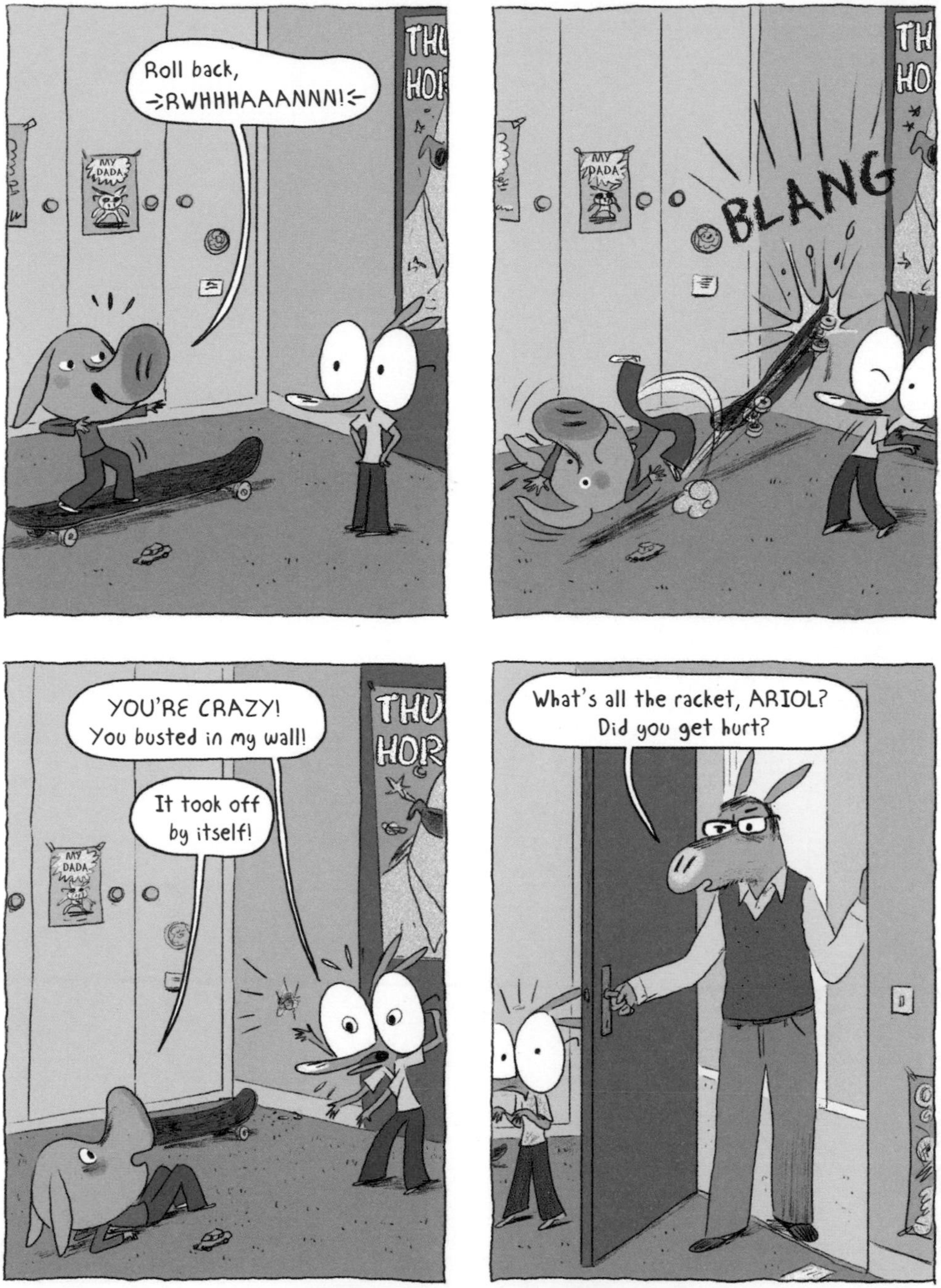
Roll back,
RWHHHAAANNN!
BLANG
YOU'RE CRAZY! You busted in my wall!
It took off by itself!
What's all the racket, ARIOL? Did you get hurt?

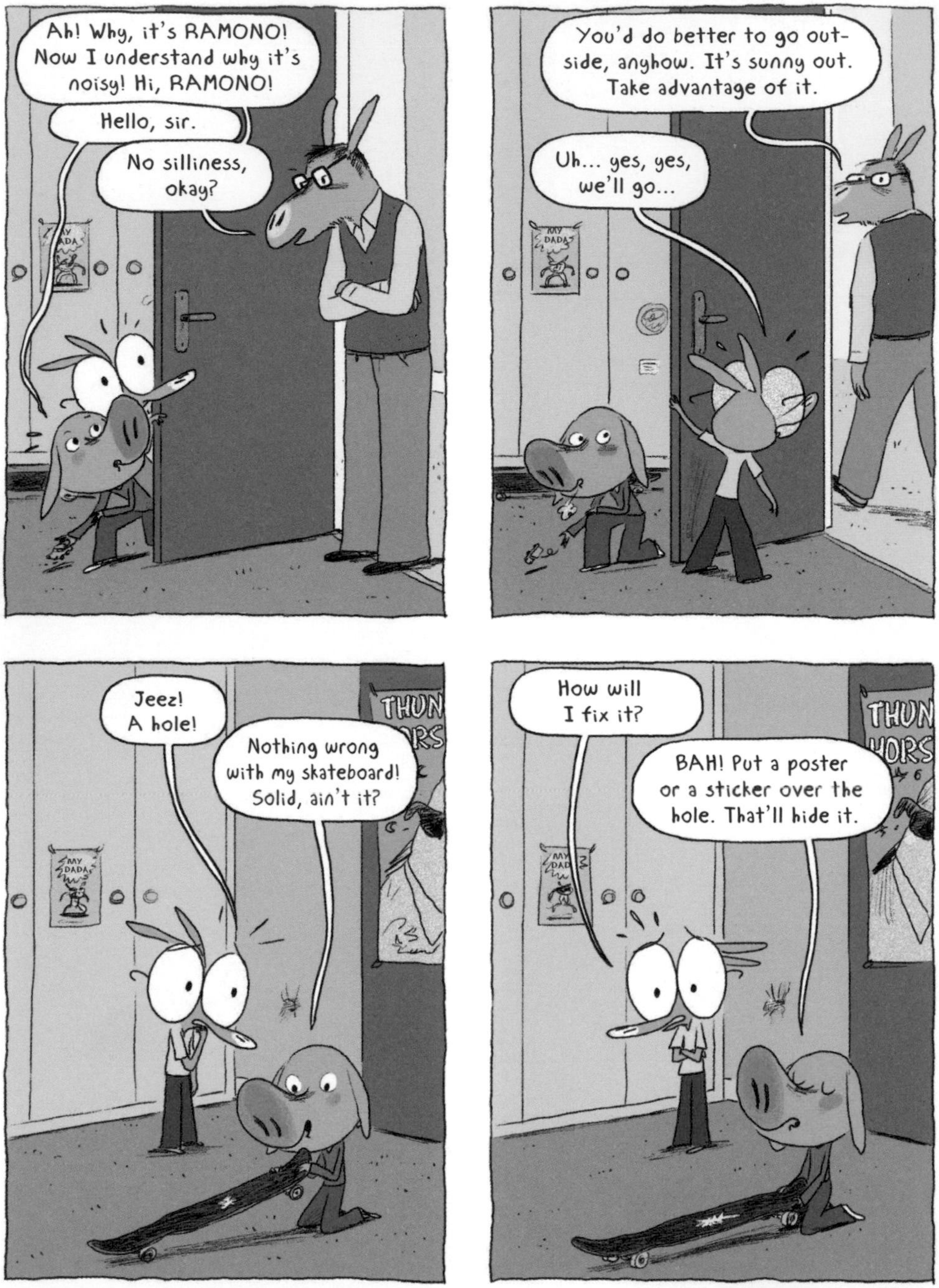
Ah! Why, it's RAMONO! Now I understand why it's noisy! Hi, RAMONO!
Hello, sir.
No silliness, okay?
You'd do better to go outside, anyhow. It's sunny out. Take advantage of it.
Uh... yes, yes, we'll go...
MY DADA
Jeez! A hole!
Nothing wrong with my skateboard! Solid, ain't it?
THUN
ORS
How will I fix it?
BAH! Put a poster or a sticker over the hole. That'll hide it.

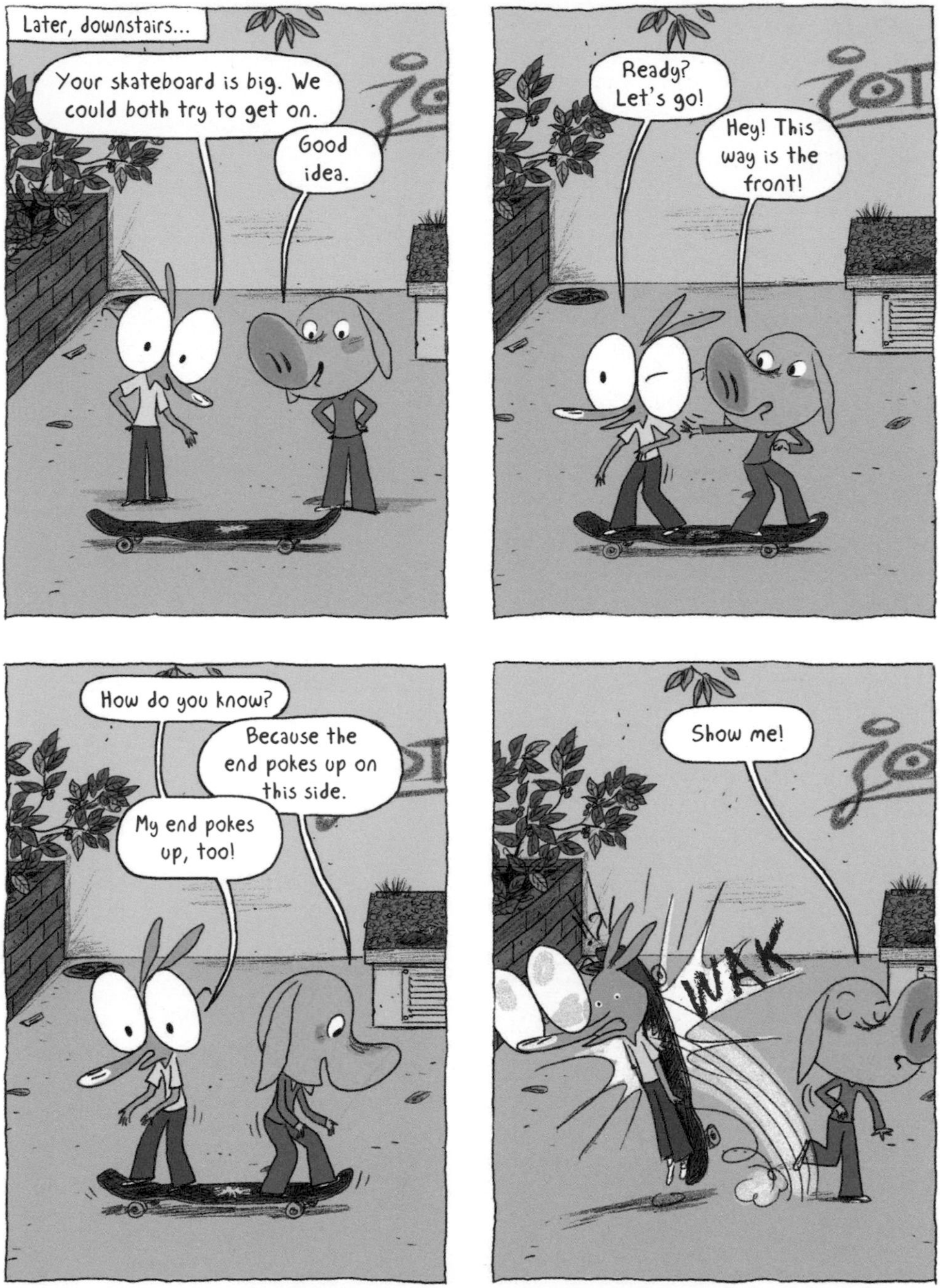

Later, downstairs...
Your skateboard is big. We could both try to get on.
Good idea.
Ready? Let's go!
Hey! This way is the front!
How do you know?
Because the end pokes up on this side.
My end pokes up, too!
Show me!
WAK

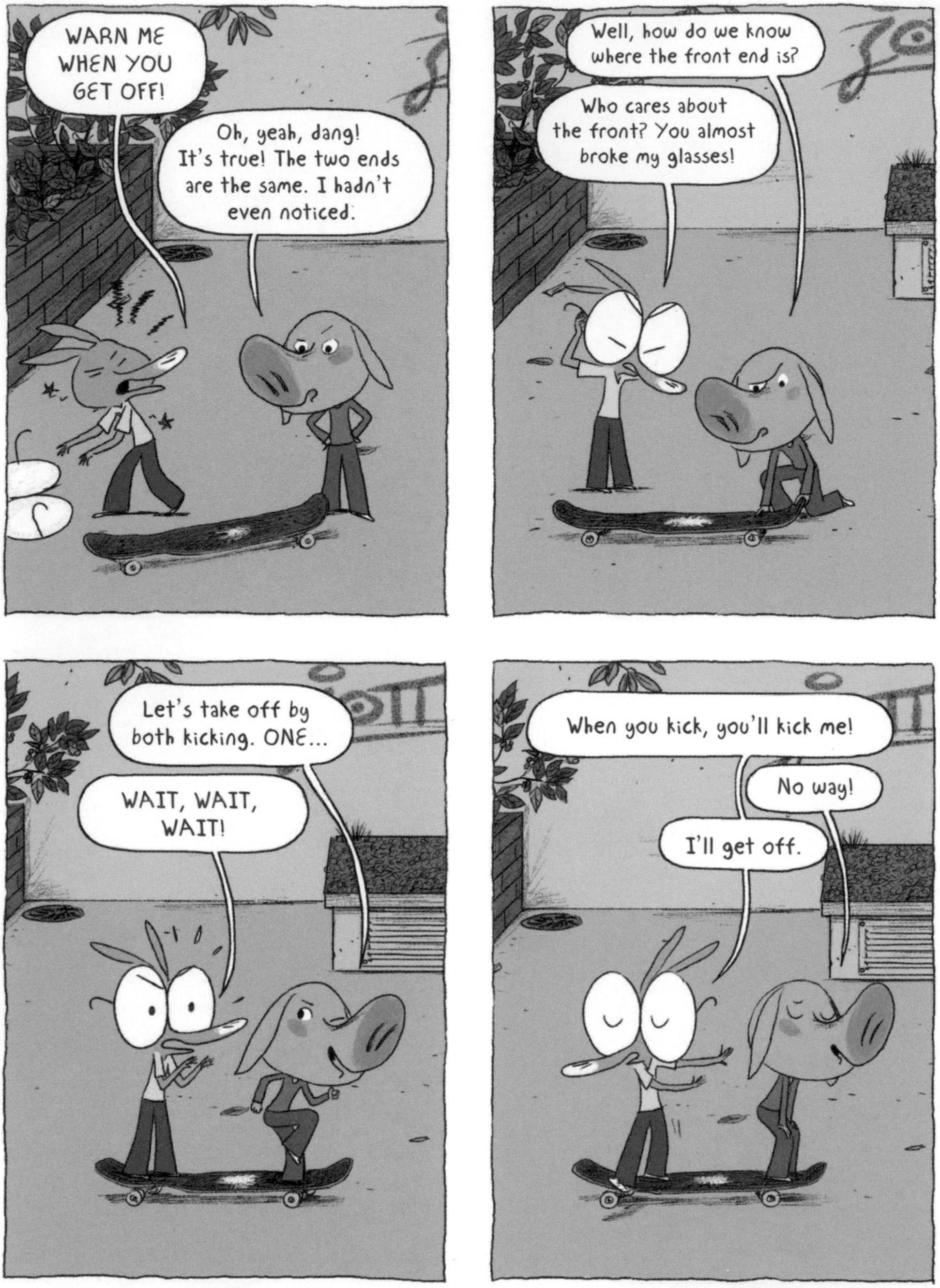
WARN ME WHEN YOU GET OFF!
Oh, yeah, dang! It's true! The two ends are the same. I hadn't even noticed.
Well, how do we know where the front end is?
Who cares about the front? You almost broke my glasses!
Let's take off by both kicking. ONE...
WAIT, WAIT, WAIT!
When you kick, you'll kick me!
No way!
I'll get off.

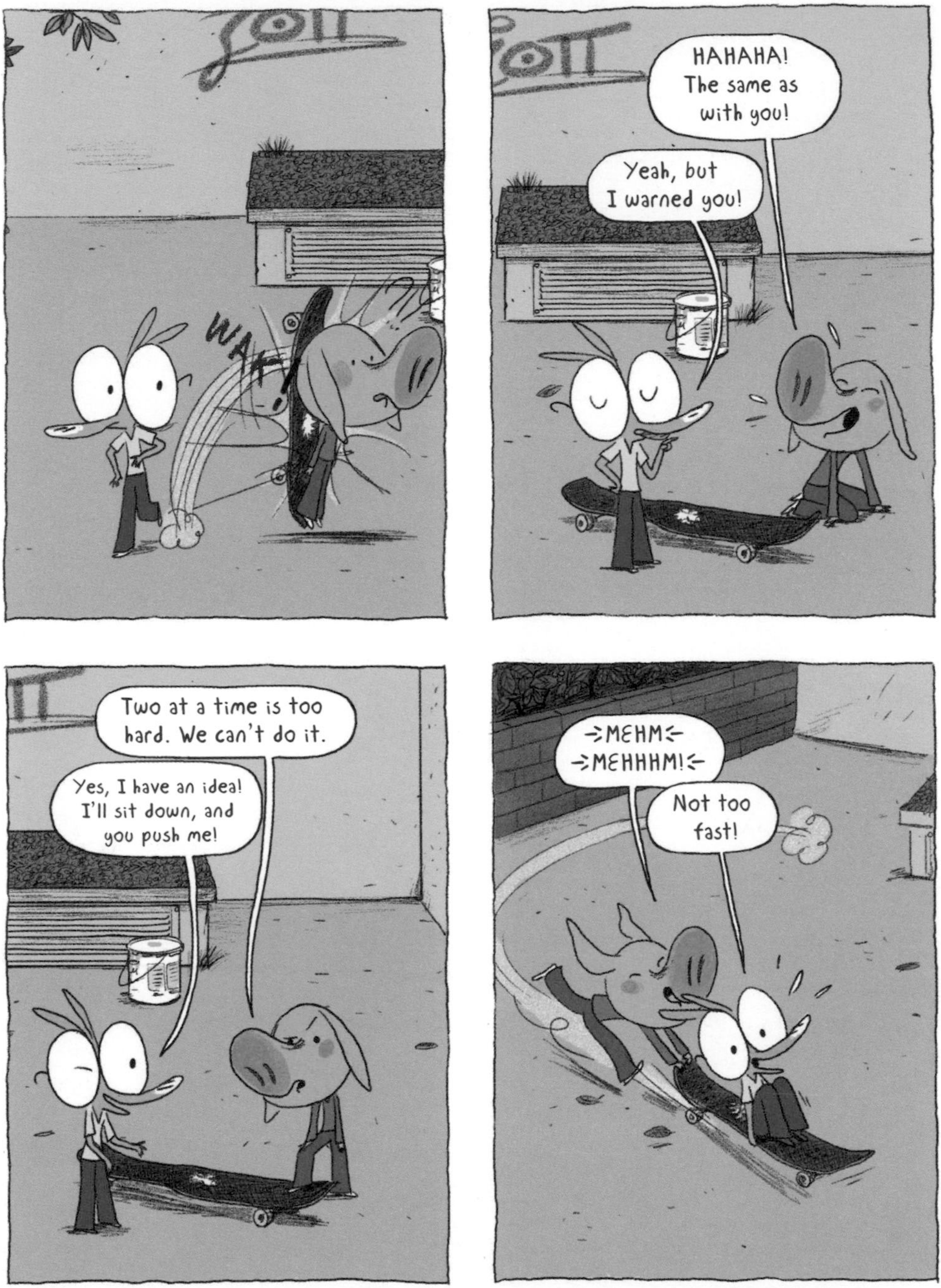
WAK!
HAHAHA! The same as with you!
Yeah, but I warned you!
Two at a time is too hard. We can't do it.
Yes, I have an idea! I'll sit down, and you push me!
MEHM MEHHHM!
Not too fast!

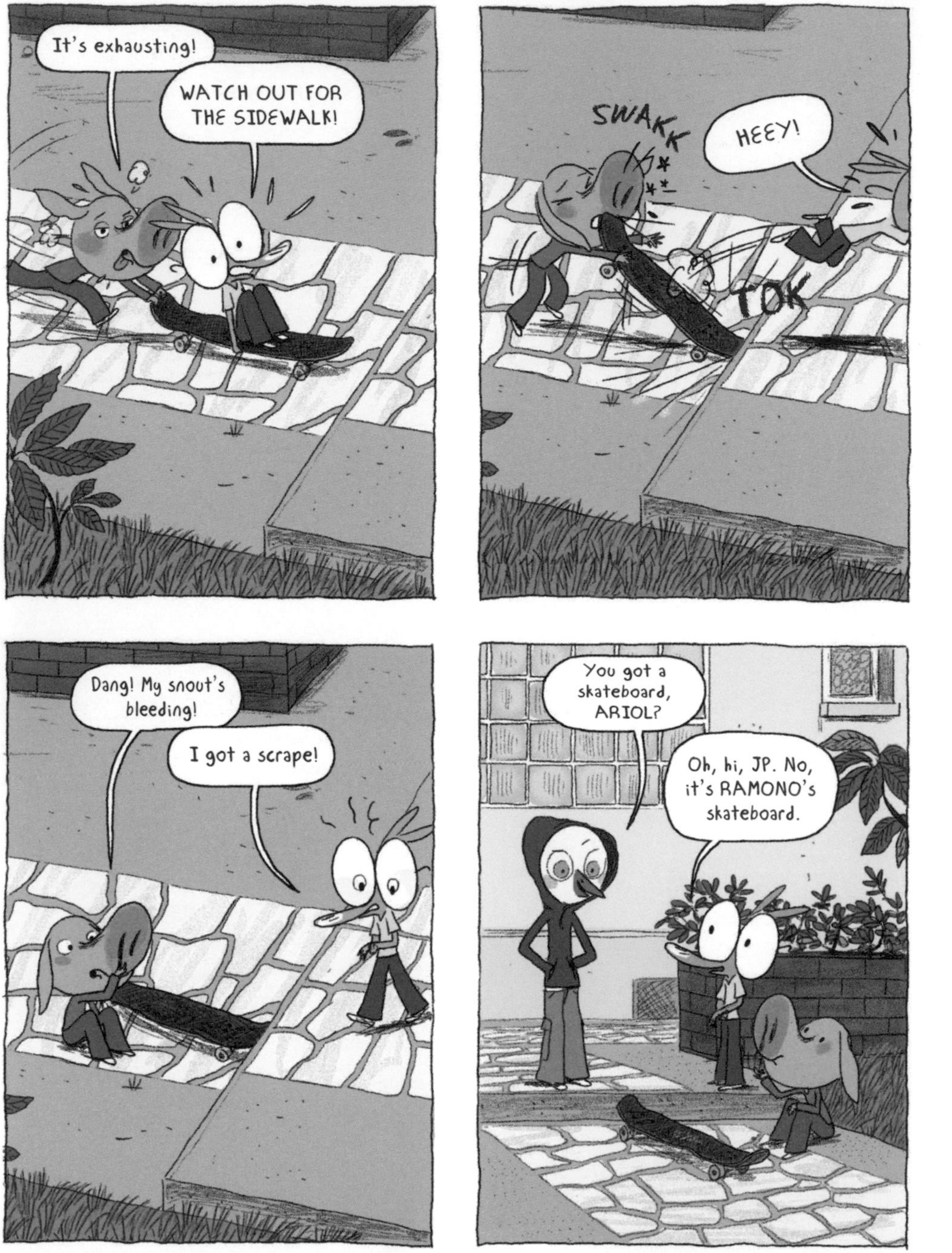
It's exhausting!
WATCH OUT FOR THE SIDEWALK!
SWAKK
HEEY!
TOK
Dang! My snout's bleeding!
I got a scrape!
You got a skateboard, ARIOL?
Oh, hi, JP. No, it's RAMONO's skateboard.

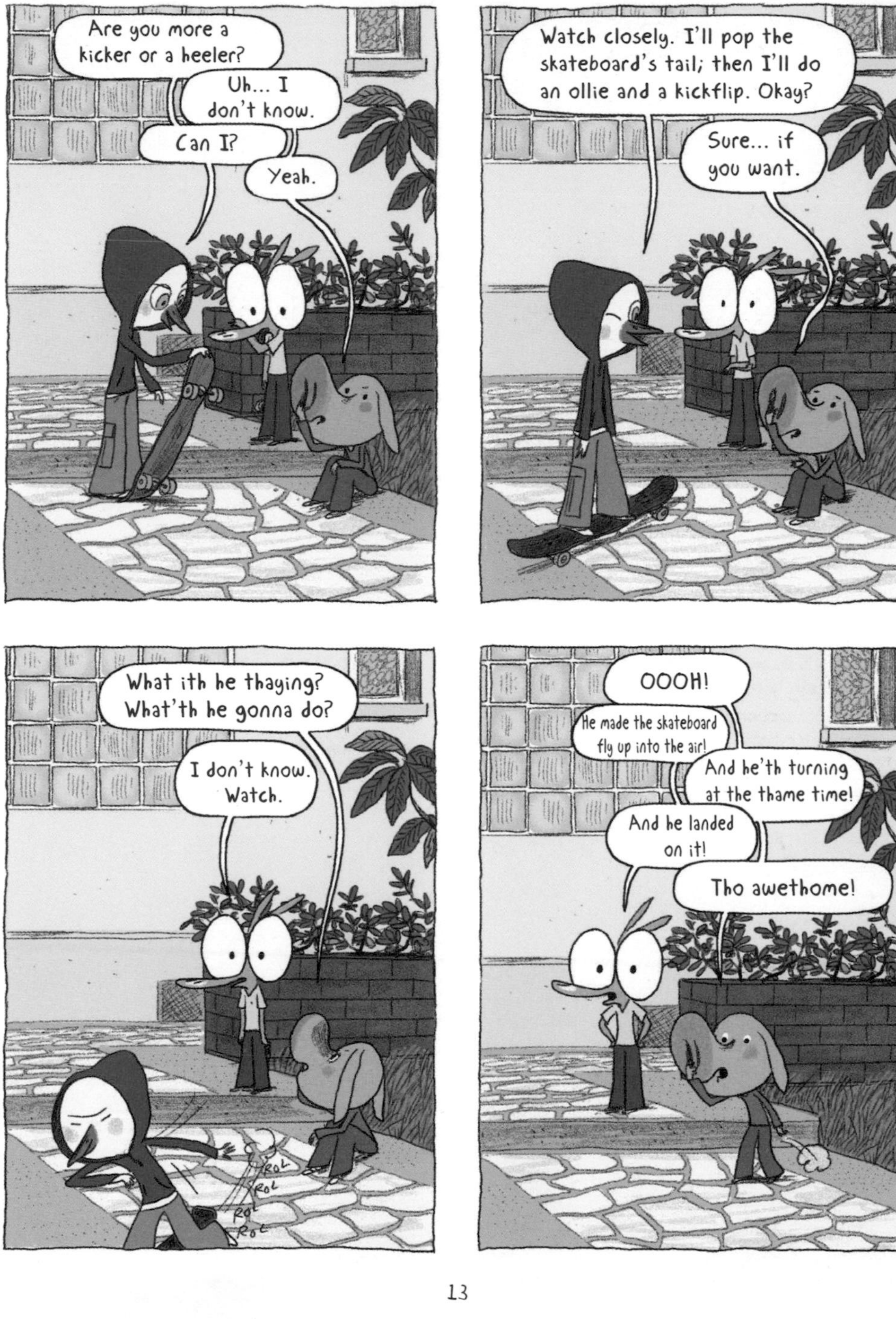
Are you more a kicker or a heeler?
Uh... I don't know.
Can I?
Yeah.
Watch closely. I'll pop the skateboard's tail; then I'll do an ollie and a kickflip. Okay?
Sure... if you want.
What ith he thaying? What'th he gonna do?
I don't know. Watch.
OOOH!
He made the skateboard fly up into the air!
And he'th turning at the thame time!
And he landed on it!
Tho awethome!

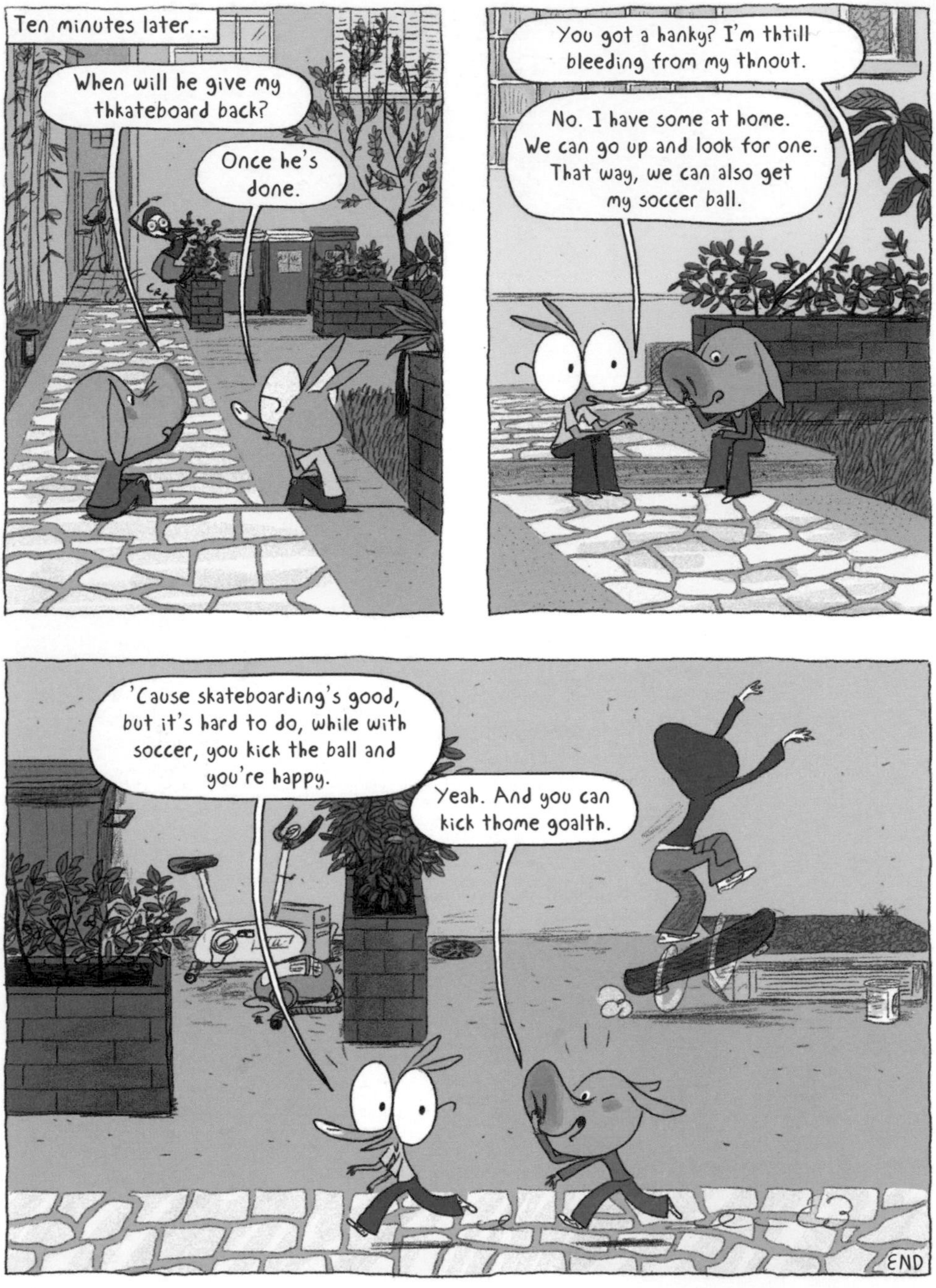
Ten minutes later...
When will he give my thkateboard back?
Once he's done.
You got a hanky? I'm thtill bleeding from my thnout.
No. I have some at home. We can go up and look for one. That way, we can also get my soccer ball.
'Cause skateboarding's good, but it's hard to do, while with soccer, you kick the ball and you're happy.
Yeah. And you can kick thome goalth.
END

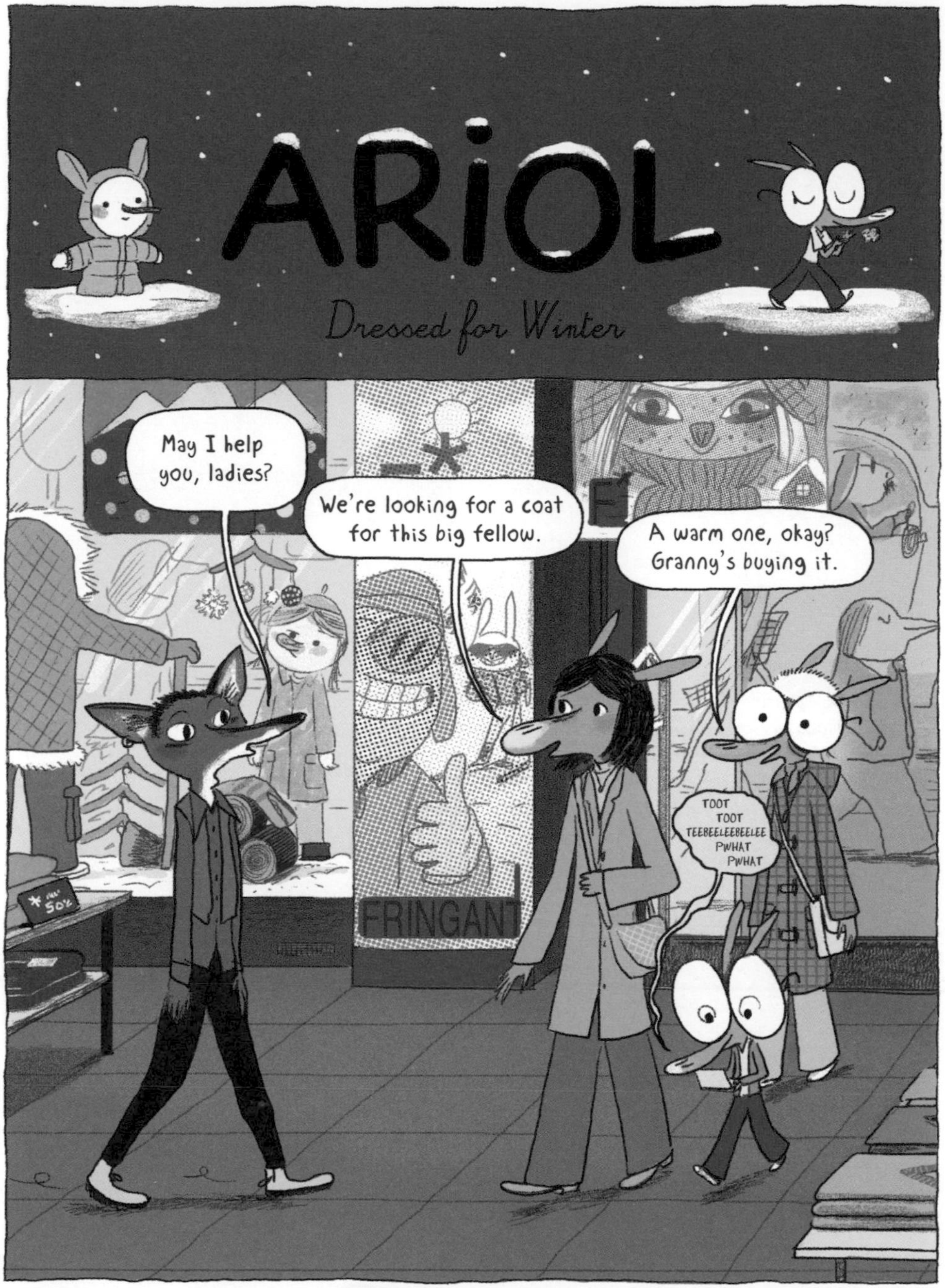
ARiOL
Dressed for Winter
May I help you, ladies?
We're looking for a coat for this big fellow.
A warm one, okay? Granny's buying it.
TOOT TOOT TEEBEELEEBEELEE PWHAT PWHAT
FRINGANT
50%

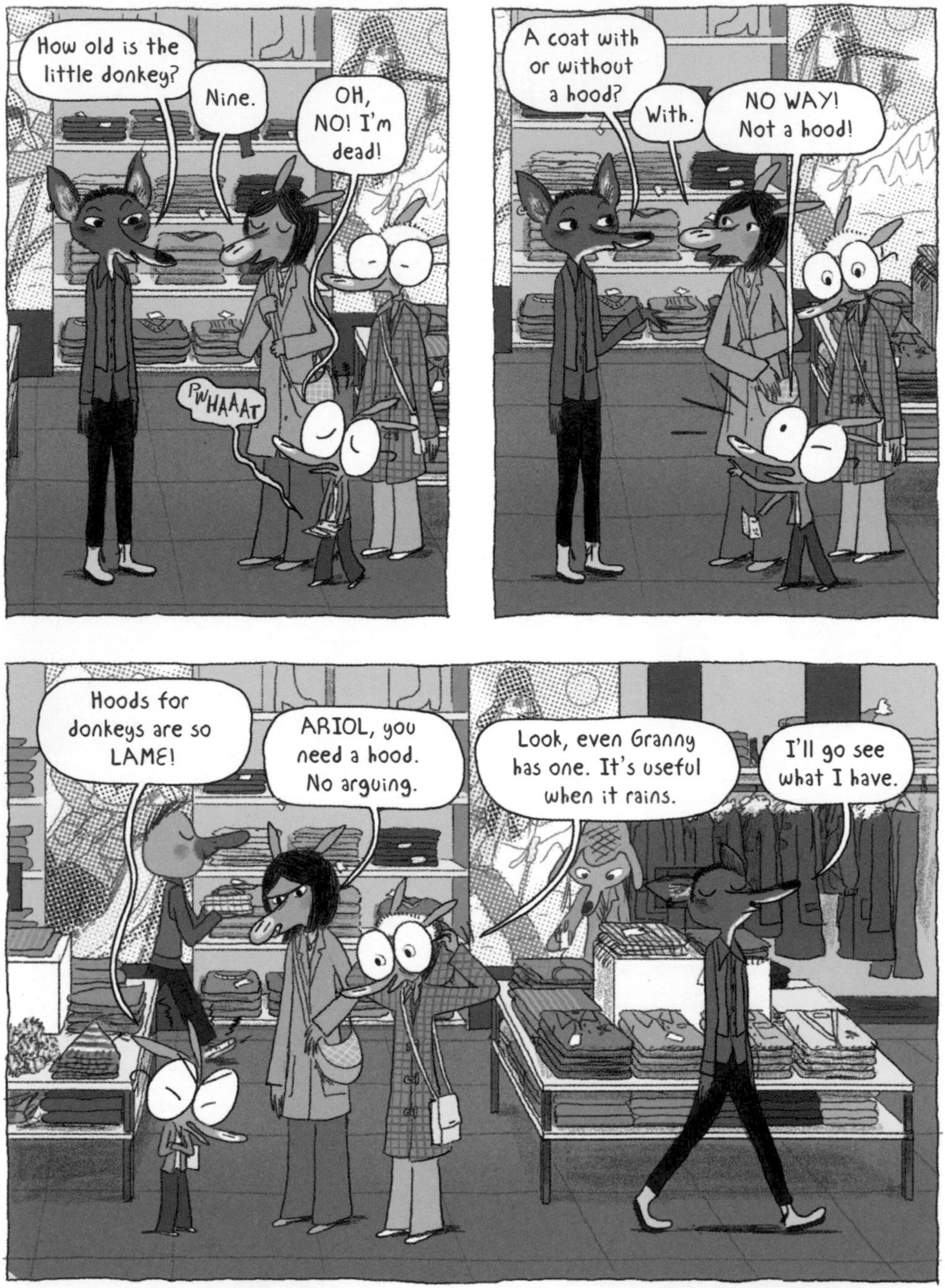
How old is the little donkey?
Nine.
OH, NO! I'm dead!
PWHAAAT
A coat with or without a hood?
With.
NO WAY! Not a hood!
Hoods for donkeys are so LAME!
ARIOL, you need a hood. No arguing.
Look, even Granny has one. It's useful when it rains.
I'll go see what I have.

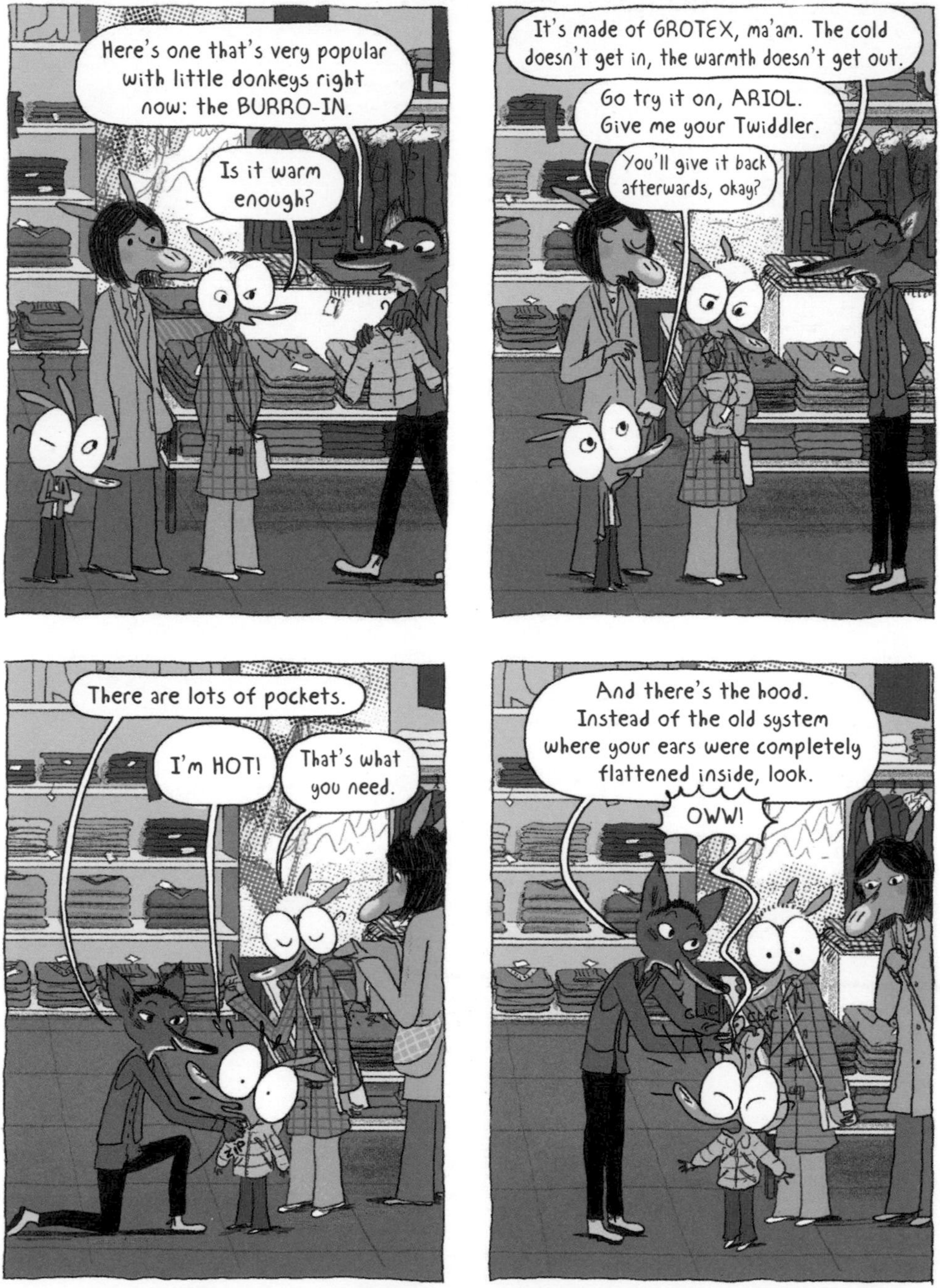
Here's one that's very popular with little donkeys right now: the BURRO-IN.
Is it warm enough?
It's made of GROTEX, ma'am. The cold doesn't get in, the warmth doesn't get out.
Go try it on, ARIOL. Give me your Twiddler.
You'll give it back afterwards, okay?
There are lots of pockets.
I'm HOT!
That's what you need.
ZIP
And there's the hood. Instead of the old system where your ears were completely flattened inside, look.
OWW!
CLIC
CLIC

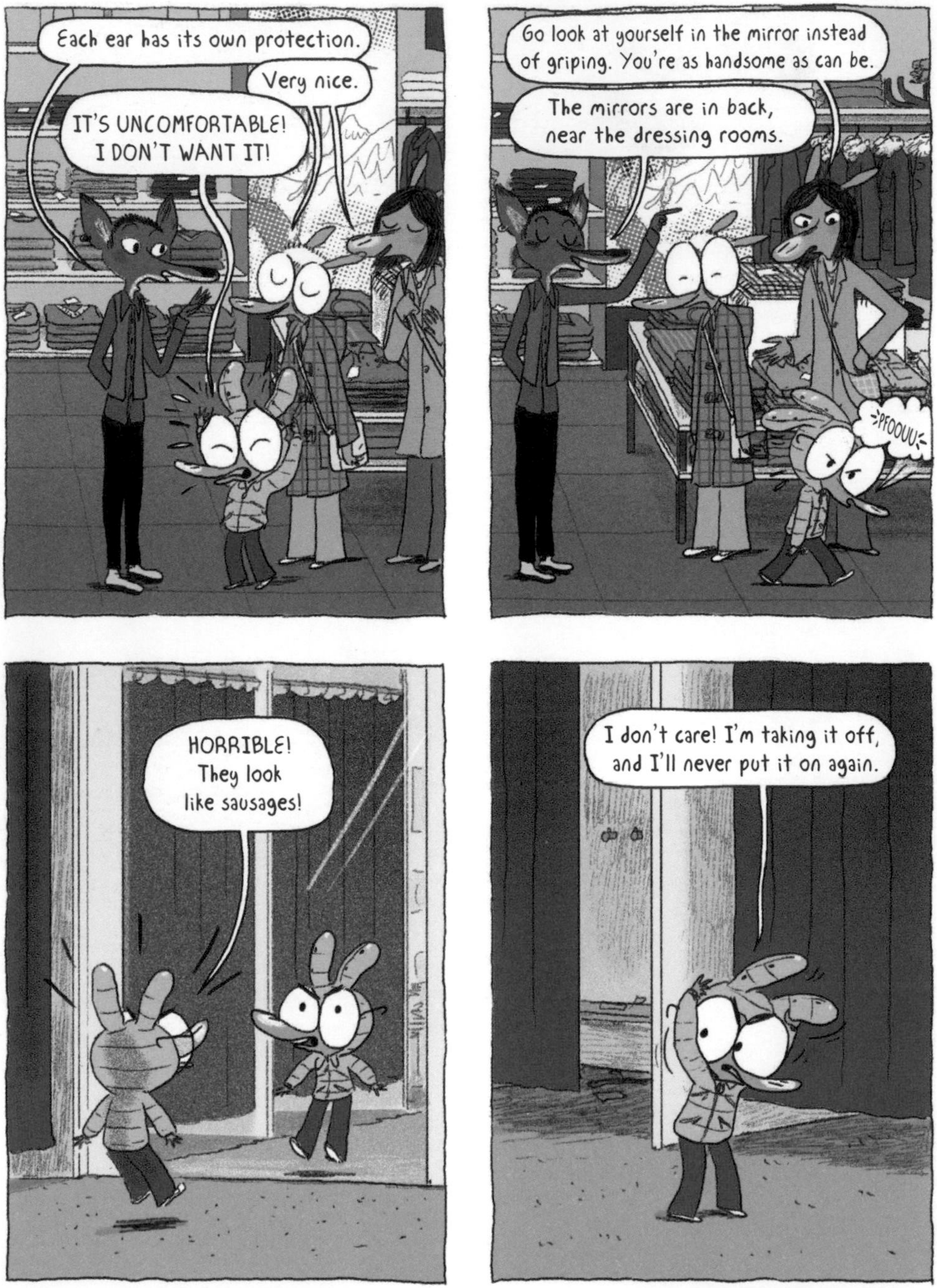
Each ear has its own protection.
Very nice.
IT'S UNCOMFORTABLE! I DON'T WANT IT!
Go look at yourself in the mirror instead of griping. You're as handsome as can be.
The mirrors are in back, near the dressing rooms.
PFOOUU
HORRIBLE! They look like sausages!
I don't care! I'm taking it off, and I'll never put it on again.

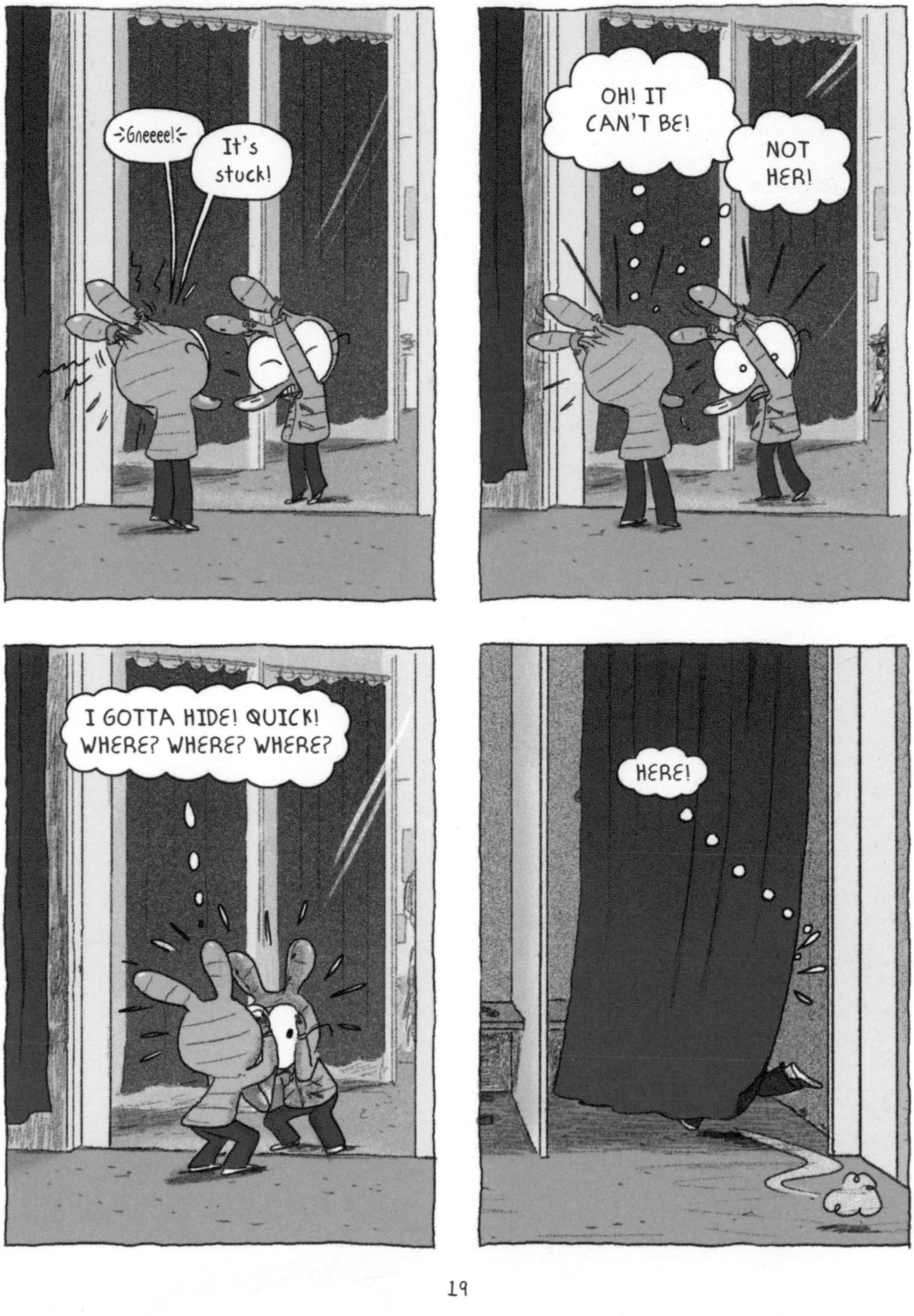

-Gneeee!-
It's stuck!
OH! IT CAN'T BE!
NOT HER!
I GOTTA HIDE! QUICK! WHERE? WHERE? WHERE?
HERE!

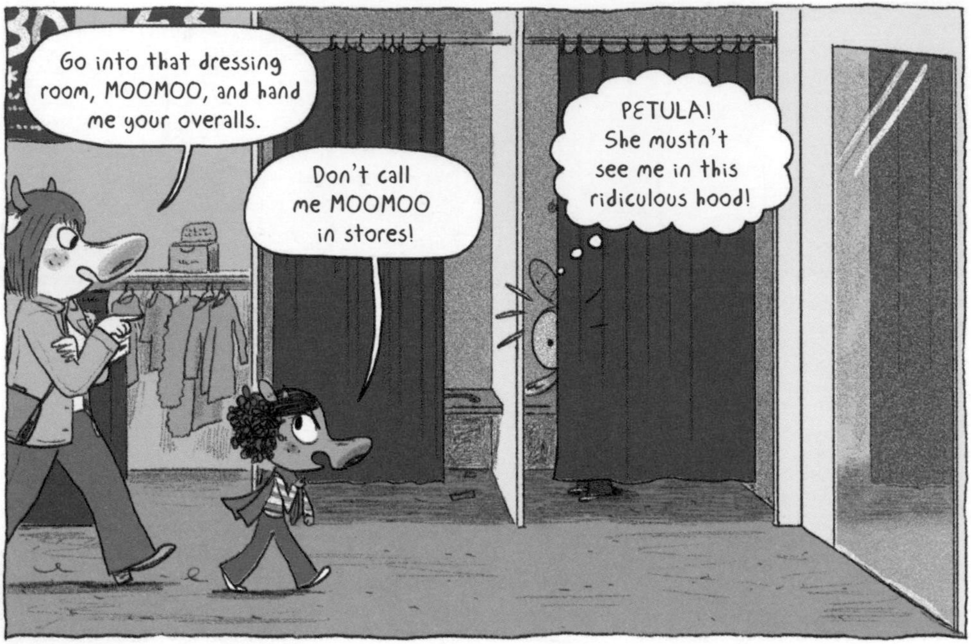
Go into that dressing room, MOOMOO, and hand me your overalls.
Don't call me MOOMOO in stores!
PETULA! She mustn't see me in this ridiculous hood!

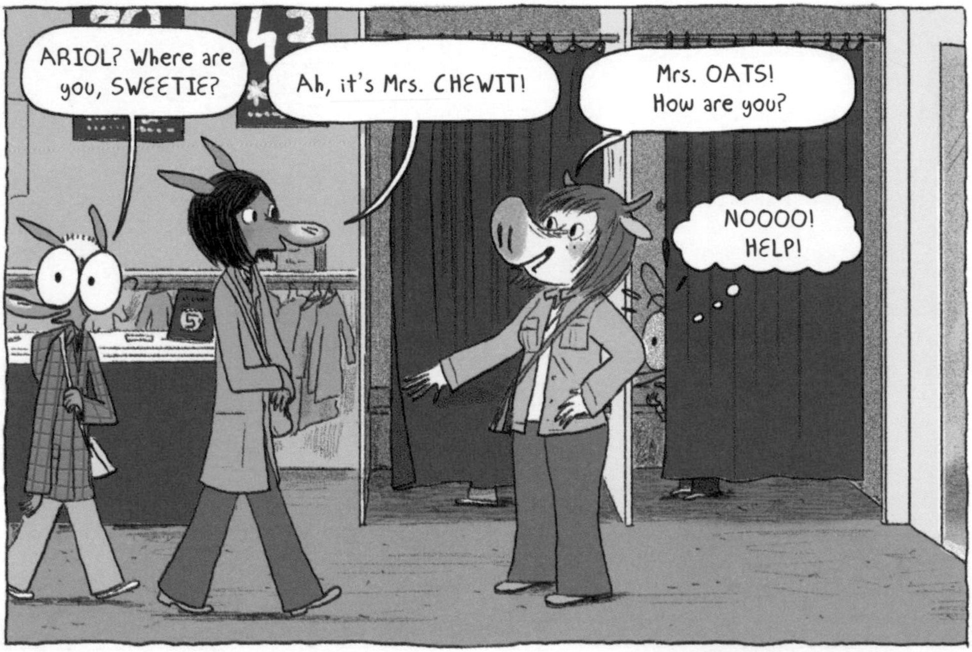
ARIOL? Where are you, SWEETIE?
Ah, it's Mrs. CHEWIT!
Mrs. OATS! How are you?
NOOOO! HELP!

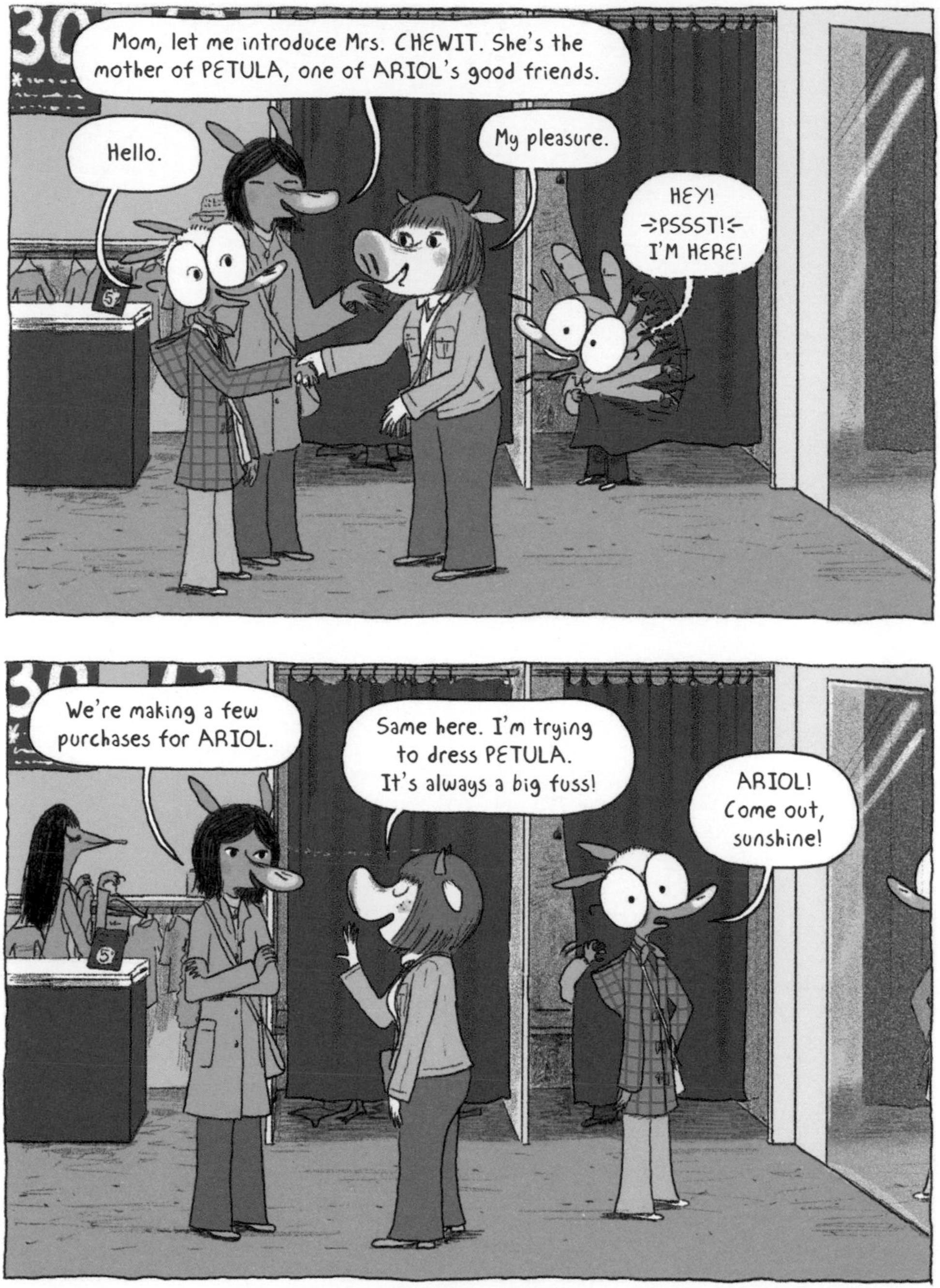
Mom, let me introduce Mrs. CHEWIT. She's the mother of PETULA, one of ARIOL's good friends.
Hello.
My pleasure.
HEY! PSSST! I'M HERE!
We're making a few purchases for ARIOL.
Same here. I'm trying to dress PETULA. It's always a big fuss!
ARIOL! Come out, sunshine!

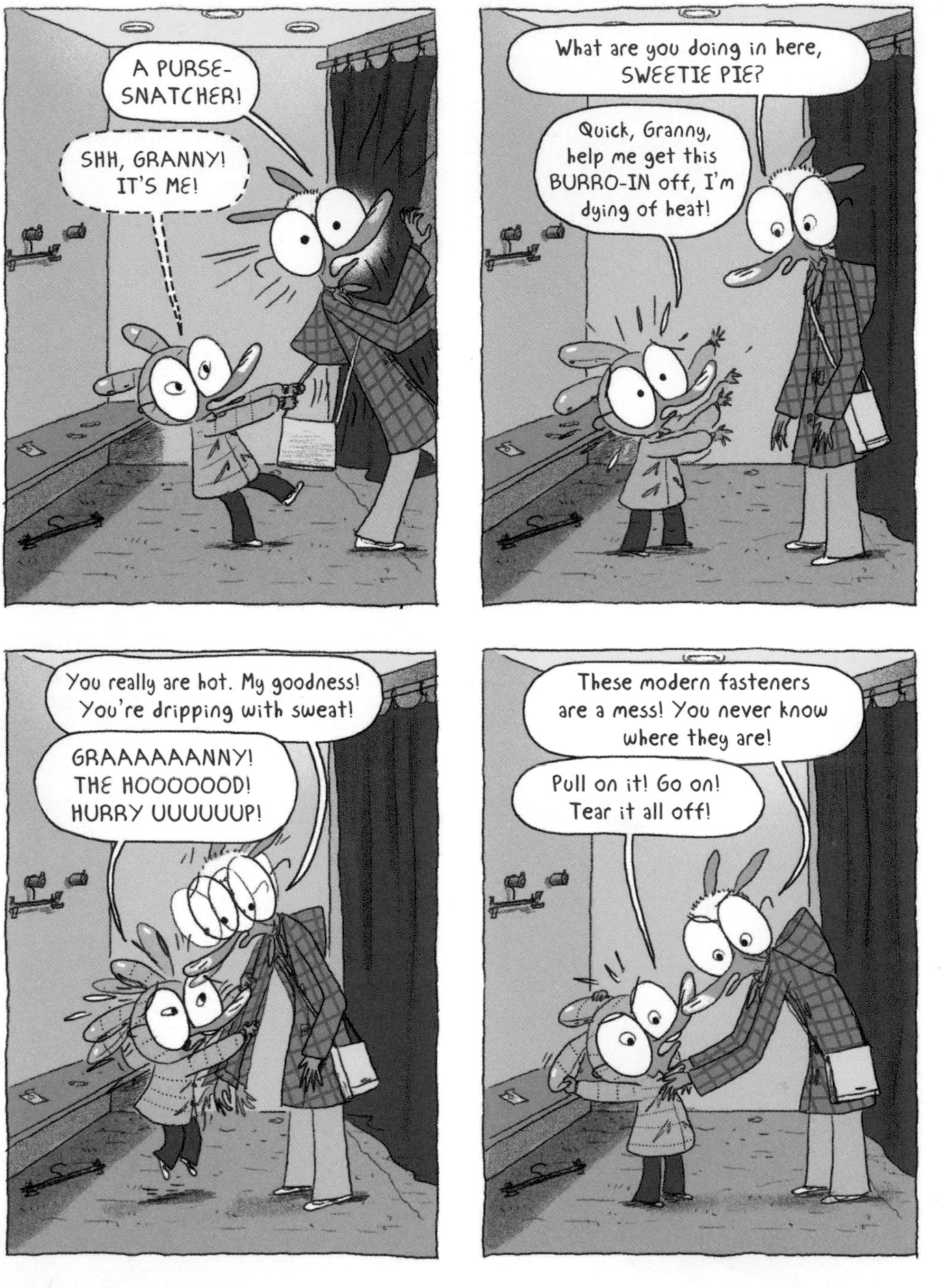

A PURSE-SNATCHER!
SHH, GRANNY! IT'S ME!
What are you doing in here, SWEETIE PIE?
Quick, Granny, help me get this BURRO-IN off, I'm dying of heat!
You really are hot. My goodness! You're dripping with sweat!
GRAAAAAANNY! THE HOOOOOOD! HURRY UUUUUUP!
These modern fasteners are a mess! You never know where they are!
Pull on it! Go on! Tear it all off!

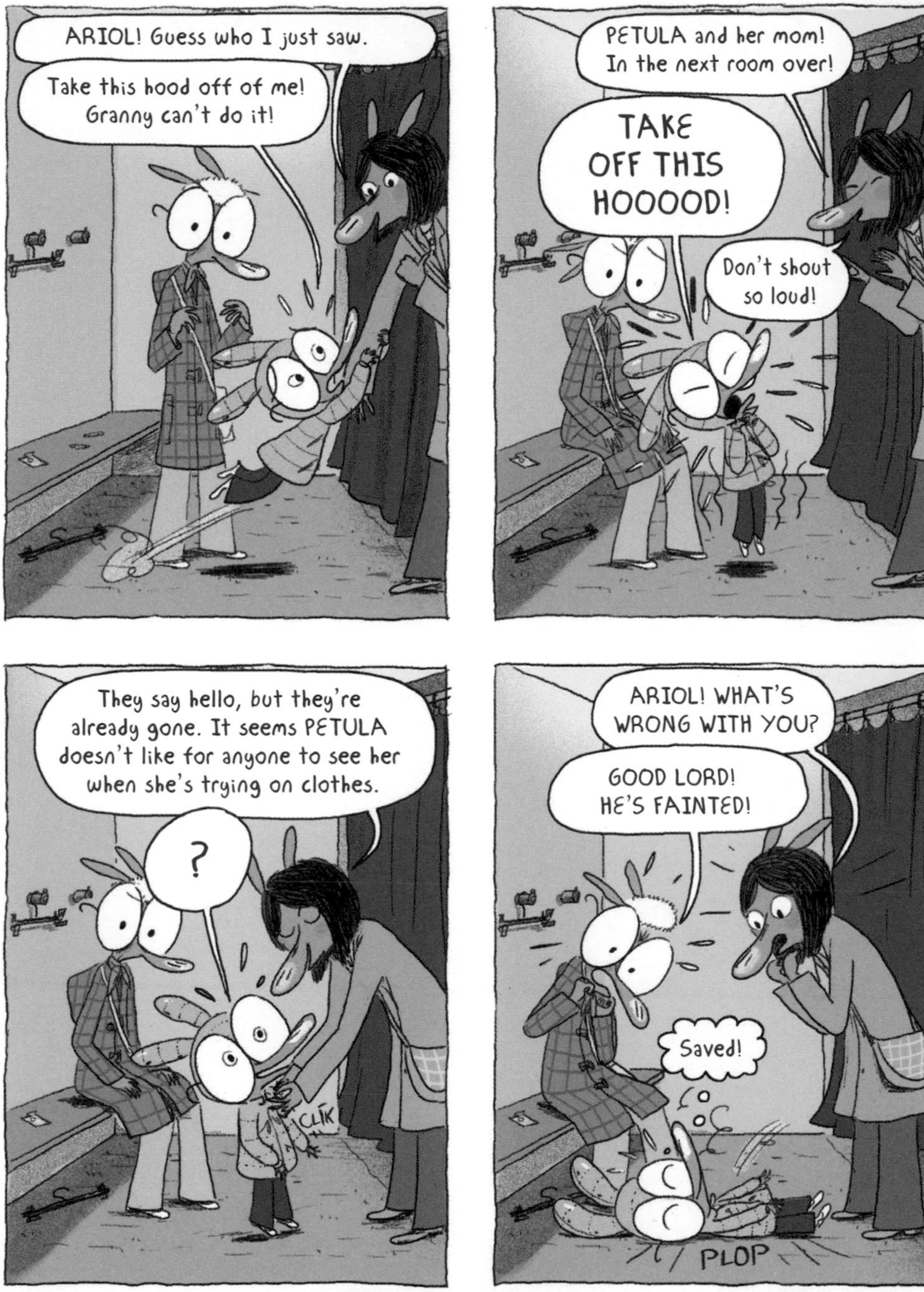
ARIOL! Guess who I just saw.
Take this hood off of me! Granny can't do it!
PETULA and her mom! In the next room over!
TAKE OFF THIS HOOOOD!
Don't shout so loud!
They say hello, but they're already gone. It seems PETULA doesn't like for anyone to see her when she's trying on clothes.
?
CLIK
ARIOL! WHAT'S WRONG WITH YOU?
GOOD LORD! HE'S FAINTED!
Saved!
PLOP

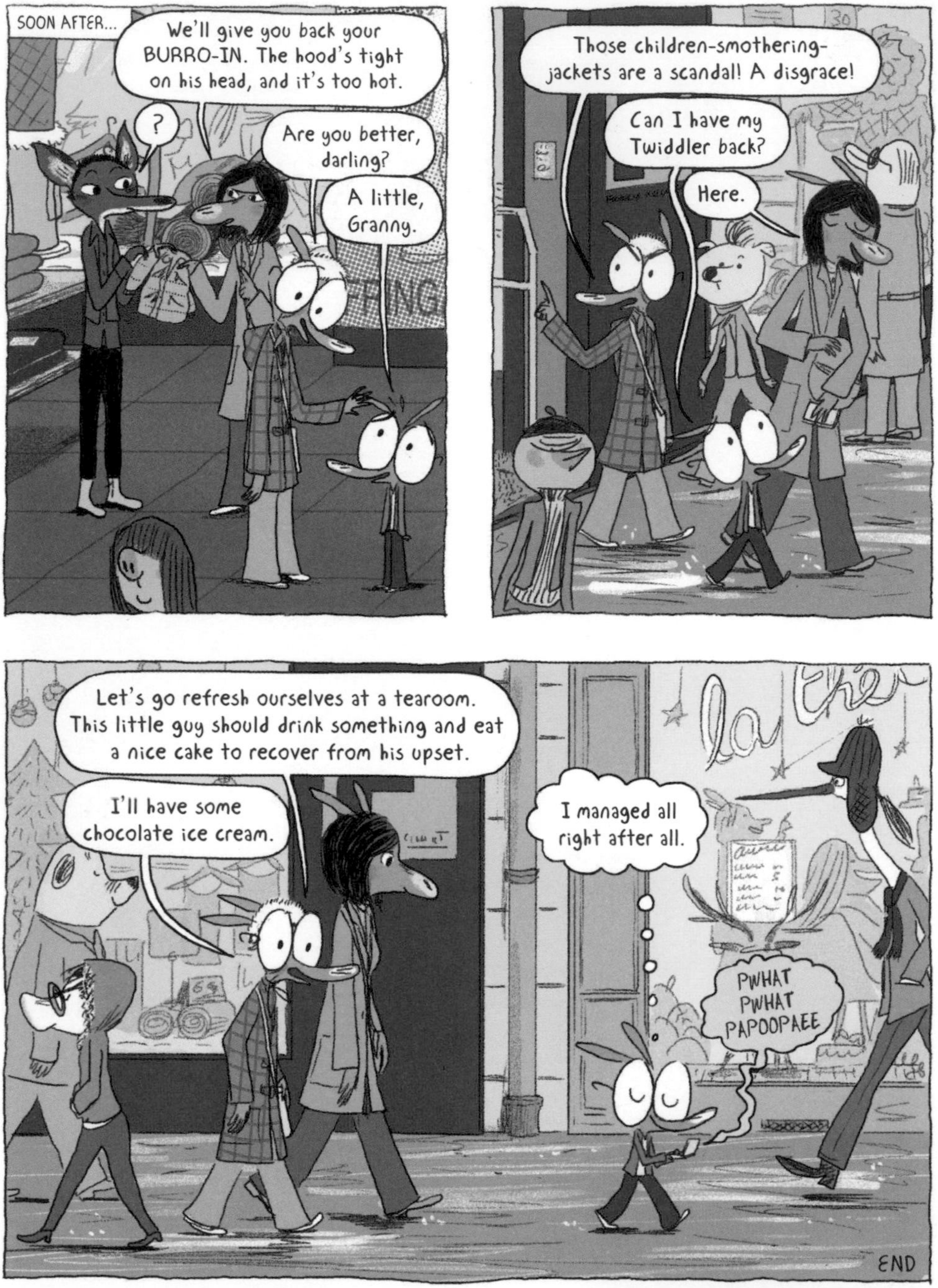
SOON AFTER...
We'll give you back your BURRO-IN. The hood's tight on his head, and it's too hot.
?
Are you better, darling?
A little, Granny.
Those children-smothering-jackets are a scandal! A disgrace!
Can I have my Twiddler back?
Here.
Let's go refresh ourselves at a tearoom. This little guy should drink something and eat a nice cake to recover from his upset.
I'll have some chocolate ice cream.
I managed all right after all.
PWHAT PWHAT PAPOOPAEE
END

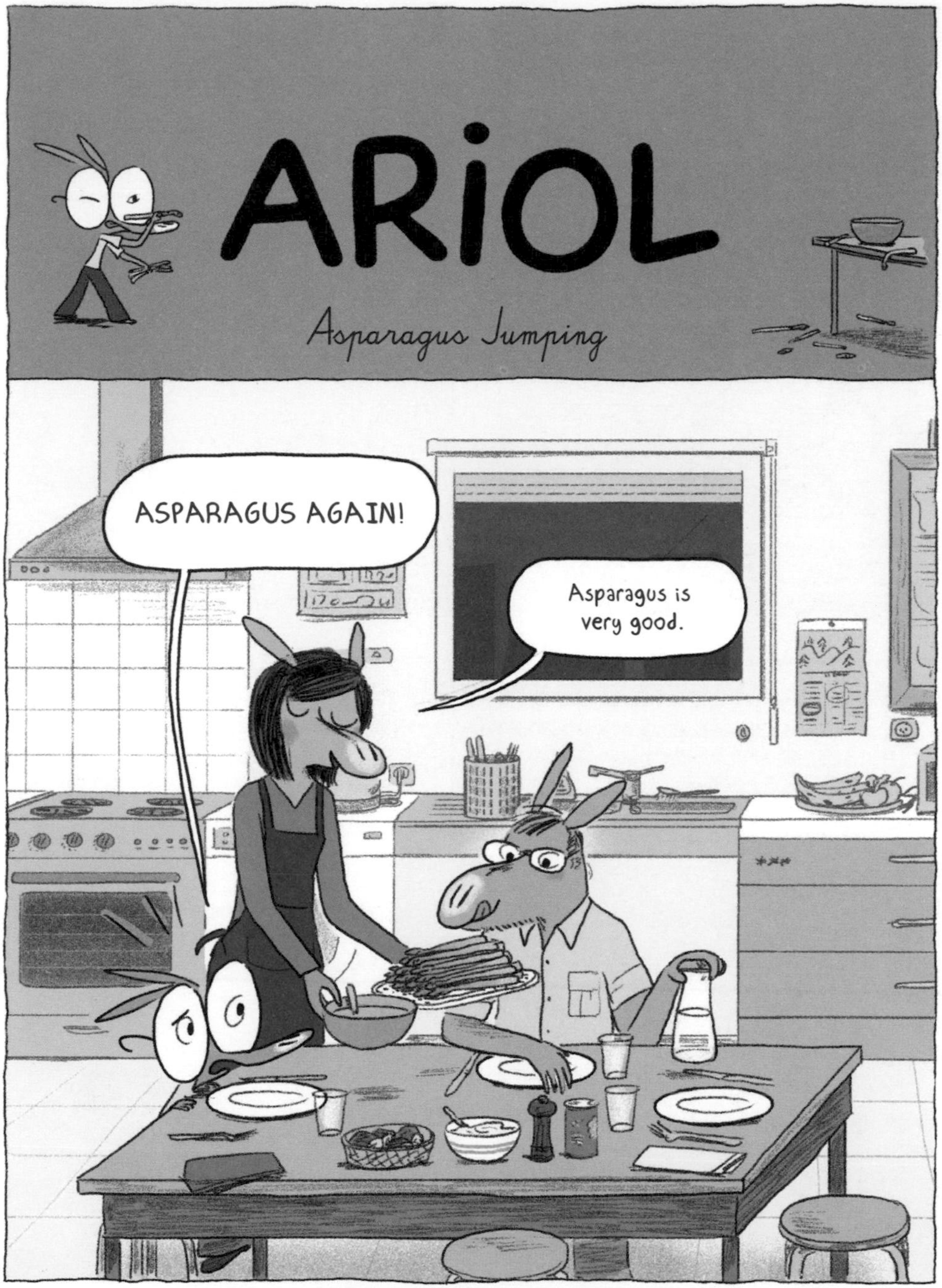
ARiOL
Asparagus Jumping
ASPARAGUS AGAIN!
Asparagus is very good.

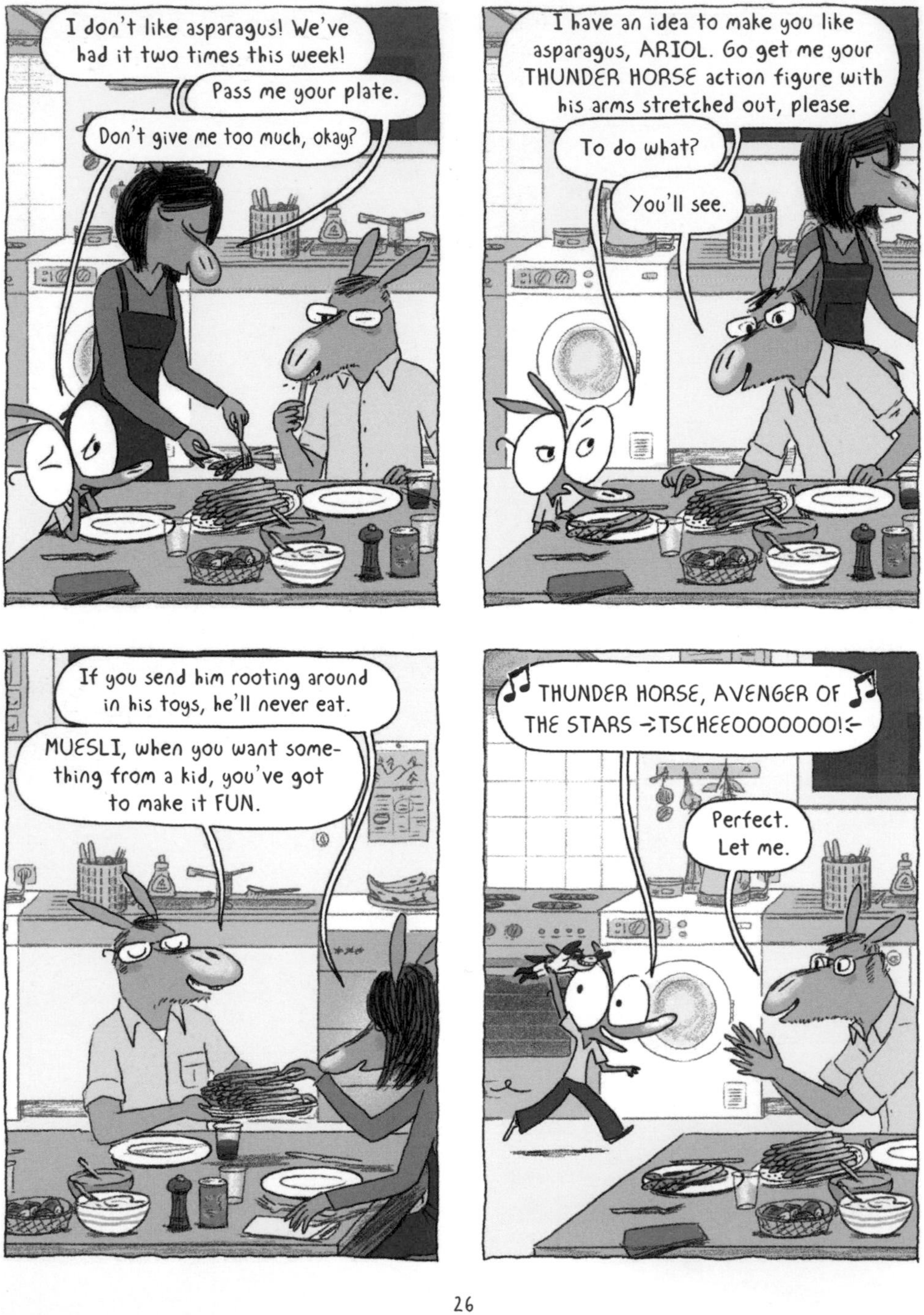
I don't like asparagus! We've had it two times this week!
Pass me your plate.
Don't give me too much, okay?
I have an idea to make you like asparagus, ARIOL. Go get me your THUNDER HORSE action figure with his arms stretched out, please.
To do what?
You'll see.
If you send him rooting around in his toys, he'll never eat.
MUESLI, when you want something from a kid, you've got to make it FUN.
THUNDER HORSE, AVENGER OF THE STARS ⇥TSCHEEOOOOOOO!⇤
Perfect. Let me.

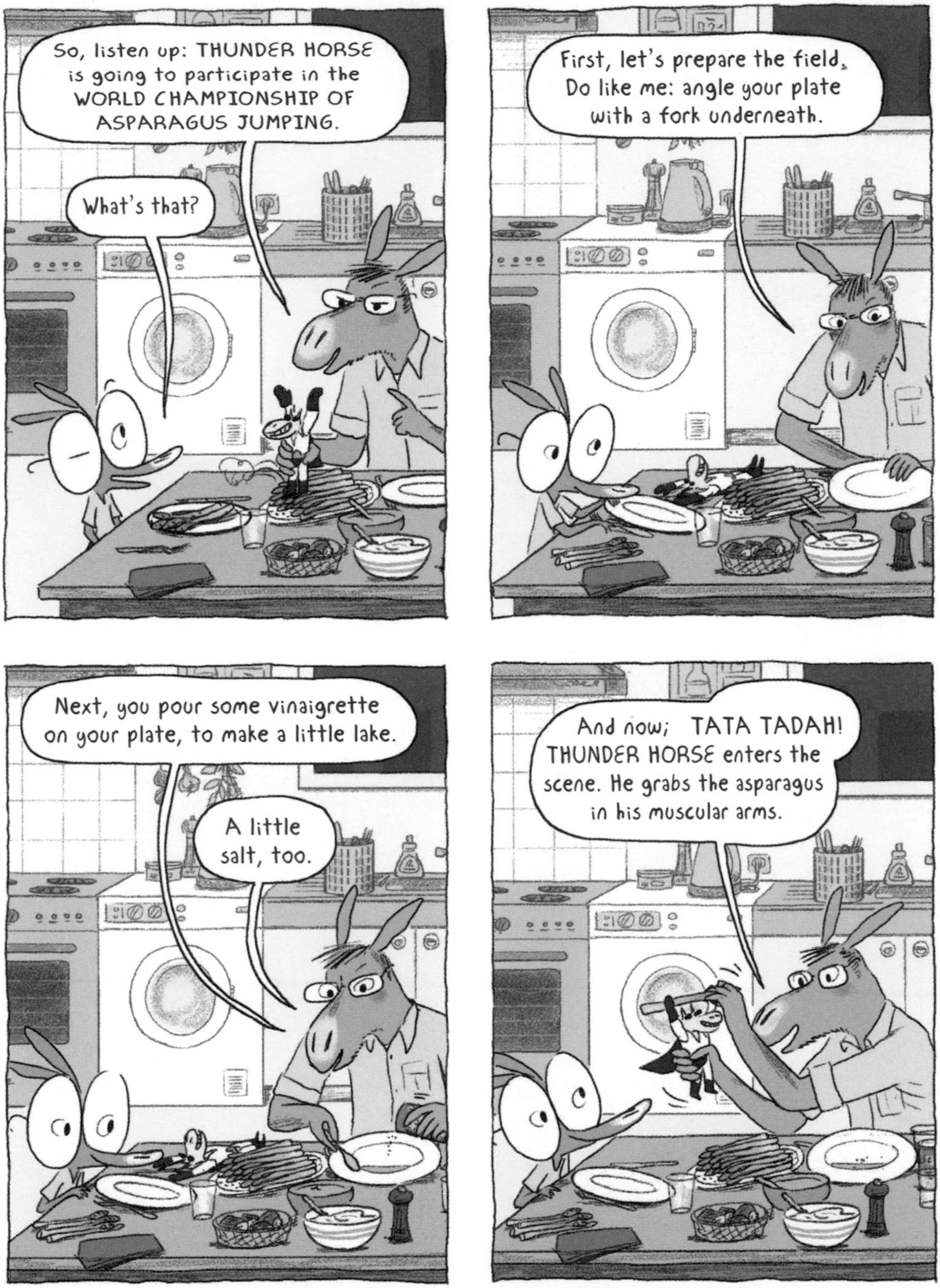
So, listen up: THUNDER HORSE is going to participate in the WORLD CHAMPIONSHIP OF ASPARAGUS JUMPING.
What's that?
First, let's prepare the field. Do like me: angle your plate with a fork underneath.
Next, you pour some vinaigrette on your plate, to make a little lake.
A little salt, too.
And now; TATA TADAH! THUNDER HORSE enters the scene. He grabs the asparagus in his muscular arms.

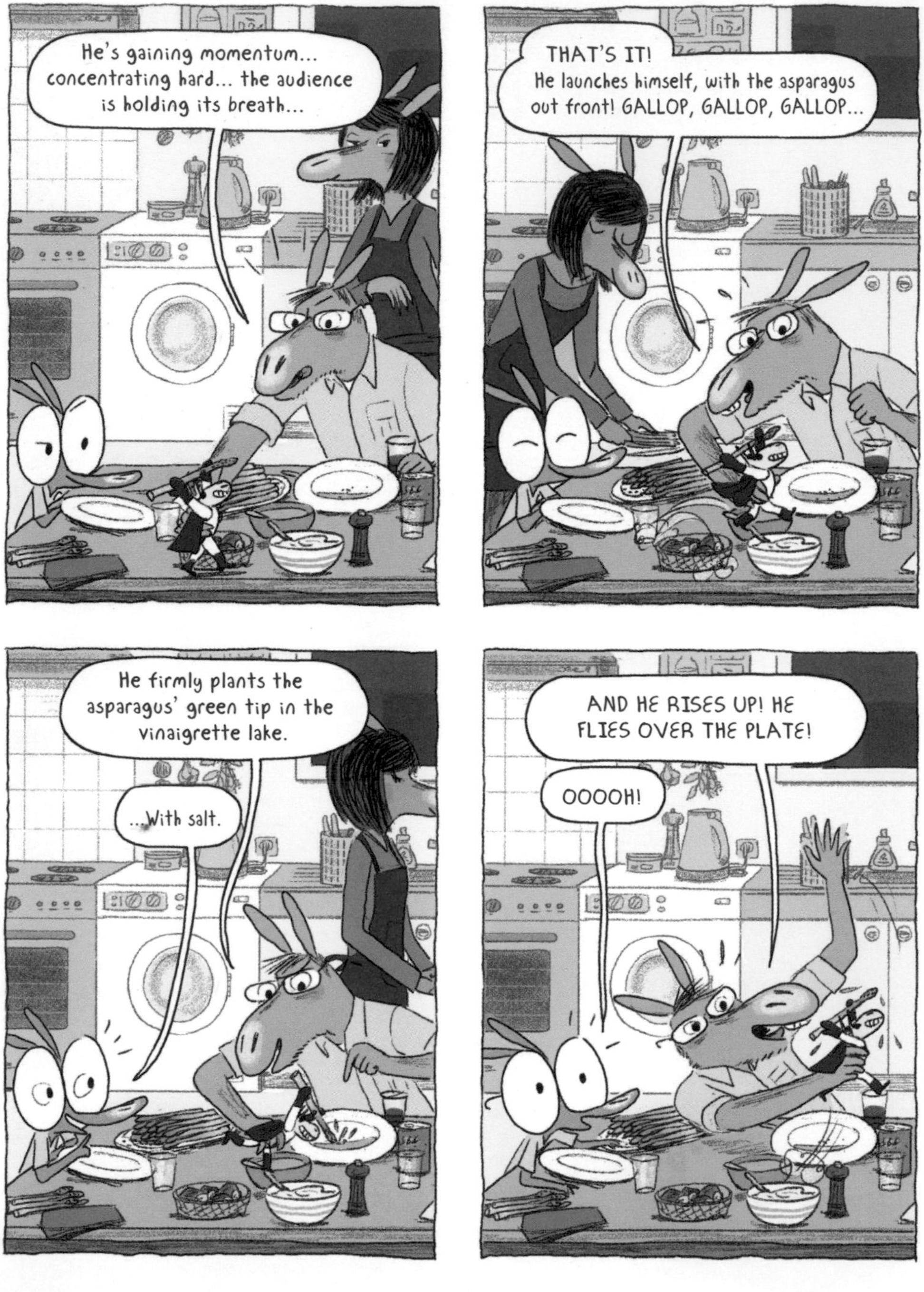
He's gaining momentum... concentrating hard... the audience is holding its breath...
THAT'S IT!
He launches himself, with the asparagus out front! GALLOP, GALLOP, GALLOP...
He firmly plants the asparagus' green tip in the vinaigrette lake.
...With salt.
AND HE RISES UP! HE FLIES OVER THE PLATE!
OOOOH!

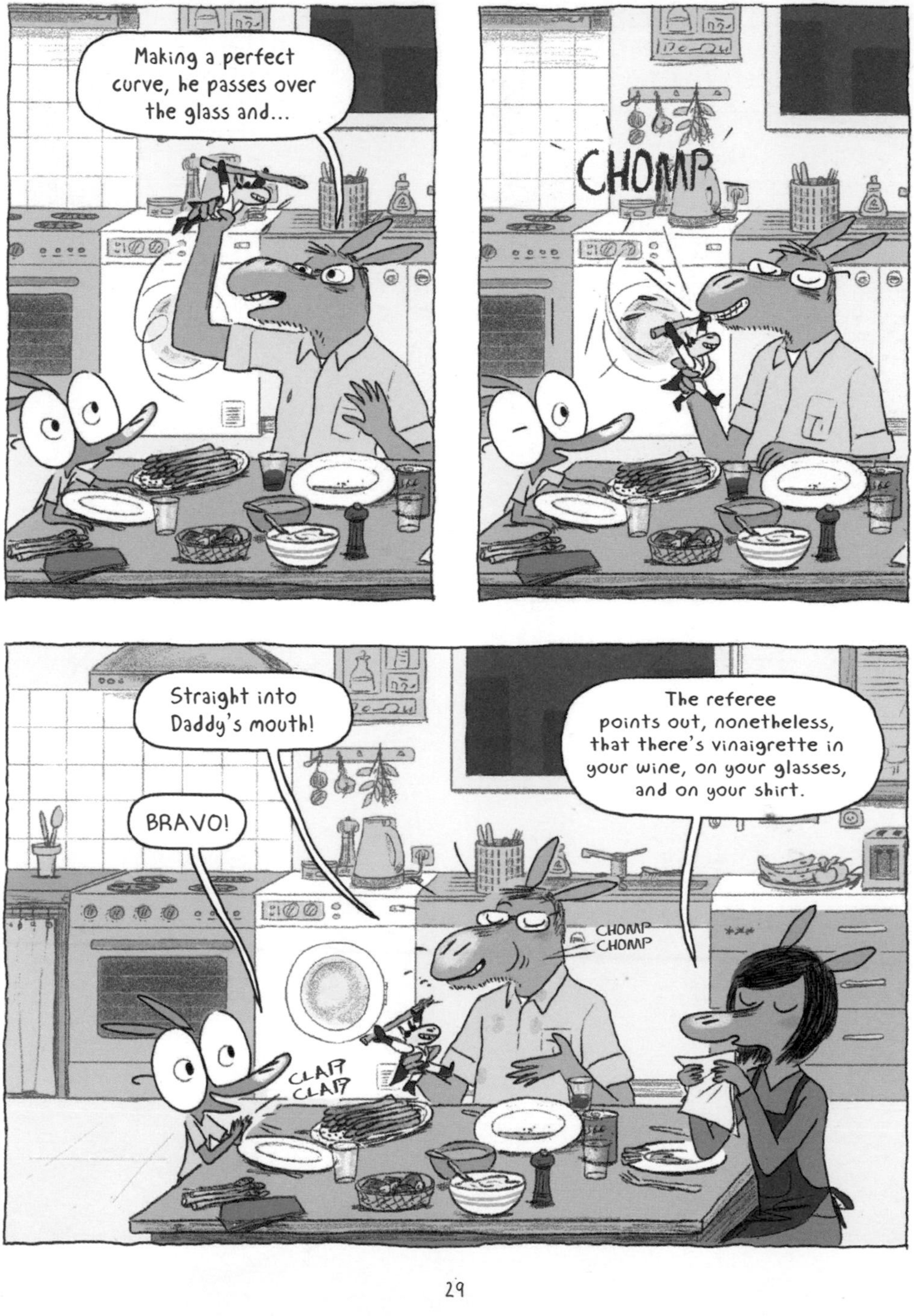
Making a perfect curve, he passes over the glass and...
CHOMP
Straight into Daddy's mouth!
BRAVO!
The referee points out, nonetheless, that there's vinaigrette in your wine, on your glasses, and on your shirt.
CHOMP CHOMP
CLAP CLAP

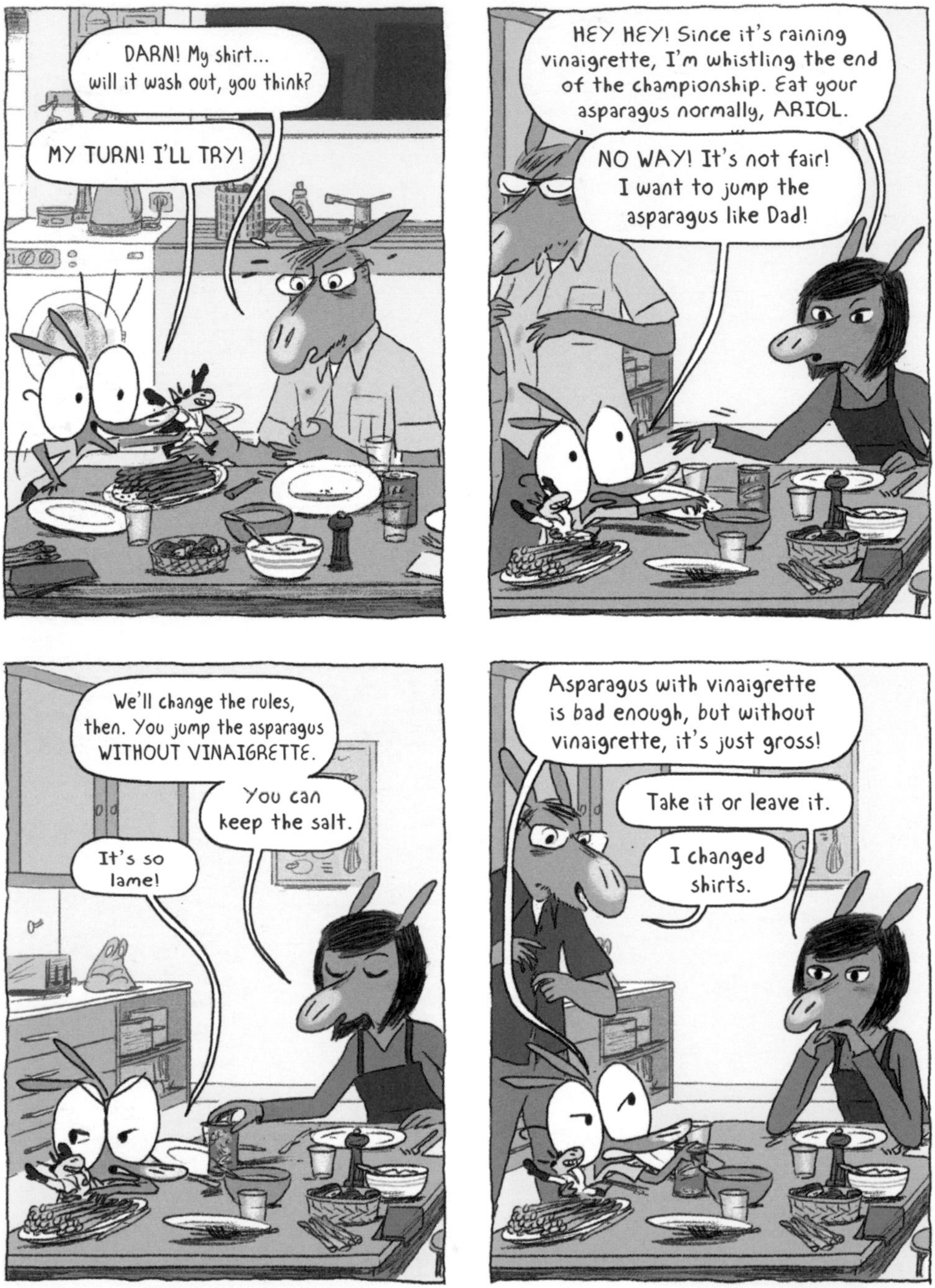
DARN! My shirt... will it wash out, you think?
MY TURN! I'LL TRY!
HEY HEY! Since it's raining vinaigrette, I'm whistling the end of the championship. Eat your asparagus normally, ARIOL.
NO WAY! It's not fair! I want to jump the asparagus like Dad!
We'll change the rules, then. You jump the asparagus WITHOUT VINAIGRETTE.
You can keep the salt.
It's so lame!
Asparagus with vinaigrette is bad enough, but without vinaigrette, it's just gross!
Take it or leave it.
I changed shirts.

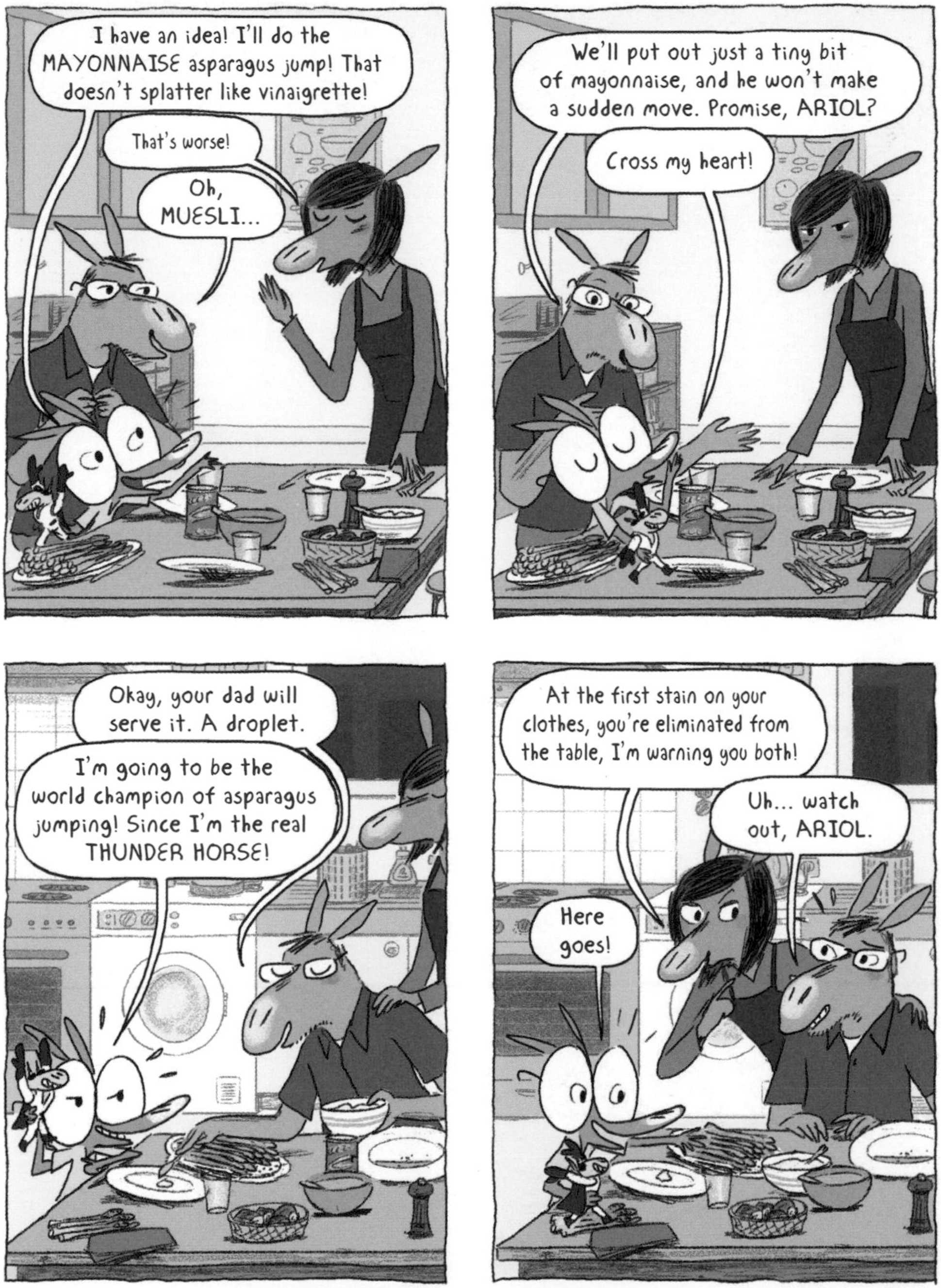
I have an idea! I'll do the MAYONNAISE asparagus jump! That doesn't splatter like vinaigrette!
That's worse!
Oh, MUESLI...
We'll put out just a tiny bit of mayonnaise, and he won't make a sudden move. Promise, ARIOL?
Cross my heart!
Okay, your dad will serve it. A droplet.
I'm going to be the world champion of asparagus jumping! Since I'm the real THUNDER HORSE!
At the first stain on your clothes, you're eliminated from the table, I'm warning you both!
Uh... watch out, ARIOL.
Here goes!

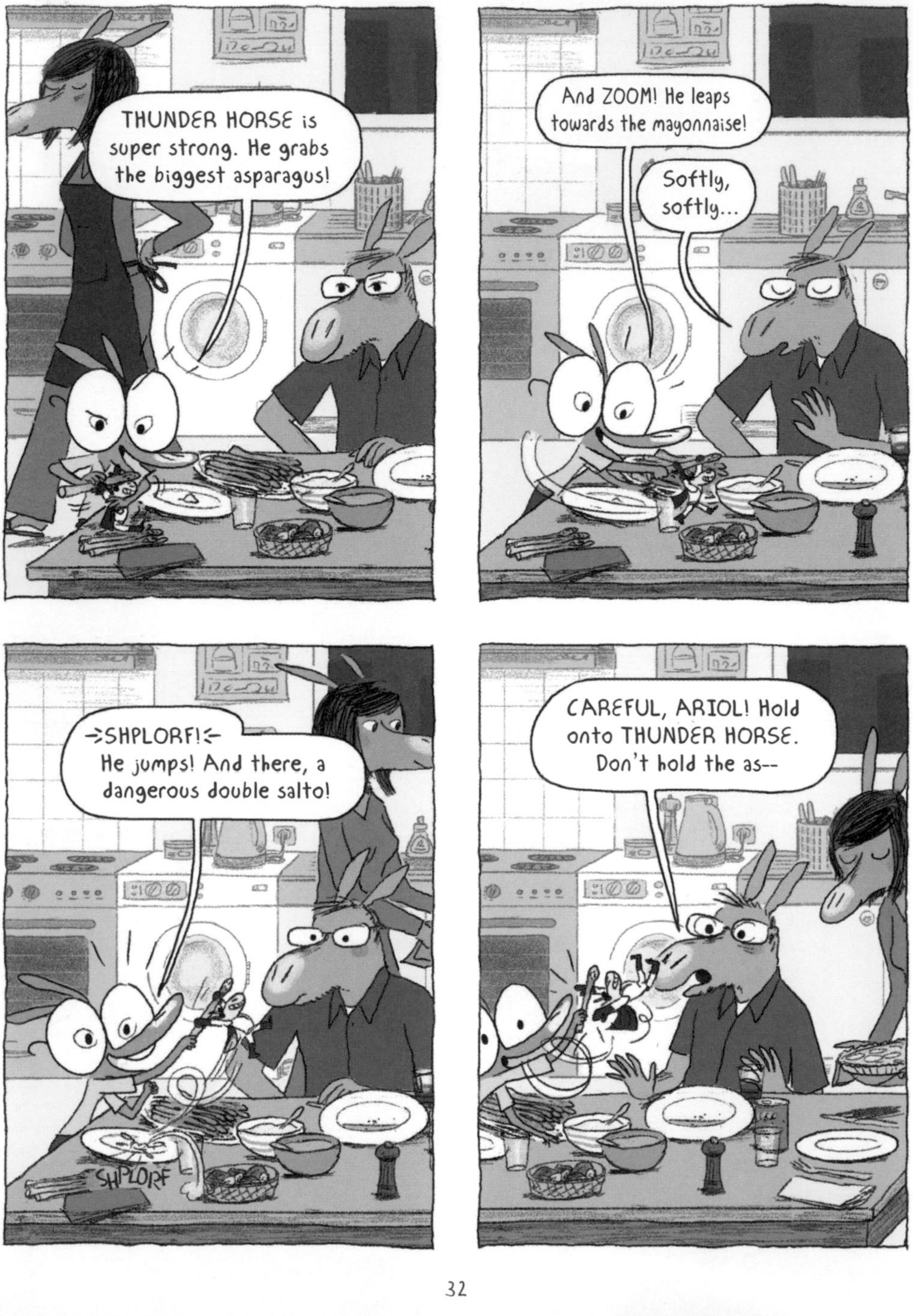
THUNDER HORSE is super strong. He grabs the biggest asparagus!
And ZOOM! He leaps towards the mayonnaise!
Softly, softly...
SHPLORF!
He jumps! And there, a dangerous double salto!
SHPLORF
CAREFUL, ARIOL! Hold onto THUNDER HORSE. Don't hold the as--

...
WOOSH
WOOSH
WOOOOSH
SPLASH
--paragus.
That's what they call getting "asperged."

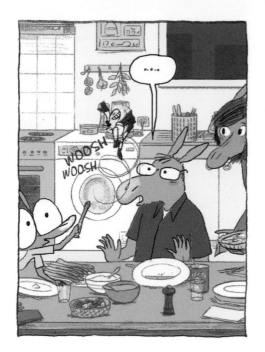

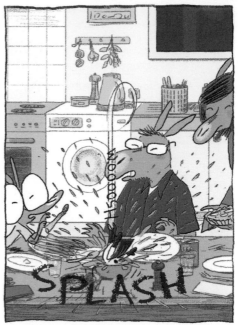

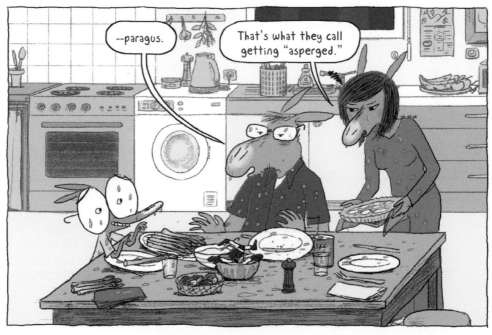

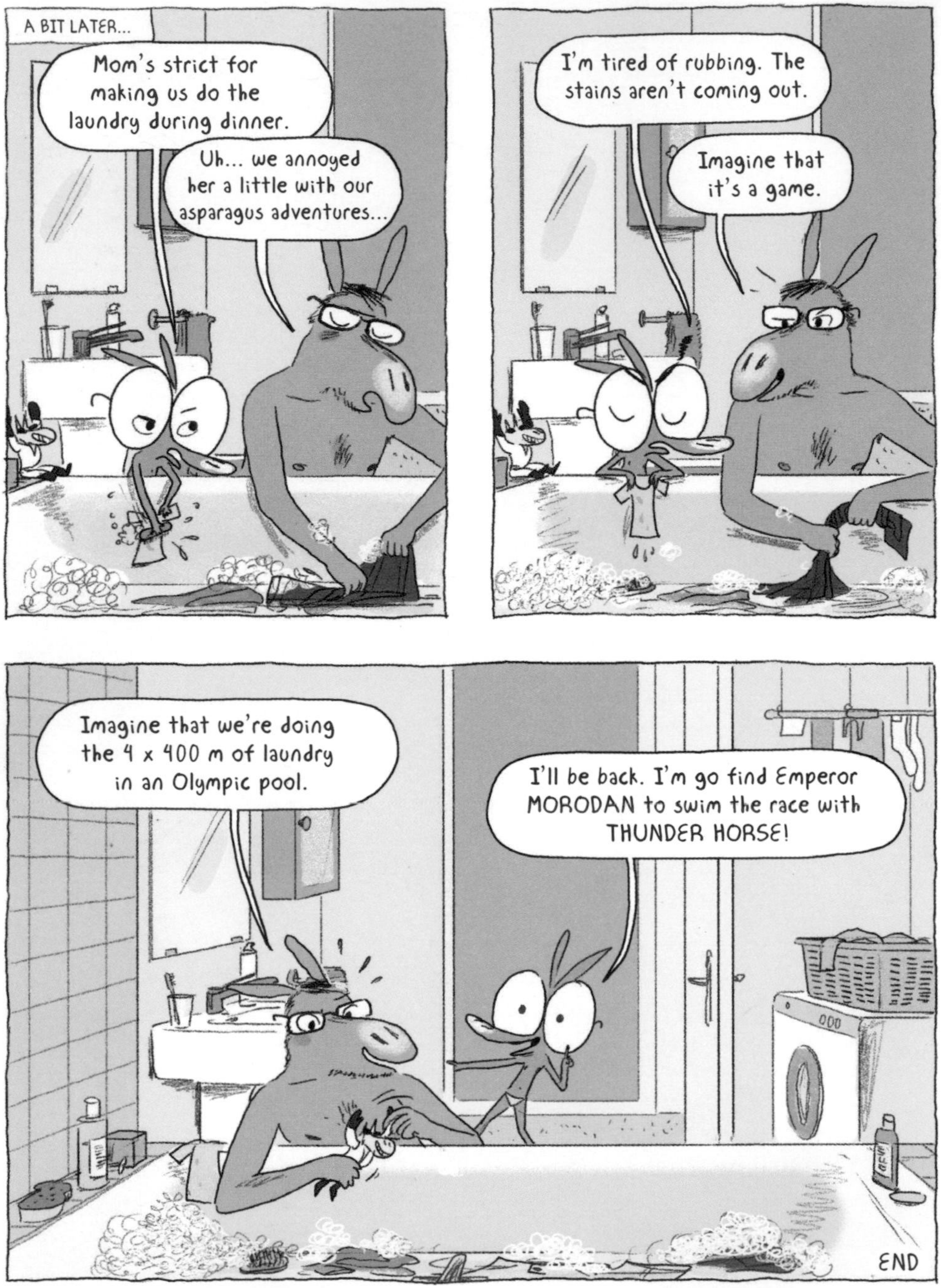
A BIT LATER...
Mom's strict for making us do the laundry during dinner.
Uh... we annoyed her a little with our asparagus adventures...
I'm tired of rubbing. The stains aren't coming out.
Imagine that it's a game.
Imagine that we're doing the 4 x 400 m of laundry in an Olympic pool.
I'll be back. I'm go find Emperor MORODAN to swim the race with THUNDER HORSE!
END

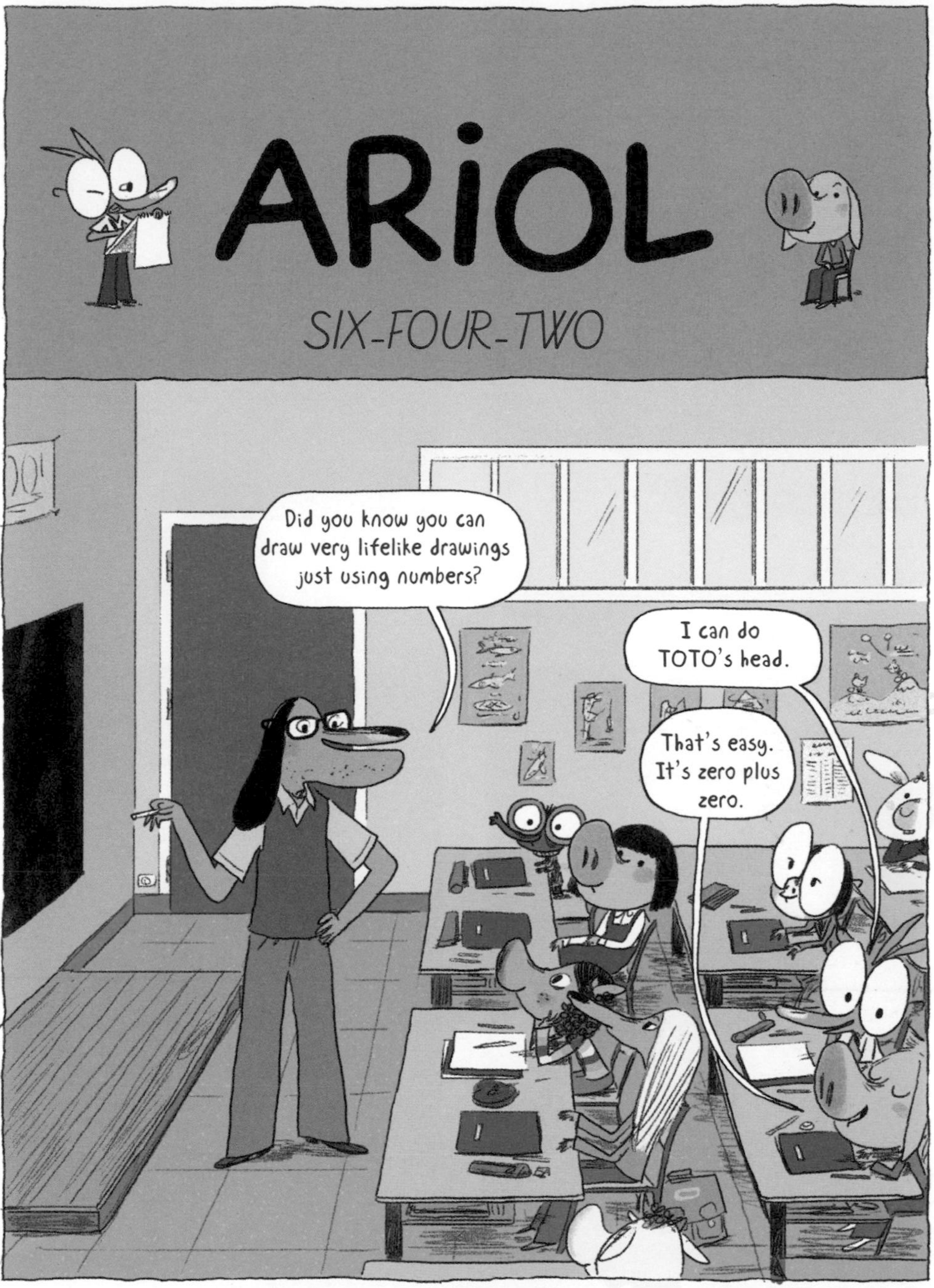
ARiOL
SIX-FOUR-TWO
Did you know you can draw very lifelike drawings just using numbers?
I can do TOTO's head.
That's easy. It's zero plus zero.

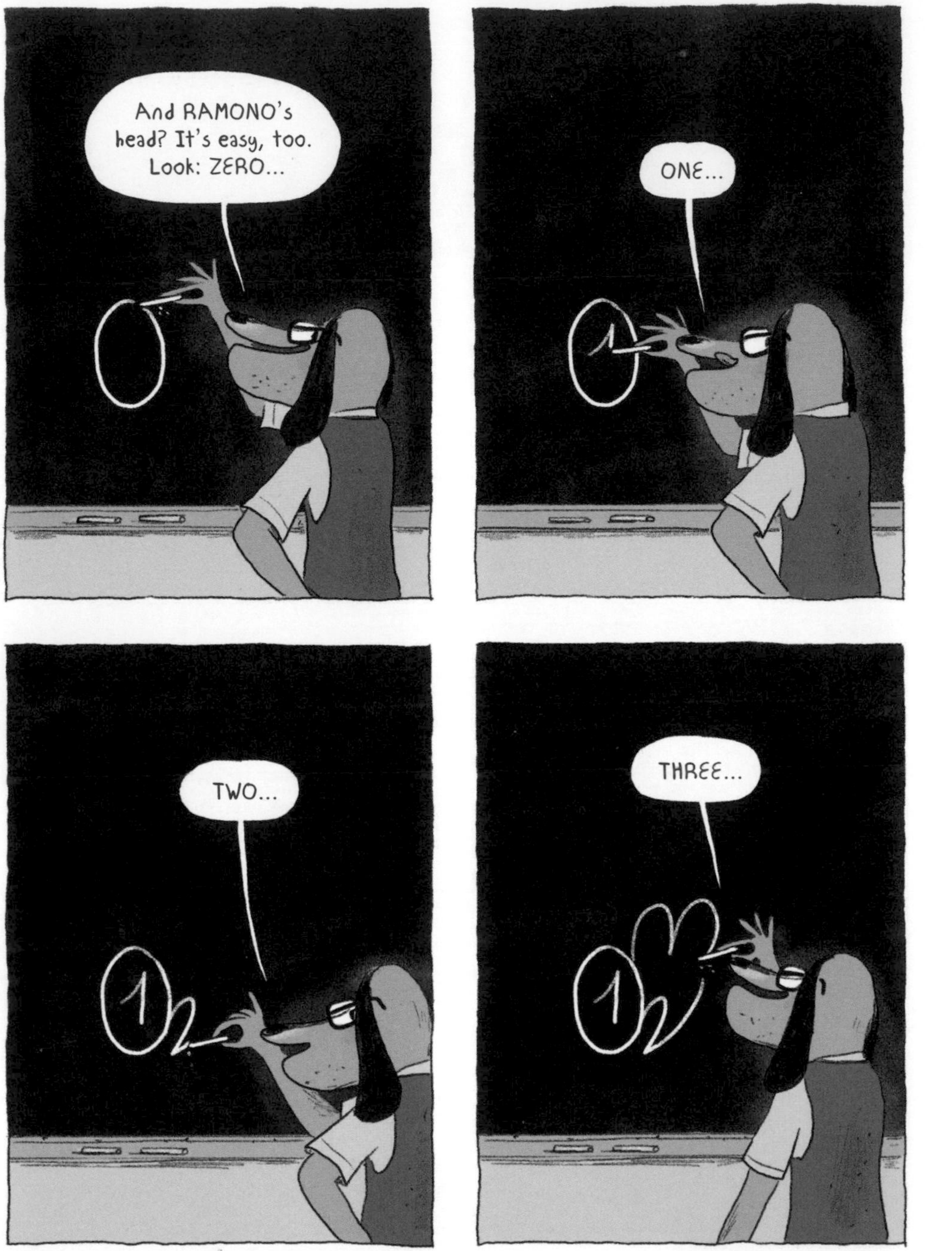
And RAMONO's head? It's easy, too. Look: ZERO...
ONE...
TWO...
THREE...

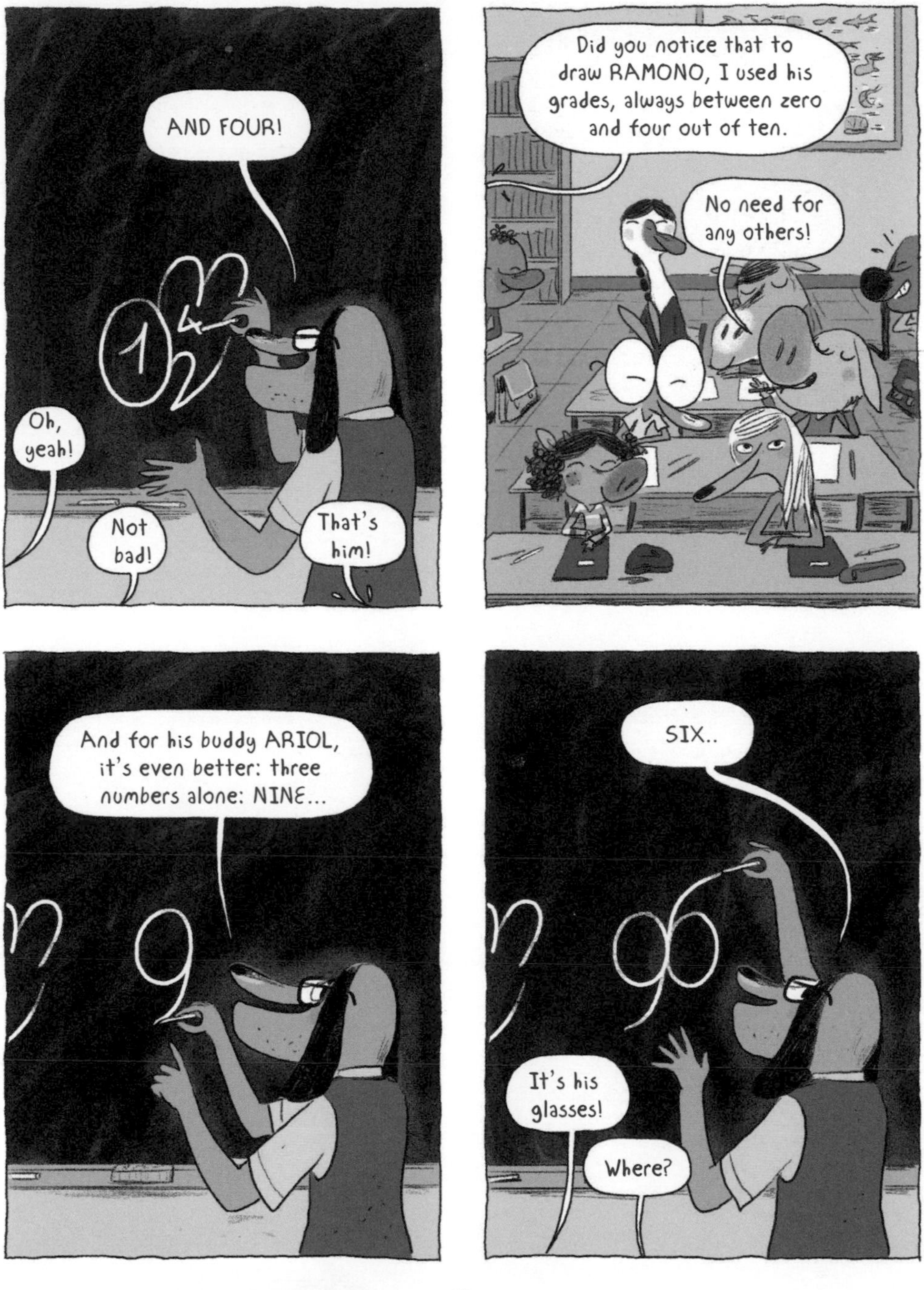
AND FOUR!
Oh, yeah!
Not bad!
That's him!
Did you notice that to draw RAMONO, I used his grades, always between zero and four out of ten.
No need for any others!
And for his buddy ARIOL, it's even better: three numbers alone: NINE...
SIX..
It's his glasses!
Where?

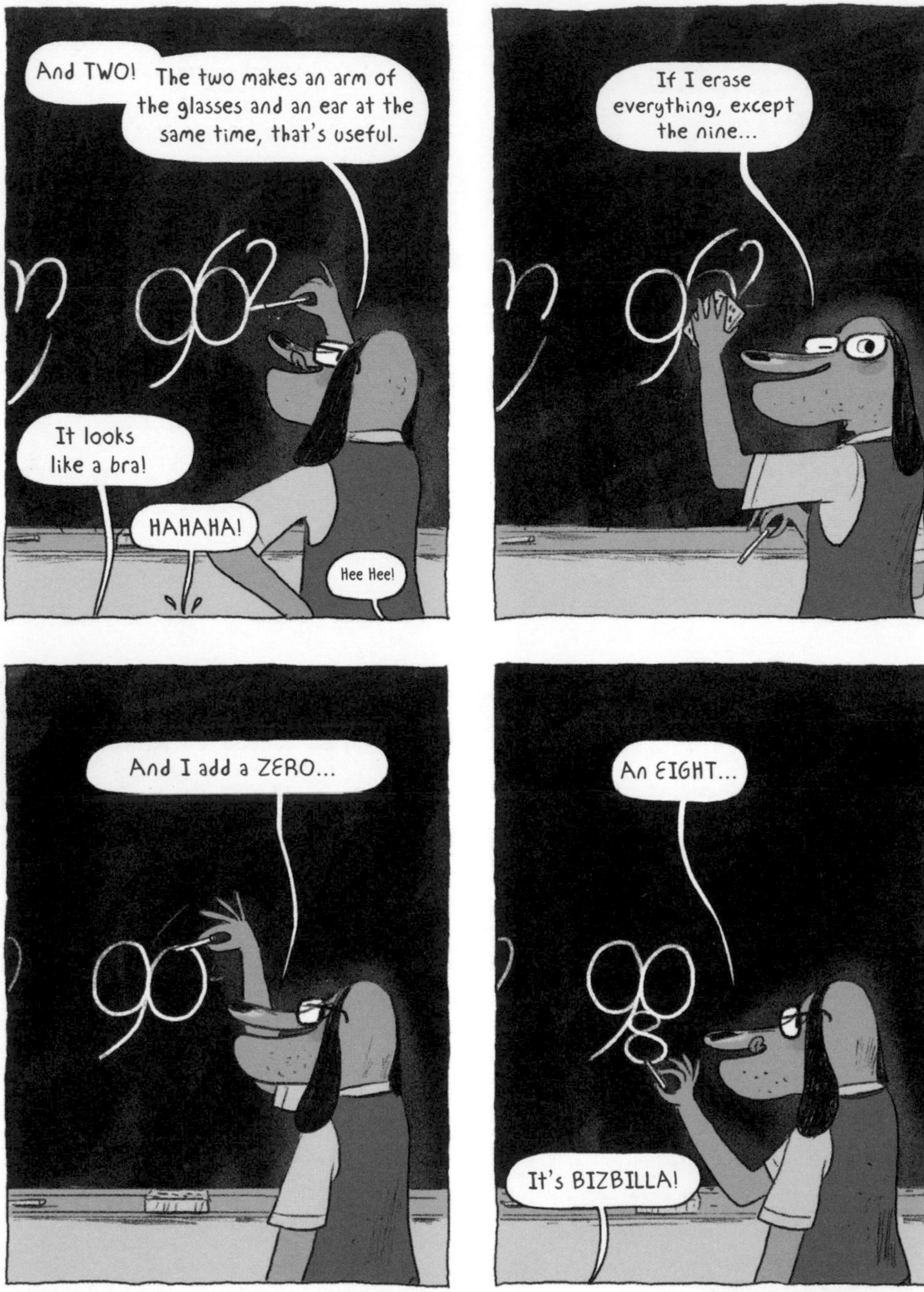
And TWO!
The two makes an arm of the glasses and an ear at the same time, that's useful.
It looks like a bra!
HAHAHA!
Hee Hee!
If I erase everything, except the nine...
And I add a ZERO...
An EIGHT...
It's BIZBILLA!

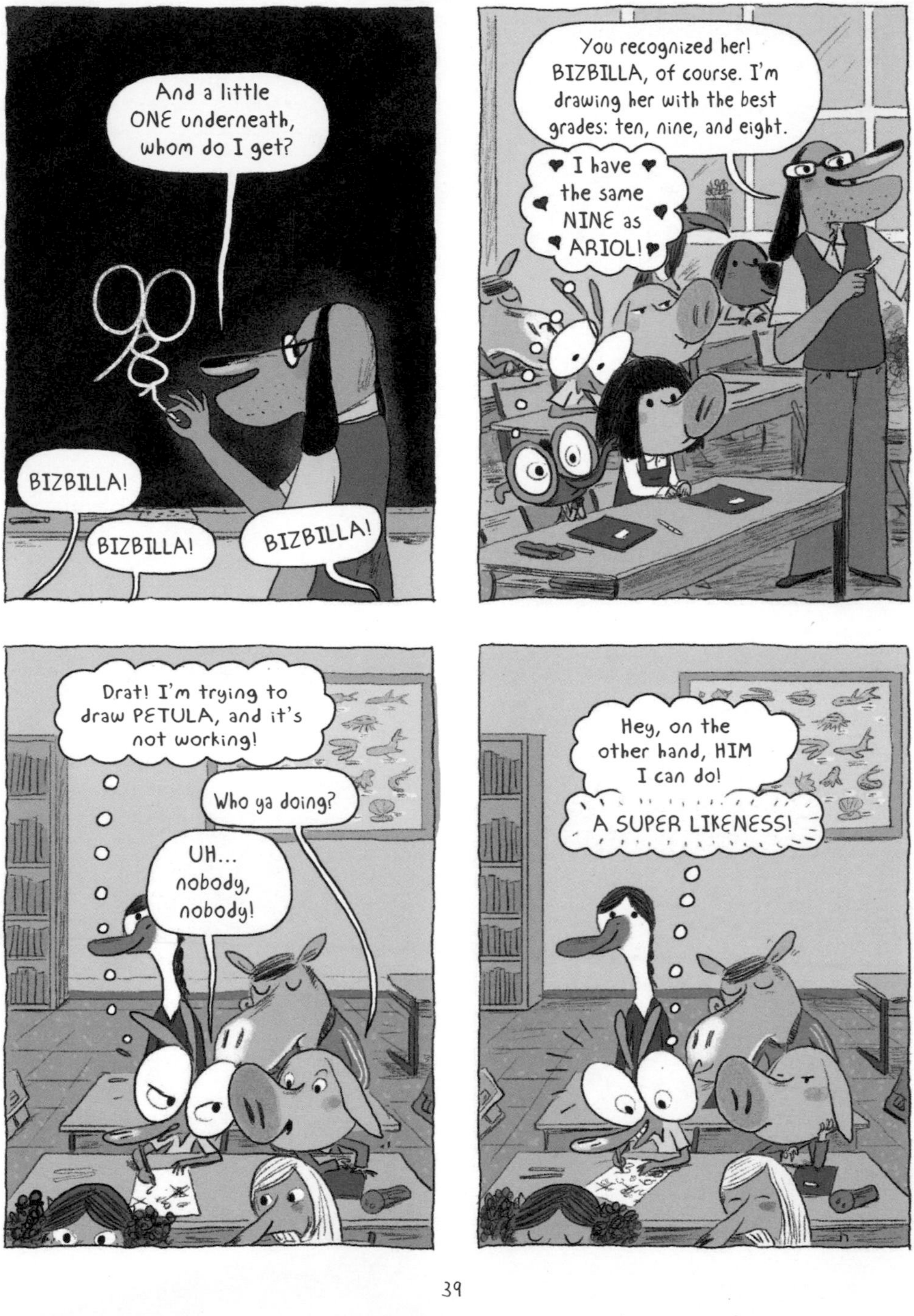

And a little ONE underneath, whom do I get?
BIZBILLA!
BIZBILLA!
BIZBILLA!
You recognized her! BIZBILLA, of course. I'm drawing her with the best grades: ten, nine, and eight.
I have the same NINE as ARIOL!
Drat! I'm trying to draw PETULA, and it's not working!
Who ya doing?
UH... nobody, nobody!
Hey, on the other hand, HIM I can do!
A SUPER LIKENESS!

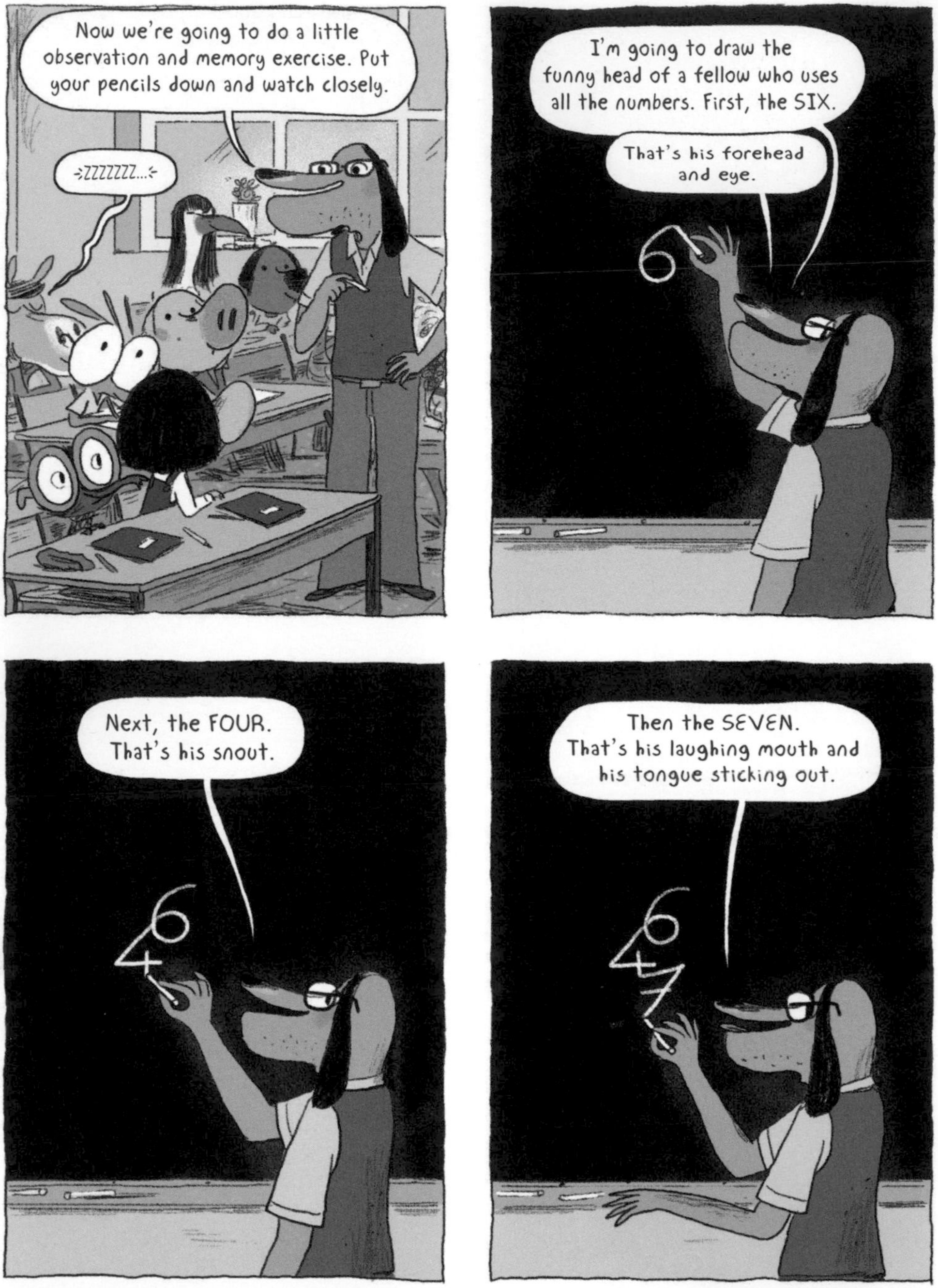
Now we're going to do a little observation and memory exercise. Put your pencils down and watch closely.
ZZZZZZZ...
I'm going to draw the funny head of a fellow who uses all the numbers. First, the SIX.
That's his forehead and eye.
Next, the FOUR. That's his snout.
Then the SEVEN. That's his laughing mouth and his tongue sticking out.

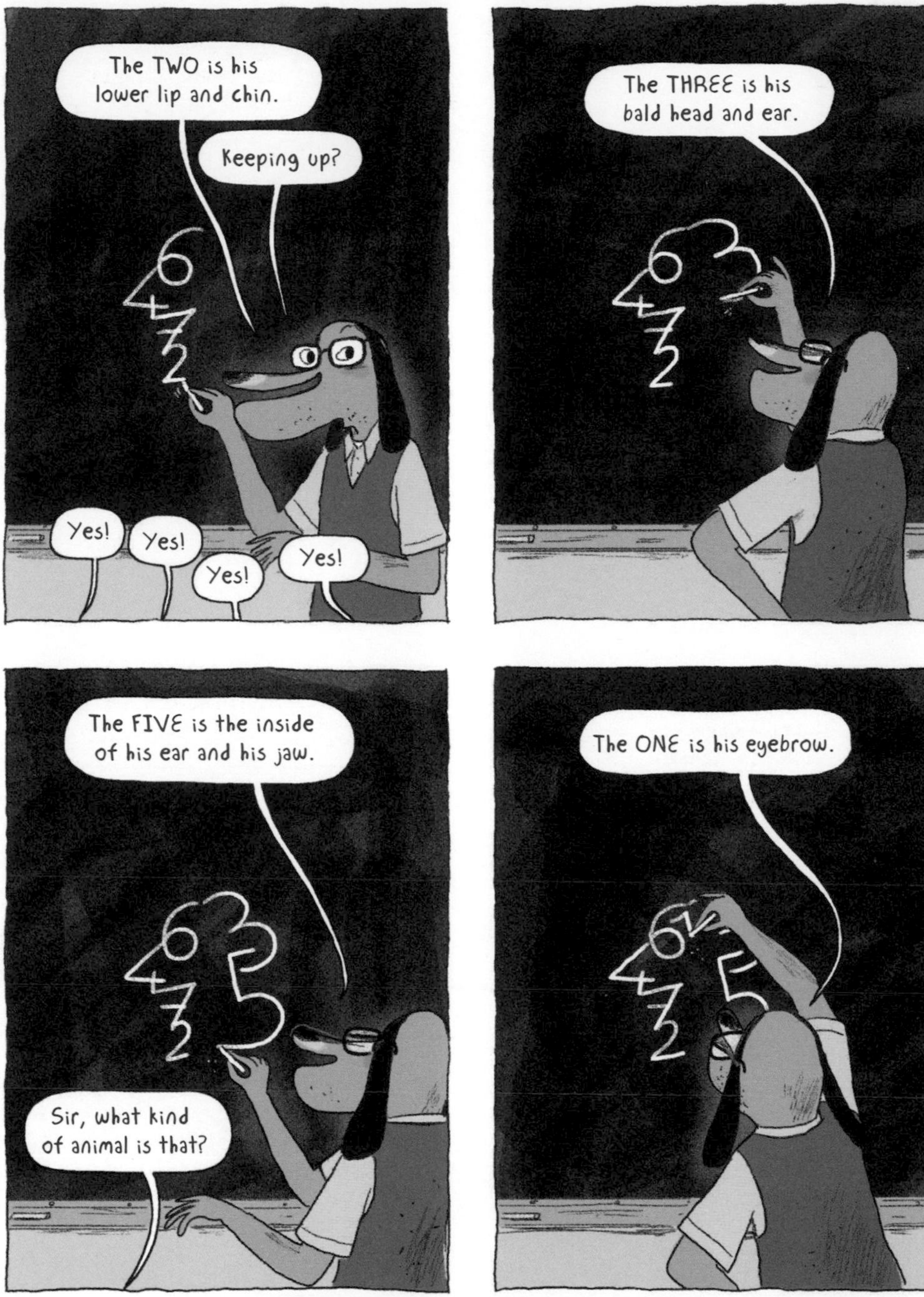
The TWO is his lower lip and chin.
Keeping up?
Yes!
Yes!
Yes!
Yes!
The THREE is his bald head and ear.
The FIVE is the inside of his ear and his jaw.
Sir, what kind of animal is that?
The ONE is his eyebrow.

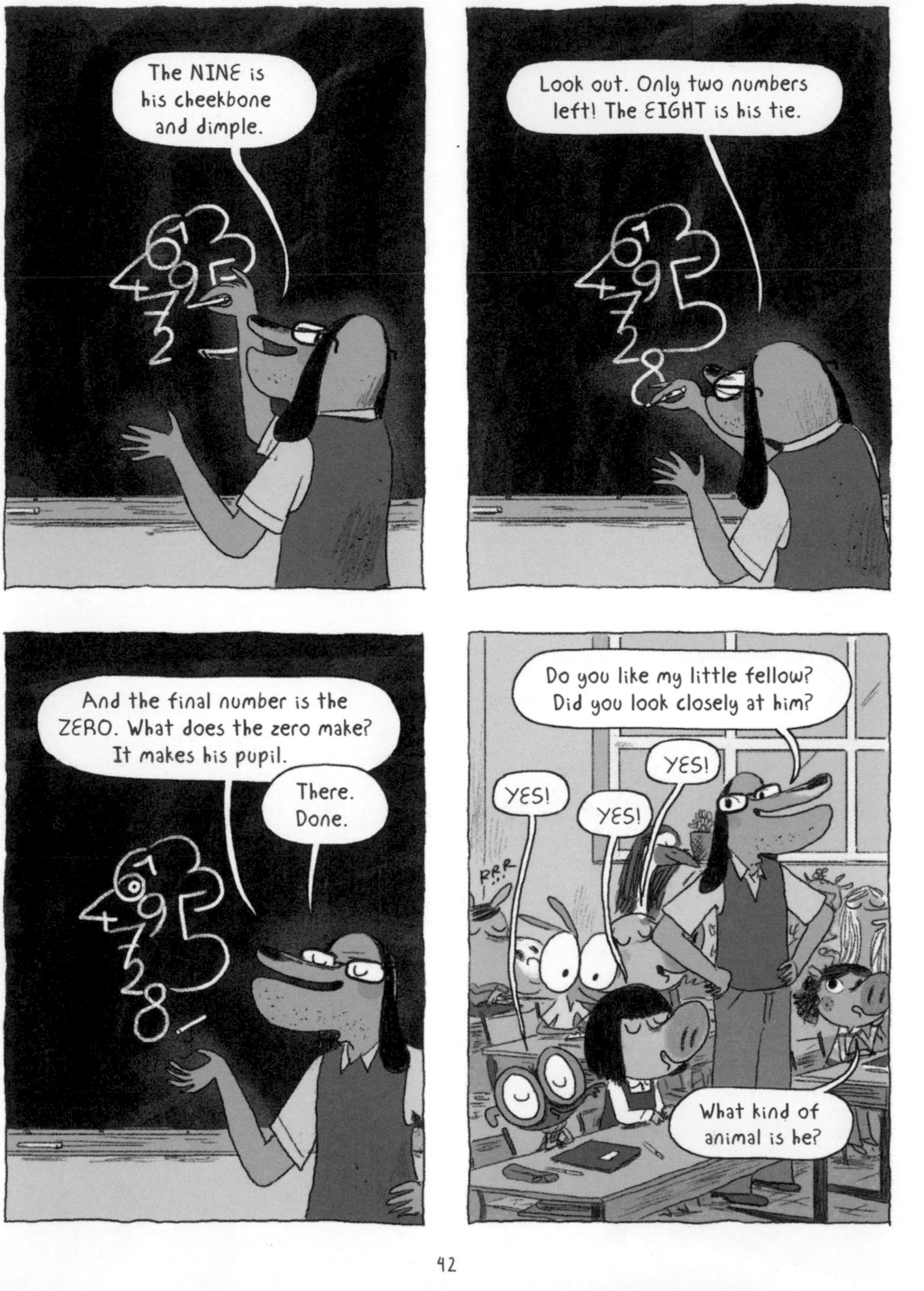
The NINE is his cheekbone and dimple.
Look out. Only two numbers left! The EIGHT is his tie.
And the final number is the ZERO. What does the zero make? It makes his pupil.
There. Done.
Do you like my little fellow? Did you look closely at him?
YES!
YES!
YES!
RRR
What kind of animal is he?

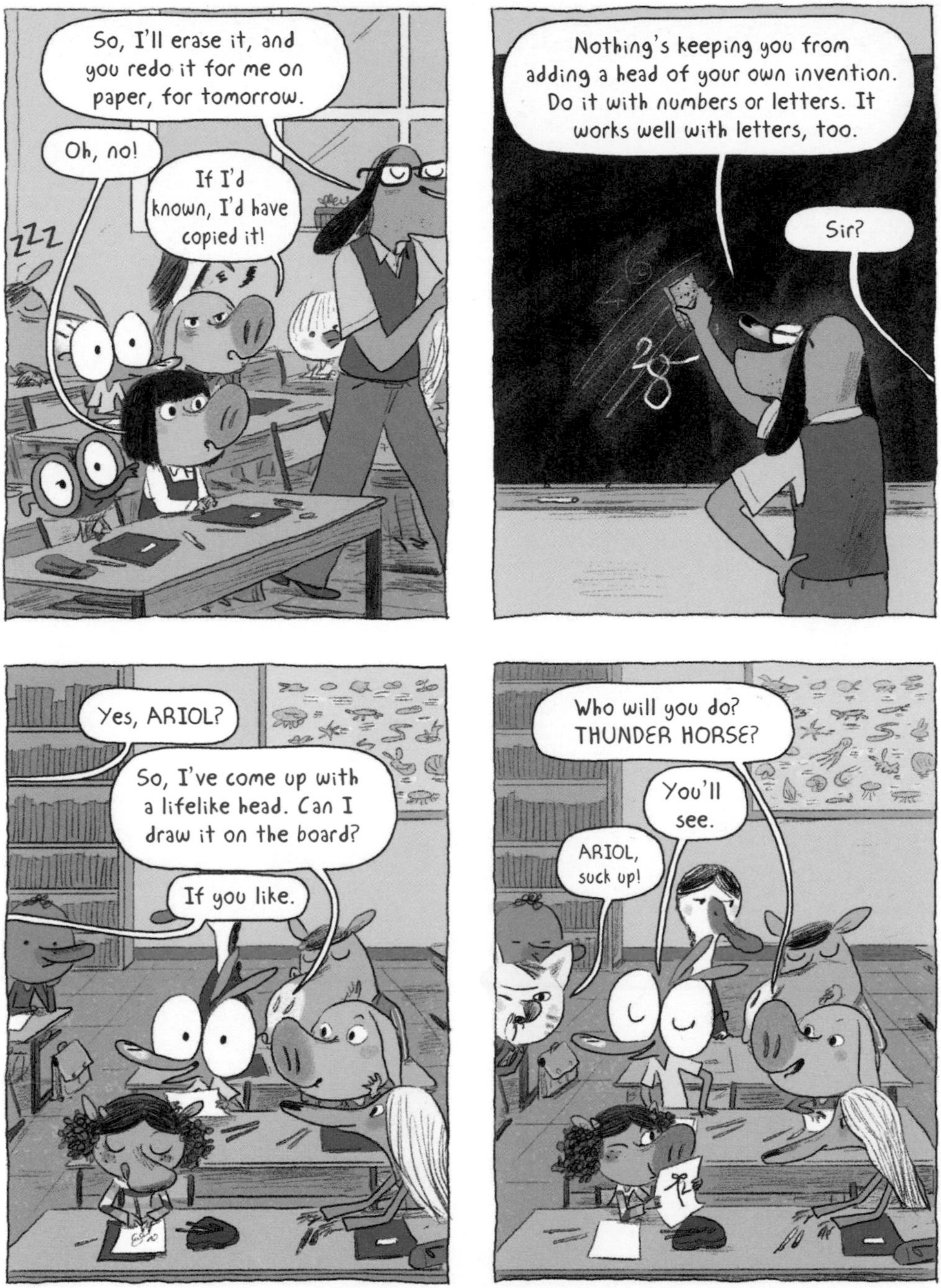

So, I'll erase it, and you redo it for me on paper, for tomorrow.
Oh, no!
If I'd known, I'd have copied it!
Nothing's keeping you from adding a head of your own invention. Do it with numbers or letters. It works well with letters, too.
Sir?
Yes, ARIOL?
So, I've come up with a lifelike head. Can I draw it on the board?
If you like.
Who will you do? THUNDER HORSE?
You'll see.
ARIOL, suck up!

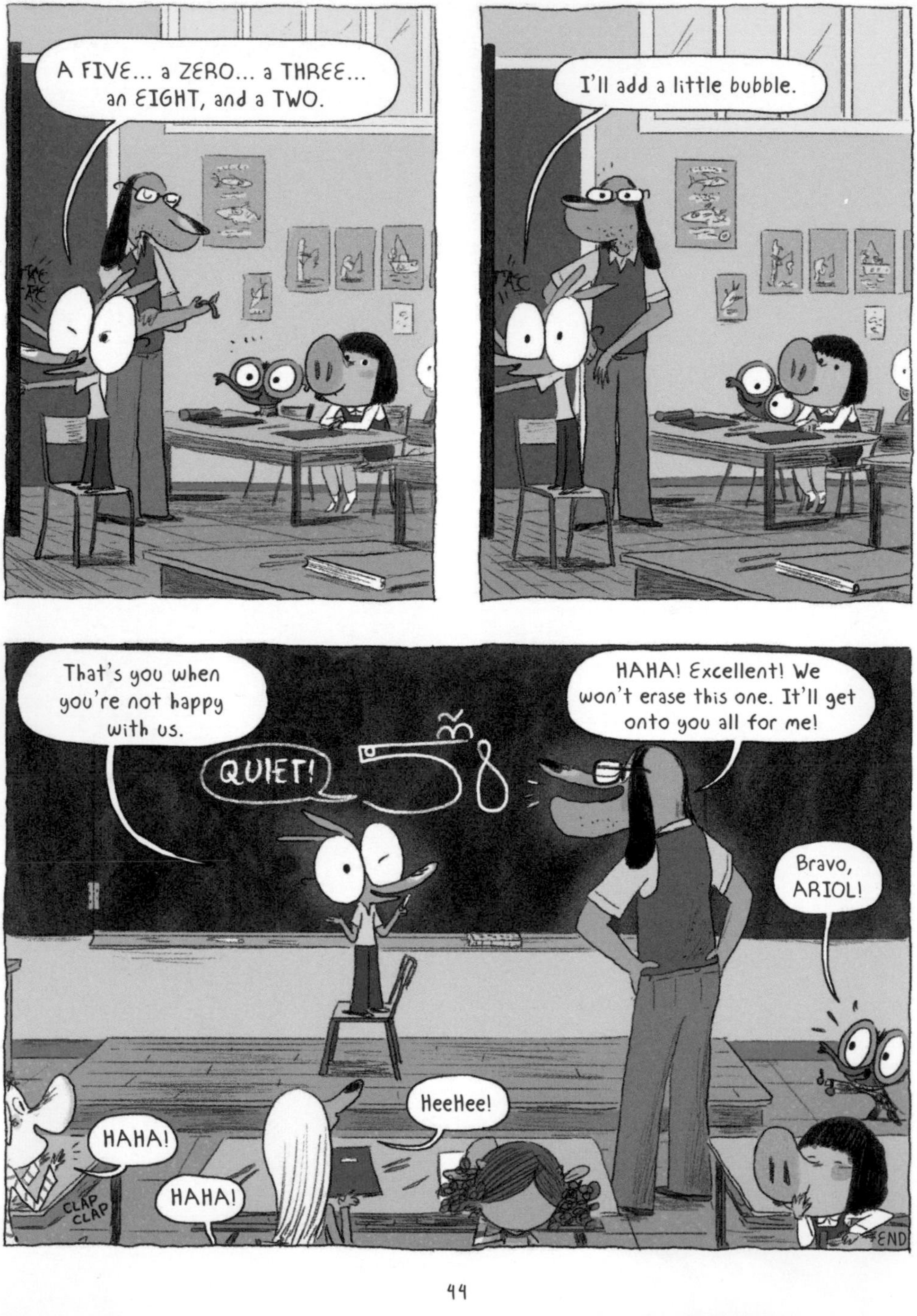
A FIVE... a ZERO... a THREE... an EIGHT, and a TWO.
I'll add a little bubble.
That's you when you're not happy with us.
QUIET!
HAHA! Excellent! We won't erase this one. It'll get onto you all for me!
Bravo, ARIOL!
HeeHee!
HAHA!
HAHA!
CLAP CLAP
END

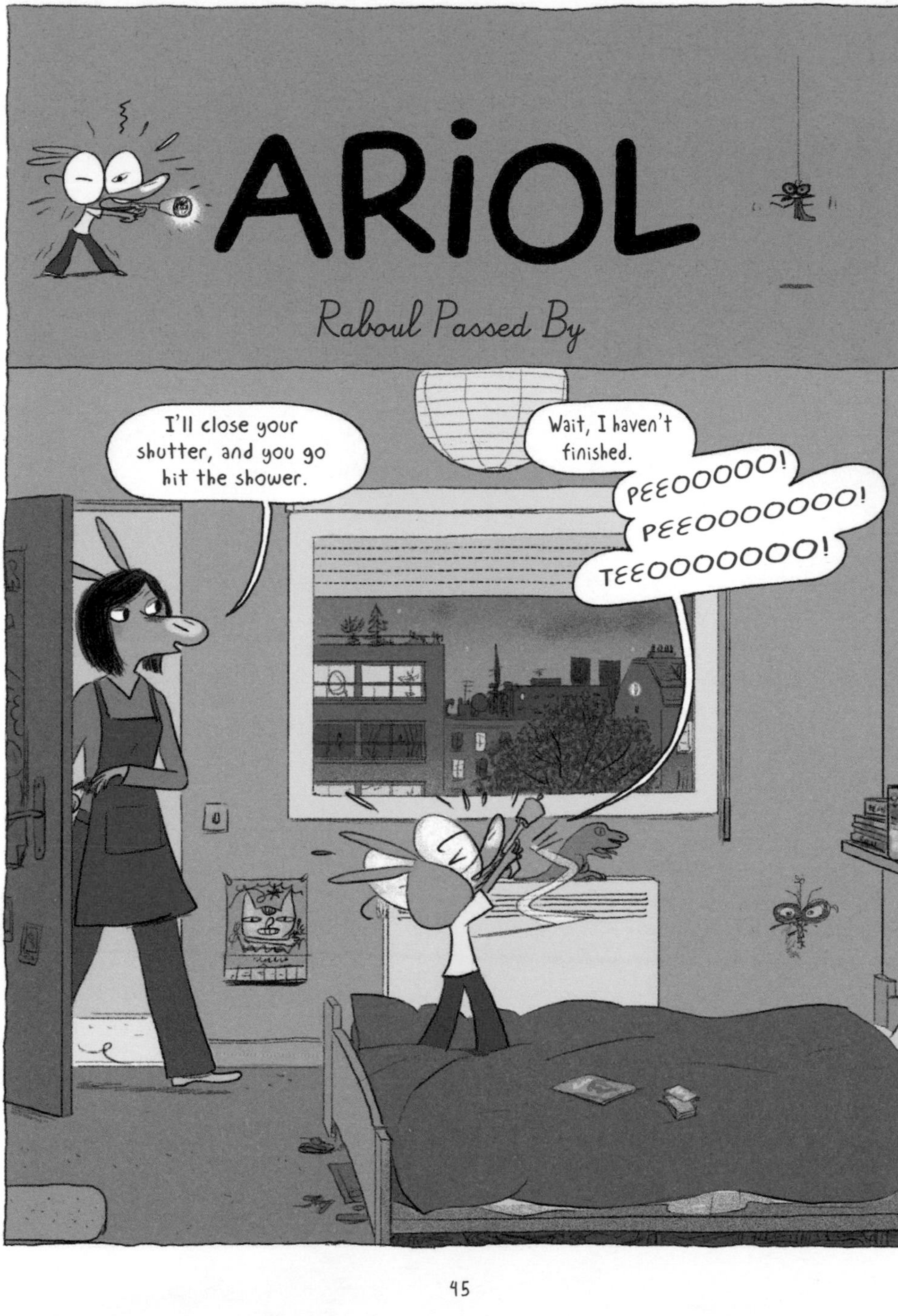
ARiOL
Raboul Passed By
I'll close your shutter, and you go hit the shower.
Wait, I haven't finished.
PEEOOOOO! PEEOOOOOOOO! TEEOOOOOOOO!

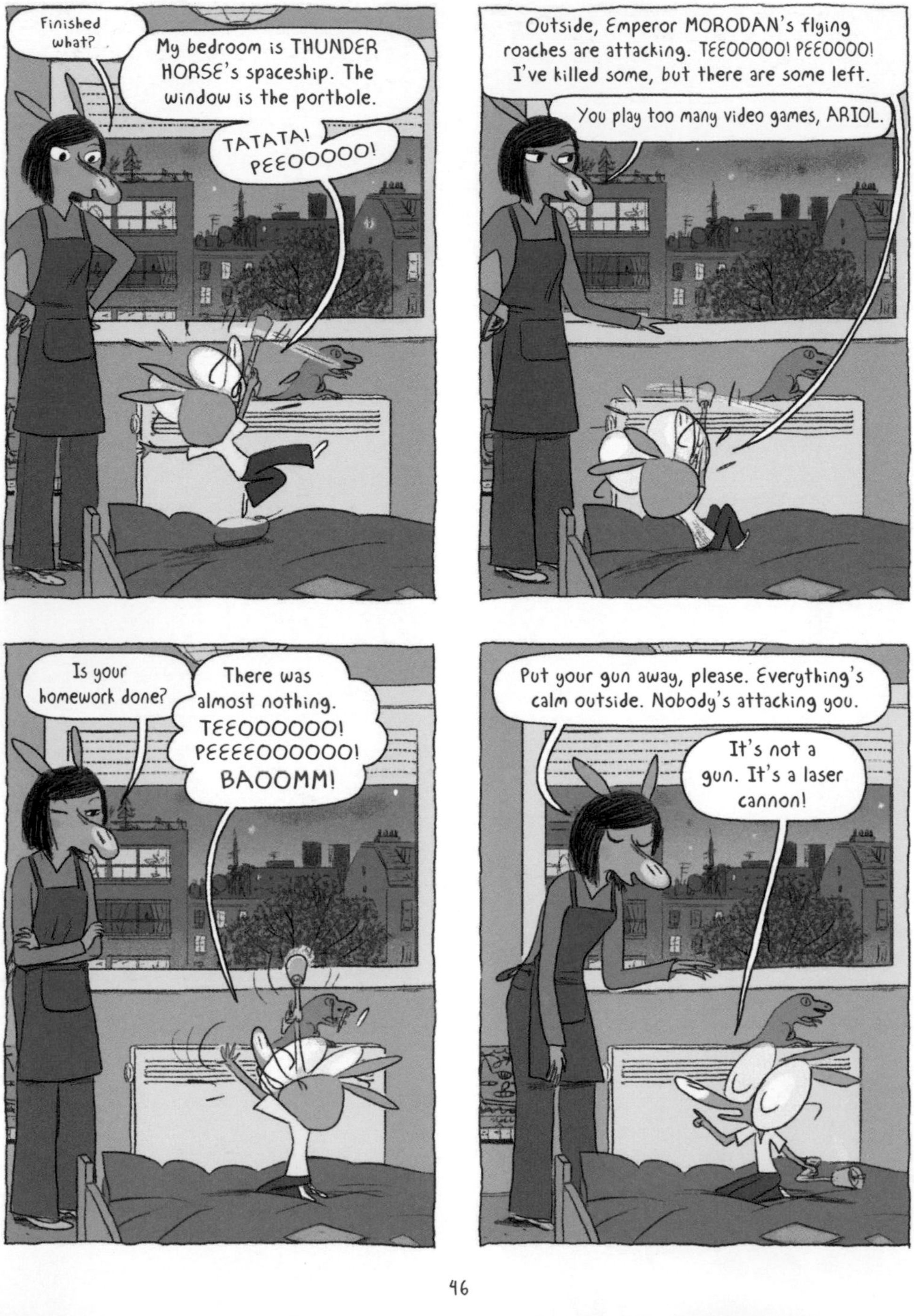
Finished what?
My bedroom is THUNDER HORSE's spaceship. The window is the porthole.
TATATA! PEEOOOOO!
Outside, Emperor MORODAN's flying roaches are attacking. TEEOOOOO! PEEOOOO! I've killed some, but there are some left.
You play too many video games, ARIOL.
Is your homework done?
There was almost nothing. TEEOOOOOO! PEEEEOOOOOO! BAOOMM!
Put your gun away, please. Everything's calm outside. Nobody's attacking you.
It's not a gun. It's a laser cannon!

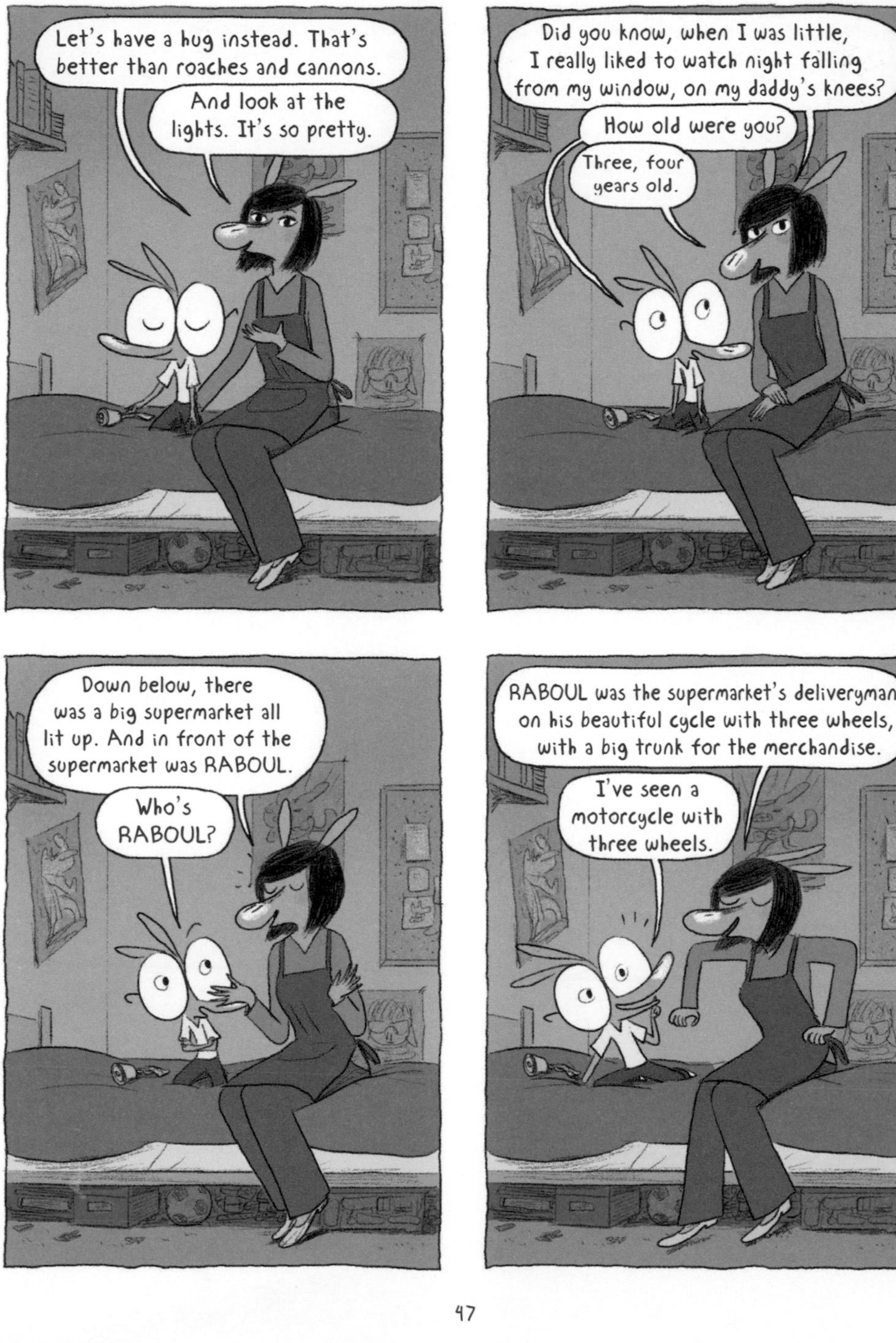
Let's have a hug instead. That's better than roaches and cannons.
And look at the lights. It's so pretty.
Did you know, when I was little, I really liked to watch night falling from my window, on my daddy's knees?
How old were you?
Three, four years old.
Down below, there was a big supermarket all lit up. And in front of the supermarket was RABOUL.
Who's RABOUL?
RABOUL was the supermarket's deliveryman, on his beautiful cycle with three wheels, with a big trunk for the merchandise.
I've seen a motorcycle with three wheels.

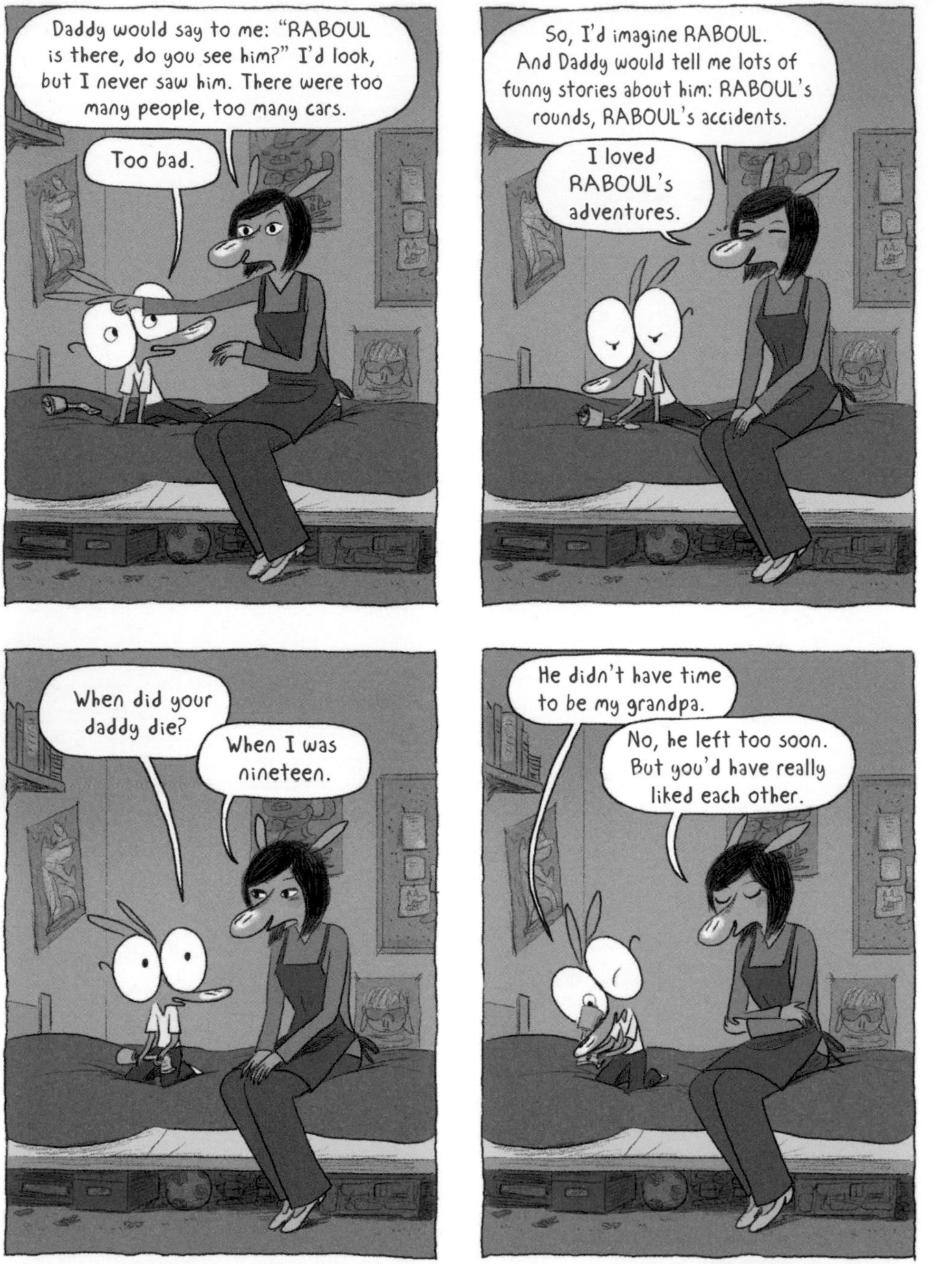
Daddy would say to me: "RABOUL is there, do you see him?" I'd look, but I never saw him. There were too many people, too many cars.
Too bad.
So, I'd imagine RABOUL. And Daddy would tell me lots of funny stories about him: RABOUL's rounds, RABOUL's accidents.
I loved RABOUL's adventures.
When did your daddy die?
When I was nineteen.
He didn't have time to be my grandpa.
No, he left too soon. But you'd have really liked each other.

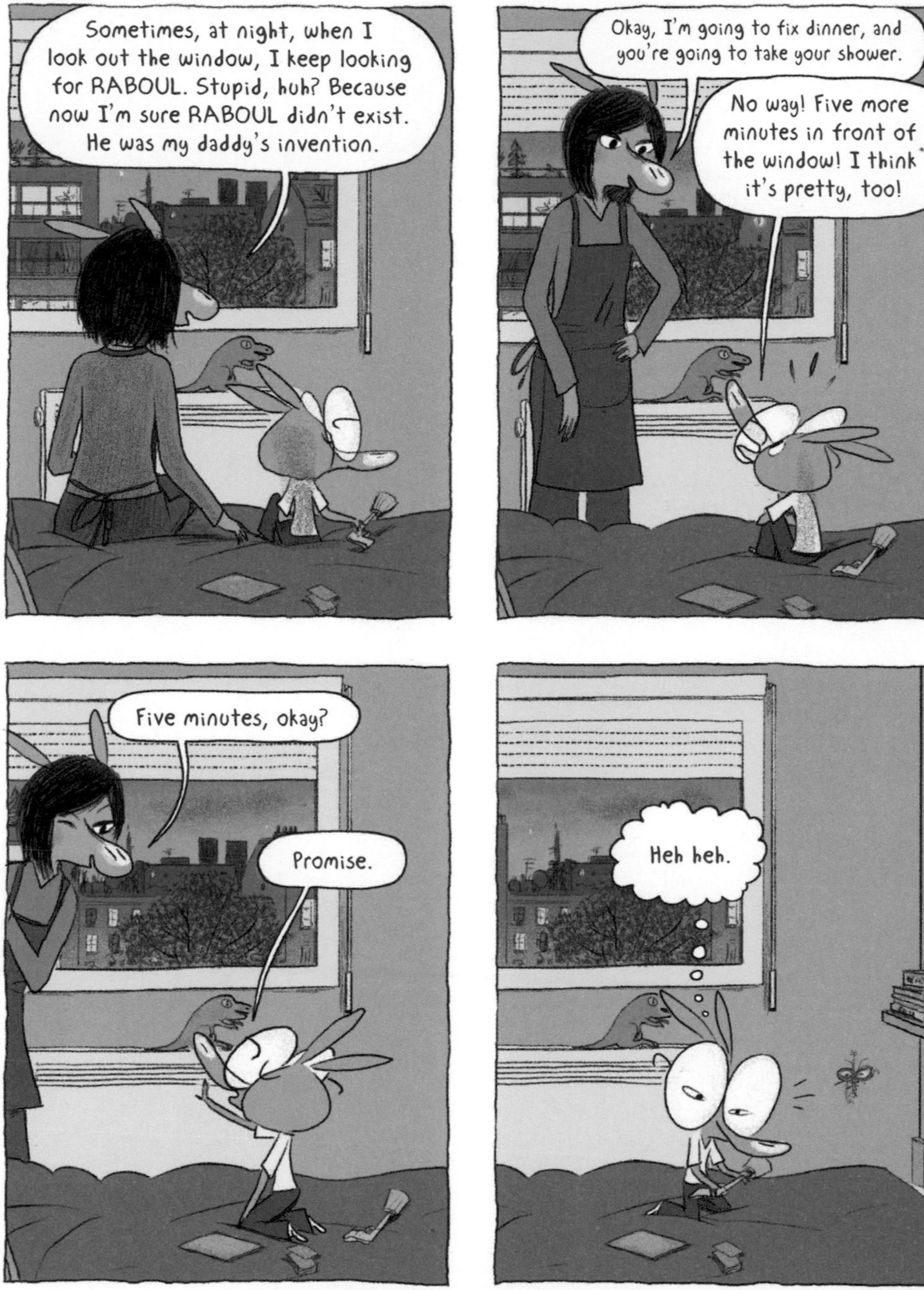
Sometimes, at night, when I look out the window, I keep looking for RABOUL. Stupid, huh? Because now I'm sure RABOUL didn't exist. He was my daddy's invention.
Okay, I'm going to fix dinner, and you're going to take your shower.
No way! Five more minutes in front of the window! I think it's pretty, too!
Five minutes, okay?
Promise.
Heh heh.

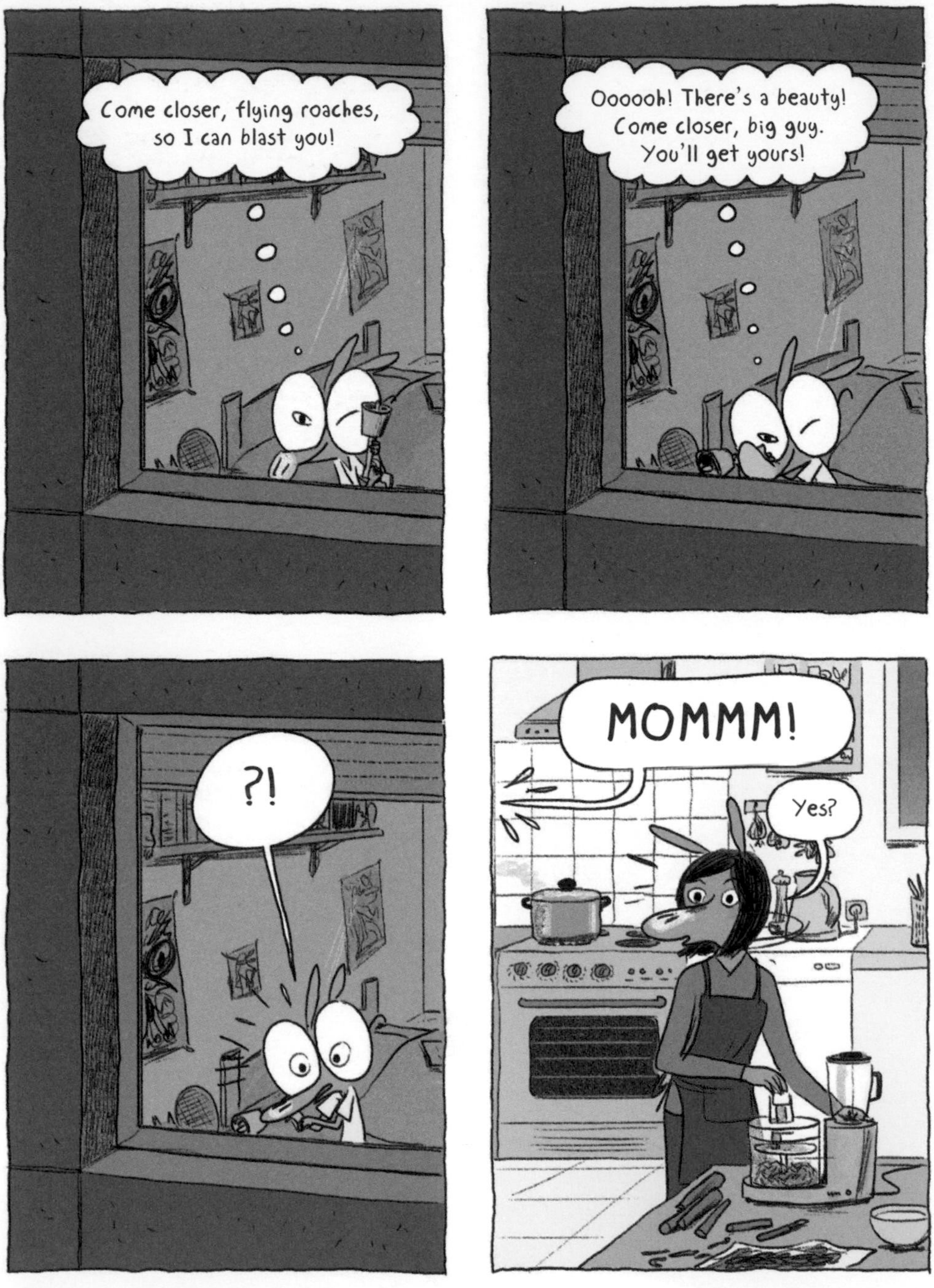
Come closer, flying roaches, so I can blast you!
Oooooh! There's a beauty! Come closer, big guy. You'll get yours!
?!
MOMMM!
Yes?

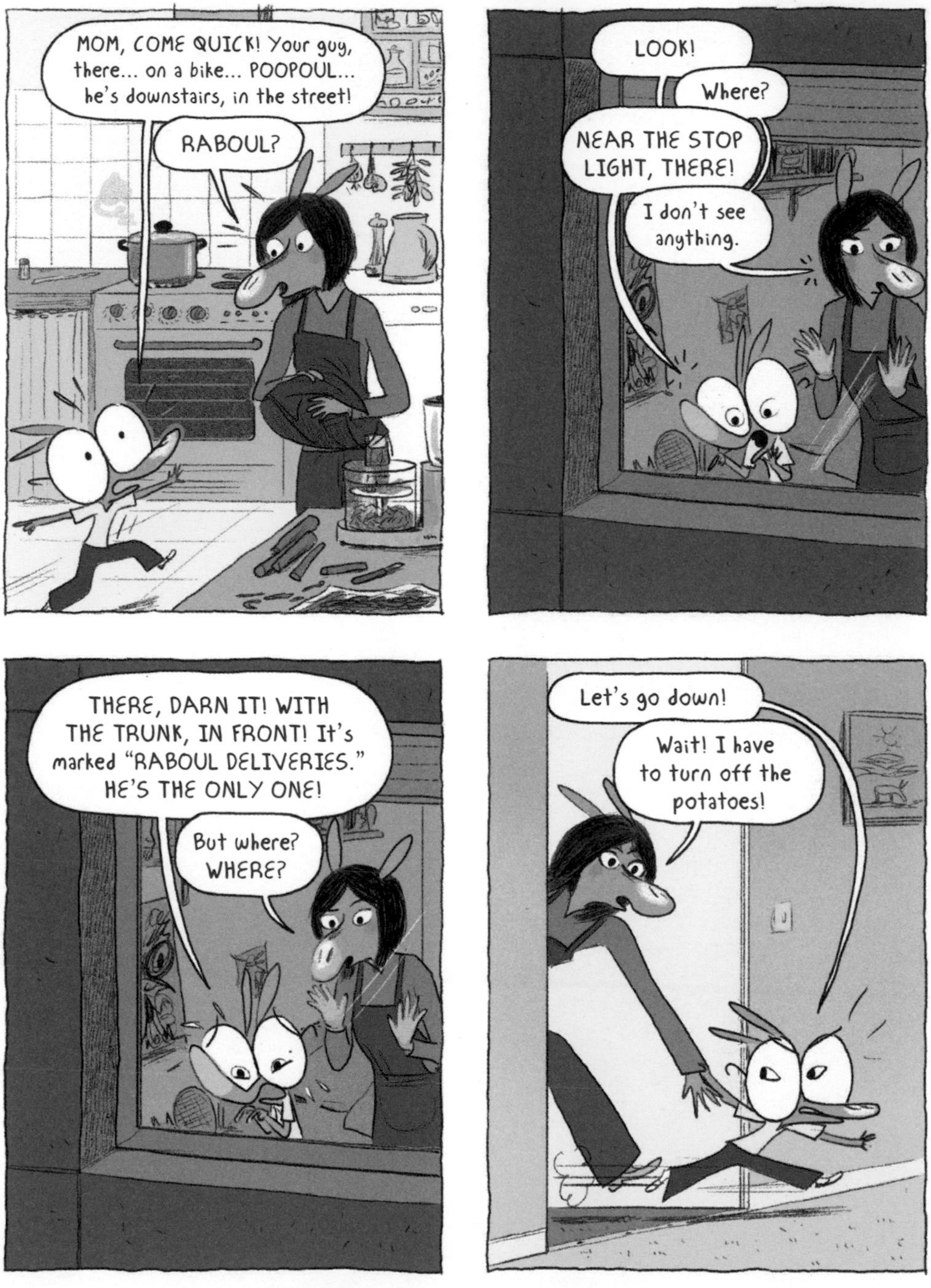

MOM, COME QUICK! Your guy, there... on a bike... POOPOUL... he's downstairs, in the street!
RABOUL?
LOOK!
Where?
NEAR THE STOP LIGHT, THERE!
I don't see anything.
THERE, DARN IT! WITH THE TRUNK, IN FRONT! It's marked "RABOUL DELIVERIES." HE'S THE ONLY ONE!
But where? WHERE?
Let's go down!
Wait! I have to turn off the potatoes!

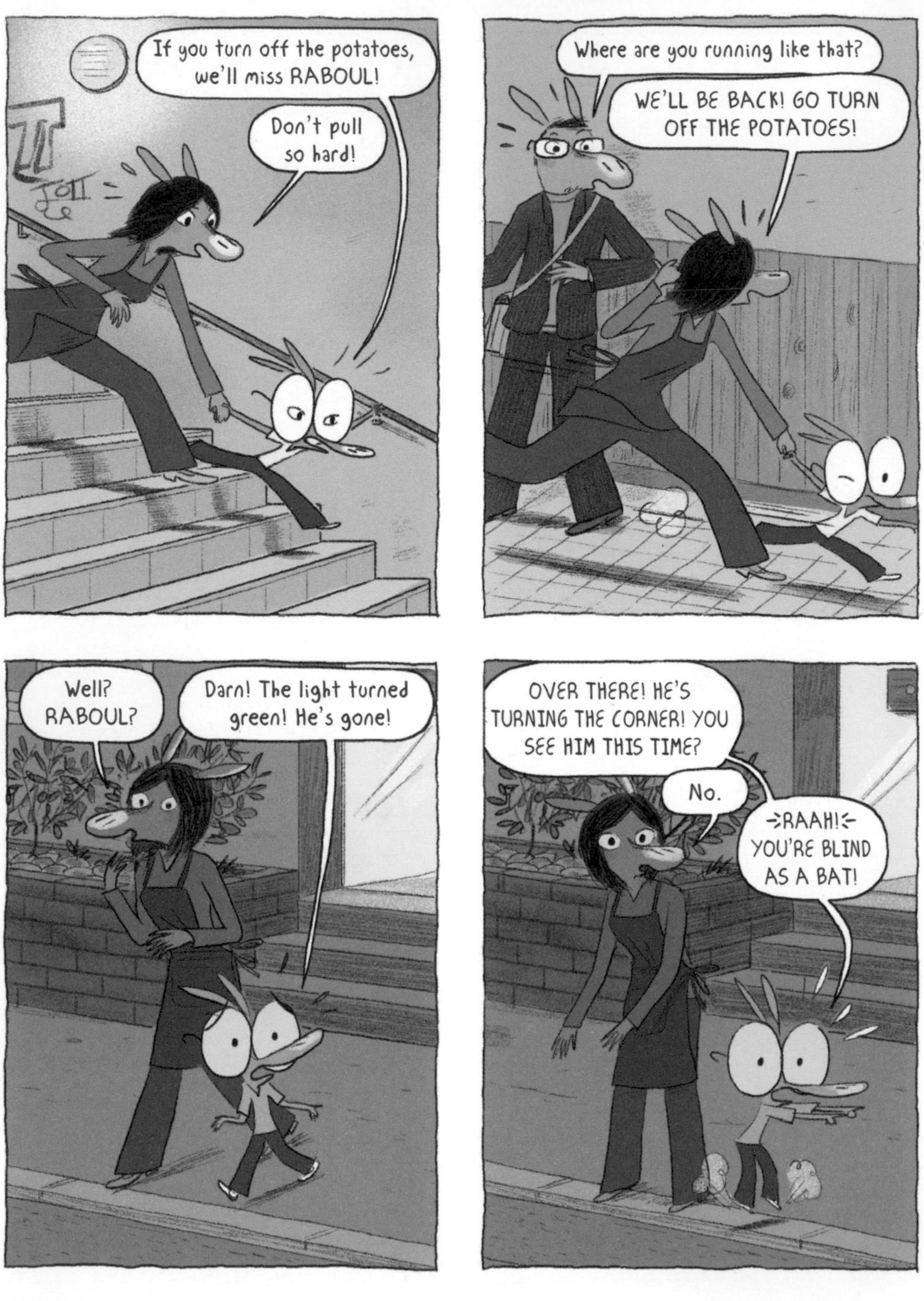
If you turn off the potatoes, we'll miss RABOUL!
Don't pull so hard!
Where are you running like that?
WE'LL BE BACK! GO TURN OFF THE POTATOES!
Well? RABOUL?
Darn! The light turned green! He's gone!
OVER THERE! HE'S TURNING THE CORNER! YOU SEE HIM THIS TIME?
No.
RAAH!
YOU'RE BLIND AS A BAT!

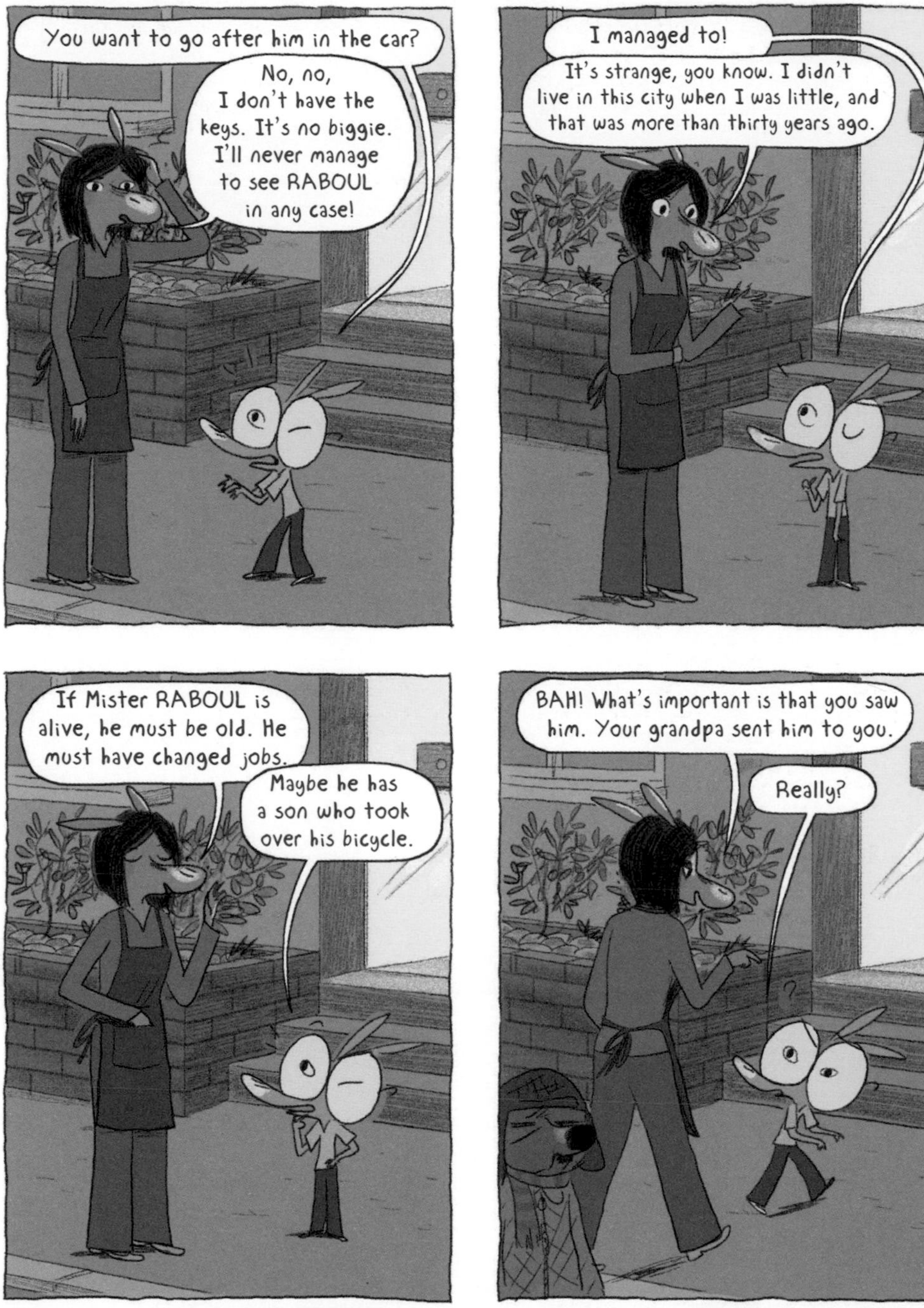
You want to go after him in the car?
No, no, I don't have the keys. It's no biggie. I'll never manage to see RABOUL in any case!
I managed to!
It's strange, you know. I didn't live in this city when I was little, and that was more than thirty years ago.
If Mister RABOUL is alive, he must be old. He must have changed jobs.
Maybe he has a son who took over his bicycle.
BAH! What's important is that you saw him. Your grandpa sent him to you.
Really?
?

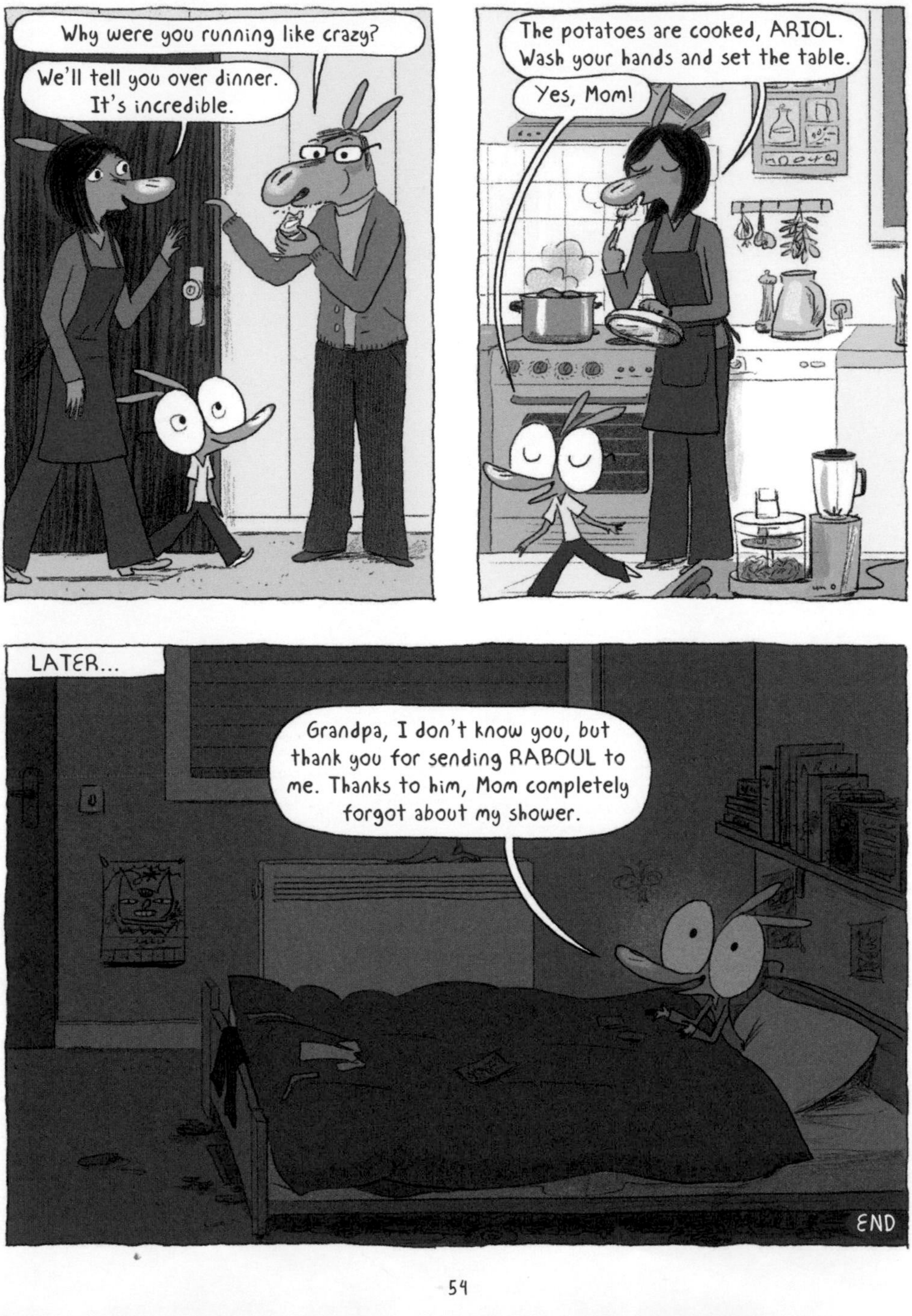
Why were you running like crazy?
We'll tell you over dinner. It's incredible.
The potatoes are cooked, ARIOL. Wash your hands and set the table.
Yes, Mom!
LATER...
Grandpa, I don't know you, but thank you for sending RABOUL to me. Thanks to him, Mom completely forgot about my shower.
END

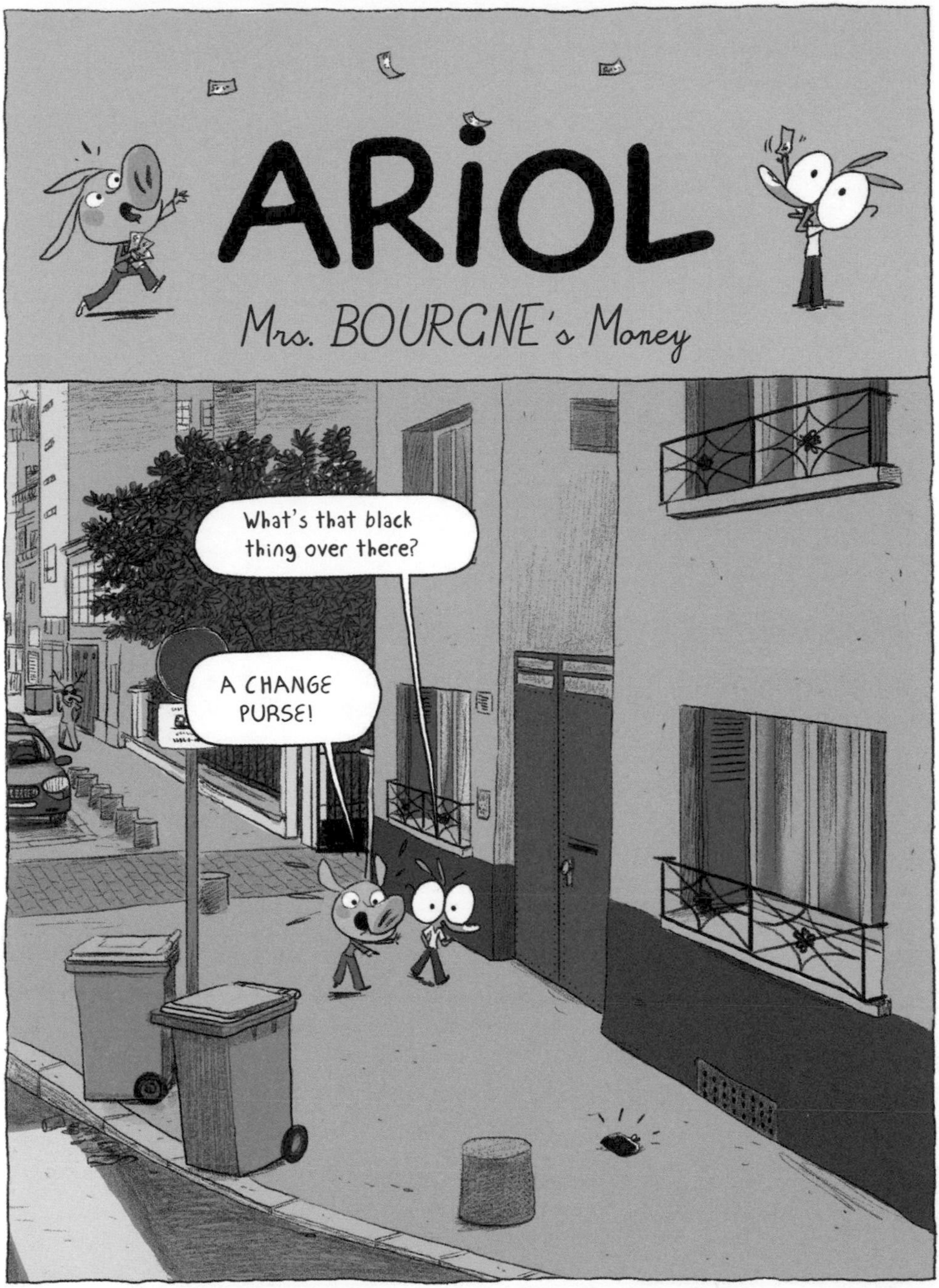
ARIOL
Mrs. BOURGNE's Money
What's that black thing over there?
A CHANGE PURSE!

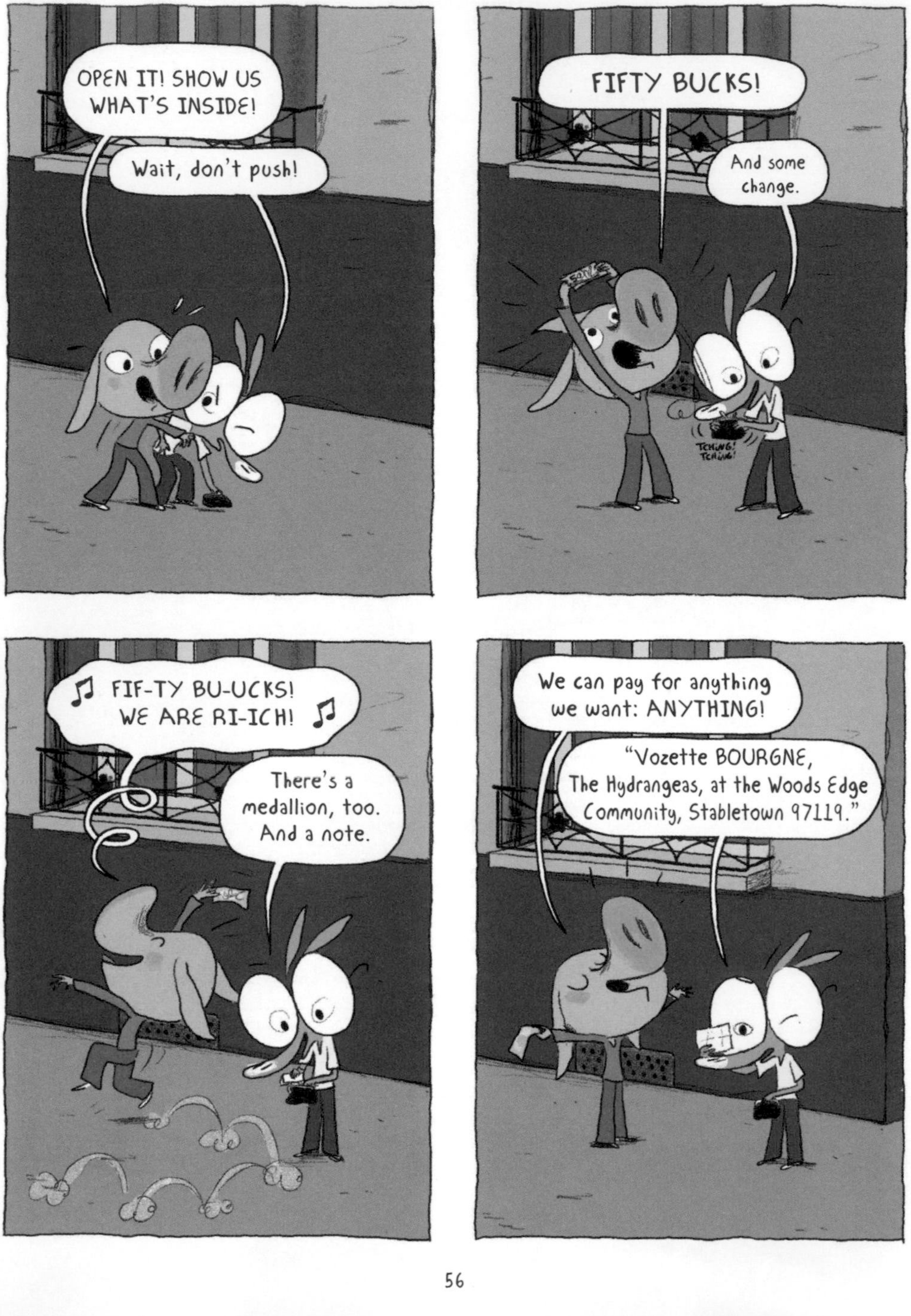
OPEN IT! SHOW US WHAT'S INSIDE!
Wait, don't push!
FIFTY BUCKS!
And some change.
TCHING! TCHING!
♫ FIF-TY BU-UCKS! WE ARE RI-ICH! ♫
There's a medallion, too. And a note.
We can pay for anything we want: ANYTHING!
"Vozette BOURGNE, The Hydrangeas, at the Woods Edge Community, Stabletown 97119."

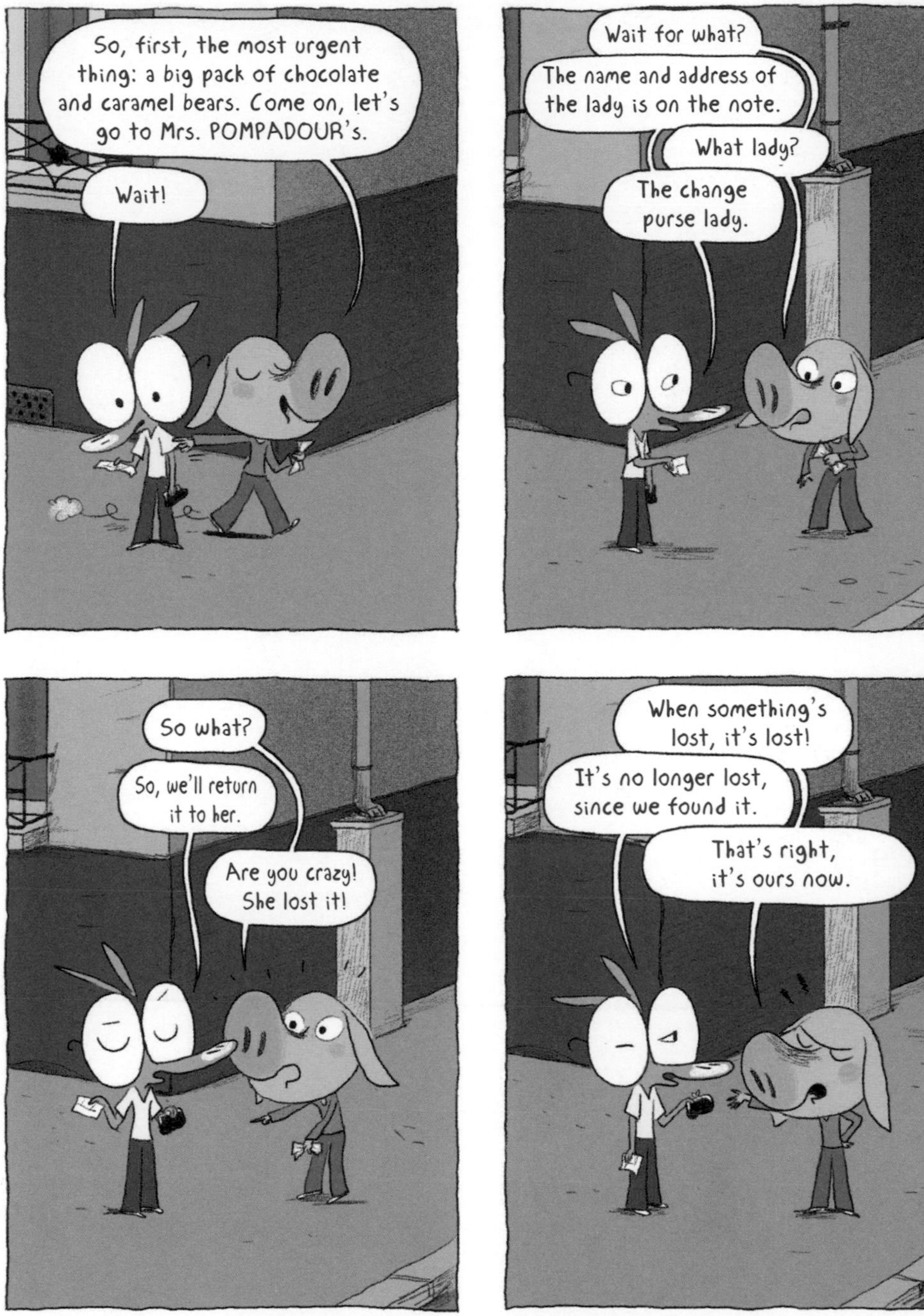
So, first, the most urgent thing: a big pack of chocolate and caramel bears. Come on, let's go to Mrs. POMPADOUR's.
Wait!
Wait for what?
The name and address of the lady is on the note.
What lady?
The change purse lady.
So what?
So, we'll return it to her.
Are you crazy! She lost it!
When something's lost, it's lost!
It's no longer lost, since we found it.
That's right, it's ours now.

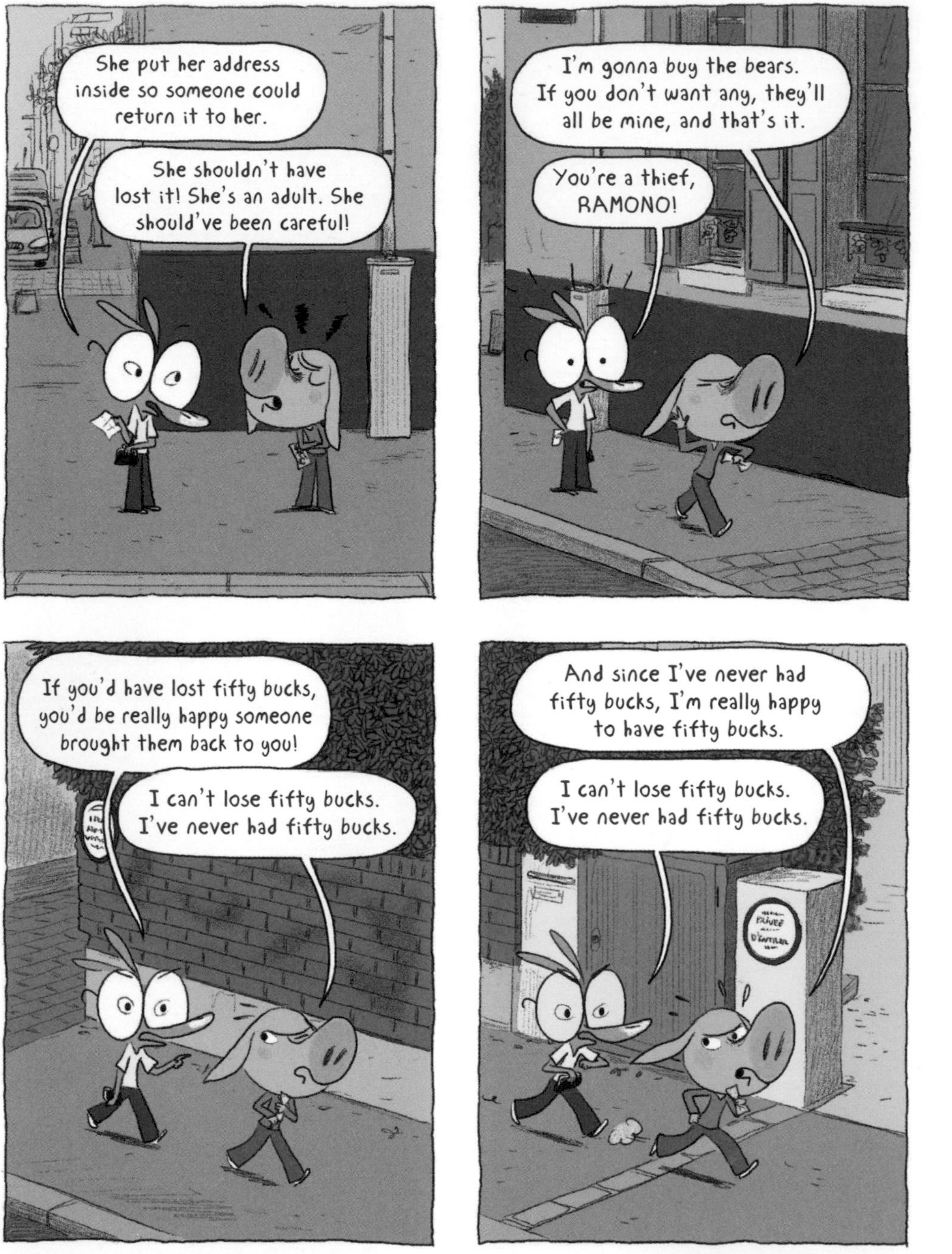

She put her address inside so someone could return it to her.
She shouldn't have lost it! She's an adult. She should've been careful!
I'm gonna buy the bears. If you don't want any, they'll all be mine, and that's it.
You're a thief, RAMONO!
If you'd have lost fifty bucks, you'd be really happy someone brought them back to you!
I can't lose fifty bucks. I've never had fifty bucks.
And since I've never had fifty bucks, I'm really happy to have fifty bucks.
I can't lose fifty bucks. I've never had fifty bucks.

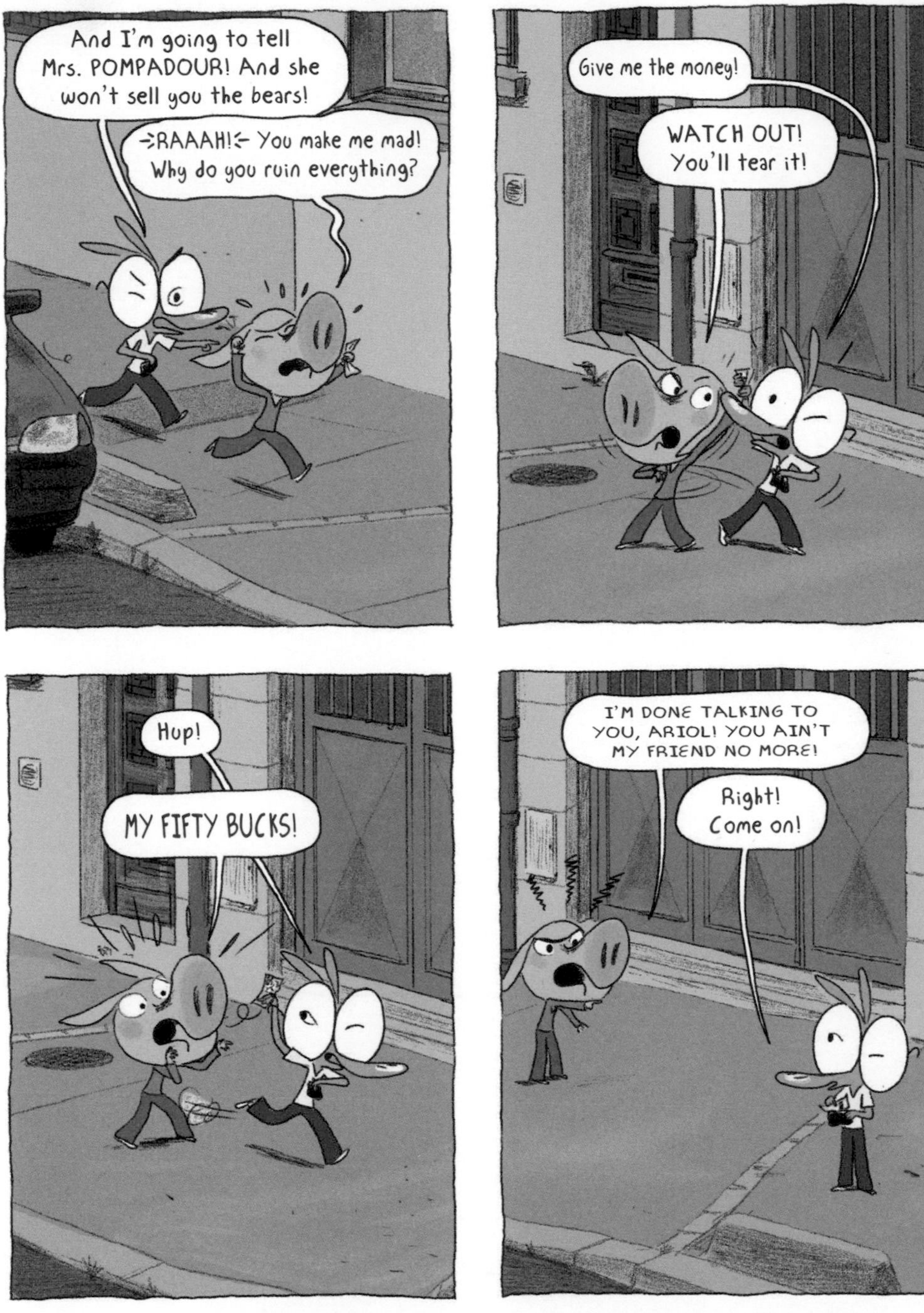

And I'm going to tell Mrs. POMPADOUR! And she won't sell you the bears!
RAAAH! You make me mad! Why do you ruin everything?
Give me the money!
WATCH OUT! You'll tear it!
Hup!
MY FIFTY BUCKS!
I'M DONE TALKING TO YOU, ARIOL! YOU AIN'T MY FRIEND NO MORE!
Right! Come on!

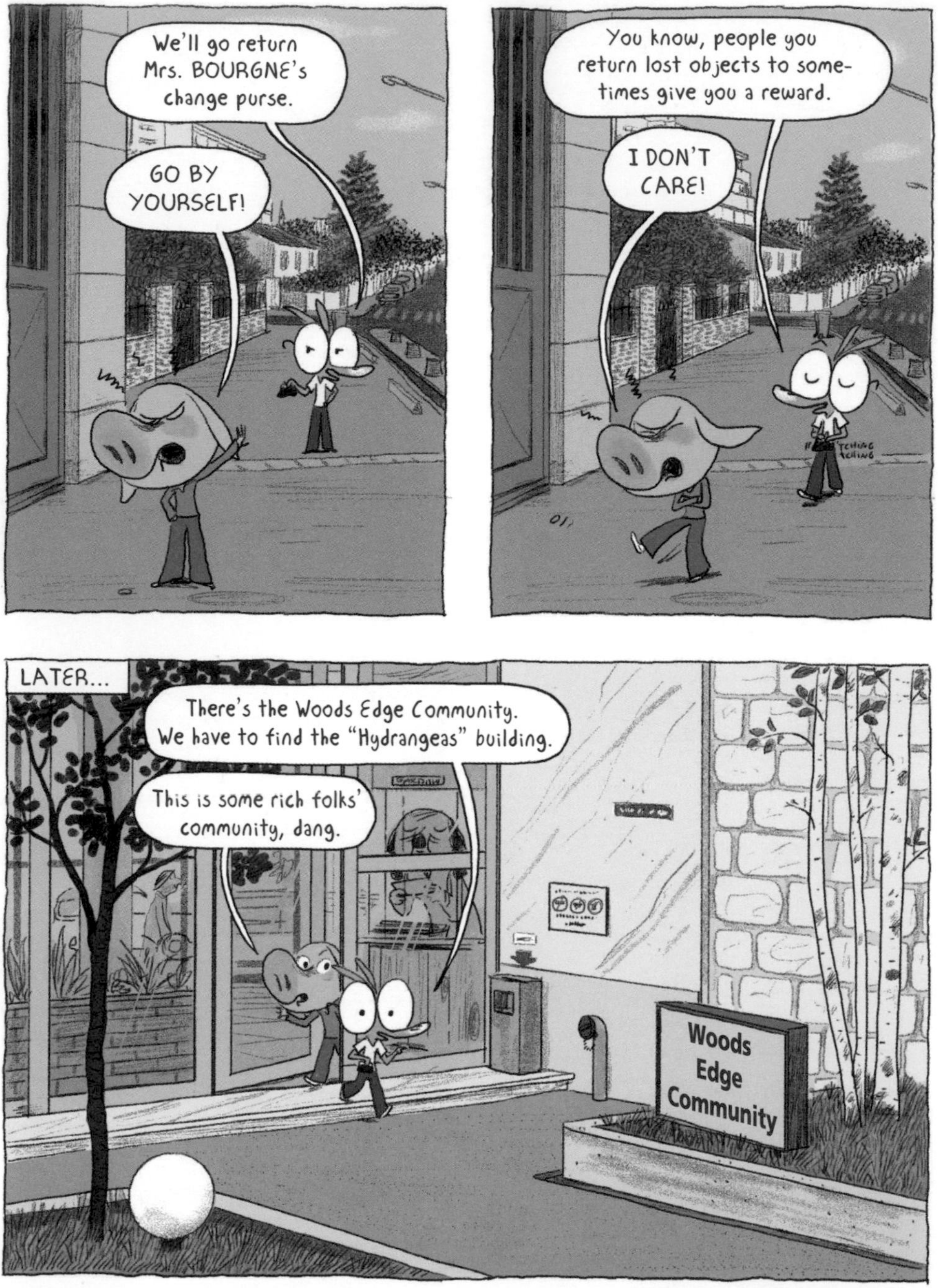
We'll go return Mrs. BOURGNE's change purse.
GO BY YOURSELF!
You know, people you return lost objects to some-times give you a reward.
I DON'T CARE!
LATER...
There's the Woods Edge Community. We have to find the "Hydrangeas" building.
This is some rich folks' community, dang.
Woods Edge Community

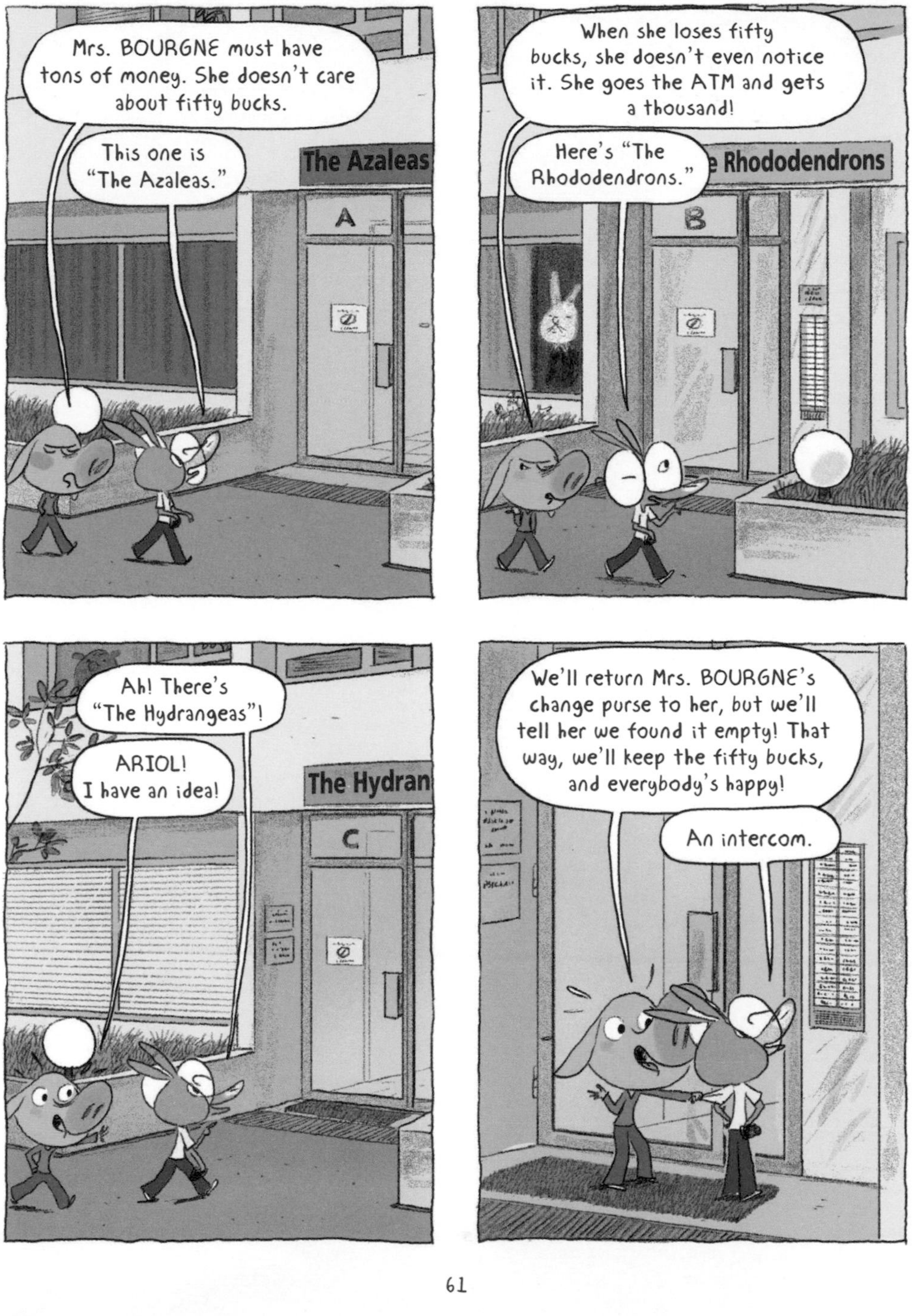

Mrs. BOURGNE must have tons of money. She doesn't care about fifty bucks.
This one is "The Azaleas."
The Azaleas
A
When she loses fifty bucks, she doesn't even notice it. She goes the ATM and gets a thousand!
Here's "The Rhododendrons."
e Rhododendrons
B
Ah! There's "The Hydrangeas"!
ARIOL! I have an idea!
The Hydran
C
We'll return Mrs. BOURGNE's change purse to her, but we'll tell her we found it empty! That way, we'll keep the fifty bucks, and everybody's happy!
An intercom.

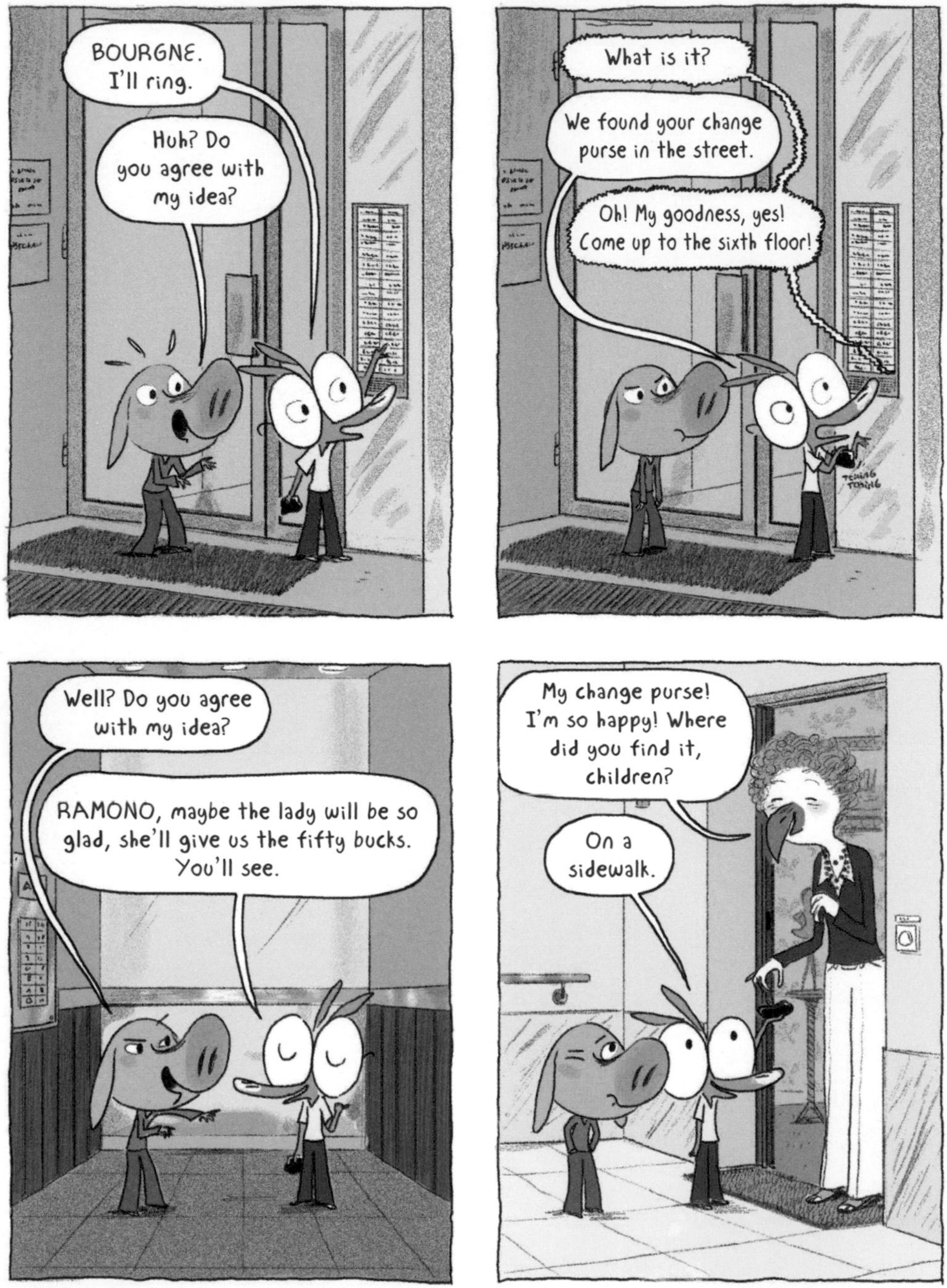
BOURGNE. I'll ring.
Huh? Do you agree with my idea?
What is it?
We found your change purse in the street.
Oh! My goodness, yes! Come up to the sixth floor!
TCHING TCHING
Well? Do you agree with my idea?
RAMONO, maybe the lady will be so glad, she'll give us the fifty bucks. You'll see.
My change purse! I'm so happy! Where did you find it, children?
On a sidewalk.

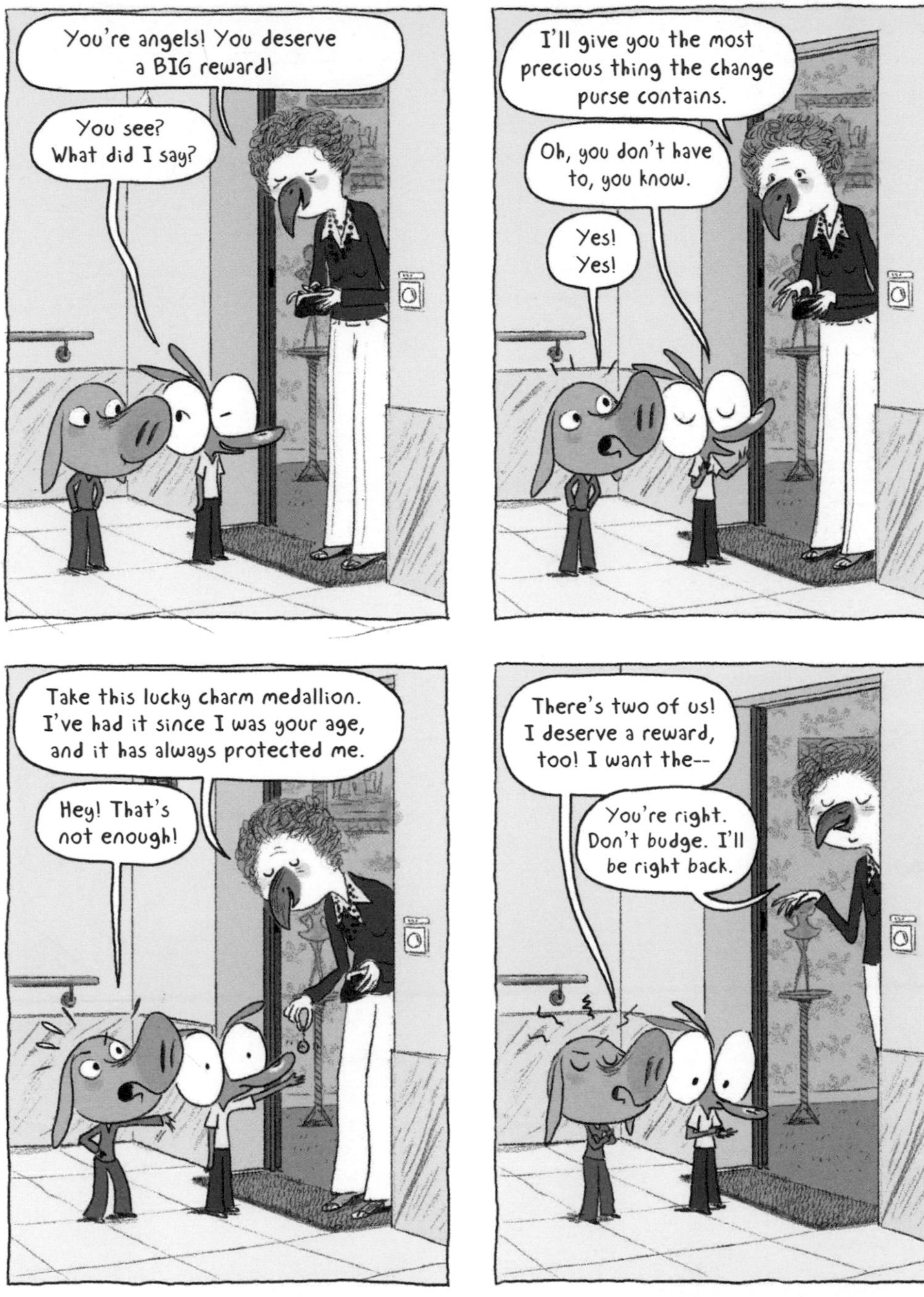
You're angels! You deserve a BIG reward!
You see? What did I say?
I'll give you the most precious thing the change purse contains.
Oh, you don't have to, you know.
Yes! Yes!
Take this lucky charm medallion. I've had it since I was your age, and it has always protected me.
Hey! That's not enough!
There's two of us! I deserve a reward, too! I want the--
You're right. Don't budge. I'll be right back.

Here's a little pack of honey candies. You can share it.
But...
With Mrs. BOURGNE's thanks!
CLAC
Uh... will you give me some candy?
Woods Edge ommunity
Ask your lucky charm!
END

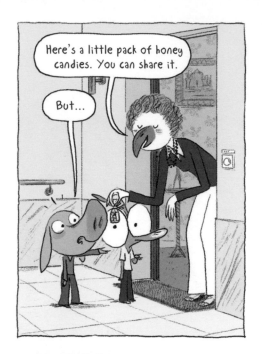

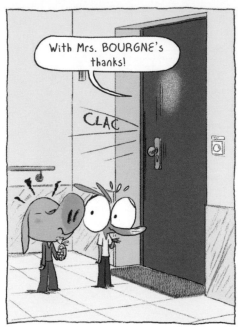

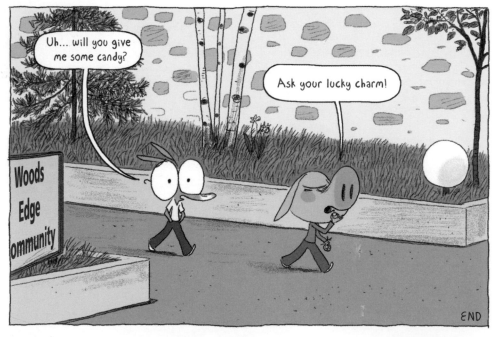

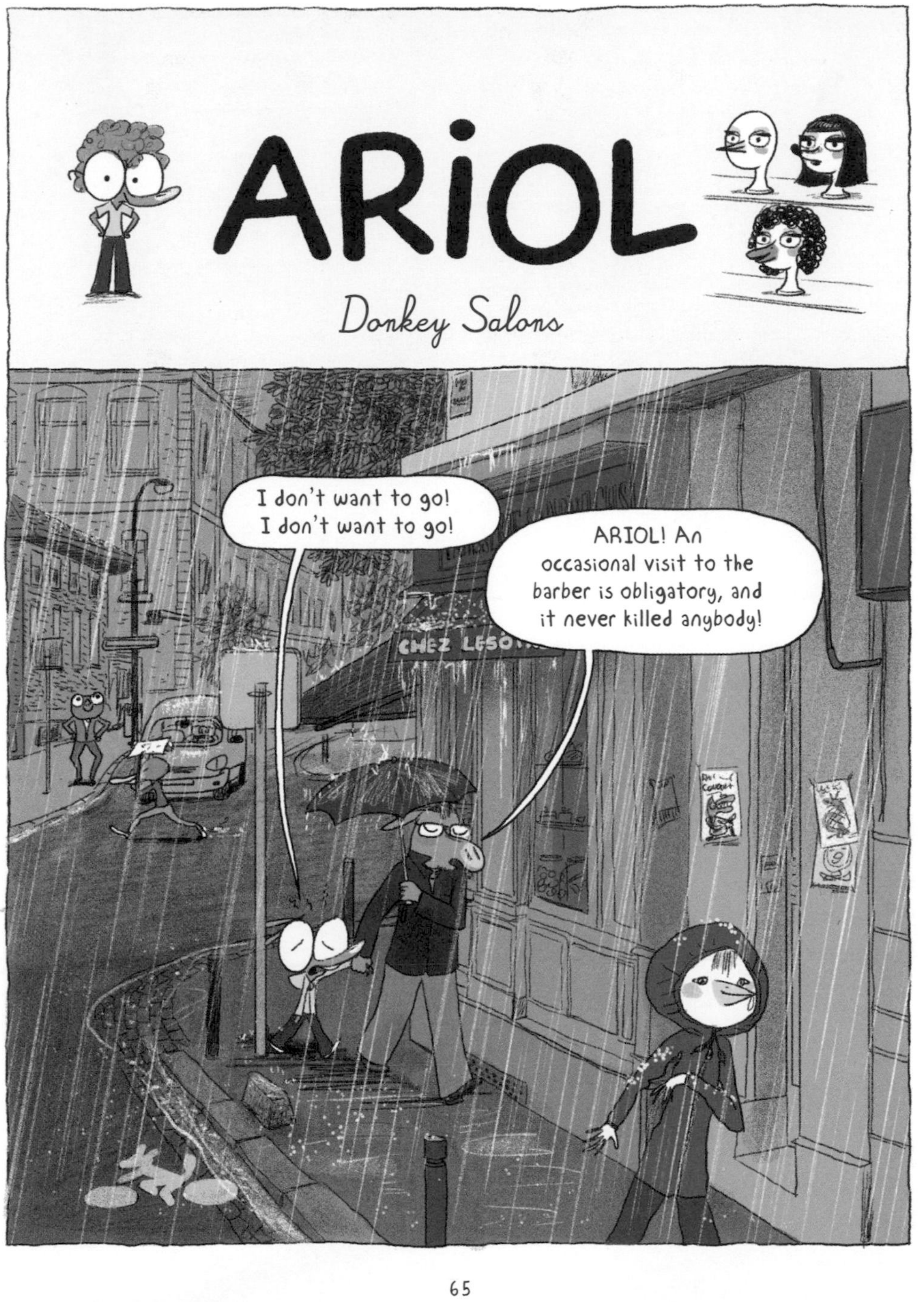
ARiOL
Donkey Salons
I don't want to go! I don't want to go!
ARIOL! An occasional visit to the barber is obligatory, and it never killed anybody!
CHEZ LESO

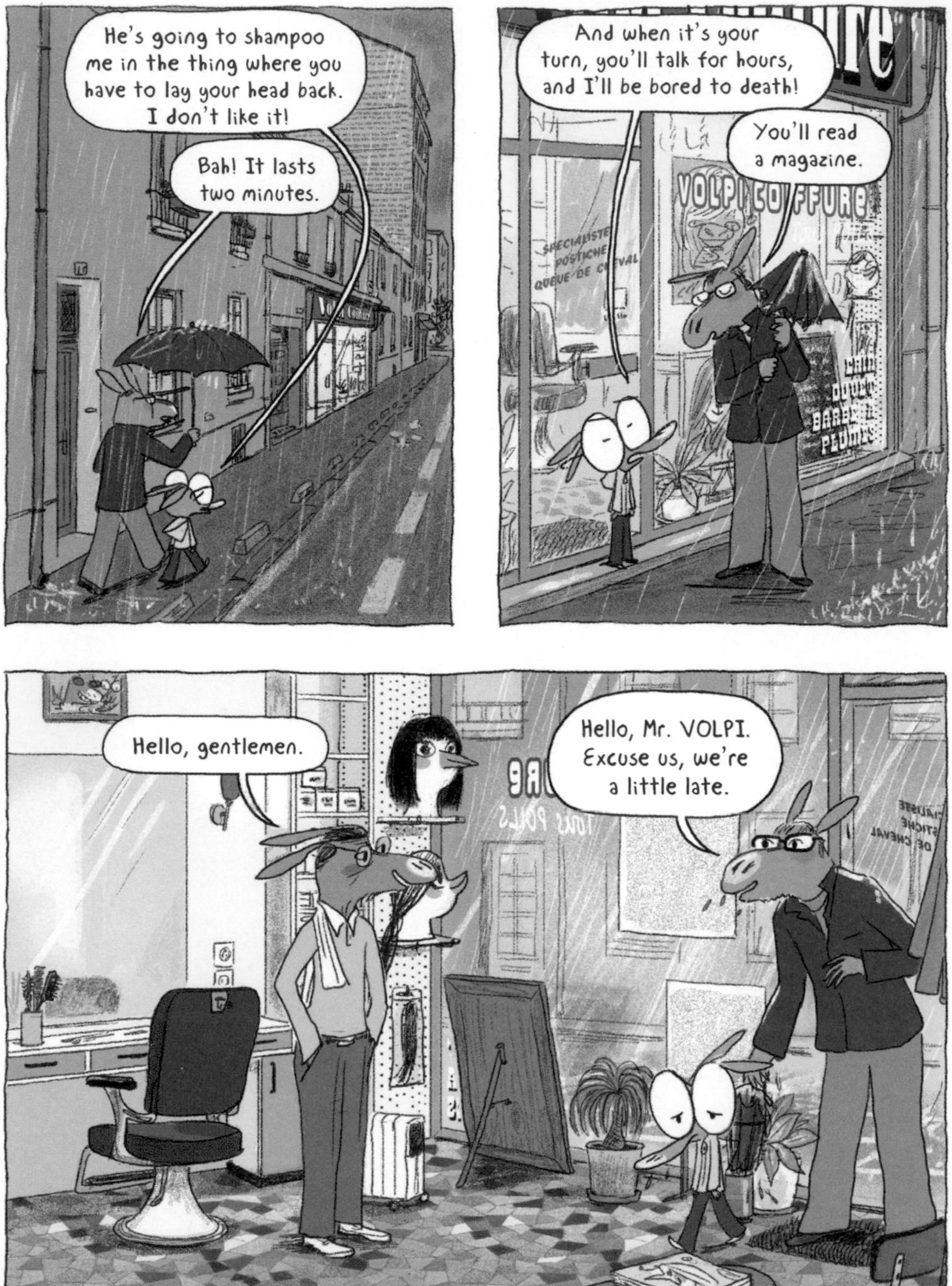
He's going to shampoo me in the thing where you have to lay your head back. I don't like it!
Bah! It lasts two minutes.
And when it's your turn, you'll talk for hours, and I'll be bored to death!
You'll read a magazine.
VOLPI COIFFURE
SPECIALISTE POSTICHE QUEUE DE CHEVAL
Hello, gentlemen.
Hello, Mr. VOLPI. Excuse us, we're a little late.

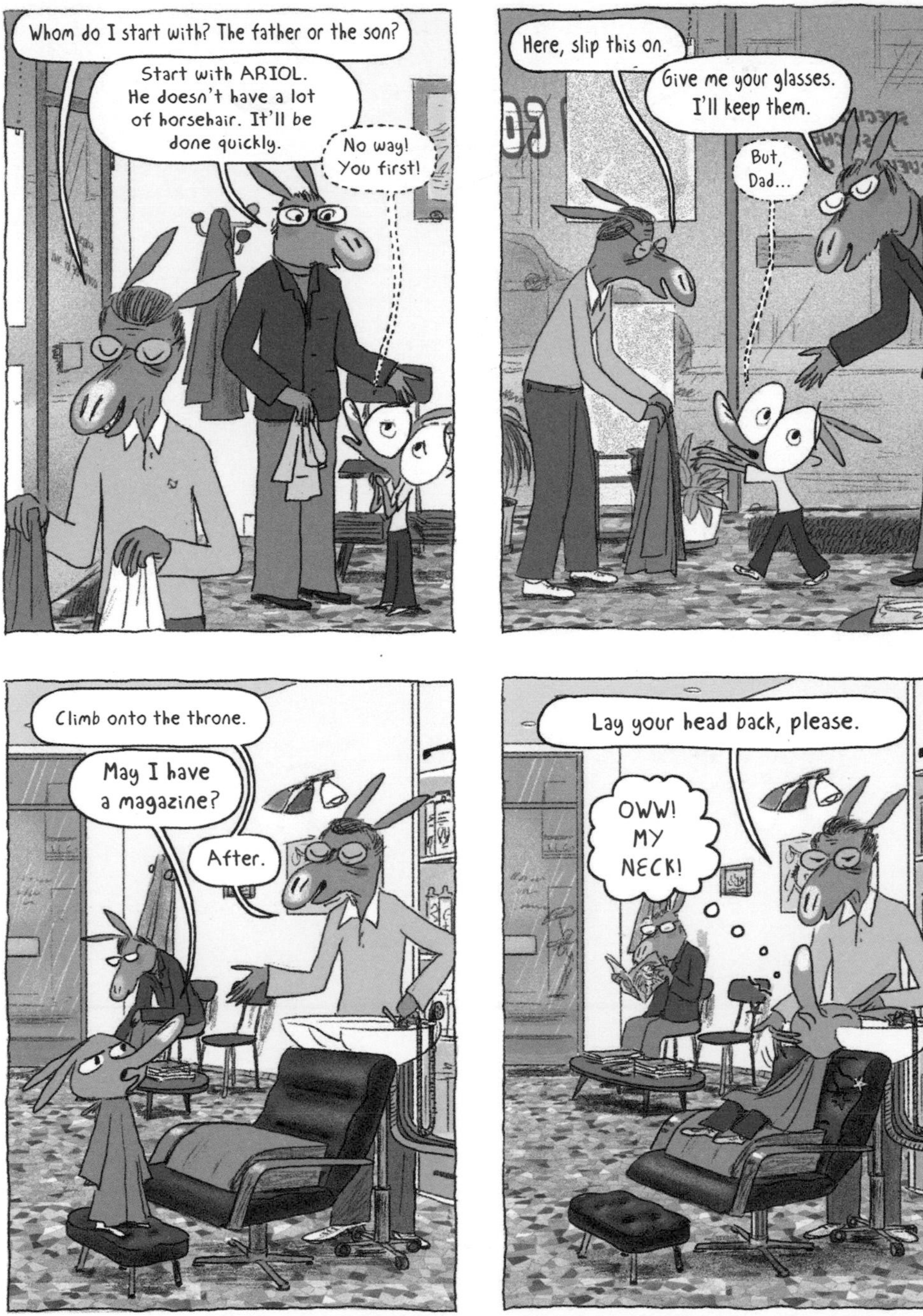
Whom do I start with? The father or the son?
Start with ARIOL. He doesn't have a lot of horsehair. It'll be done quickly.
No way! You first!
Here, slip this on.
Give me your glasses. I'll keep them.
But, Dad...
Climb onto the throne.
May I have a magazine?
After.
Lay your head back, please.
OWW! MY NECK!

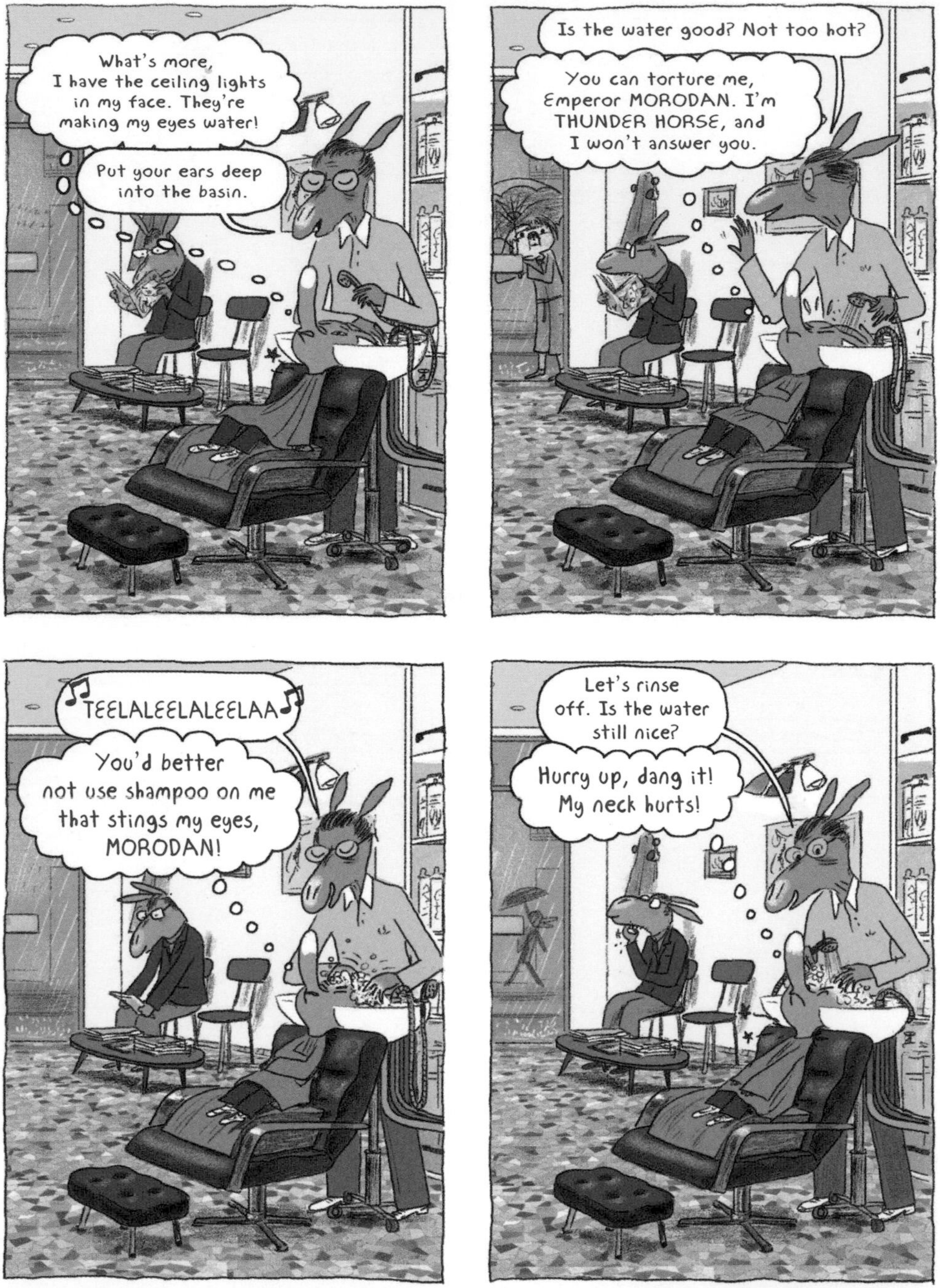
What's more, I have the ceiling lights in my face. They're making my eyes water!
Put your ears deep into the basin.
Is the water good? Not too hot?
You can torture me, Emperor MORODAN. I'm THUNDER HORSE, and I won't answer you.
TEELALEELALEELAA
You'd better not use shampoo on me that stings my eyes, MORODAN!
Let's rinse off. Is the water still nice?
Hurry up, dang it! My neck hurts!

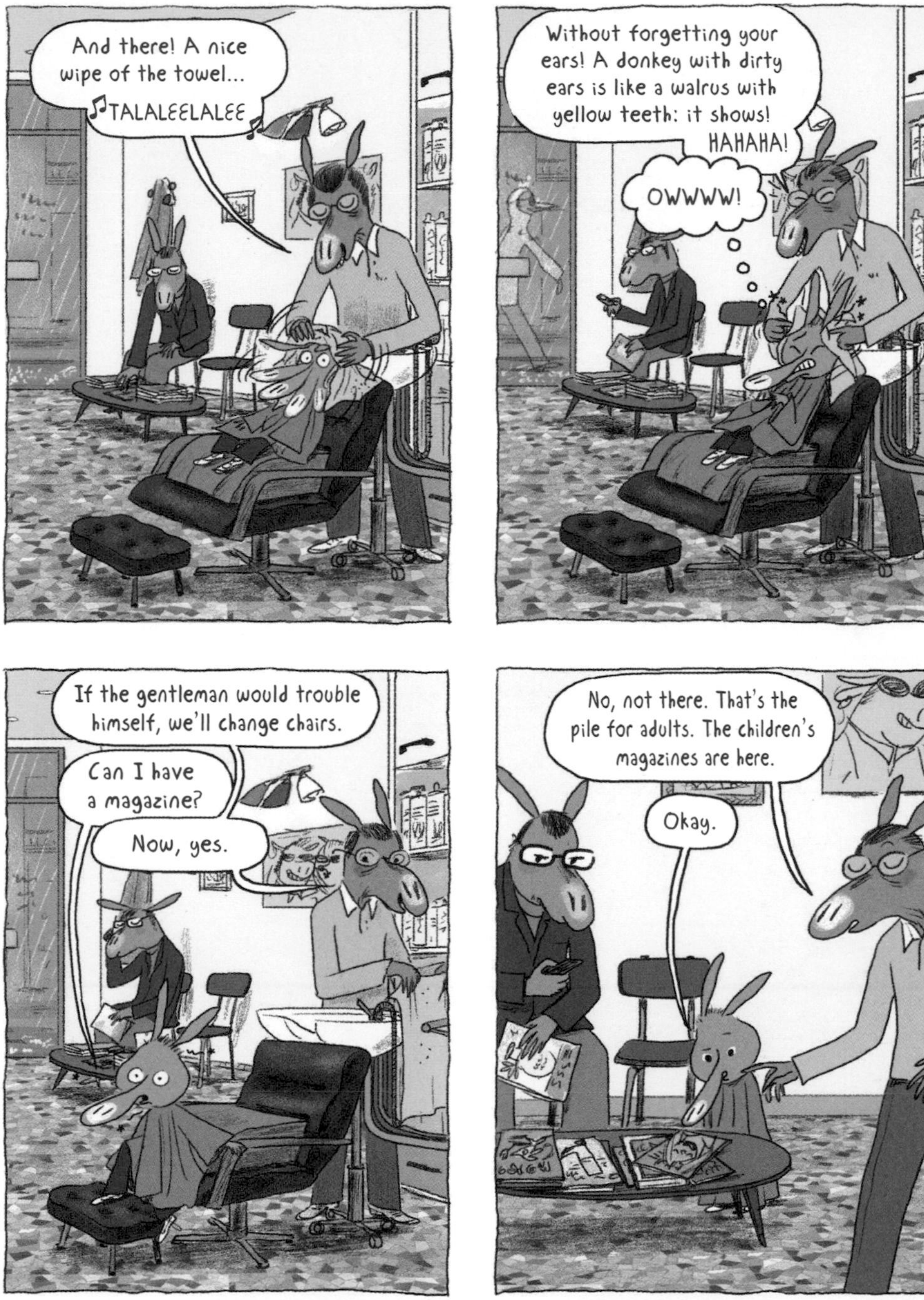
And there! A nice wipe of the towel...
♪TALALEELALEE
Without forgetting your ears! A donkey with dirty ears is like a walrus with yellow teeth: it shows! HAHAHA!
OWWWW!
If the gentleman would trouble himself, we'll change chairs.
Can I have a magazine?
Now, yes.
No, not there. That's the pile for adults. The children's magazines are here.
Okay.

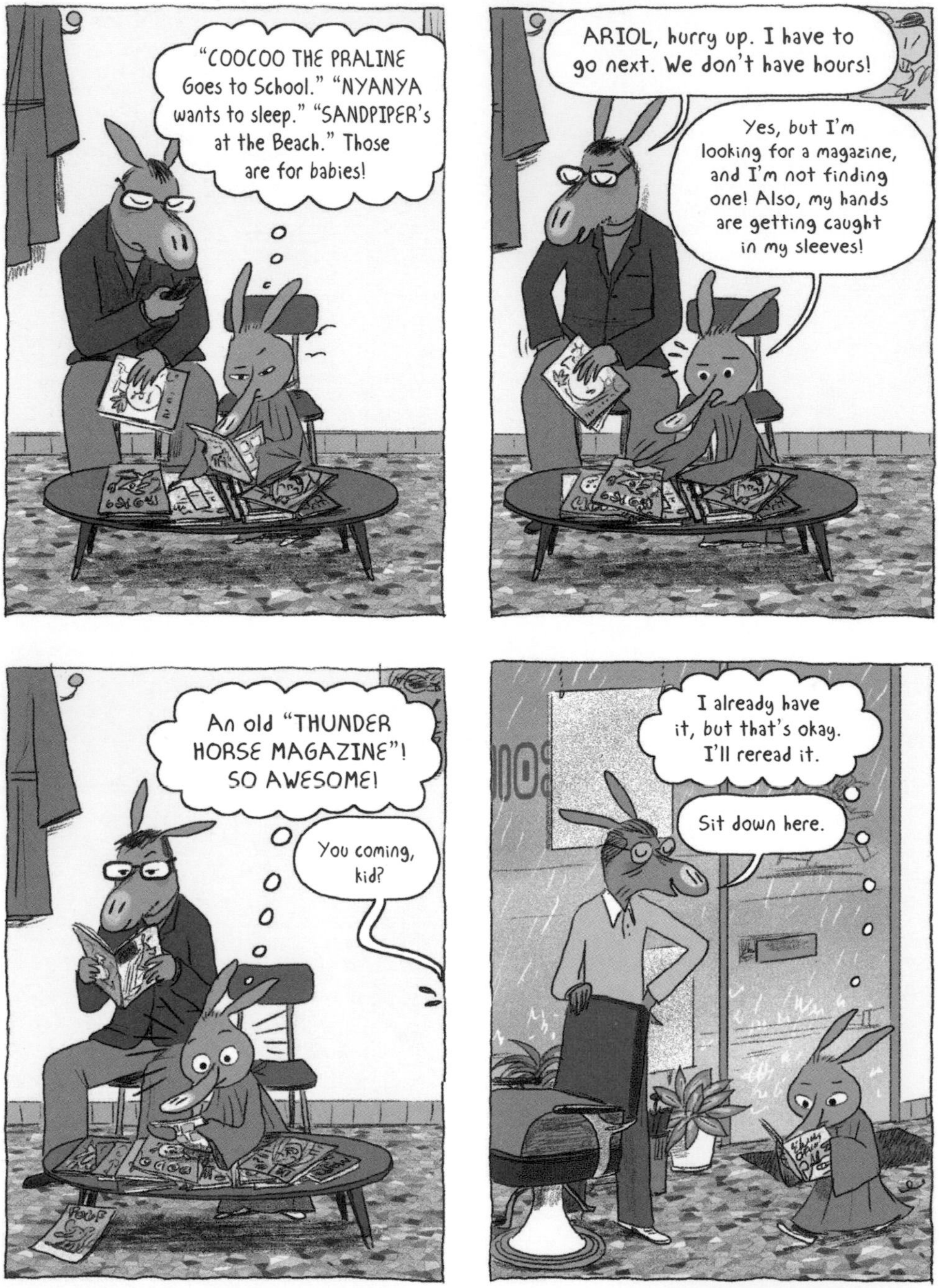
"COOCOO THE PRALINE Goes to School." "NYANYA wants to sleep." "SANDPIPER's at the Beach." Those are for babies!
ARIOL, hurry up. I have to go next. We don't have hours!
Yes, but I'm looking for a magazine, and I'm not finding one! Also, my hands are getting caught in my sleeves!
An old "THUNDER HORSE MAGAZINE"! SO AWESOME!
You coming, kid?
I already have it, but that's okay. I'll reread it.
Sit down here.

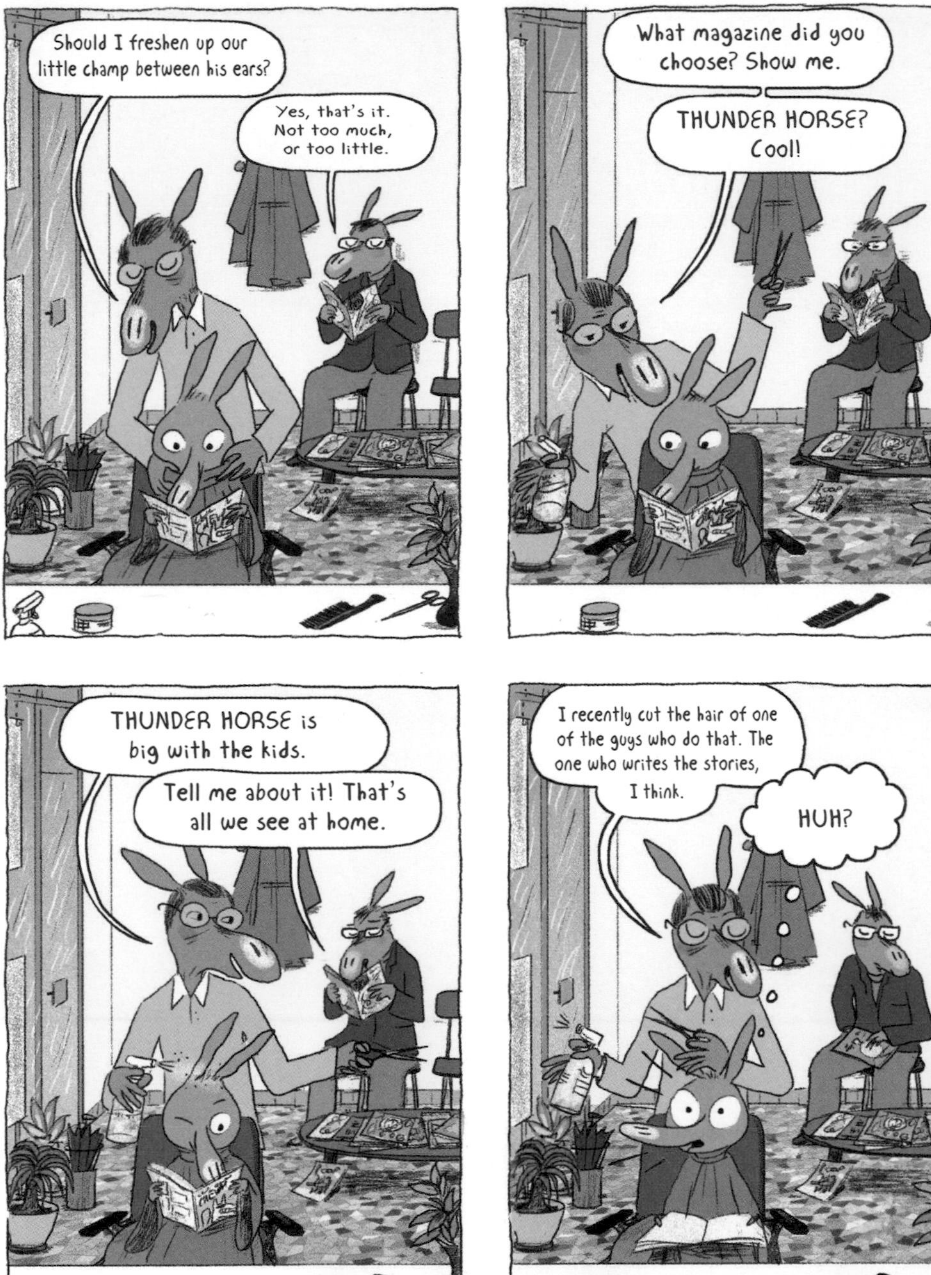
Should I freshen up our little champ between his ears?
Yes, that's it. Not too much, or too little.
What magazine did you choose? Show me.
THUNDER HORSE? Cool!
THUNDER HORSE is big with the kids.
Tell me about it! That's all we see at home.
I recently cut the hair of one of the guys who do that. The one who writes the stories, I think.
HUH?

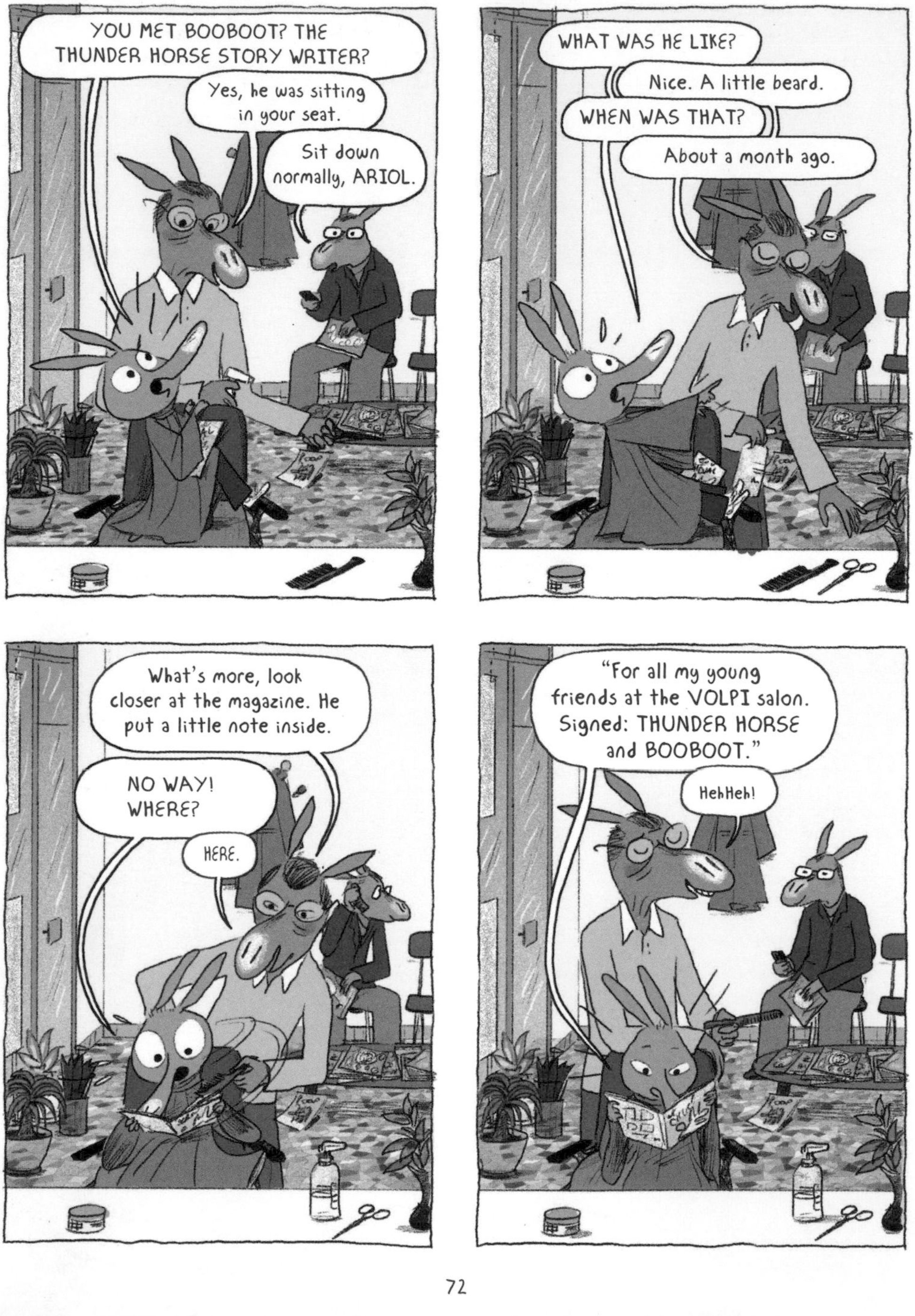
YOU MET BOOBOOT? THE THUNDER HORSE STORY WRITER?
Yes, he was sitting in your seat.
Sit down normally, ARIOL.
WHAT WAS HE LIKE?
Nice. A little beard.
WHEN WAS THAT?
About a month ago.
What's more, look closer at the magazine. He put a little note inside.
NO WAY! WHERE?
HERE.
"For all my young friends at the VOLPI salon. Signed: THUNDER HORSE and BOOBOOT."
HehHeh!

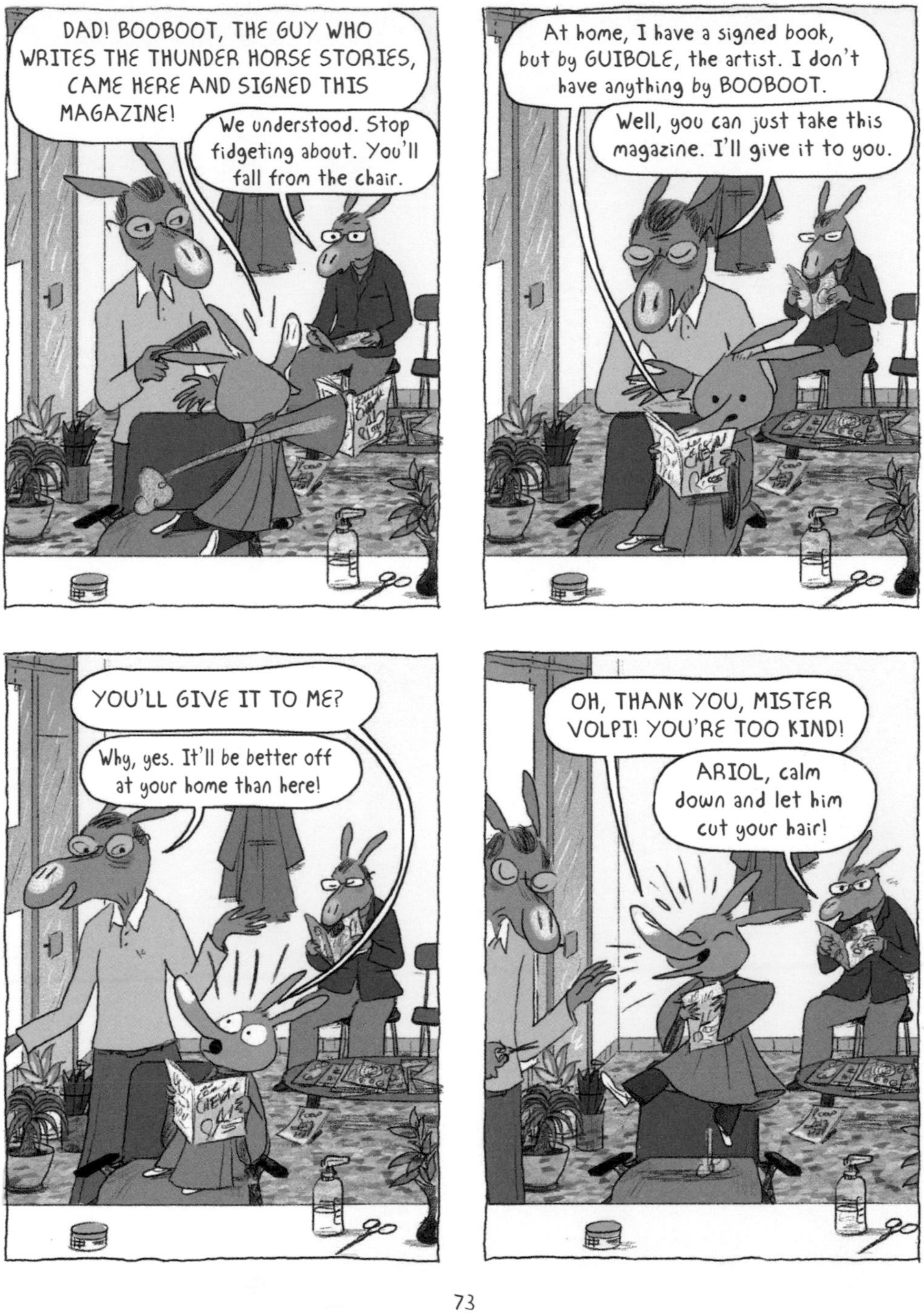
DAD! BOOBOOT, THE GUY WHO WRITES THE THUNDER HORSE STORIES, CAME HERE AND SIGNED THIS MAGAZINE!
We understood. Stop fidgeting about. You'll fall from the chair.
At home, I have a signed book, but by GUIBOLE, the artist. I don't have anything by BOOBOOT.
Well, you can just take this magazine. I'll give it to you.
YOU'LL GIVE IT TO ME?
Why, yes. It'll be better off at your home than here!
OH, THANK YOU, MISTER VOLPI! YOU'RE TOO KIND!
ARIOL, calm down and let him cut your hair!

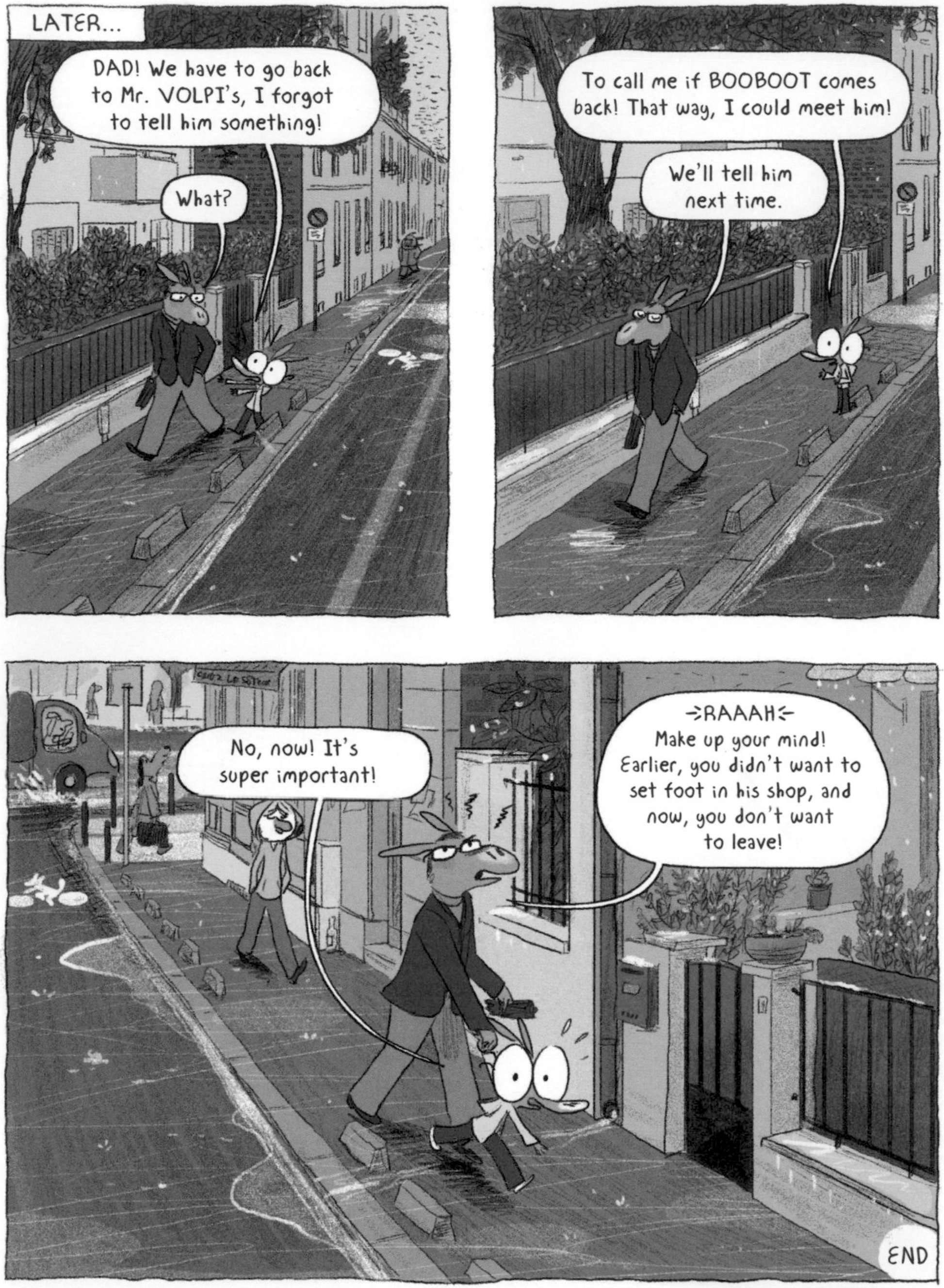

LATER...
DAD! We have to go back to Mr. VOLPI's, I forgot to tell him something!
What?
To call me if BOOBOOT comes back! That way, I could meet him!
We'll tell him next time.
No, now! It's super important!
⇒RAAAH⇐ Make up your mind! Earlier, you didn't want to set foot in his shop, and now, you don't want to leave!
END

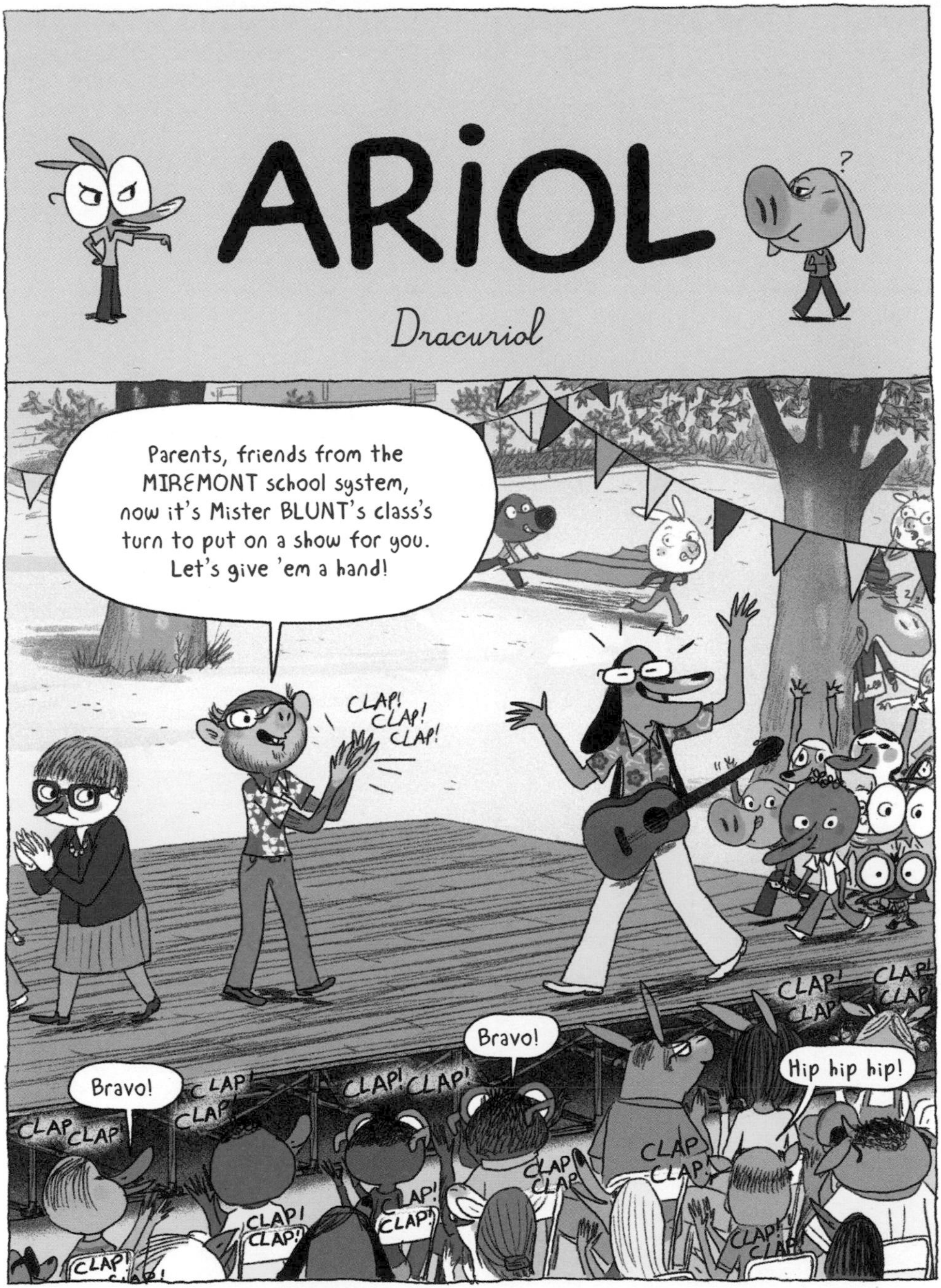
ARIOL
Dracuriol
Parents, friends from the MIREMONT school system, now it's Mister BLUNT's class's turn to put on a show for you. Let's give 'em a hand!
CLAP! CLAP! CLAP!
CLAP! CLAP!
Bravo!
Bravo!
Hip hip hip!
CLAP! CLAP!
CLAP! CLAP!
CLAP! CLAP!
CLAP! CLAP!
CLAP! CLAP!
CLAP! CLAP!
CLAP! CLAP!
CLAP! CLAP!

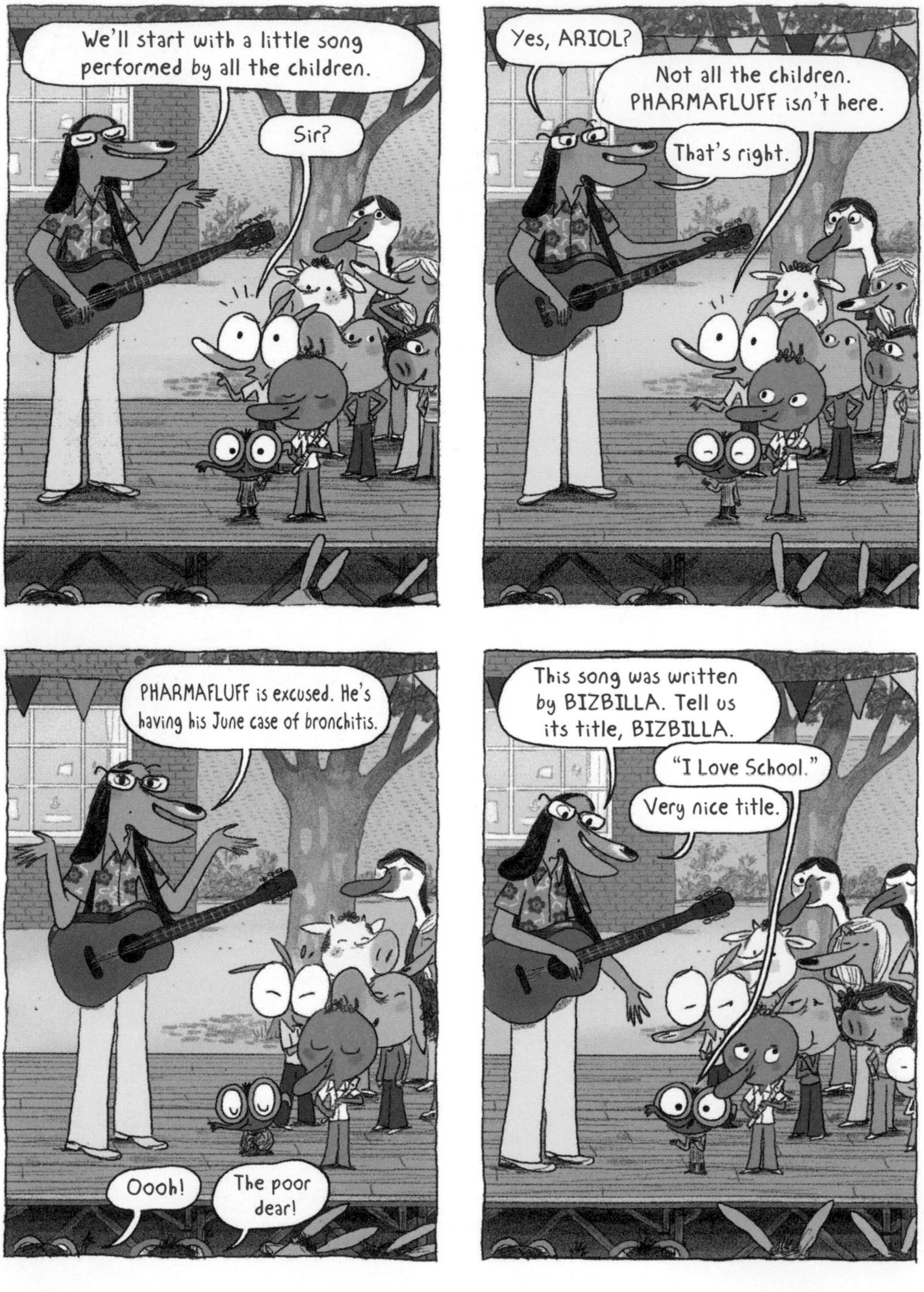

We'll start with a little song performed by all the children.
Sir?
Yes, ARIOL?
Not all the children. PHARMAFLUFF isn't here.
That's right.
PHARMAFLUFF is excused. He's having his June case of bronchitis.
Oooh!
The poor dear!
This song was written by BIZBILLA. Tell us its title, BIZBILLA.
"I Love School."
Very nice title.

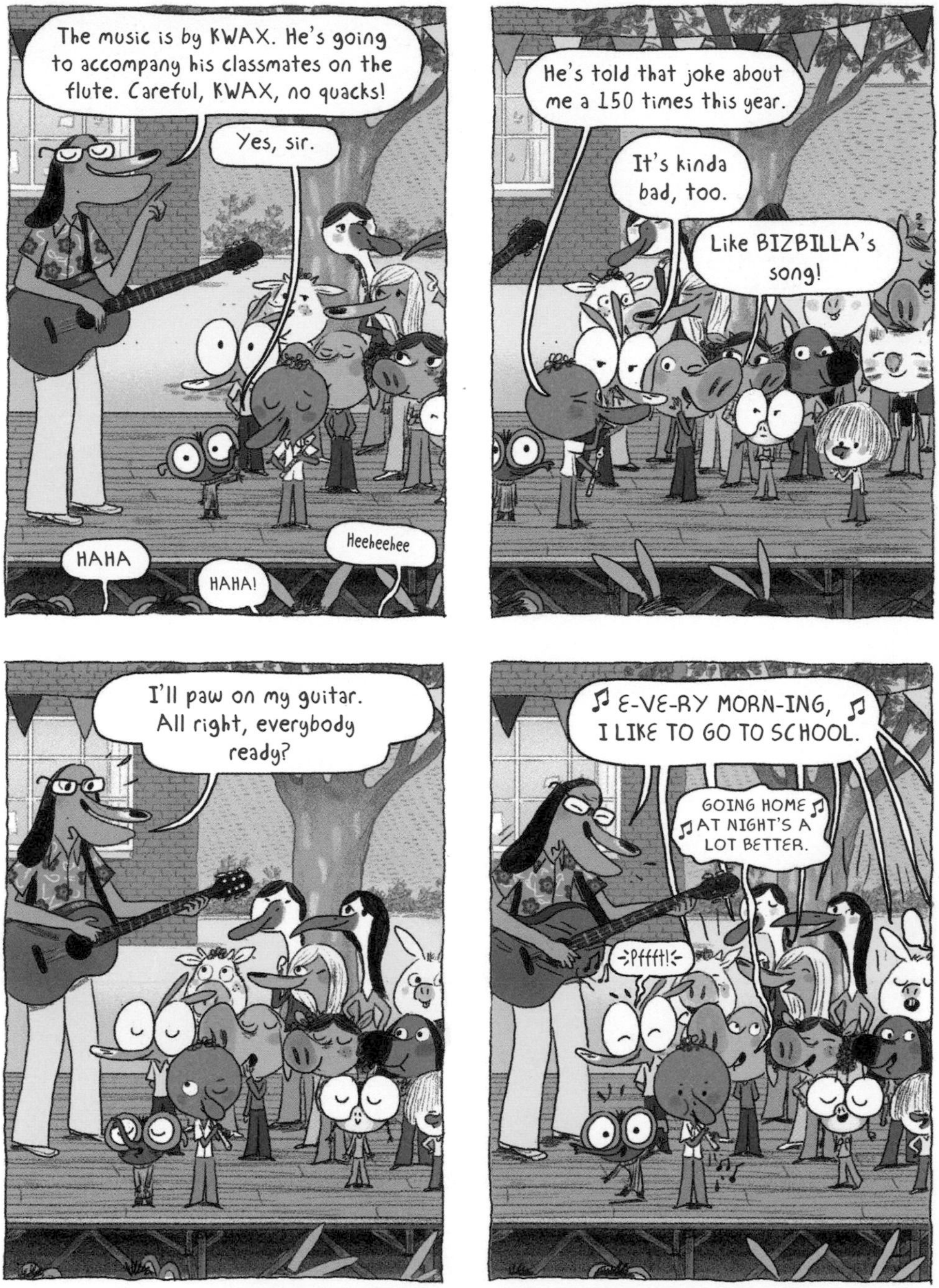

The music is by KWAX. He's going to accompany his classmates on the flute. Careful, KWAX, no quacks!
Yes, sir.
HAHA
HAHA!
Heeheehee
He's told that joke about me a 150 times this year.
It's kinda bad, too.
Like BIZBILLA's song!
I'll paw on my guitar. All right, everybody ready?
♫ E-VE-RY MORN-ING, ♫ I LIKE TO GO TO SCHOOL.
GOING HOME ♫ ♫ AT NIGHT'S A LOT BETTER.
PFFFT!

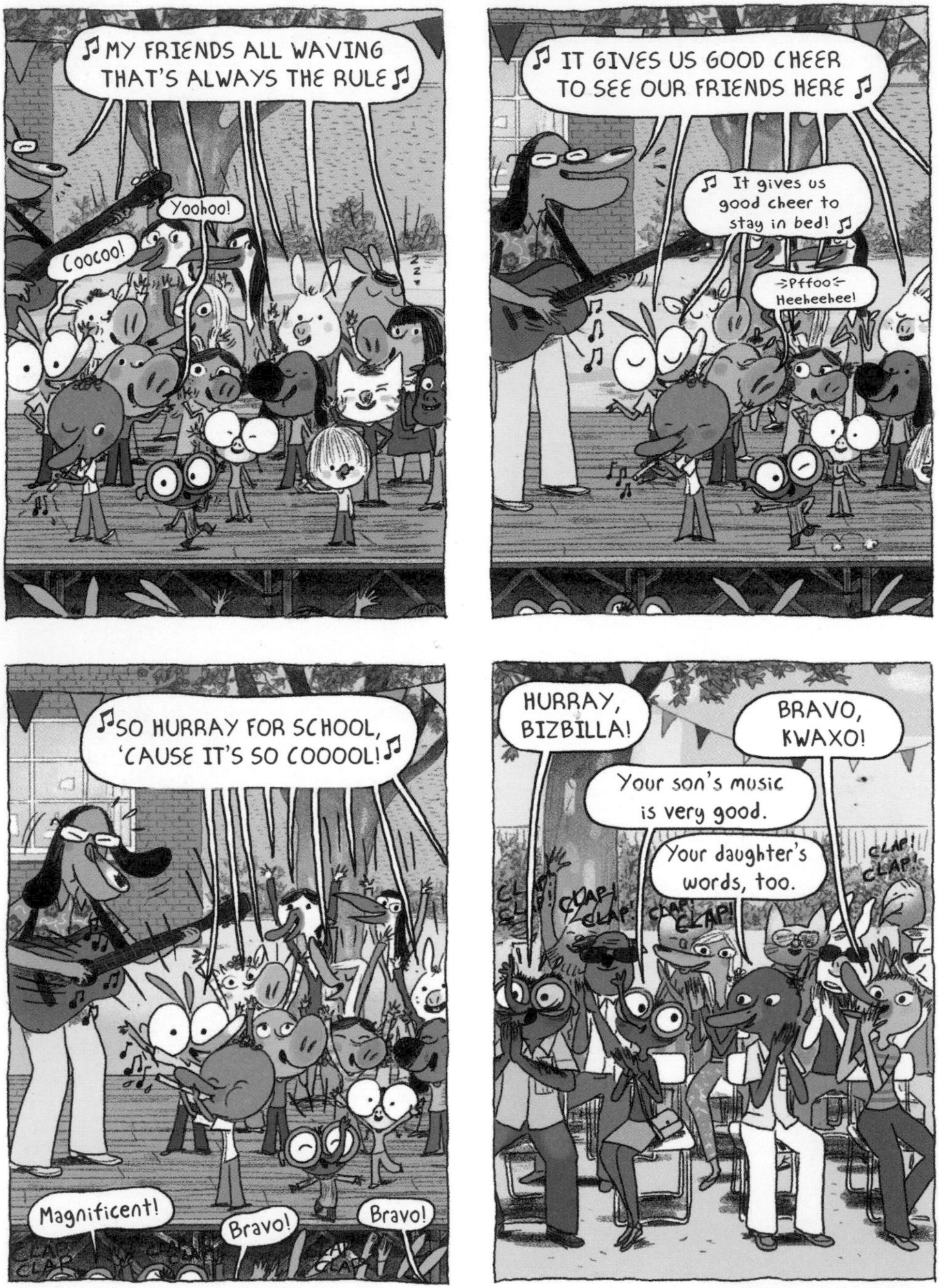
MY FRIENDS ALL WAVING THAT'S ALWAYS THE RULE
Yoohoo!
Coocoo!
IT GIVES US GOOD CHEER TO SEE OUR FRIENDS HERE
It gives us good cheer to stay in bed!
Pffoo Heeheehee!
SO HURRAY FOR SCHOOL, 'CAUSE IT'S SO COOOOL!
Magnificent!
Bravo!
Bravo!
HURRAY, BIZBILLA!
BRAVO, KWAXO!
Your son's music is very good.
Your daughter's words, too.
CLAP! CLAP!
CLAP! CLAP!
CLAP! CLAP!
CLAP! CLAP!

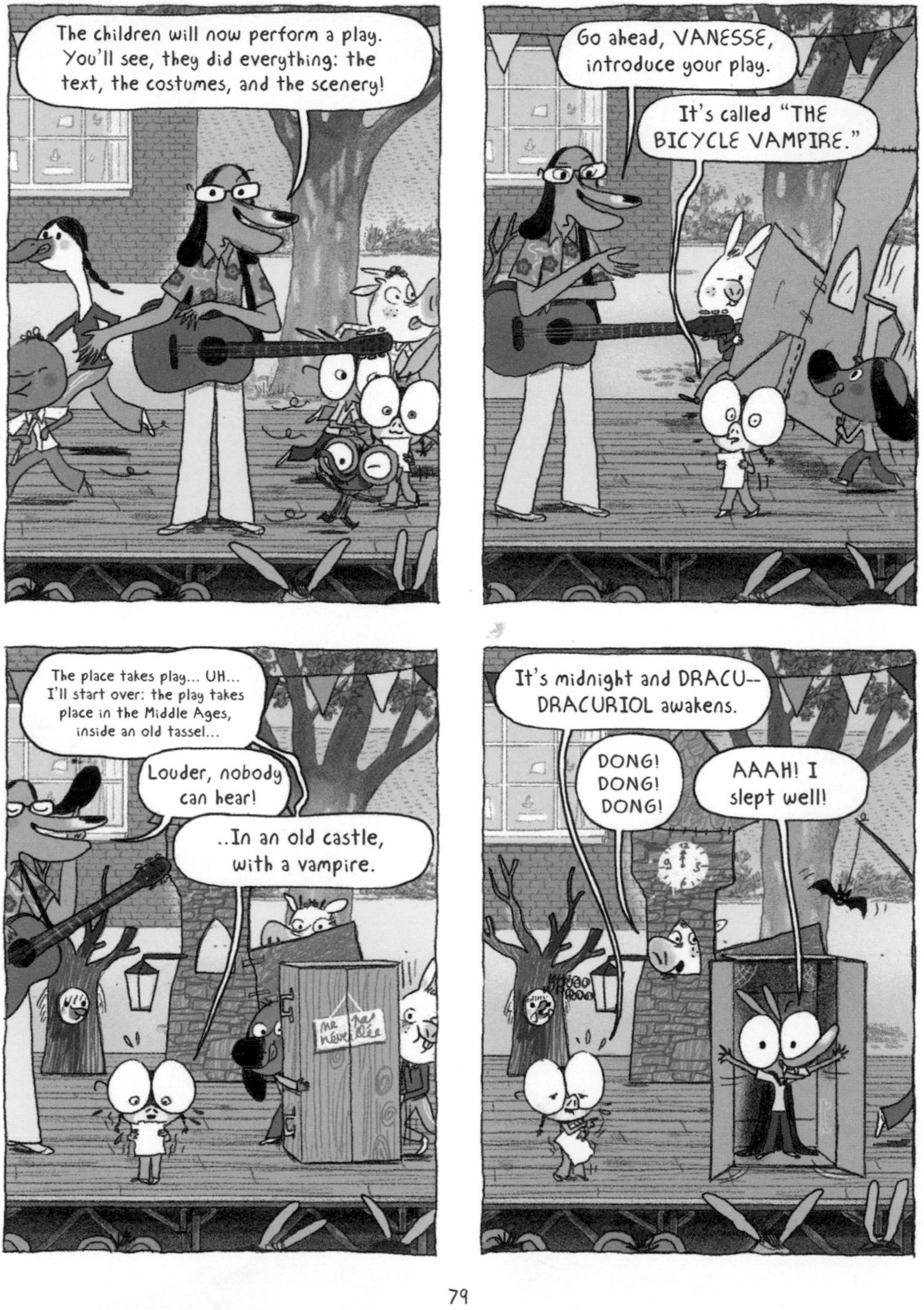
The children will now perform a play. You'll see, they did everything: the text, the costumes, and the scenery!
Go ahead, VANESSE, introduce your play.
It's called "THE BICYCLE VAMPIRE."
The place takes play... UH... I'll start over: the play takes place in the Middle Ages, inside an old tassel...
Louder, nobody can hear!
..In an old castle, with a vampire.
It's midnight and DRACU-- DRACURIOL awakens.
DONG! DONG! DONG!
AAAH! I slept well!

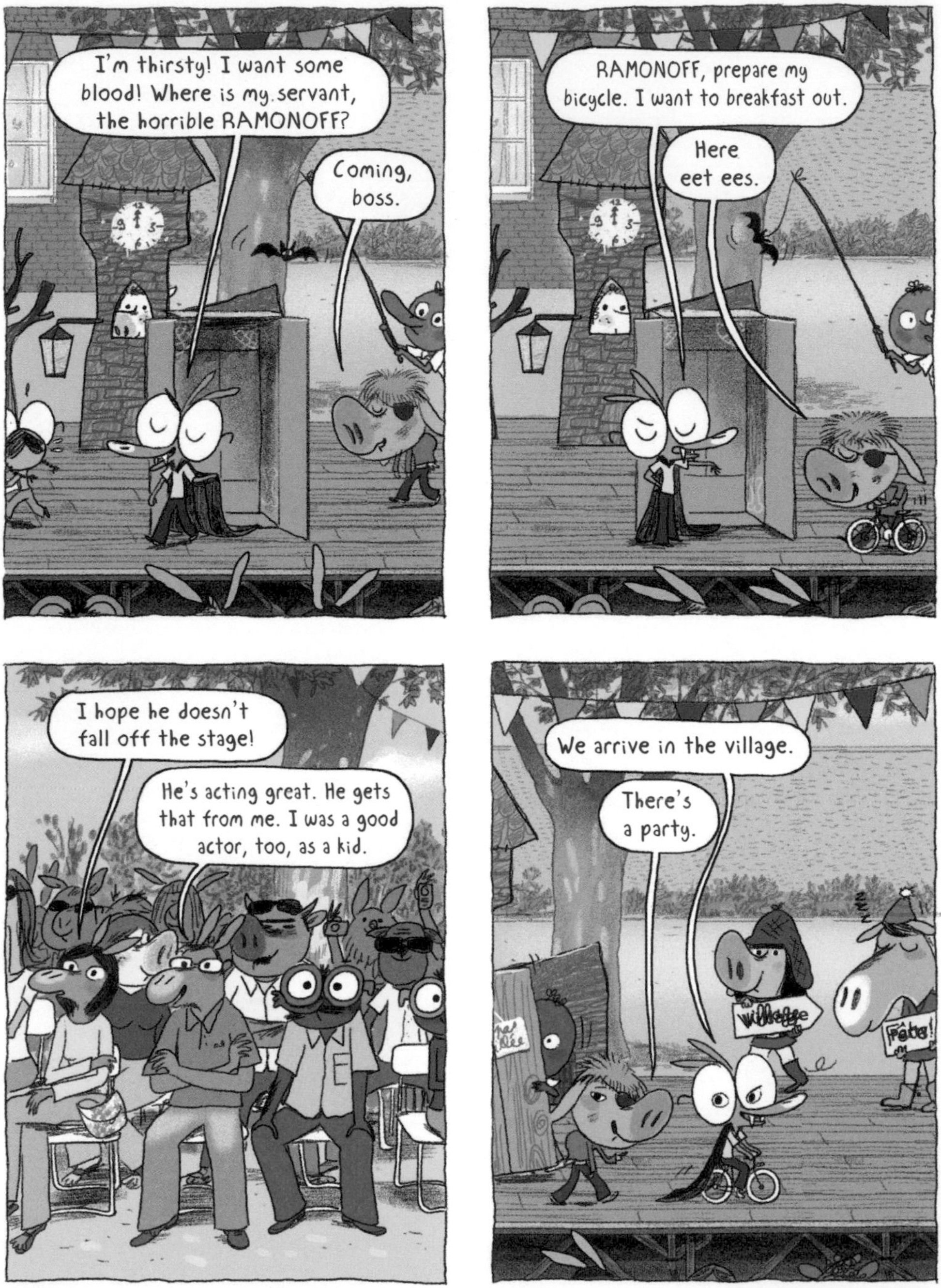
I'm thirsty! I want some blood! Where is my servant, the horrible RAMONOFF?
Coming, boss.
RAMONOFF, prepare my bicycle. I want to breakfast out.
Here eet ees.
I hope he doesn't fall off the stage!
He's acting great. He gets that from me. I was a good actor, too, as a kid.
We arrive in the village.
There's a party.
village
Fête!

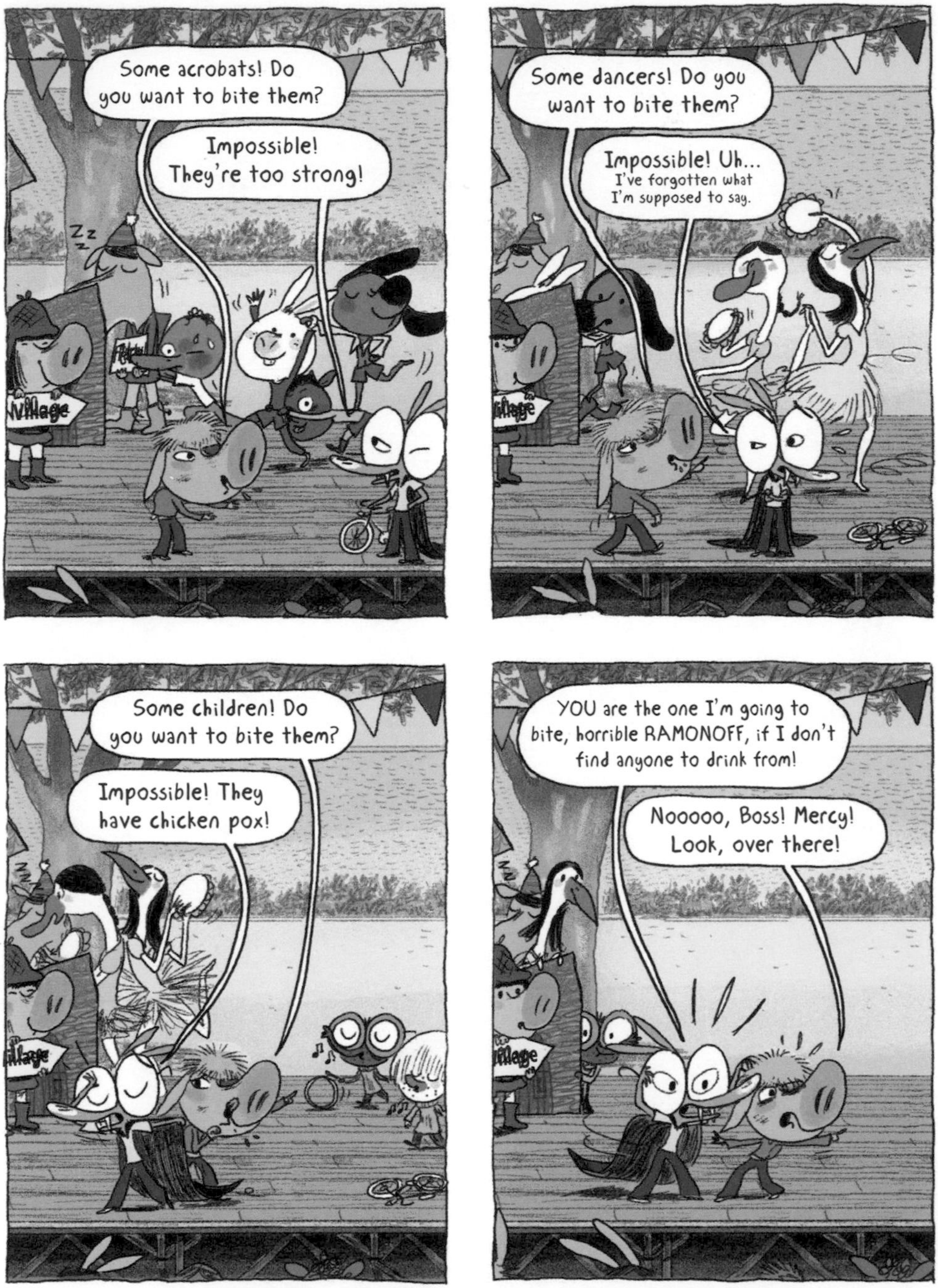
Some acrobats! Do you want to bite them?
Impossible! They're too strong!
Some dancers! Do you want to bite them?
Impossible! Uh... I've forgotten what I'm supposed to say.
Some children! Do you want to bite them?
Impossible! They have chicken pox!
YOU are the one I'm going to bite, horrible RAMONOFF, if I don't find anyone to drink from!
Nooooo, Boss! Mercy! Look, over there!

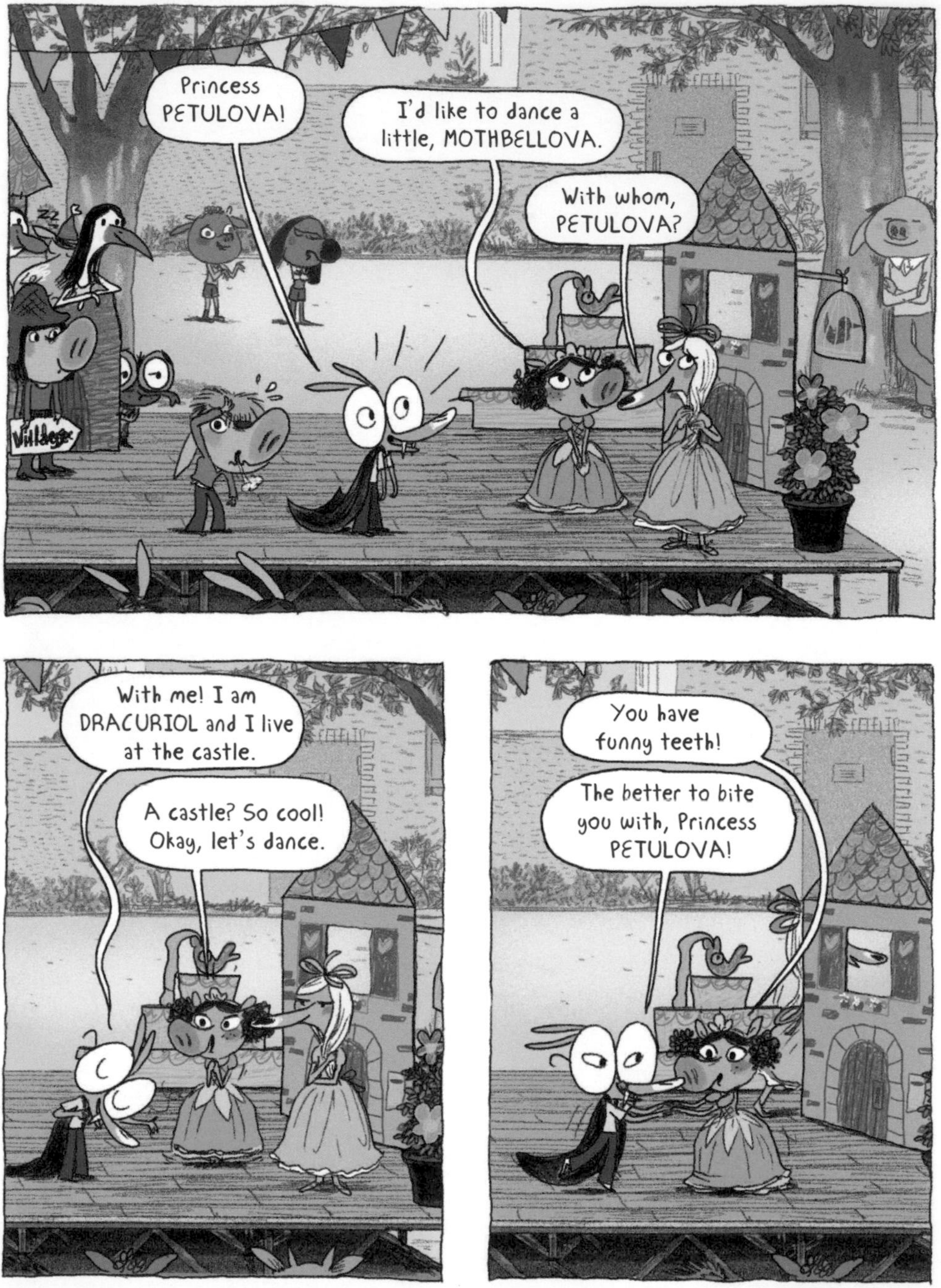
Princess PETULOVA!
I'd like to dance a little, MOTHBELLOVA.
With whom, PETULOVA?
Village
With me! I am DRACURIOL and I live at the castle.
A castle? So cool! Okay, let's dance.
You have funny teeth!
The better to bite you with, Princess PETULOVA!

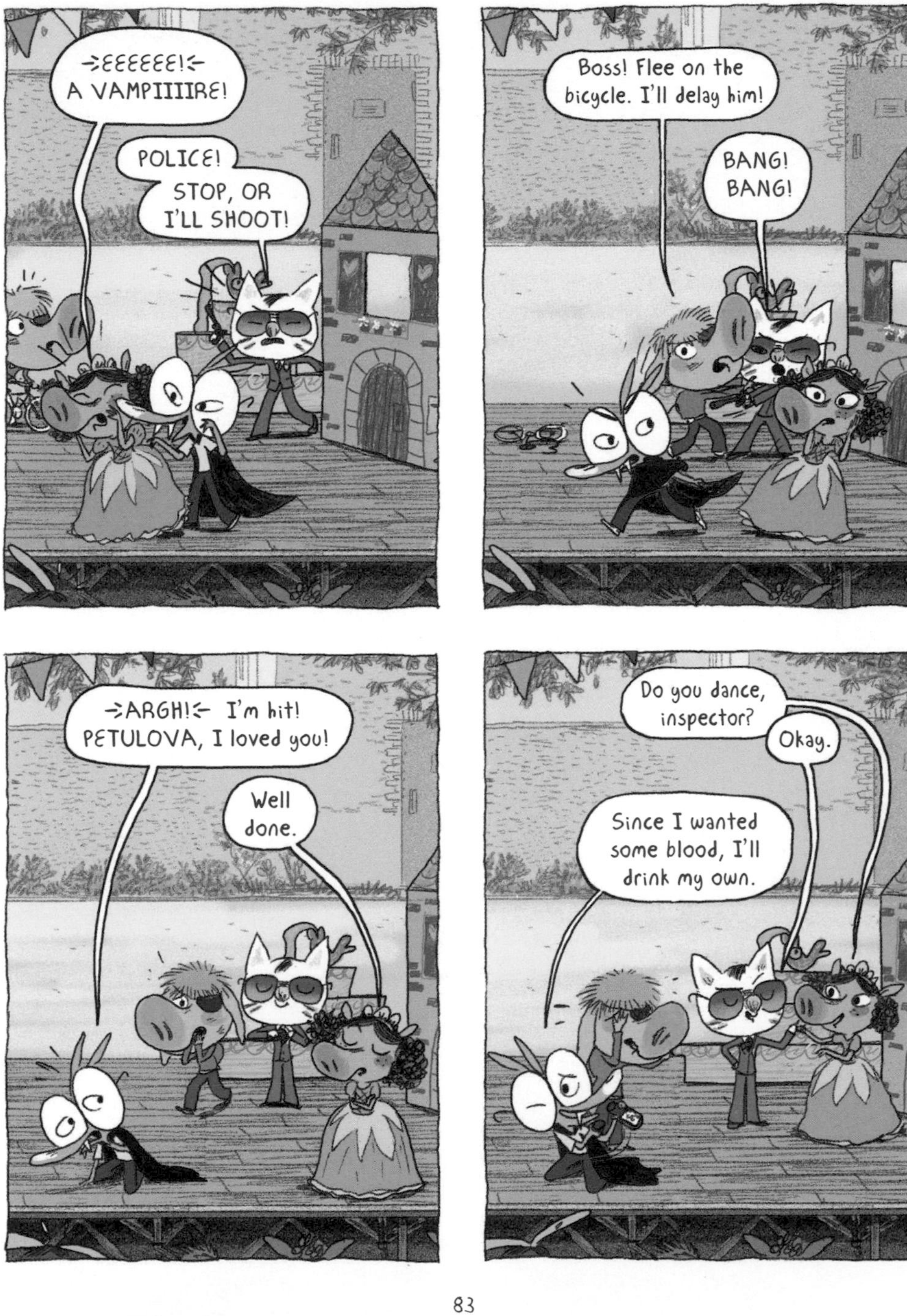
EEEEEE! A VAMPIIIIRE!
POLICE! STOP, OR I'LL SHOOT!
Boss! Flee on the bicycle. I'll delay him!
BANG! BANG!
ARGH! I'm hit! PETULOVA, I loved you!
Well done.
Do you dance, inspector?
Okay.
Since I wanted some blood, I'll drink my own.

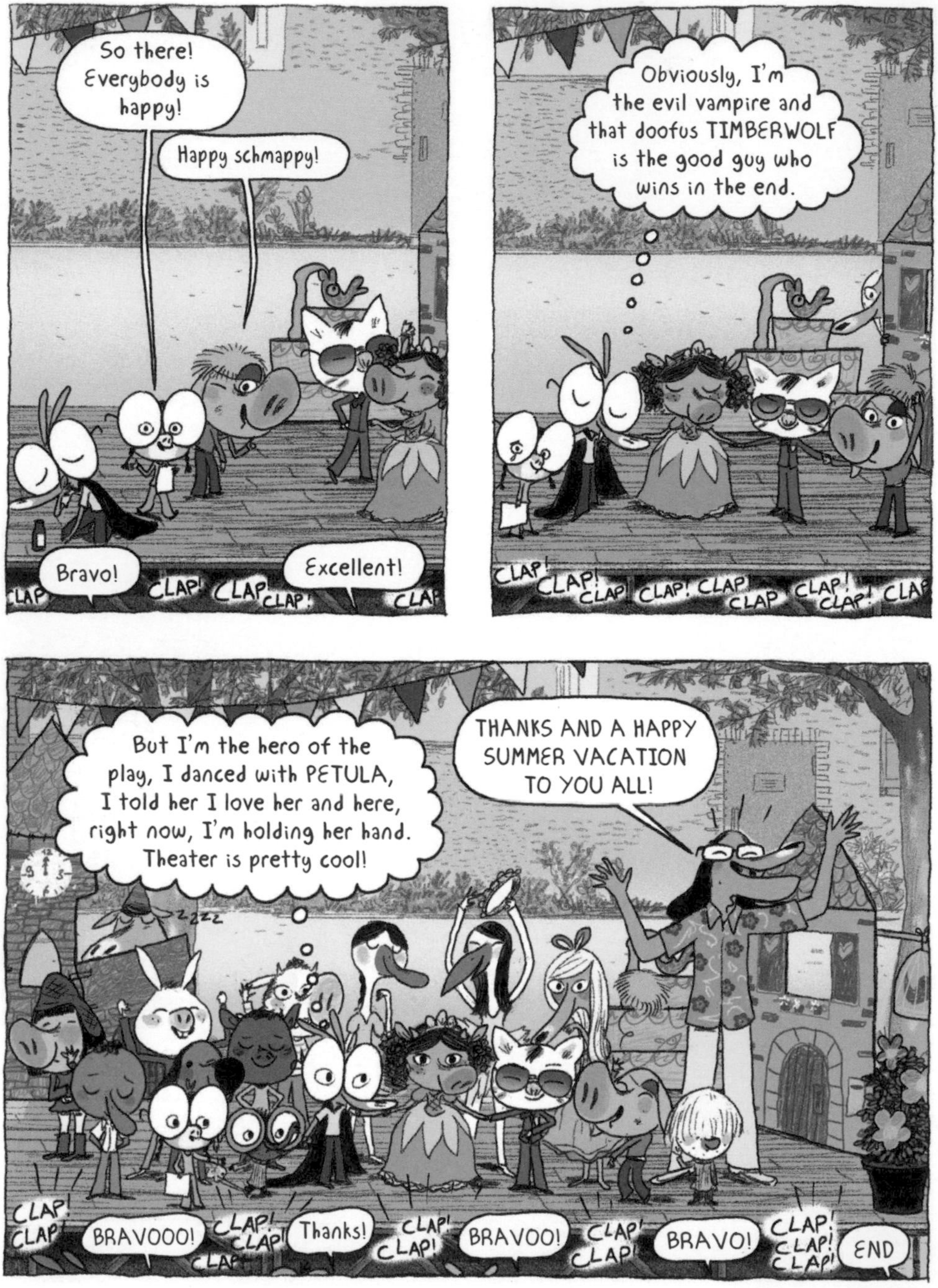
So there! Everybody is happy!
Happy schmappy!
Bravo!
CLAP! CLAP CLAP! CLAP!
Excellent!
CLAP
Obviously, I'm the evil vampire and that doofus TIMBERWOLF is the good guy who wins in the end.
CLAP! CLAP! CLAP! CLAP! CLAP! CLAP CLAP! CLAP! CLAP
But I'm the hero of the play, I danced with PETULA, I told her I love her and here, right now, I'm holding her hand. Theater is pretty cool!
THANKS AND A HAPPY SUMMER VACATION TO YOU ALL!
ZZZZ
CLAP! CLAP
BRAVOOO!
CLAP! CLAP! CLAP
Thanks!
CLAP! CLAP!
BRAVOO!
CLAP! CLAP!
BRAVO!
CLAP! CLAP! CLAP!
END

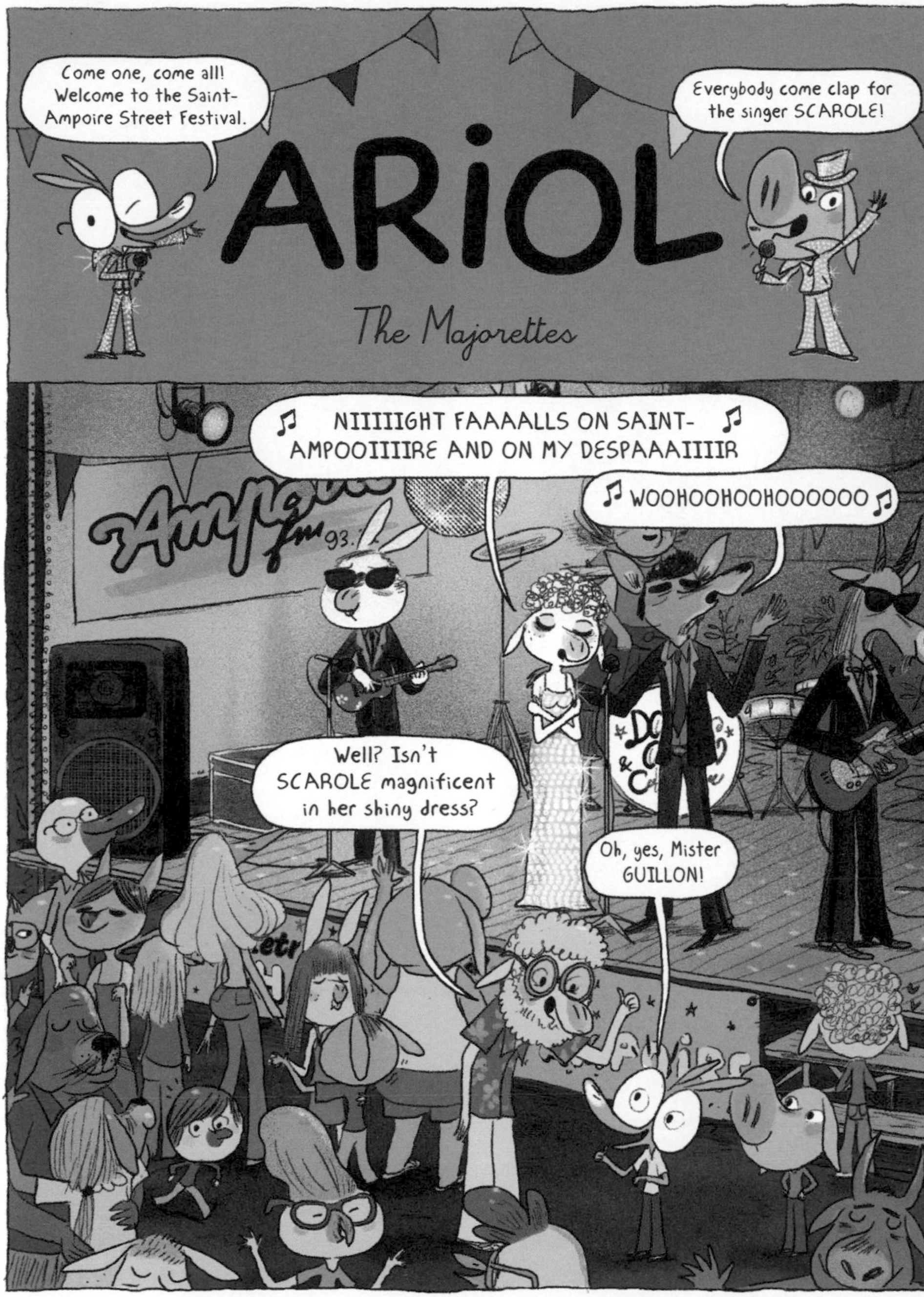
Come one, come all! Welcome to the Saint-Ampoire Street Festival.
Everybody come clap for the singer SCAROLE!
ARiOL
The Majorettes
♫ NIIIIIGHT FAAAALLS ON SAINT-AMPOOIIIIRE AND ON MY DESPAAAIIIIR ♫
♫ WOOHOOHOOHOOOOOO ♫
Well? Isn't SCAROLE magnificent in her shiny dress?
Oh, yes, Mister GUILLON!

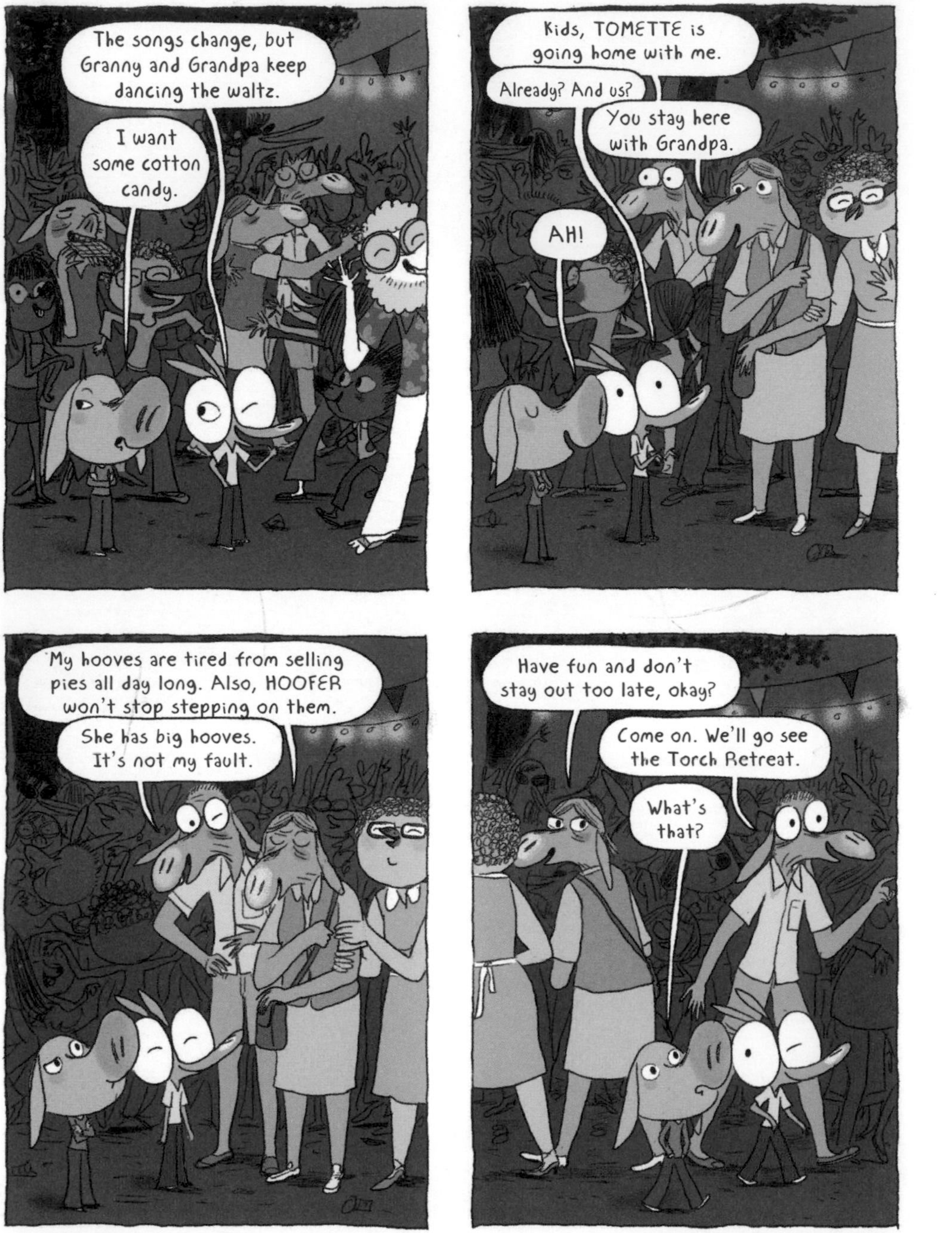
The songs change, but Granny and Grandpa keep dancing the waltz.
I want some cotton candy.
Kids, TOMETTE is going home with me.
Already? And us?
You stay here with Grandpa.
AH!
My hooves are tired from selling pies all day long. Also, HOOFER won't stop stepping on them.
She has big hooves. It's not my fault.
Have fun and don't stay out too late, okay?
Come on. We'll go see the Torch Retreat.
What's that?

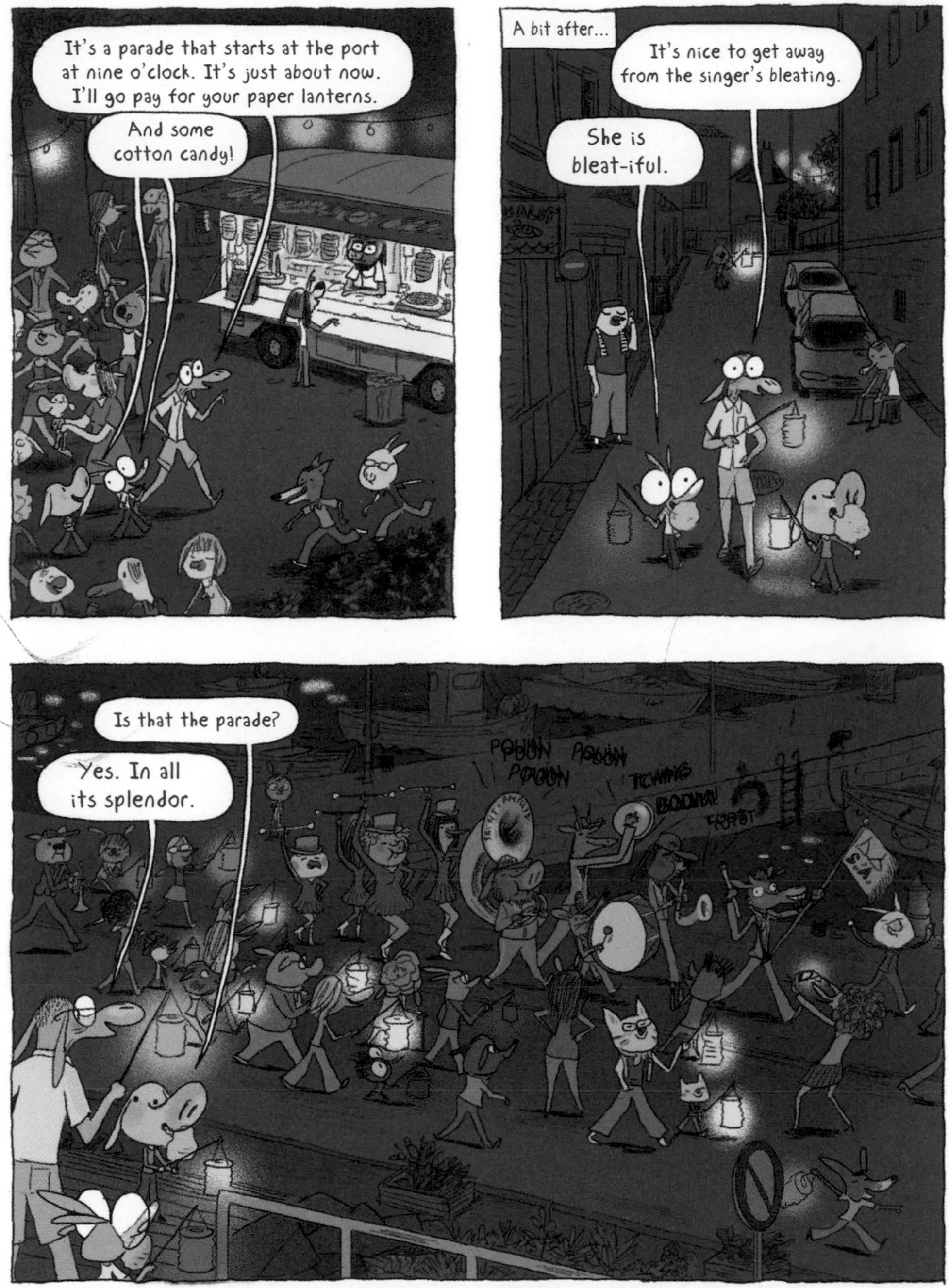
It's a parade that starts at the port at nine o'clock. It's just about now. I'll go pay for your paper lanterns.
And some cotton candy!
A bit after...
It's nice to get away from the singer's bleating.
She is bleat-iful.
Is that the parade?
Yes. In all its splendor.
TCHING

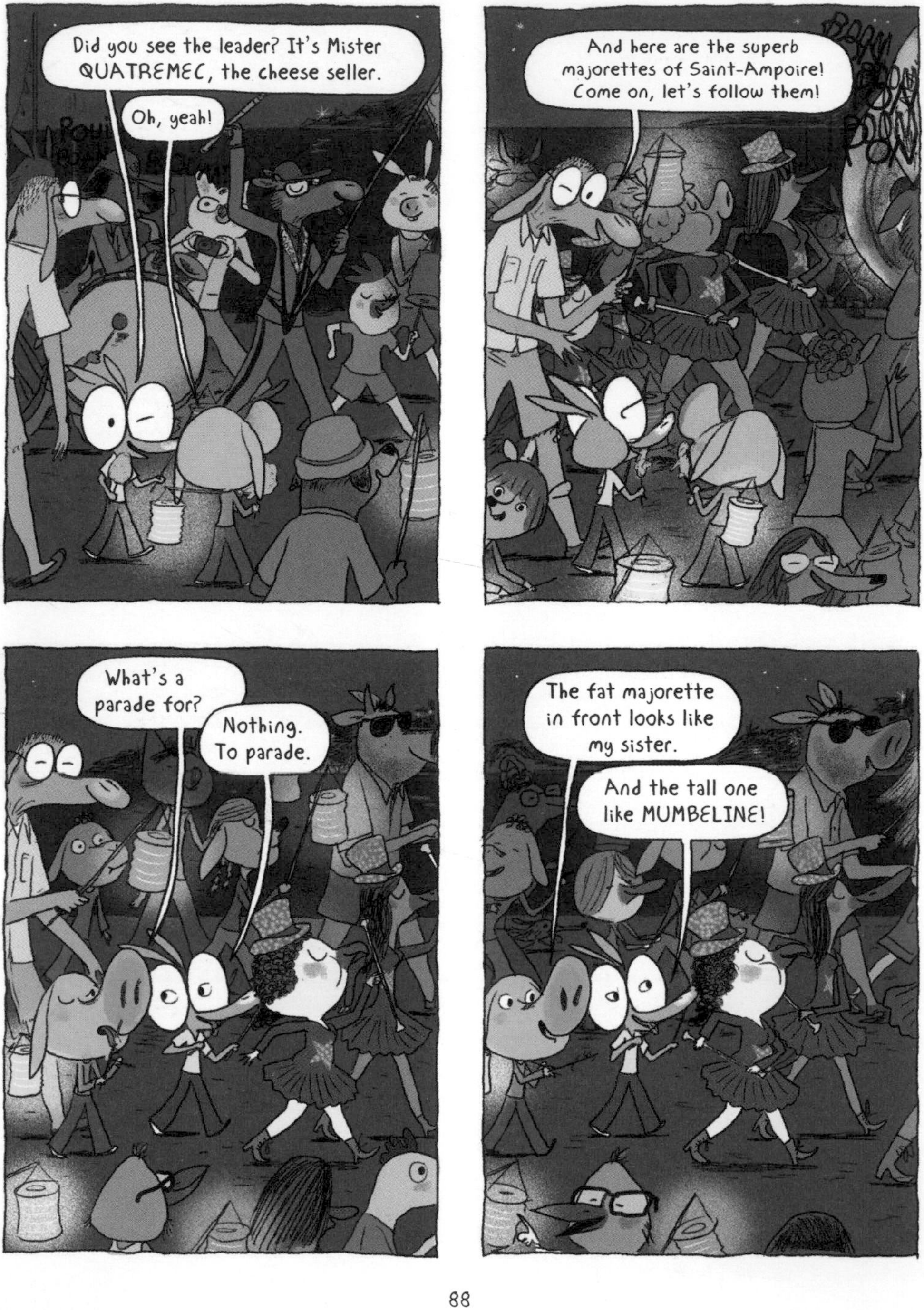
Did you see the leader? It's Mister QUATREMEC, the cheese seller.
Oh, yeah!
And here are the superb majorettes of Saint-Ampoire! Come on, let's follow them!
What's a parade for?
Nothing. To parade.
The fat majorette in front looks like my sister.
And the tall one like MUMBELINE!

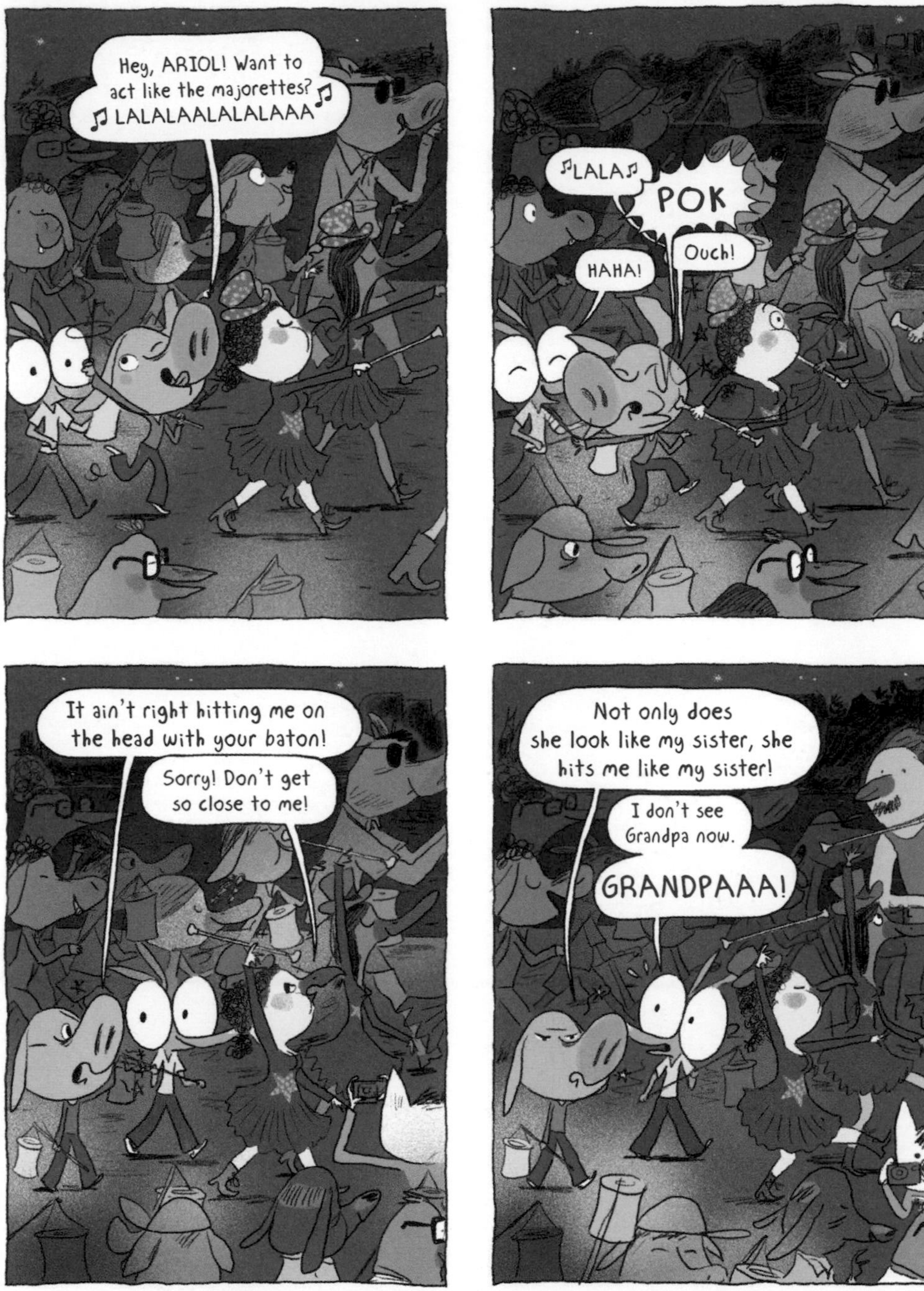
Hey, ARIOL! Want to act like the majorettes? ♫
♫ LALALAALALALAAA
♫LALA♫
POK
HAHA!
Ouch!
It ain't right hitting me on the head with your baton!
Sorry! Don't get so close to me!
Not only does she look like my sister, she hits me like my sister!
I don't see Grandpa now.
GRANDPAAA!

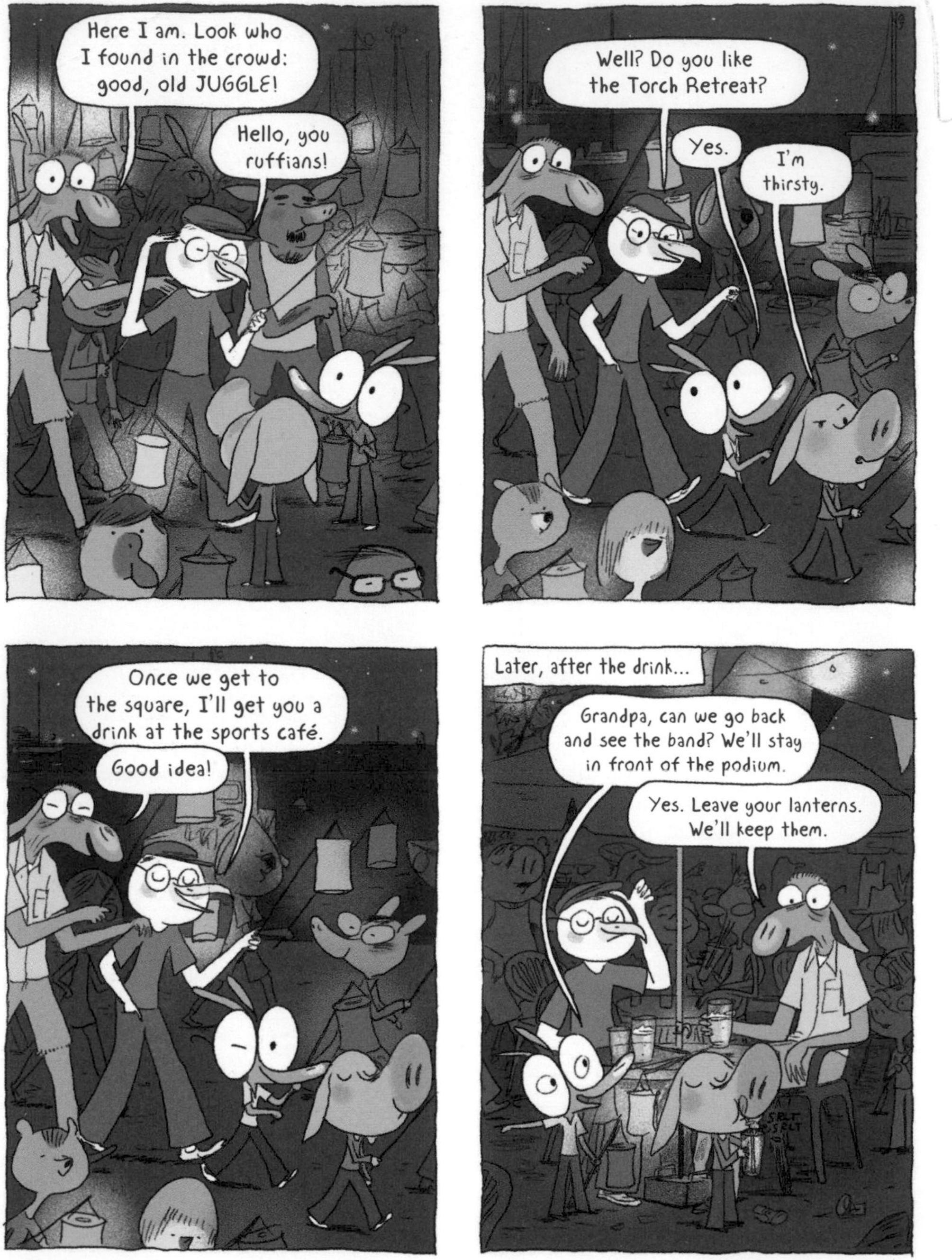
Here I am. Look who I found in the crowd: good, old JUGGLE!
Hello, you ruffians!
Well? Do you like the Torch Retreat?
Yes.
I'm thirsty.
Once we get to the square, I'll get you a drink at the sports café.
Good idea!
Later, after the drink...
Grandpa, can we go back and see the band? We'll stay in front of the podium.
Yes. Leave your lanterns. We'll keep them.

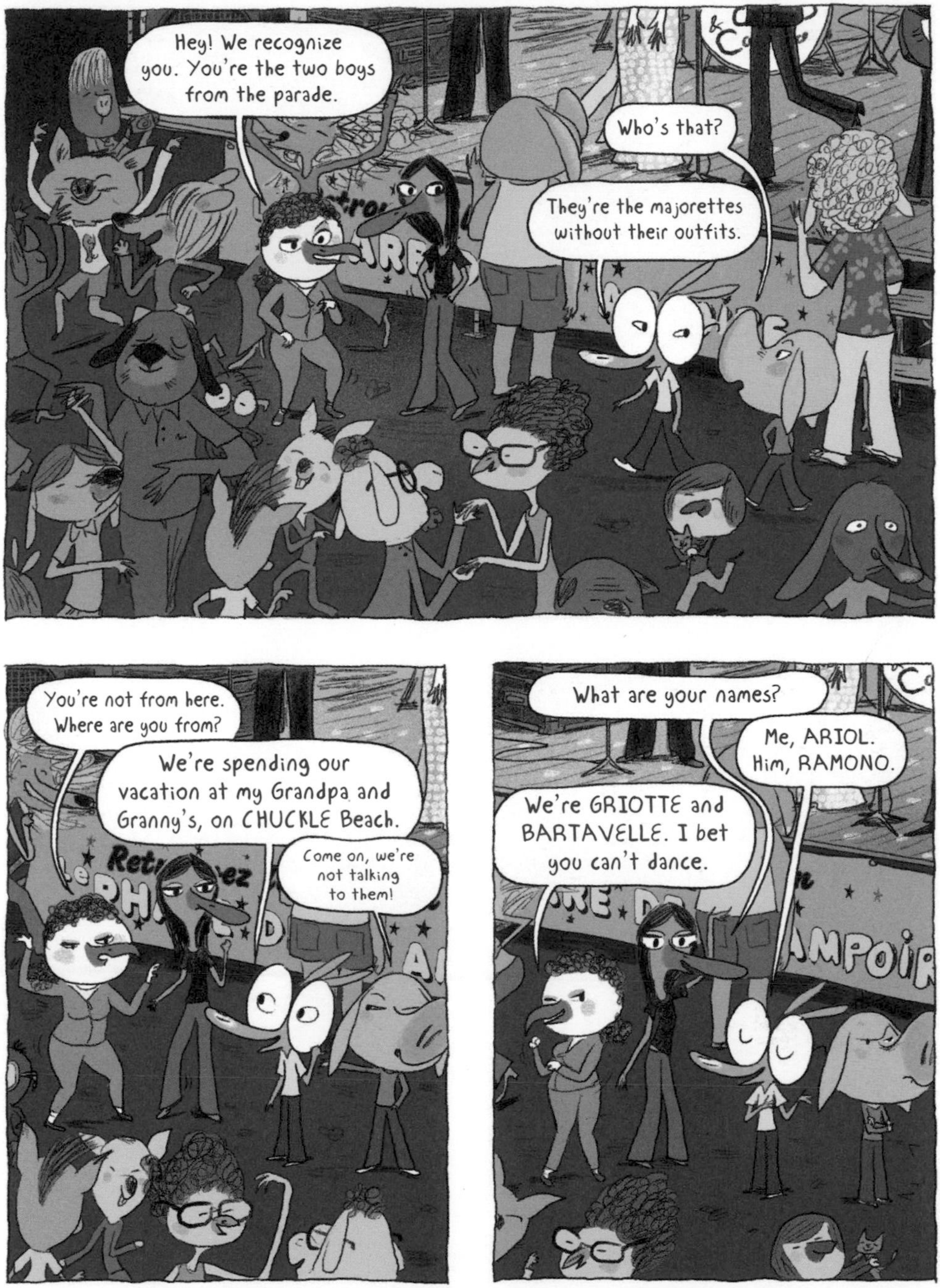
Hey! We recognize you. You're the two boys from the parade.
Who's that?
They're the majorettes without their outfits.
You're not from here. Where are you from?
We're spending our vacation at my Grandpa and Granny's, on CHUCKLE Beach.
Come on, we're not talking to them!
What are your names?
Me, ARIOL. Him, RAMONO.
We're GRIOTTE and BARTAVELLE. I bet you can't dance.

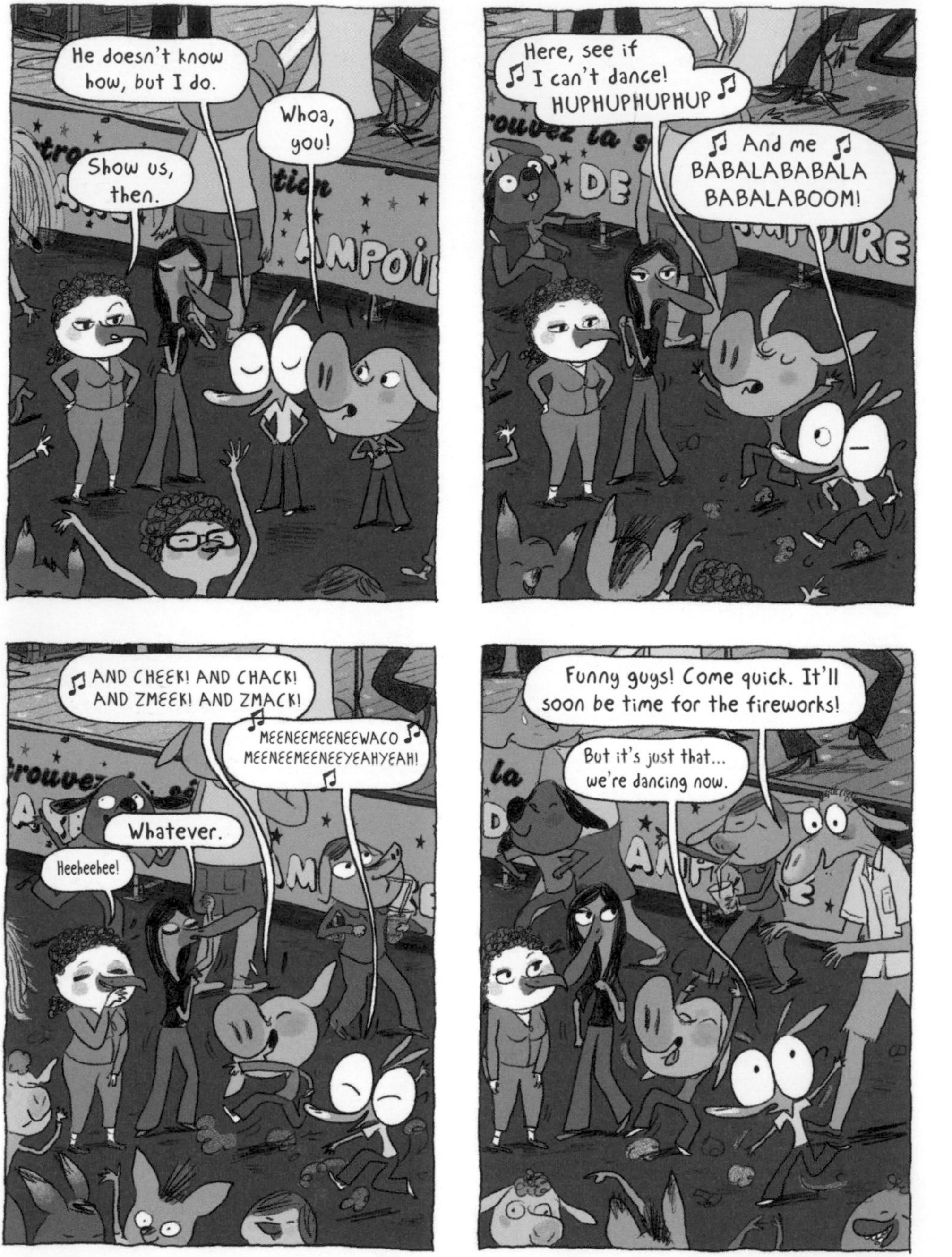

He doesn't know how, but I do.
Show us, then.
Whoa, you!
Here, see if ♫ I can't dance! HUPHUPHUPHUP ♫
♫ And me ♫ BABALABABALA BABALABOOM!
♫ AND CHEEK! AND CHACK! AND ZMEEK! AND ZMACK!
♫ MEENEEMEENEEWACO ♫ MEENEEMEENEEYEAHYEAH! ♫
Whatever.
Heeheehee!
Funny guys! Come quick. It'll soon be time for the fireworks!
But it's just that... we're dancing now.

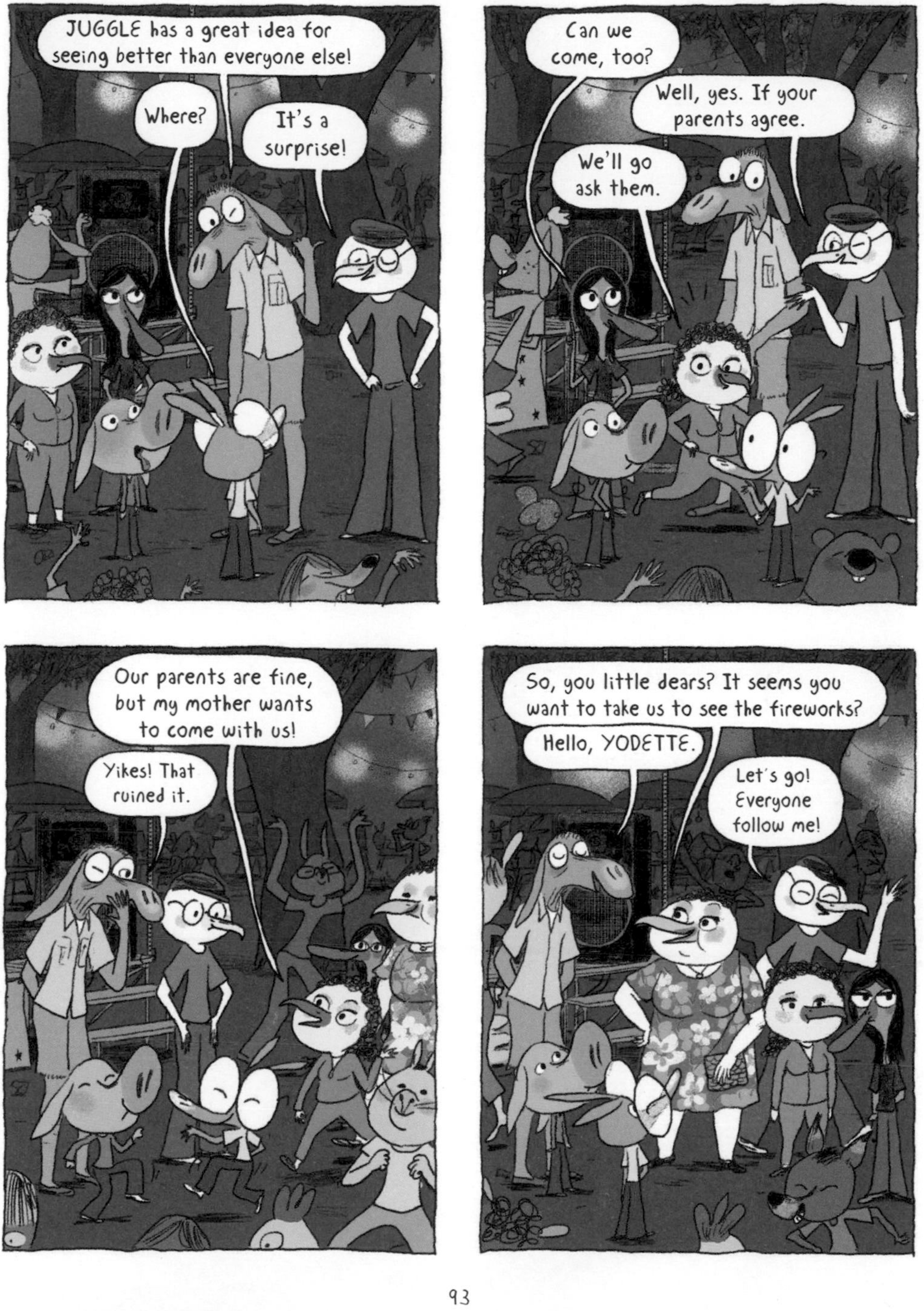
JUGGLE has a great idea for seeing better than everyone else!
Where?
It's a surprise!
Can we come, too?
Well, yes. If your parents agree.
We'll go ask them.
Our parents are fine, but my mother wants to come with us!
Yikes! That ruined it.
So, you little dears? It seems you want to take us to see the fireworks?
Hello, YODETTE.
Let's go! Everyone follow me!

A bit later, at the port...
Everyone onboard! Hurry it up!
We're going boating? That's the surprise, you little dears?
Bravo, you guessed it!
YEEAAAAH!
Let's go a little offshore to see the fireworks. There'll be fewer people, and, over the water, it'll be even more beautiful.
So cool!
Can we steer with you, Mister JUGGLE?
CHUG CHUG CHUG CHUG
IT'S ALL GOOD
TOUT VA BIEN
NEXT EPISODE: THE GRAND FINALE!

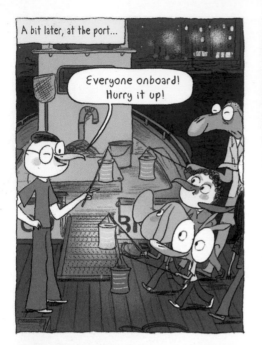

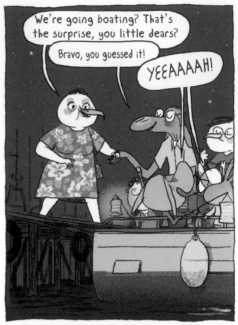

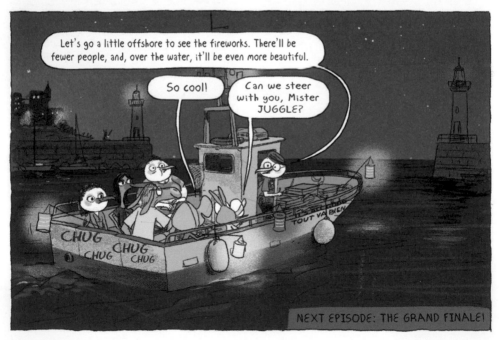

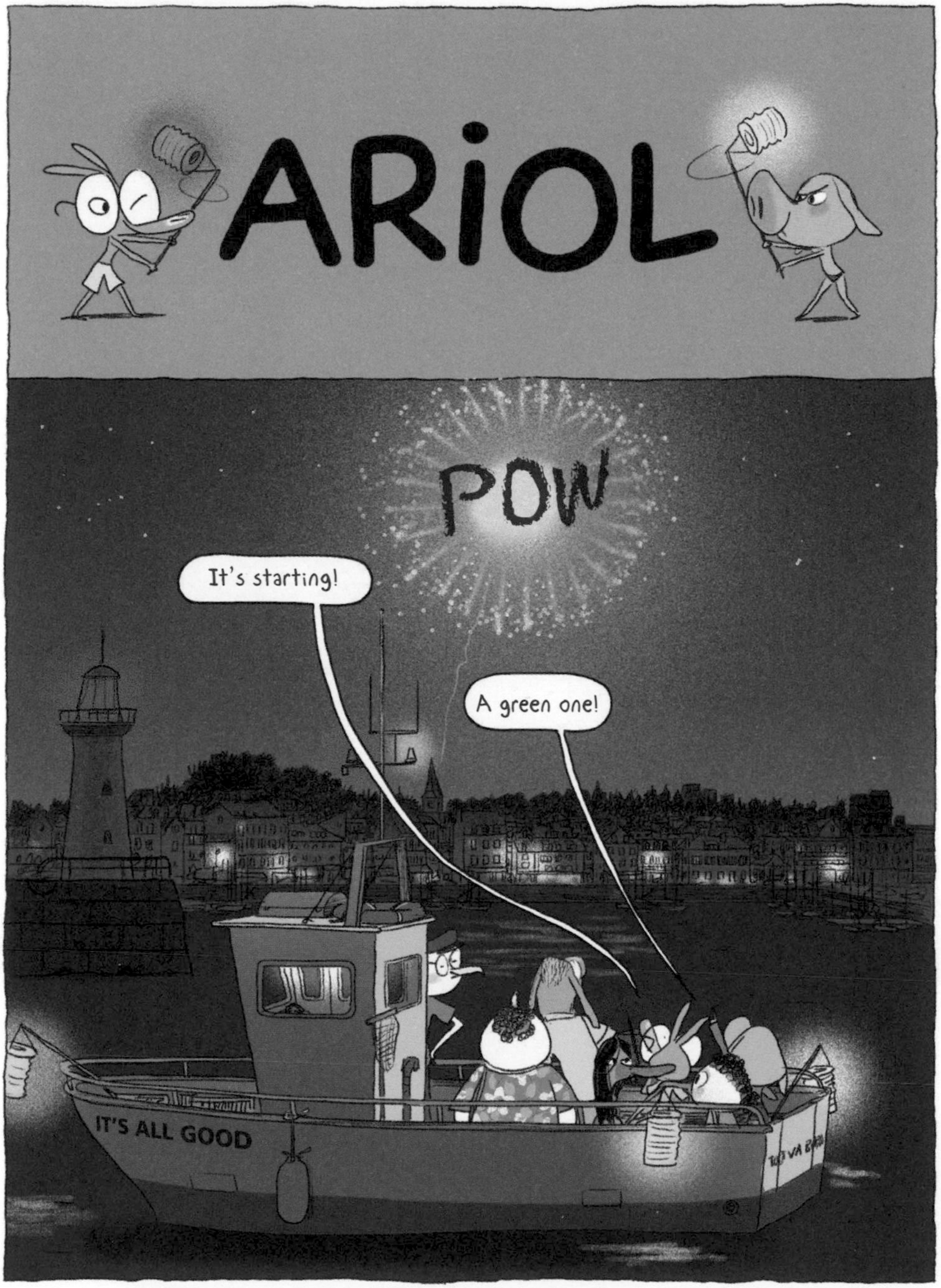
ARiOL
POW
It's starting!
A green one!
IT'S ALL GOOD

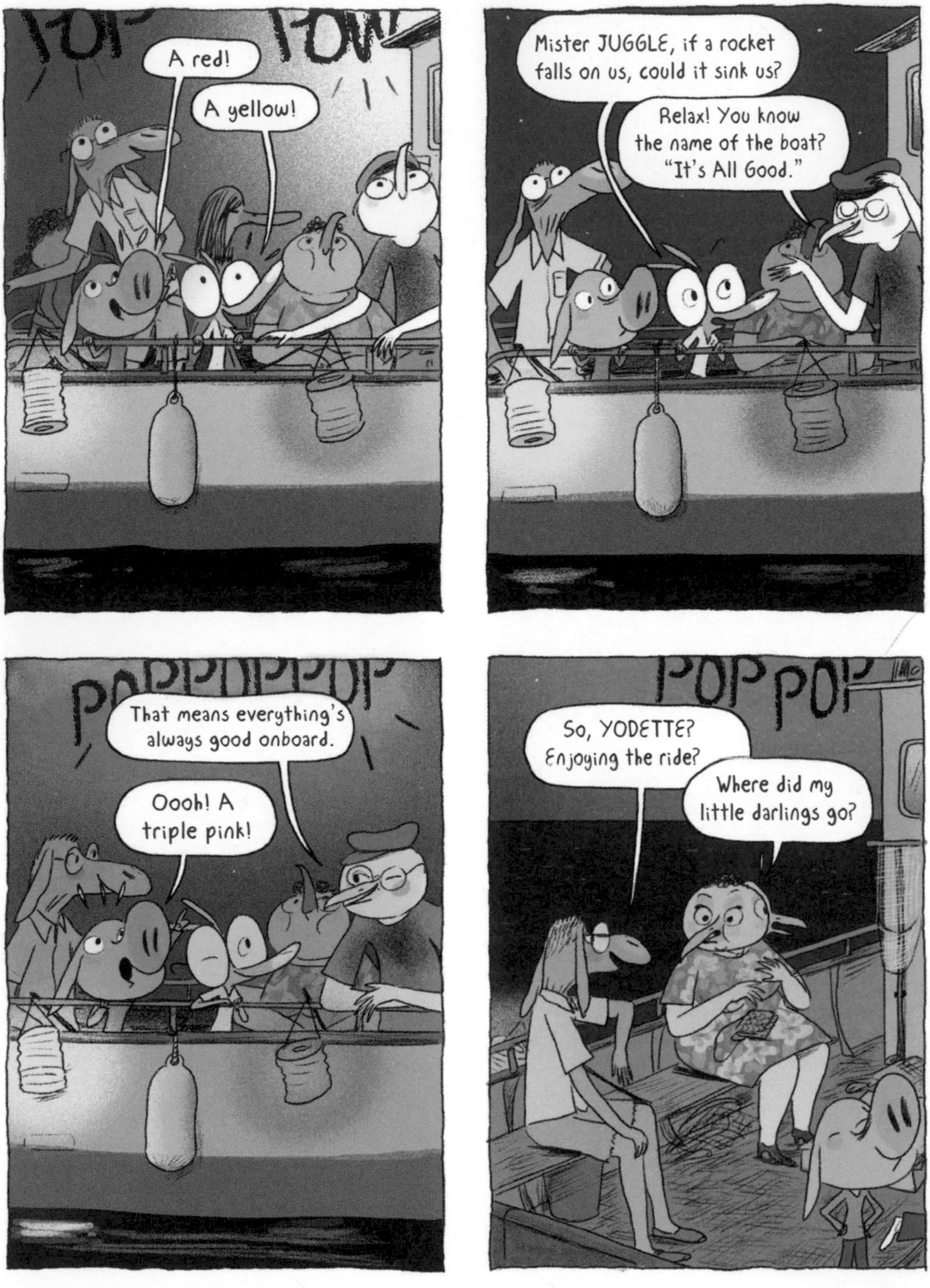
A red!
A yellow!
Mister JUGGLE, if a rocket falls on us, could it sink us?
Relax! You know the name of the boat? "It's All Good."
That means everything's always good onboard.
Oooh! A triple pink!
POP POP
So, YODETTE? Enjoying the ride?
Where did my little darlings go?

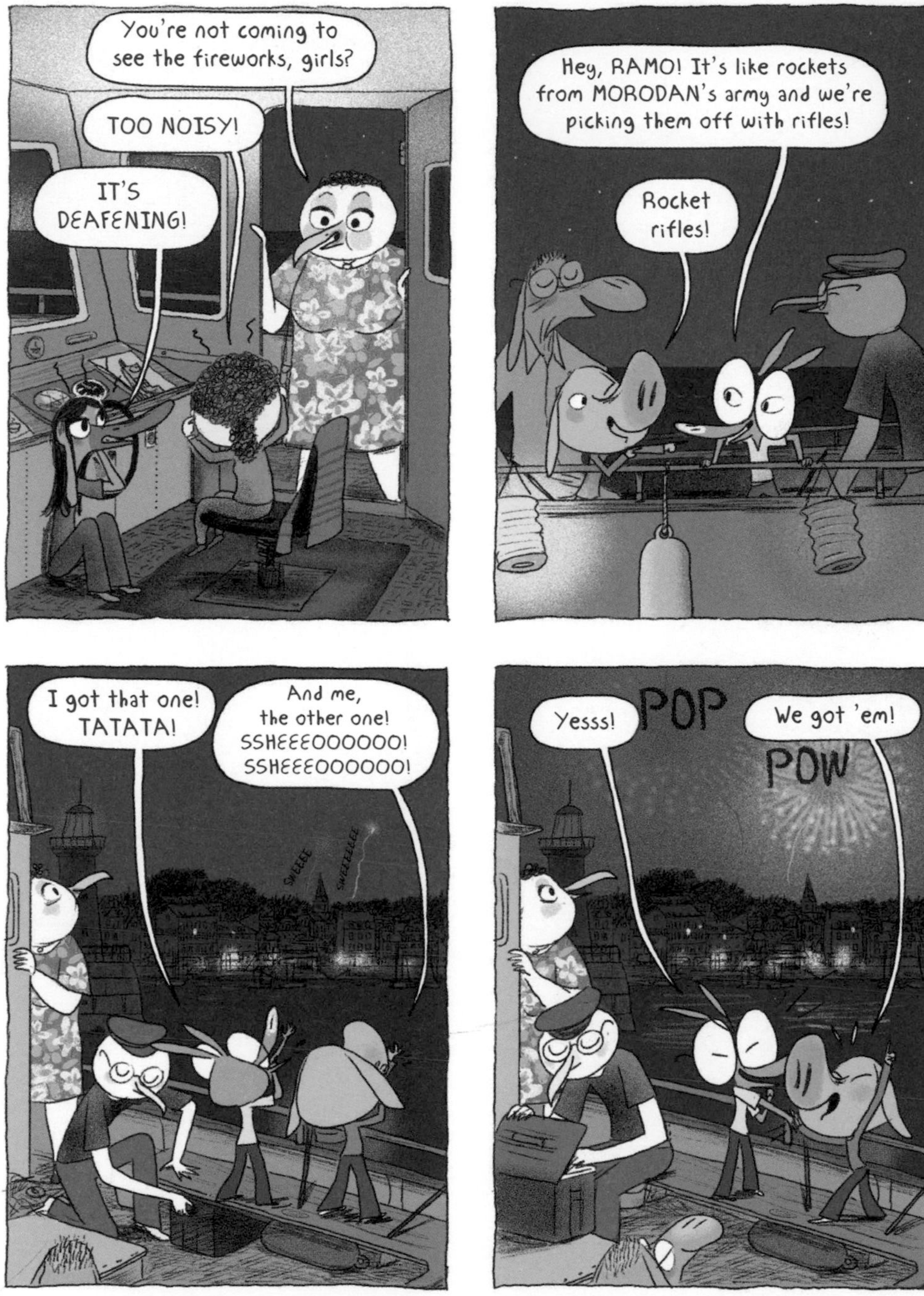

You're not coming to see the fireworks, girls?
TOO NOISY!
IT'S DEAFENING!
Hey, RAMO! It's like rockets from MORODAN's army and we're picking them off with rifles!
Rocket rifles!
I got that one! TATATA!
And me, the other one! SSHEEEOOOOOO! SSHEEEOOOOOO!
Yesss!
POP
We got 'em!
POW

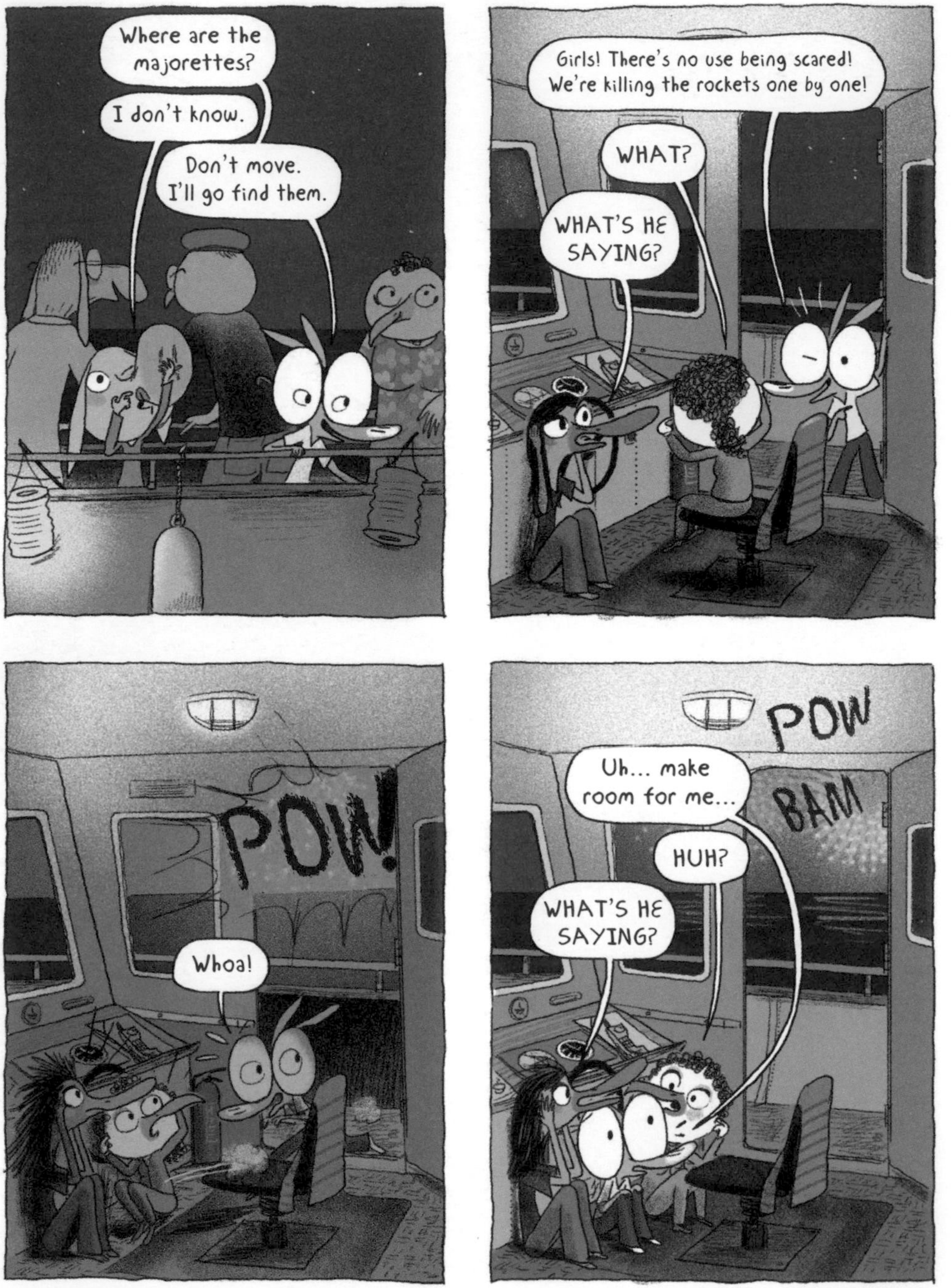
Where are the majorettes?
I don't know.
Don't move. I'll go find them.
Girls! There's no use being scared! We're killing the rockets one by one!
WHAT?
WHAT'S HE SAYING?
POW!
Whoa!
POW
Uh... make room for me...
BAM
HUH?
WHAT'S HE SAYING?

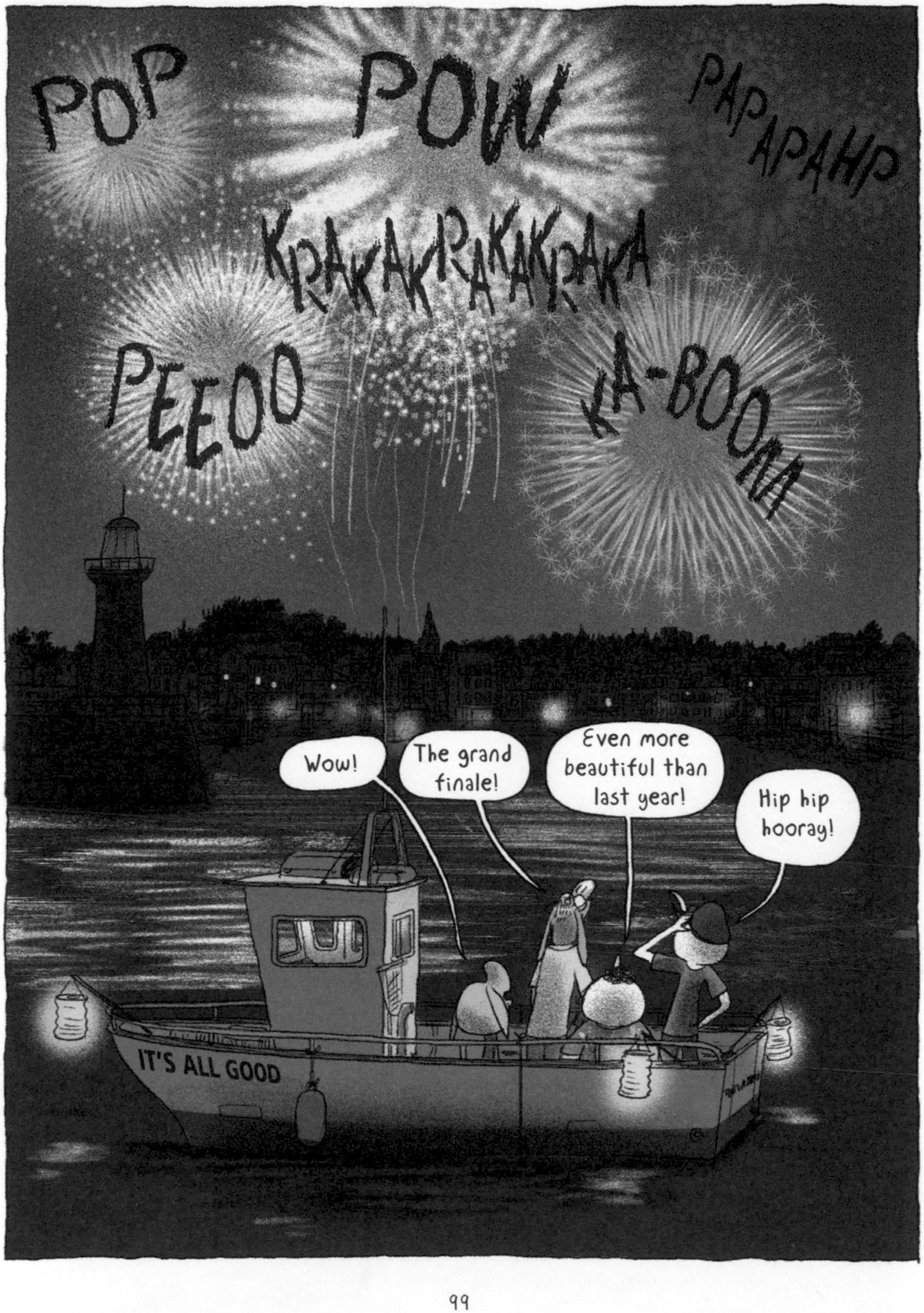
POP
POW
PAPAPAHP
KRAKAKRAKAKRAKA
PEEOO
KA-BOOM
Wow!
The grand finale!
Even more beautiful than last year!
Hip hip hooray!
IT'S ALL GOOD

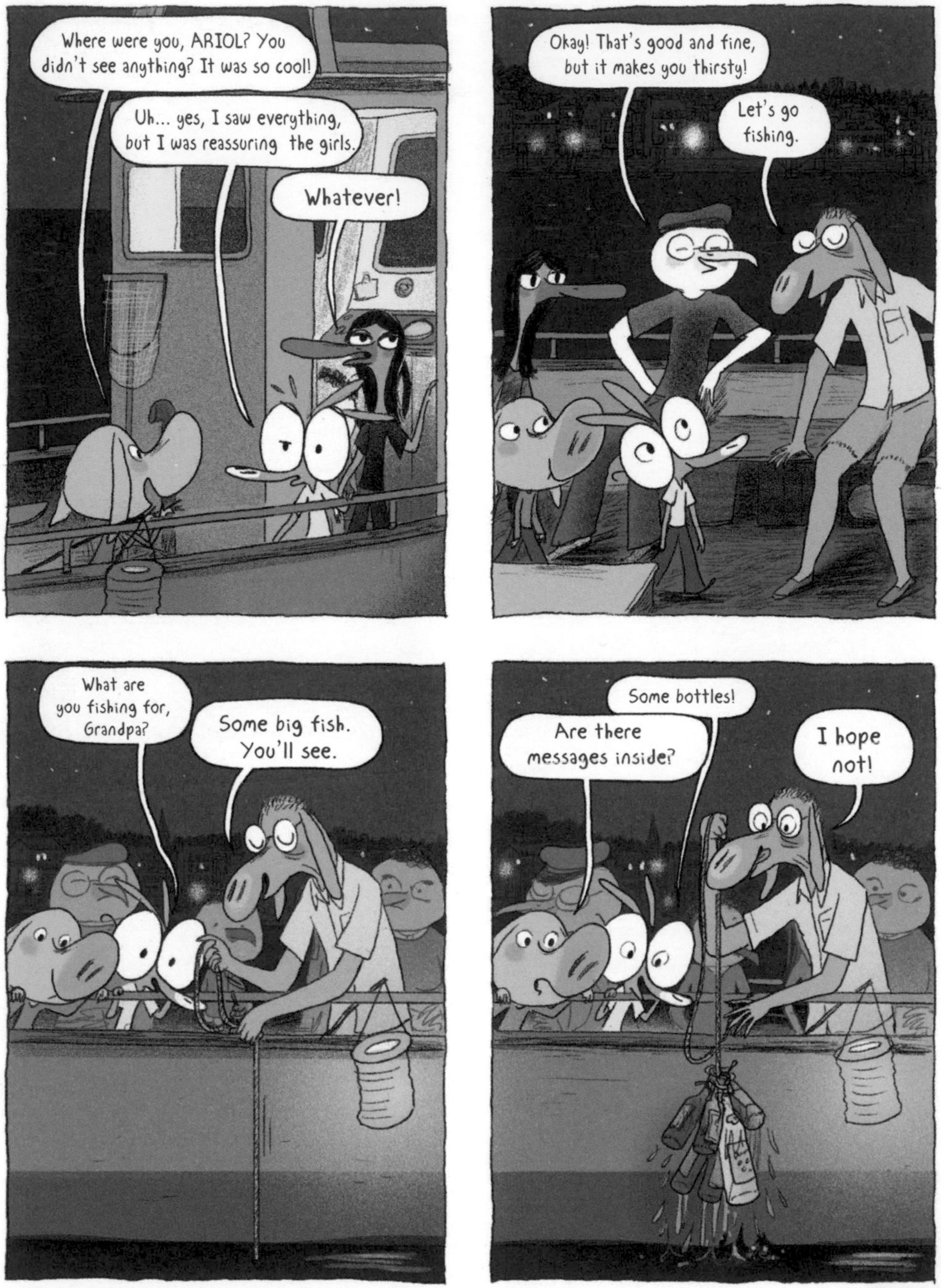

Where were you, ARIOL? You didn't see anything? It was so cool!
Uh... yes, I saw everything, but I was reassuring the girls.
Whatever!
Okay! That's good and fine, but it makes you thirsty!
Let's go fishing.
What are you fishing for, Grandpa?
Some big fish. You'll see.
Some bottles!
Are there messages inside?
I hope not!

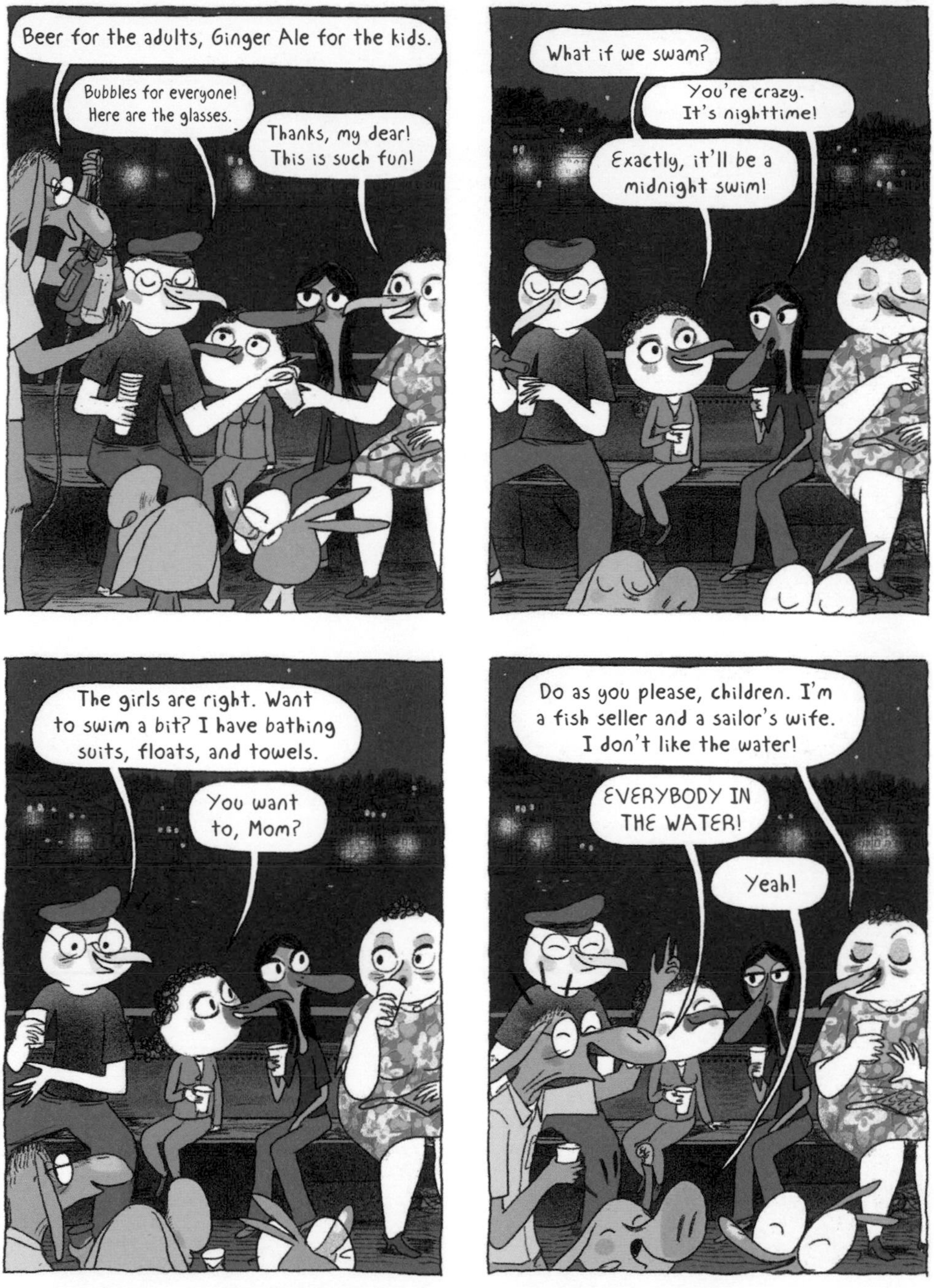
Beer for the adults, Ginger Ale for the kids.
Bubbles for everyone! Here are the glasses.
Thanks, my dear! This is such fun!
What if we swam?
You're crazy. It's nighttime!
Exactly, it'll be a midnight swim!
The girls are right. Want to swim a bit? I have bathing suits, floats, and towels.
You want to, Mom?
Do as you please, children. I'm a fish seller and a sailor's wife. I don't like the water!
EVERYBODY IN THE WATER!
Yeah!

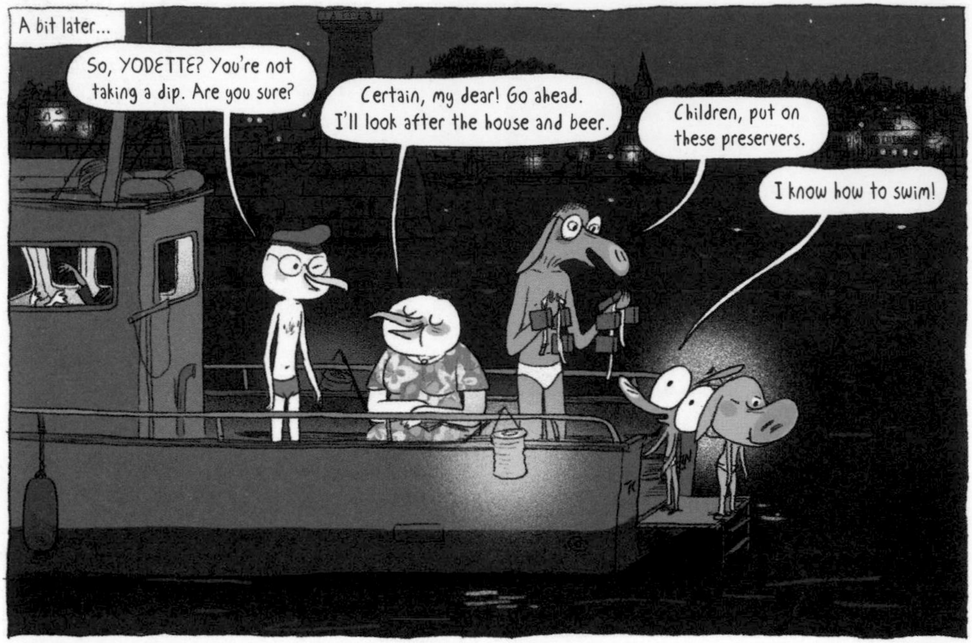
A bit later...
So, YODETTE? You're not taking a dip. Are you sure?
Certain, my dear! Go ahead. I'll look after the house and beer.
Children, put on these preservers.
I know how to swim!

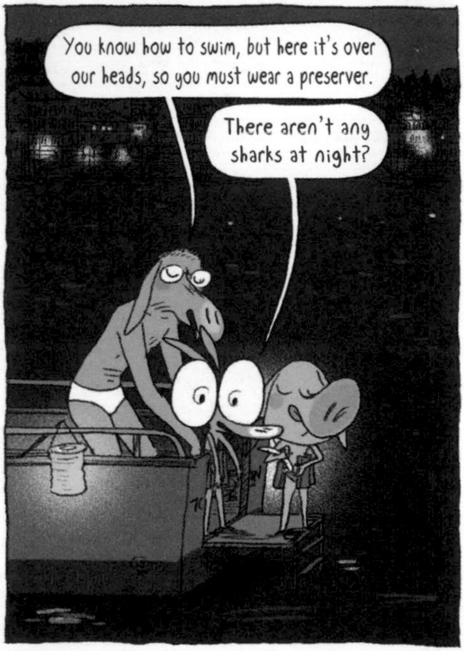
You know how to swim, but here it's over our heads, so you must wear a preserver.
There aren't any sharks at night?

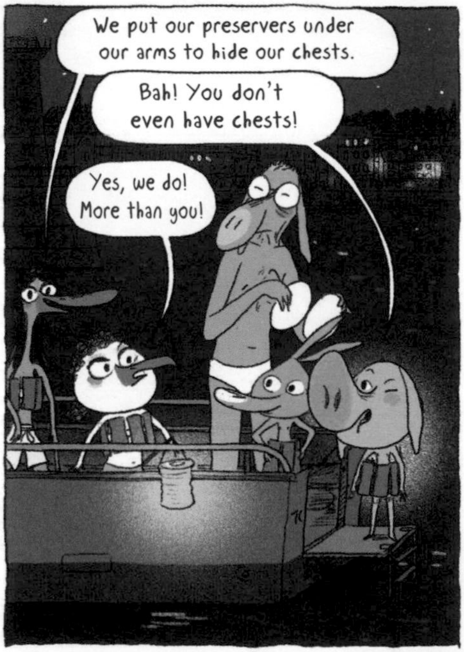
We put our preservers under our arms to hide our chests.
Bah! You don't even have chests!
Yes, we do! More than you!

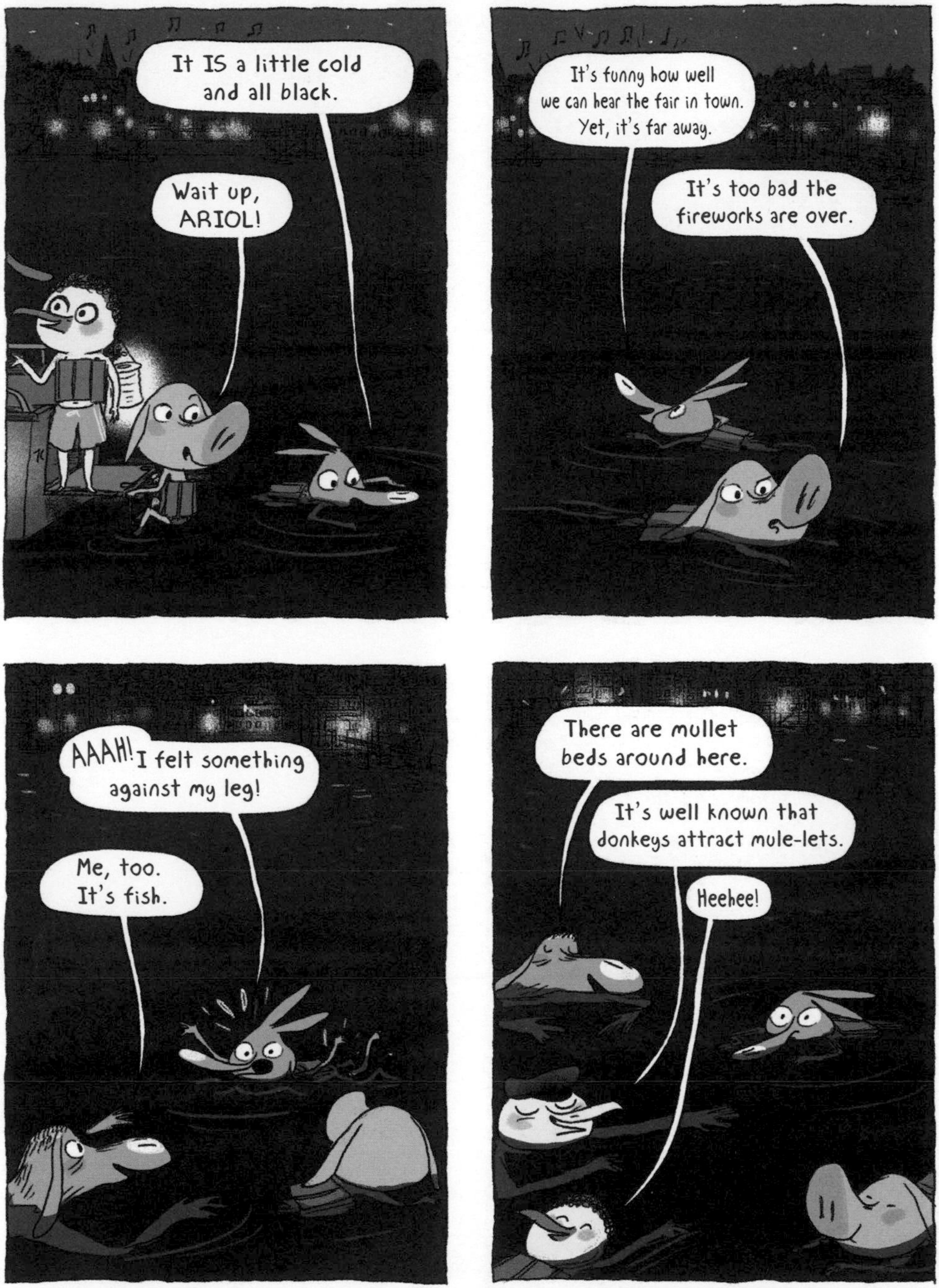
It IS a little cold and all black.
Wait up, ARIOL!
It's funny how well we can hear the fair in town. Yet, it's far away.
It's too bad the fireworks are over.
AAAH! I felt something against my leg!
Me, too. It's fish.
There are mullet beds around here.
It's well known that donkeys attract mule-lets.
Heehee!

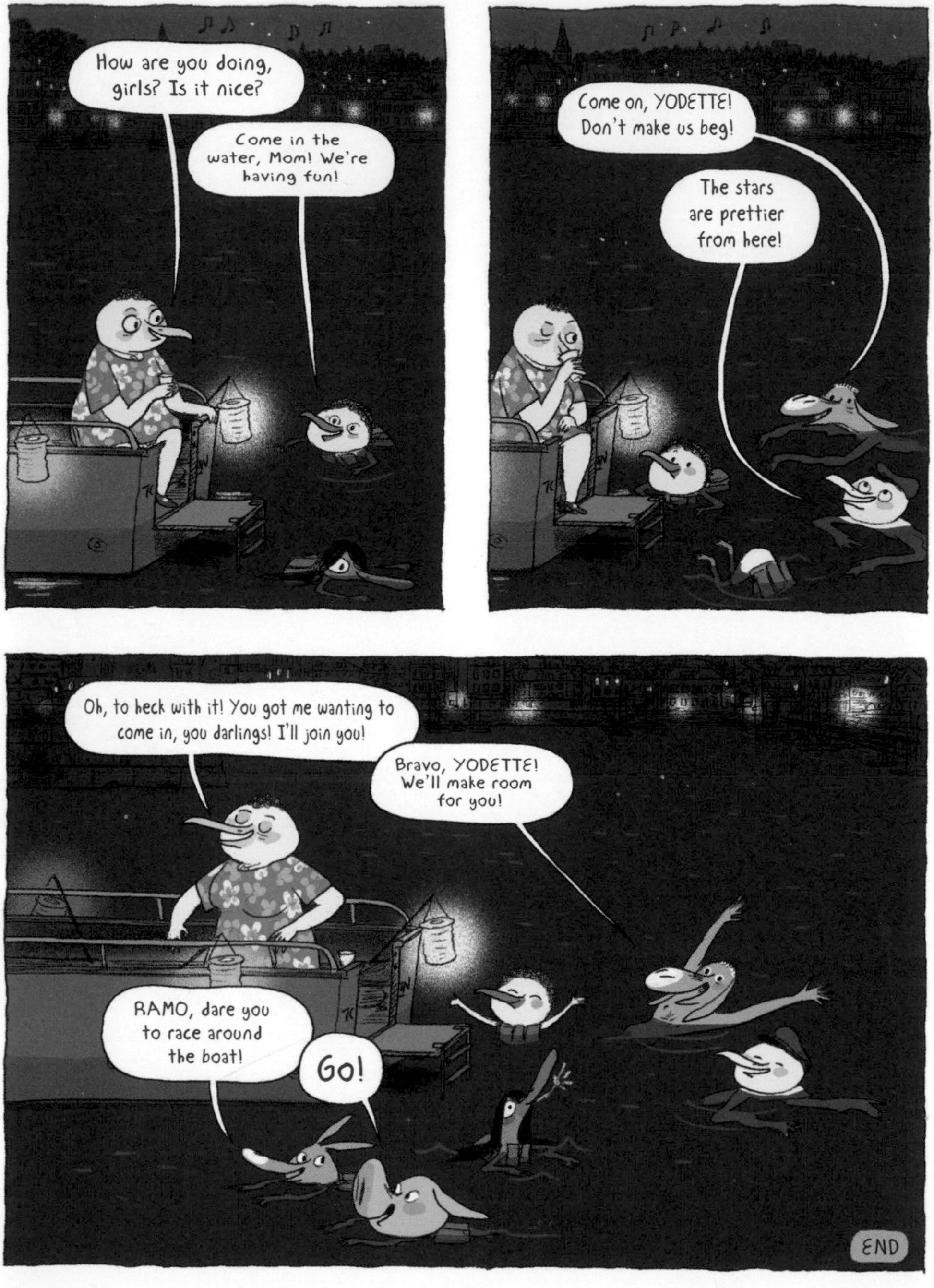
How are you doing, girls? Is it nice?
Come in the water, Mom! We're having fun!
Come on, YODETTE! Don't make us beg!
The stars are prettier from here!
Oh, to heck with it! You got me wanting to come in, you darlings! I'll join you!
Bravo, YODETTE! We'll make room for you!
RAMO, dare you to race around the boat!
GO!
END

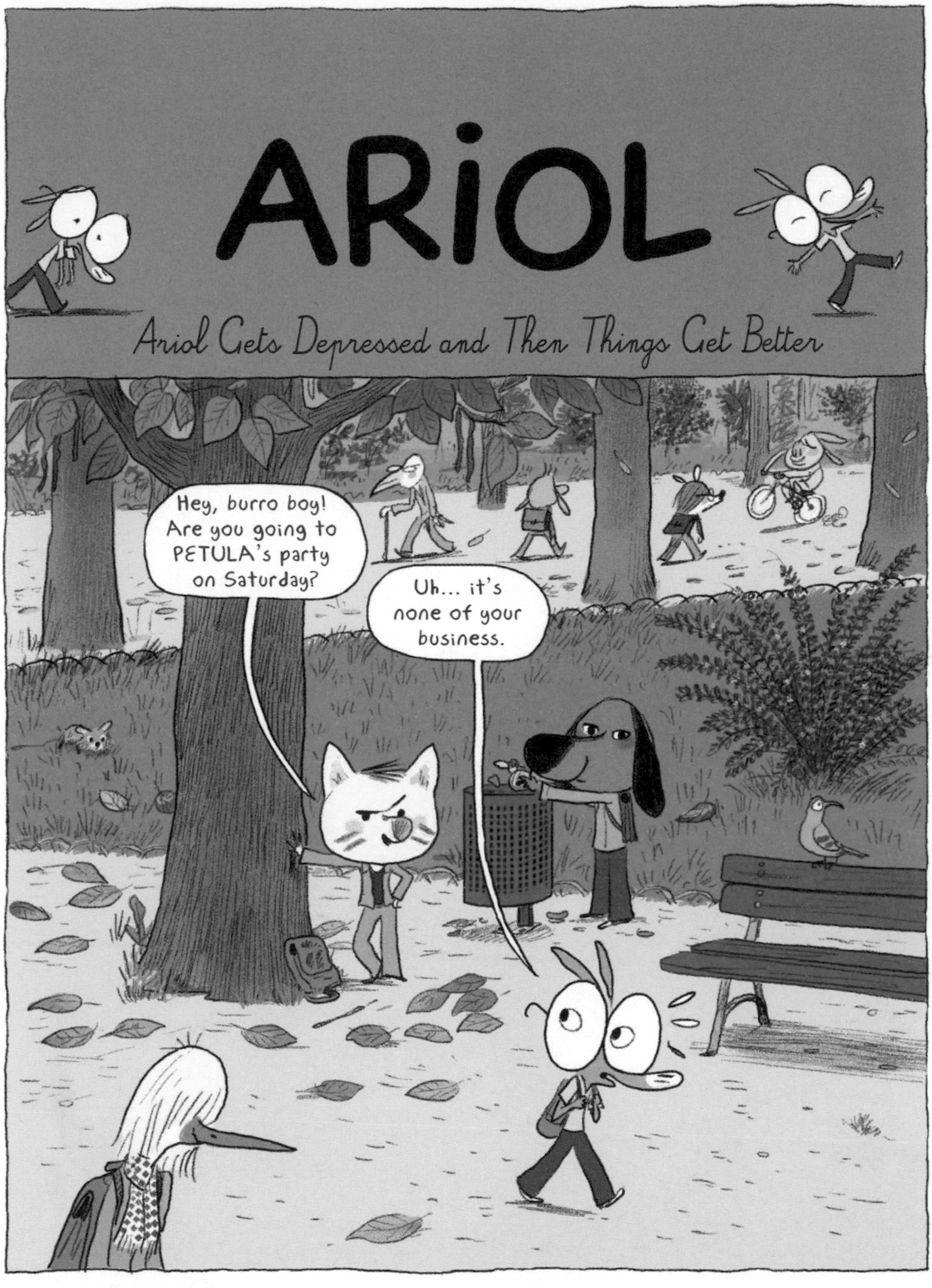
ARiOL
Ariol Gets Depressed and Then Things Get Better
Hey, burro boy! Are you going to PETULA's party on Saturday?
Uh... it's none of your business.

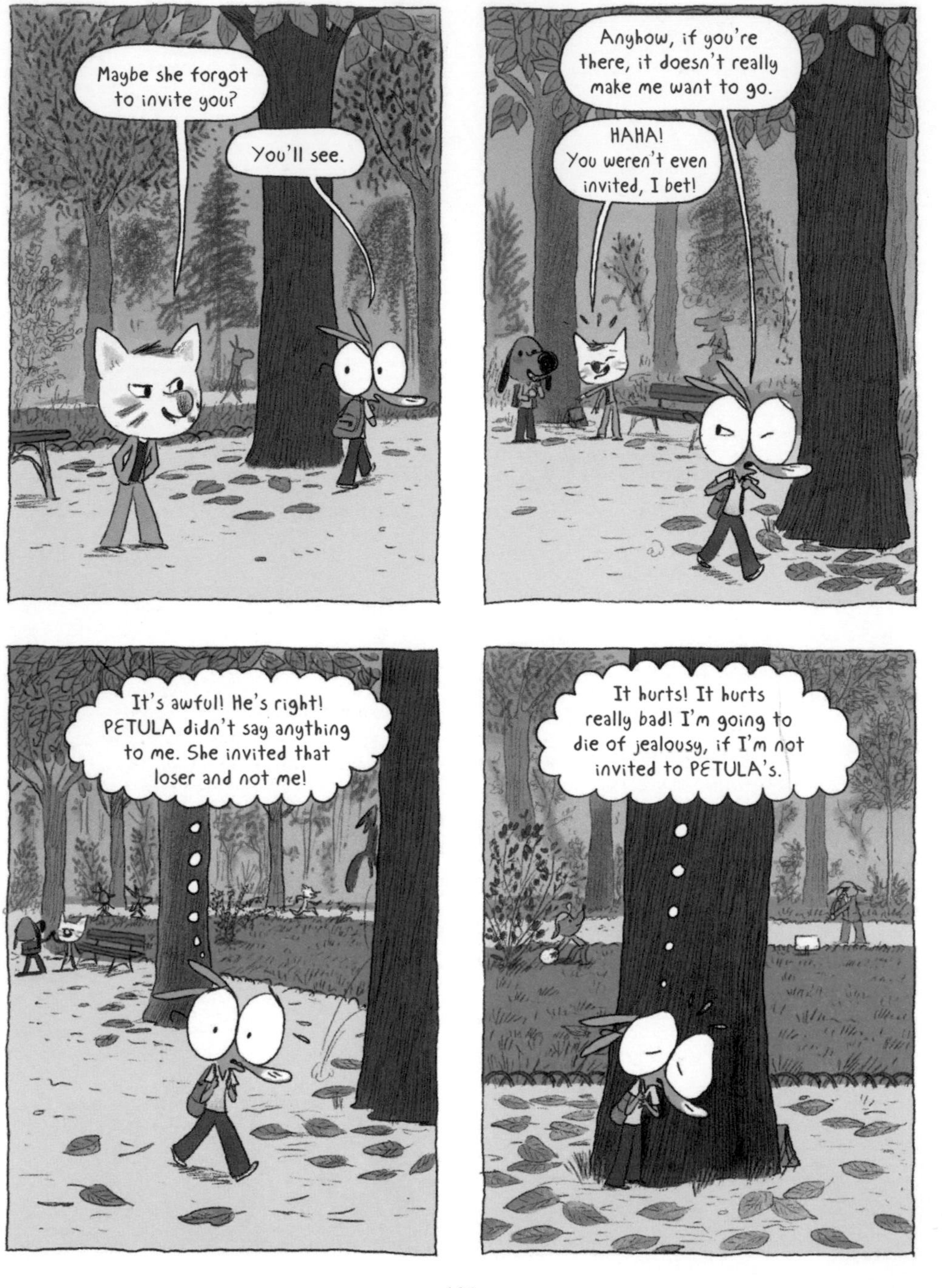
Maybe she forgot to invite you?
You'll see.
Anyhow, if you're there, it doesn't really make me want to go.
HAHA! You weren't even invited, I bet!
It's awful! He's right! PETULA didn't say anything to me. She invited that loser and not me!
It hurts! It hurts really bad! I'm going to die of jealousy, if I'm not invited to PETULA's.

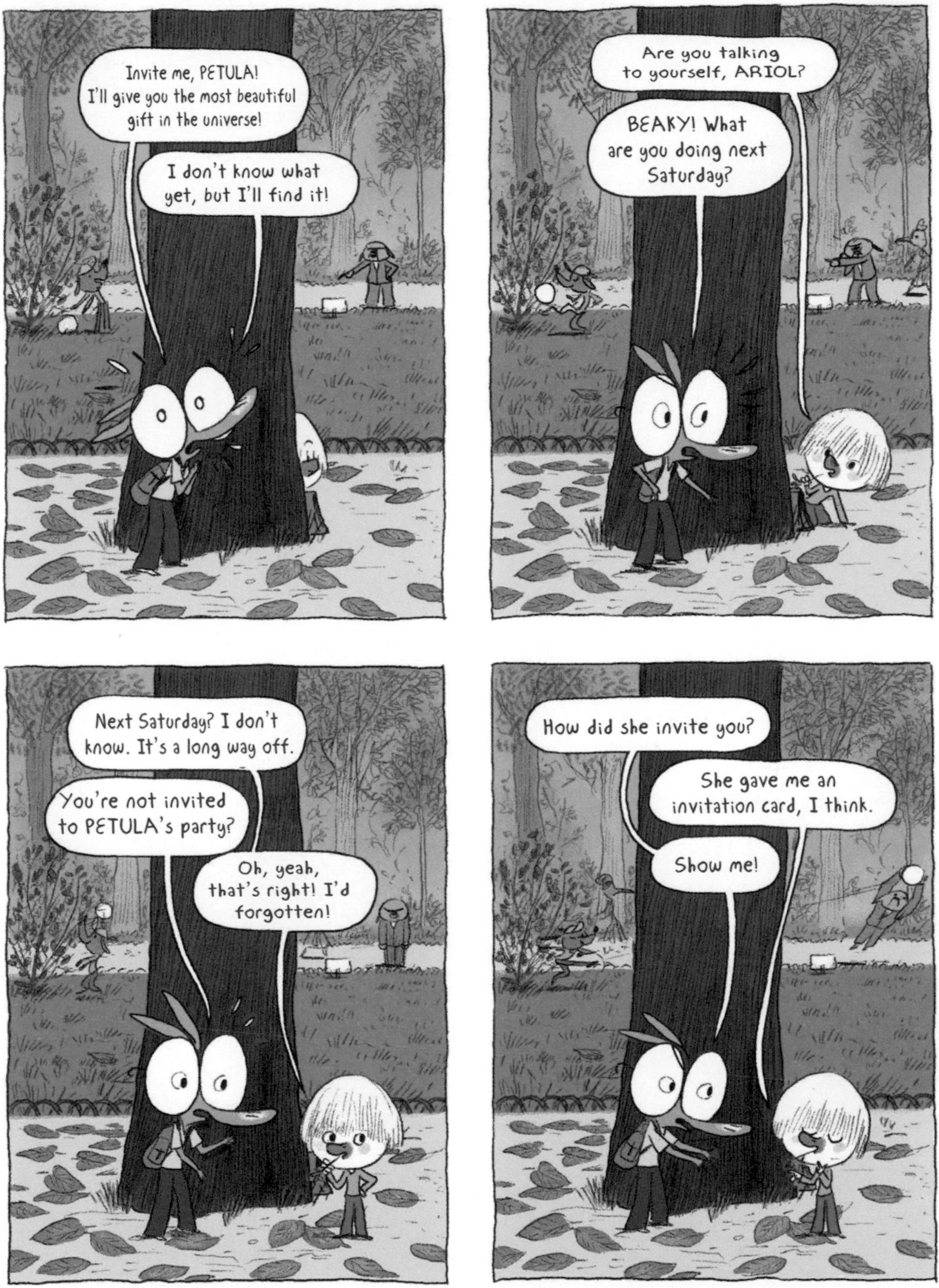
Invite me, PETULA! I'll give you the most beautiful gift in the universe!
I don't know what yet, but I'll find it!
Are you talking to yourself, ARIOL?
BEAKY! What are you doing next Saturday?
Next Saturday? I don't know. It's a long way off.
You're not invited to PETULA's party?
Oh, yeah, that's right! I'd forgotten!
How did she invite you?
She gave me an invitation card, I think.
Show me!

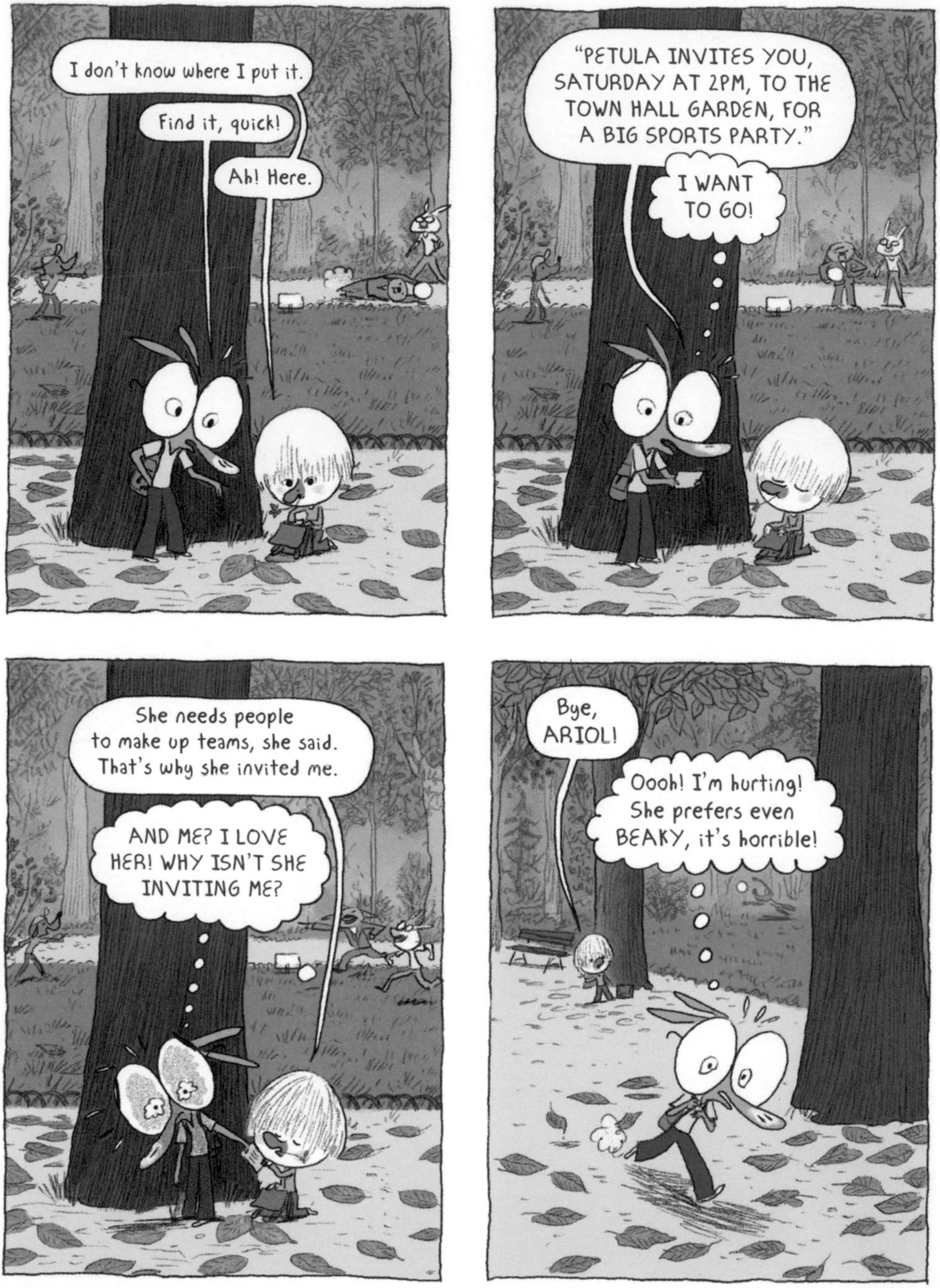
I don't know where I put it.
Find it, quick!
Ah! Here.
"PETULA INVITES YOU, SATURDAY AT 2PM, TO THE TOWN HALL GARDEN, FOR A BIG SPORTS PARTY."
I WANT TO GO!
She needs people to make up teams, she said. That's why she invited me.
AND ME? I LOVE HER! WHY ISN'T SHE INVITING ME?
Bye, ARIOL!
Oooh! I'm hurting! She prefers even BEAKY, it's horrible!

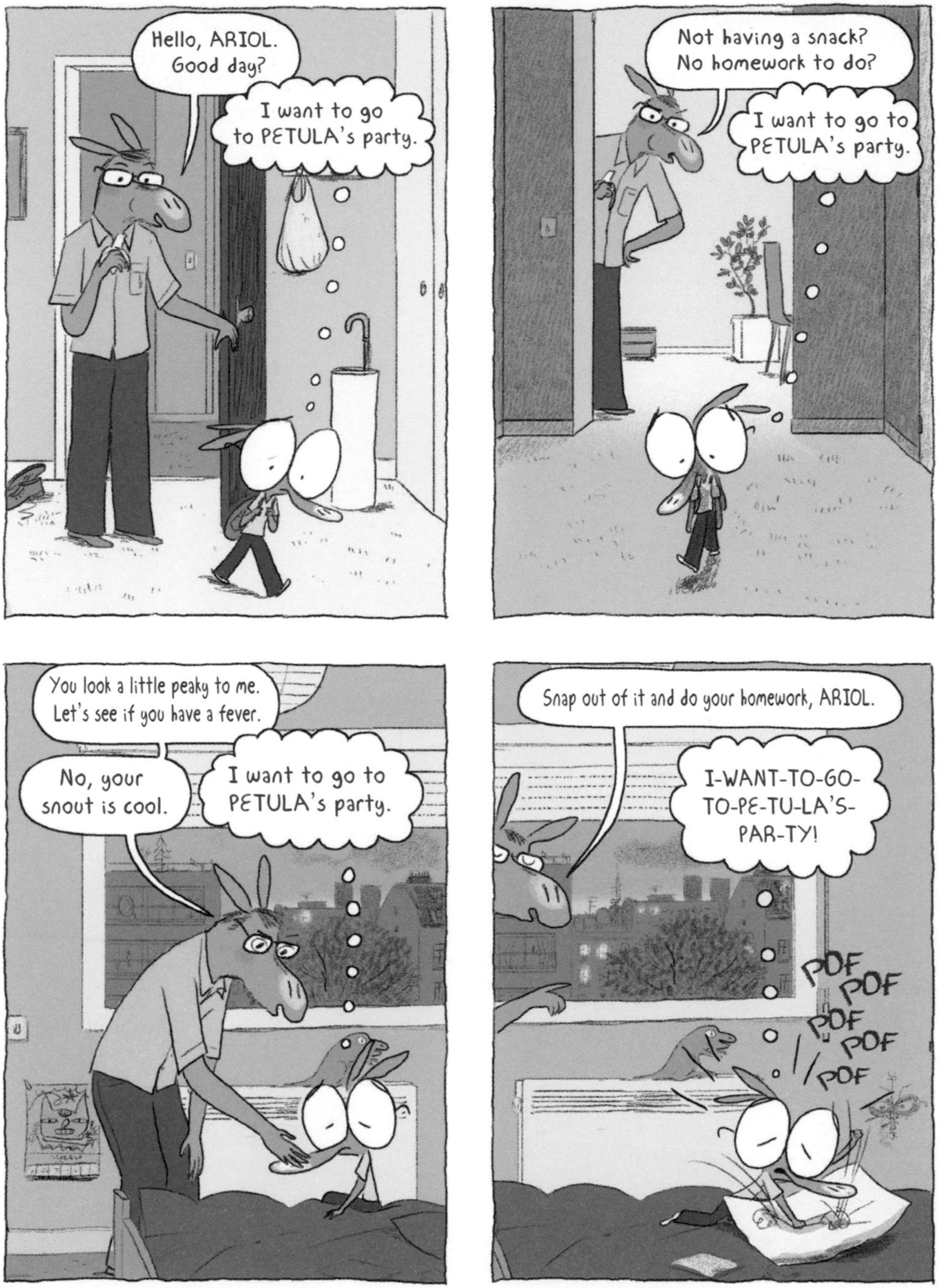
Hello, ARIOL.
Good day?
I want to go to PETULA's party.
Not having a snack?
No homework to do?
I want to go to PETULA's party.
You look a little peaky to me.
Let's see if you have a fever.
No, your snout is cool.
I want to go to PETULA's party.
Snap out of it and do your homework, ARIOL.
I-WANT-TO-GO-TO-PE-TU-LA'S-PAR-TY!
POF POF POF POF POF

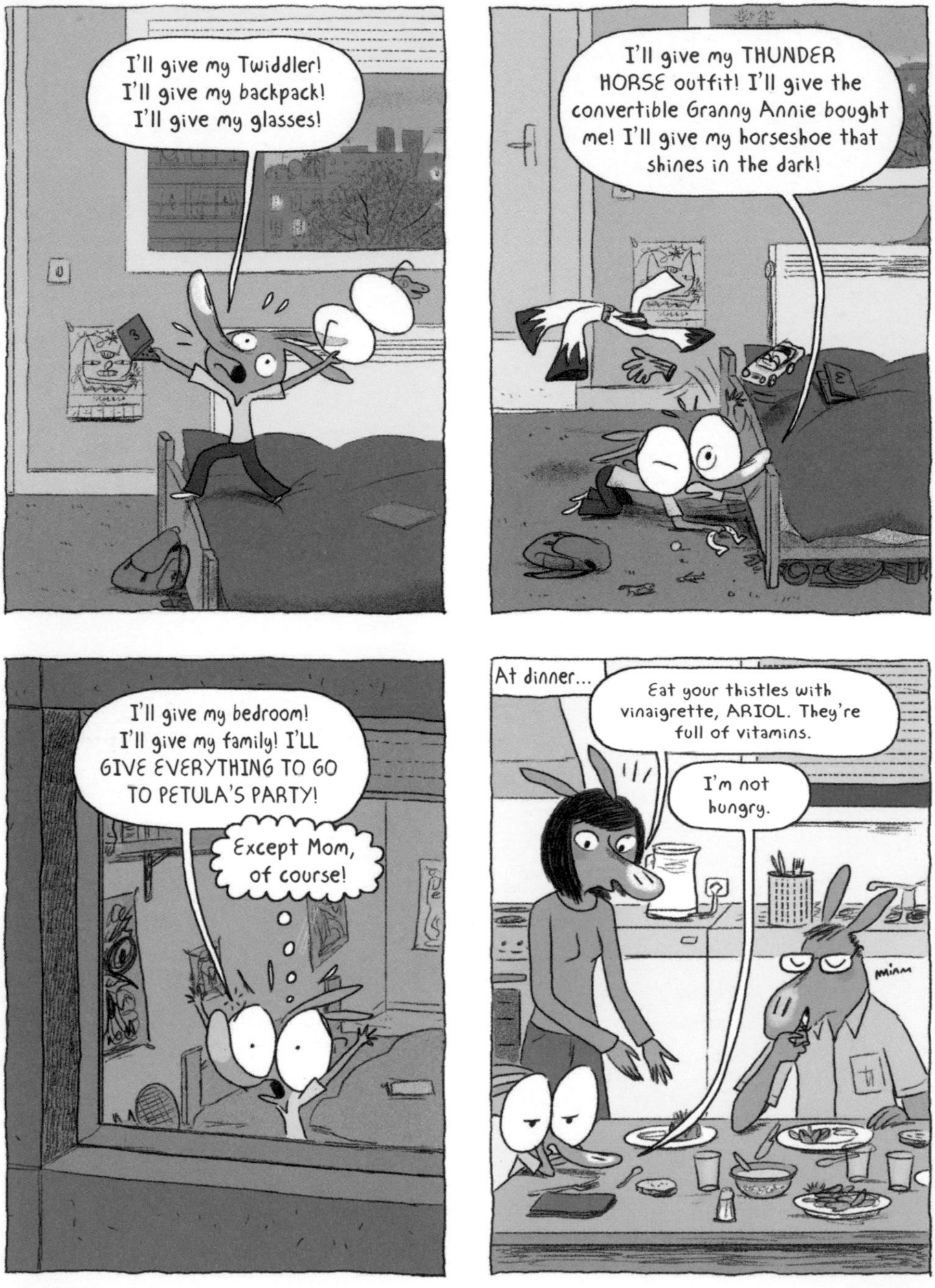
I'll give my Twiddler! I'll give my backpack! I'll give my glasses!
I'll give my THUNDER HORSE outfit! I'll give the convertible Granny Annie bought me! I'll give my horseshoe that shines in the dark!
I'll give my bedroom! I'll give my family! I'LL GIVE EVERYTHING TO GO TO PETULA'S PARTY!
Except Mom, of course!
At dinner...
Eat your thistles with vinaigrette, ARIOL. They're full of vitamins.
I'm not hungry.
MIAM

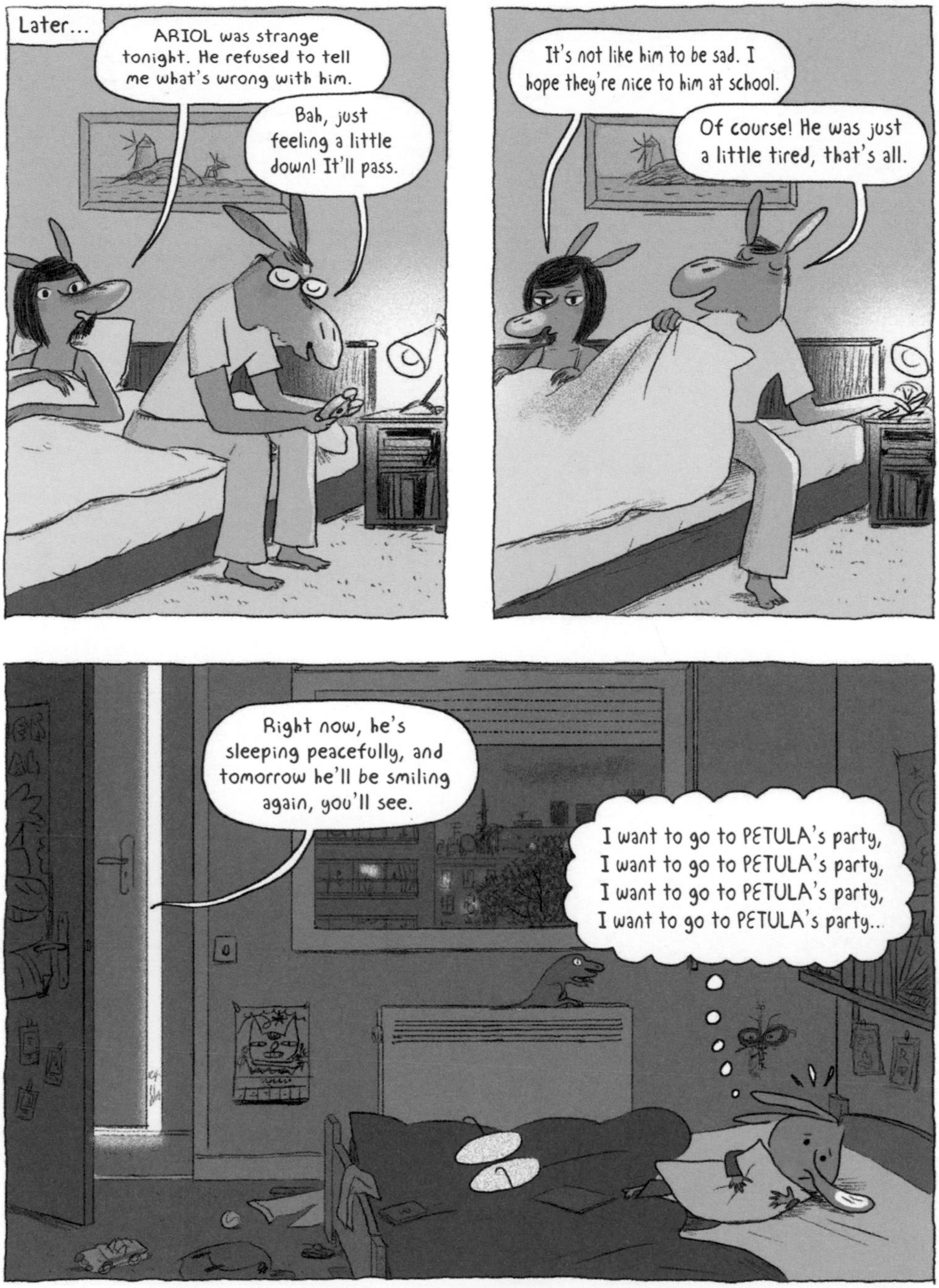
Later...
ARIOL was strange tonight. He refused to tell me what's wrong with him.
Bah, just feeling a little down! It'll pass.
It's not like him to be sad. I hope they're nice to him at school.
Of course! He was just a little tired, that's all.
Right now, he's sleeping peacefully, and tomorrow he'll be smiling again, you'll see.
I want to go to PETULA's party, I want to go to PETULA's party, I want to go to PETULA's party, I want to go to PETULA's party...

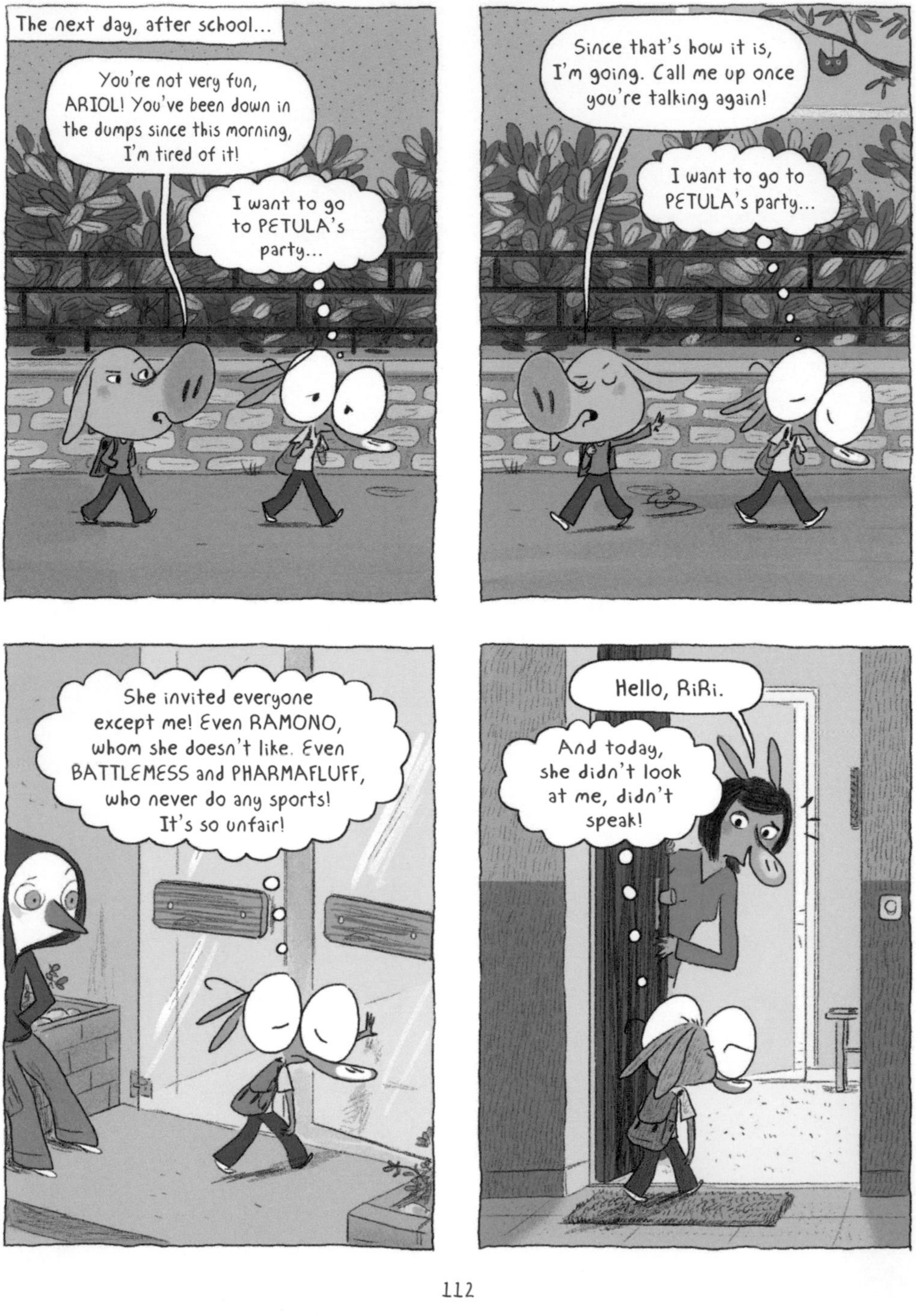
The next day, after school...
You're not very fun, ARIOL! You've been down in the dumps since this morning, I'm tired of it!
I want to go to PETULA's party...
Since that's how it is, I'm going. Call me up once you're talking again!
I want to go to PETULA's party...
She invited everyone except me! Even RAMONO, whom she doesn't like. Even BATTLEMESS and PHARMAFLUFF, who never do any sports! It's so unfair!
Hello, RiRi.
And today, she didn't look at me, didn't speak!

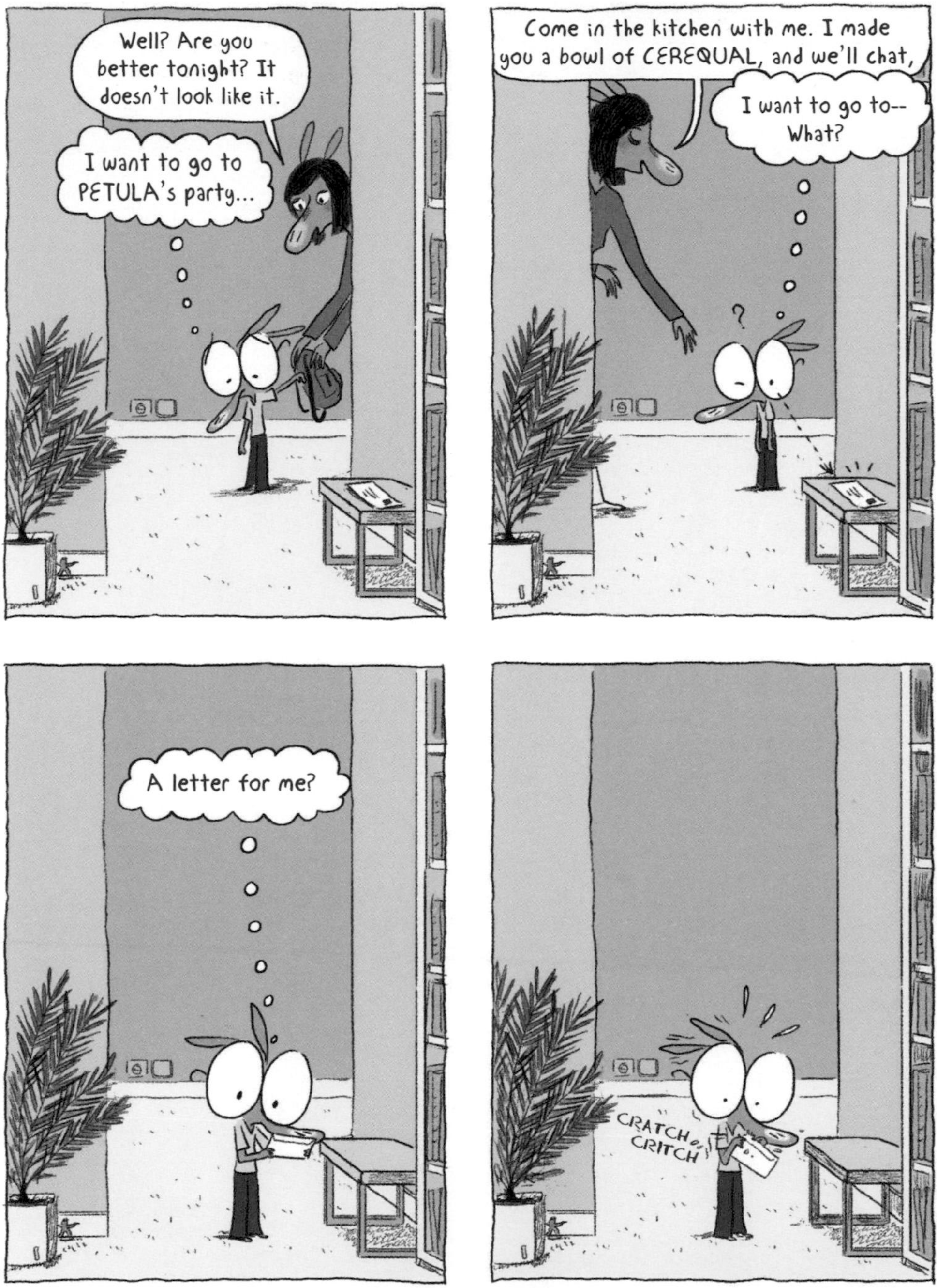
Well? Are you better tonight? It doesn't look like it.
I want to go to PETULA's party...
Come in the kitchen with me. I made you a bowl of CEREQUAL, and we'll chat,
I want to go to-- What?
?
A letter for me?
CRATCH CRITCH

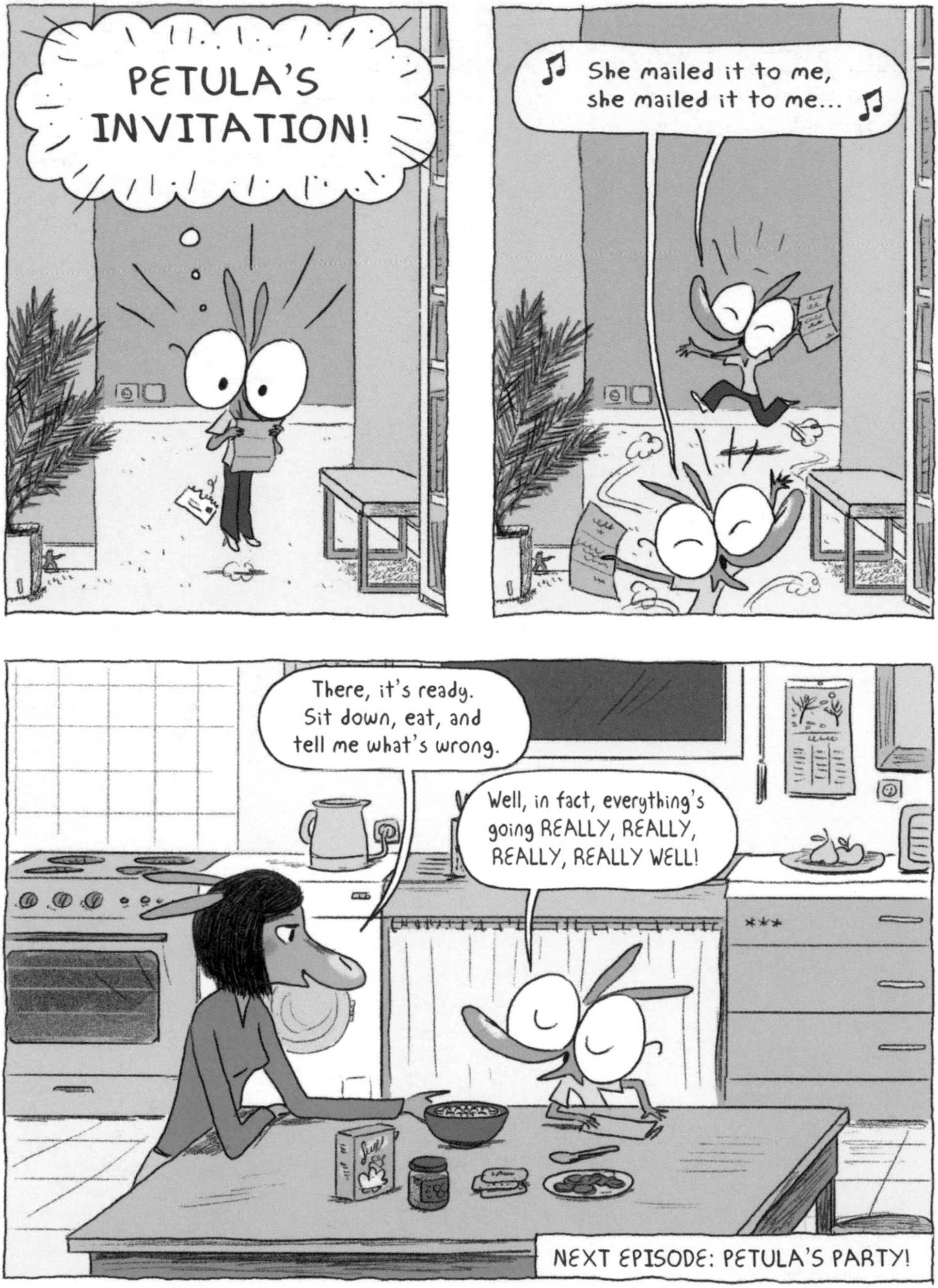
PETULA'S INVITATION!
She mailed it to me, she mailed it to me...
There, it's ready. Sit down, eat, and tell me what's wrong.
Well, in fact, everything's going REALLY, REALLY, REALLY, REALLY WELL!
NEXT EPISODE: PETULA'S PARTY!

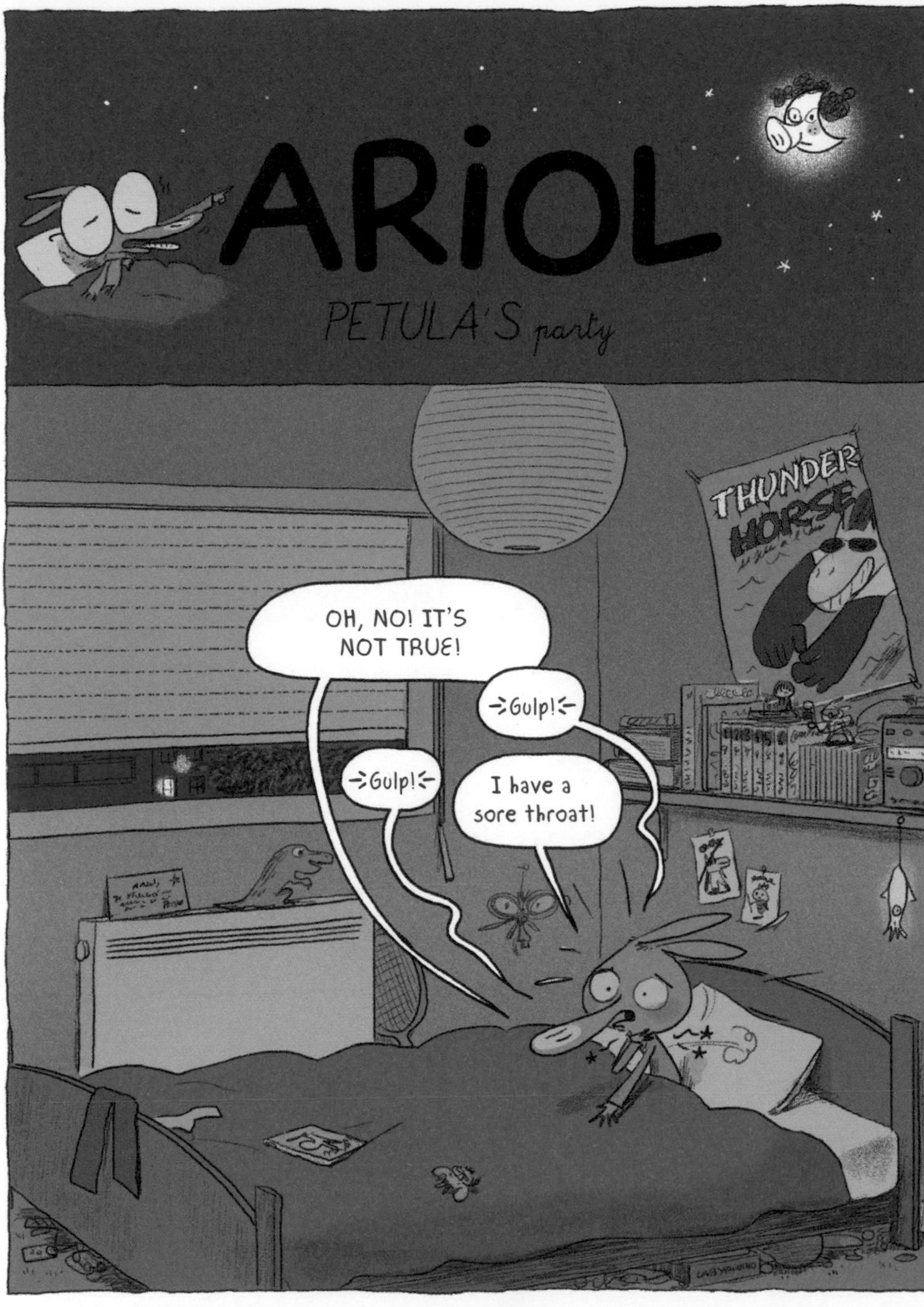
ARiOL
PETULA'S party
THUNDER HORSE
OH, NO! IT'S NOT TRUE!
Gulp!
Gulp!
I have a sore throat!

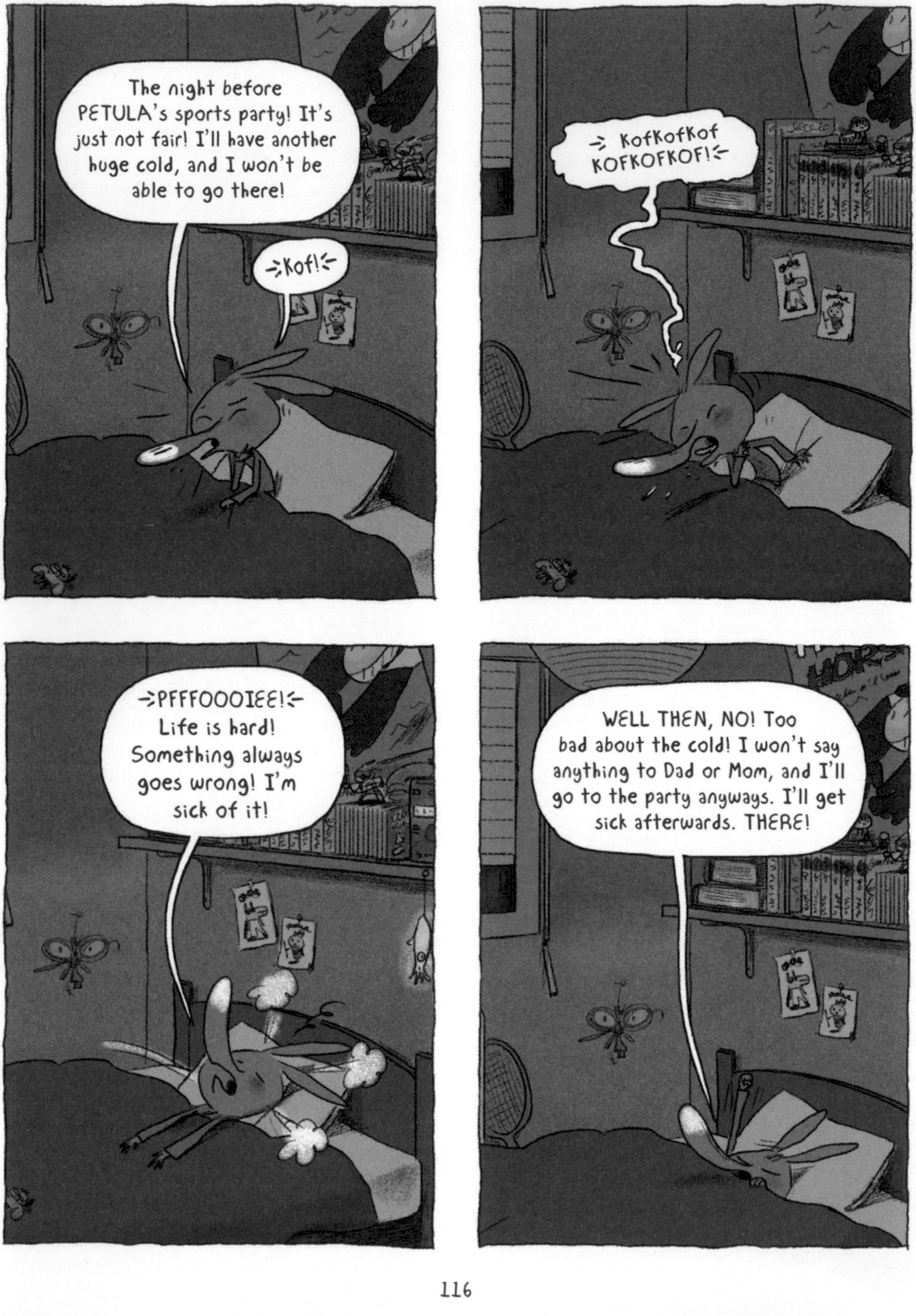
The night before PETULA's sports party! It's just not fair! I'll have another huge cold, and I won't be able to go there!
Kof!
KofKofKof KOFKOFKOF!
PFFFOOOIEE! Life is hard! Something always goes wrong! I'm sick of it!
WELL THEN, NO! Too bad about the cold! I won't say anything to Dad or Mom, and I'll go to the party anyways. I'll get sick afterwards. THERE!

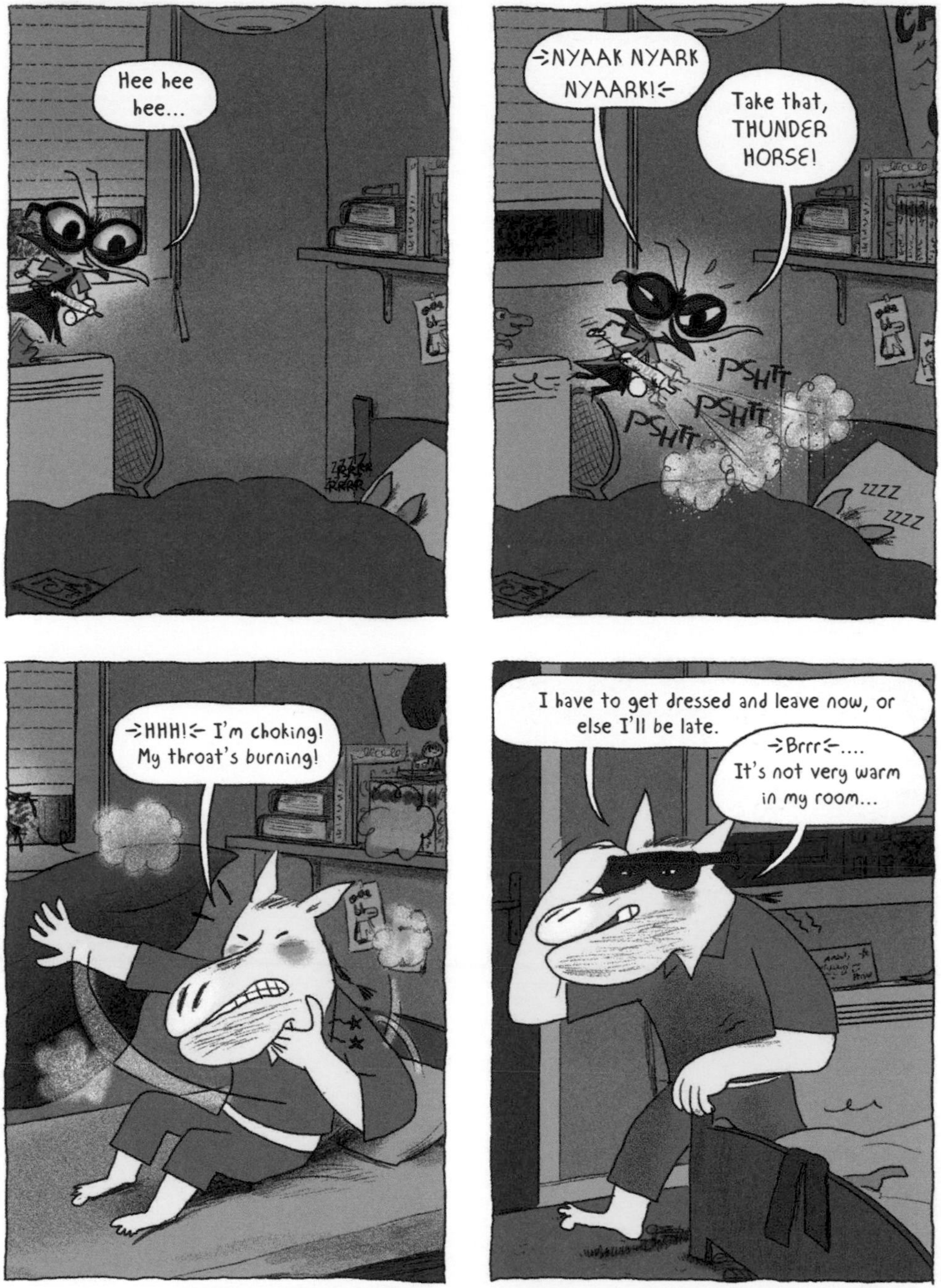

Hee hee hee...
⇒NYAAK NYARK NYAARK!⇐
Take that, THUNDER HORSE!
PSHTT
PSHTT
PSHTT
ZZZZ
ZZZZ
⇒HHH!⇐ I'm choking! My throat's burning!
I have to get dressed and leave now, or else I'll be late.
⇒Brrr⇐.... It's not very warm in my room...

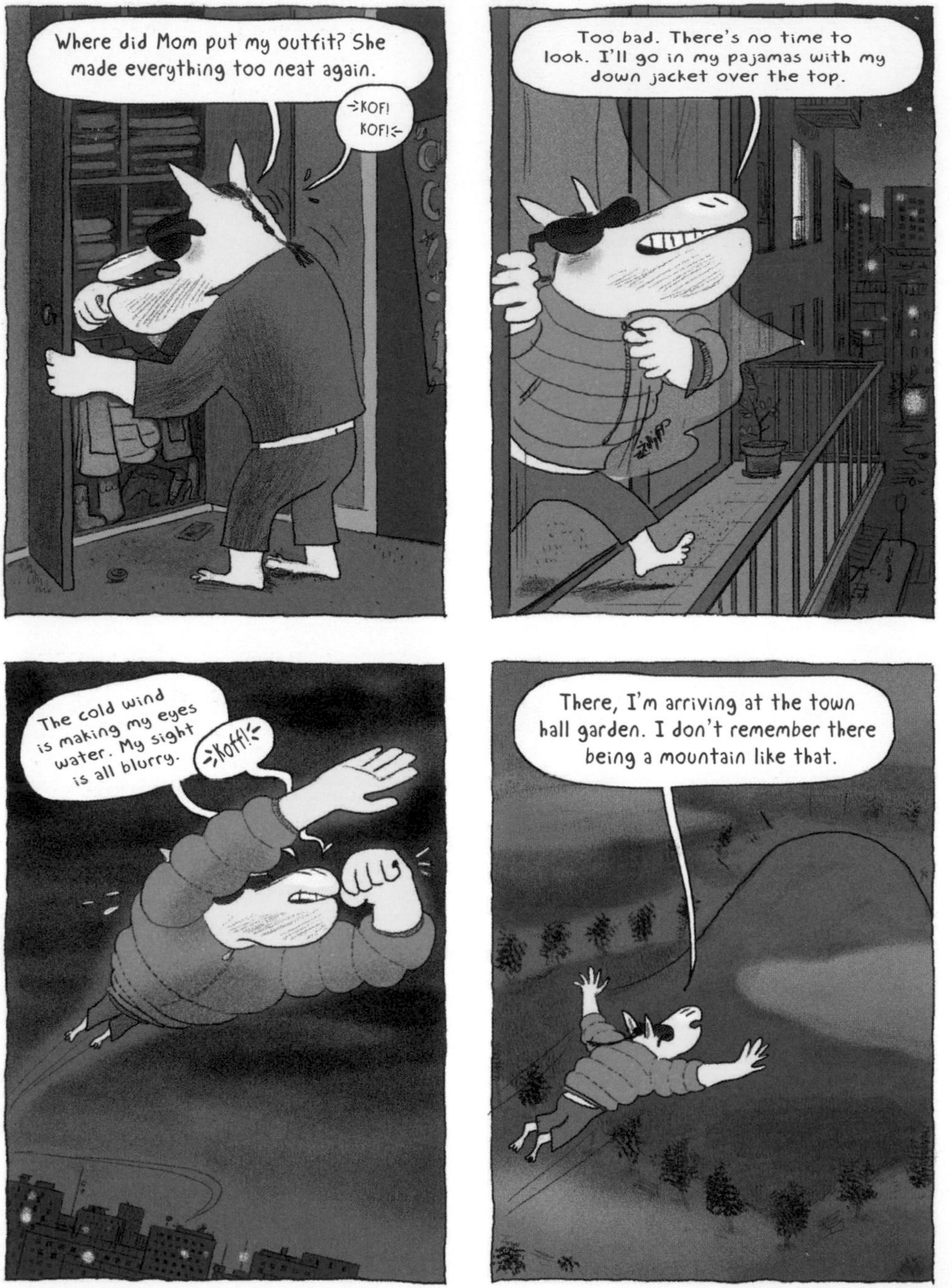
Where did Mom put my outfit? She made everything too neat again.
KOF! KOF!
Too bad. There's no time to look. I'll go in my pajamas with my down jacket over the top.
The cold wind is making my eyes water. My sight is all blurry.
Koff!
There, I'm arriving at the town hall garden. I don't remember there being a mountain like that.

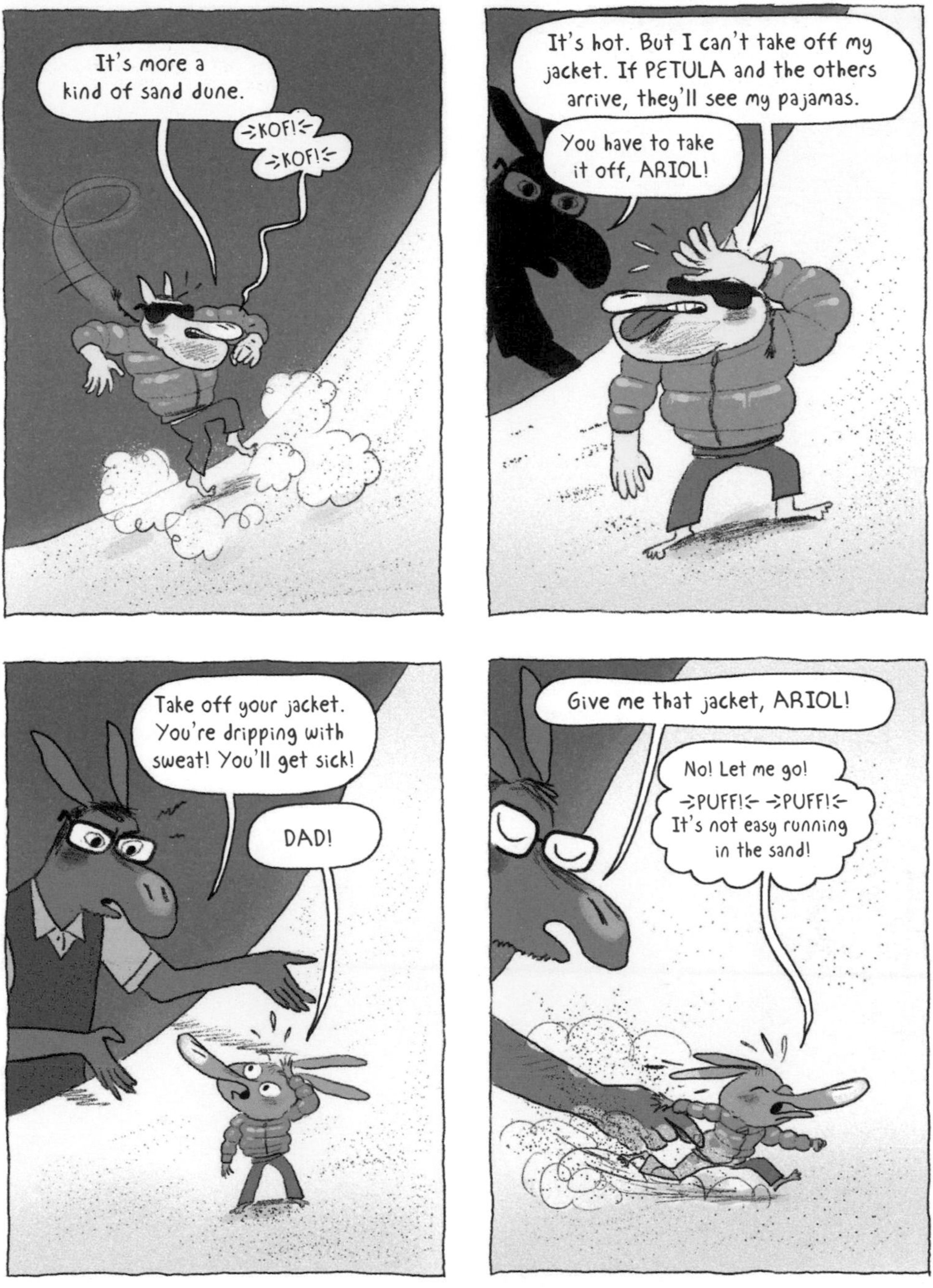
It's more a kind of sand dune.
⇒KOF!⇐
⇒KOF!⇐
It's hot. But I can't take off my jacket. If PETULA and the others arrive, they'll see my pajamas.
You have to take it off, ARIOL!
Take off your jacket. You're dripping with sweat! You'll get sick!
DAD!
Give me that jacket, ARIOL!
No! Let me go! ⇒PUFF!⇐ ⇒PUFF!⇐ It's not easy running in the sand!

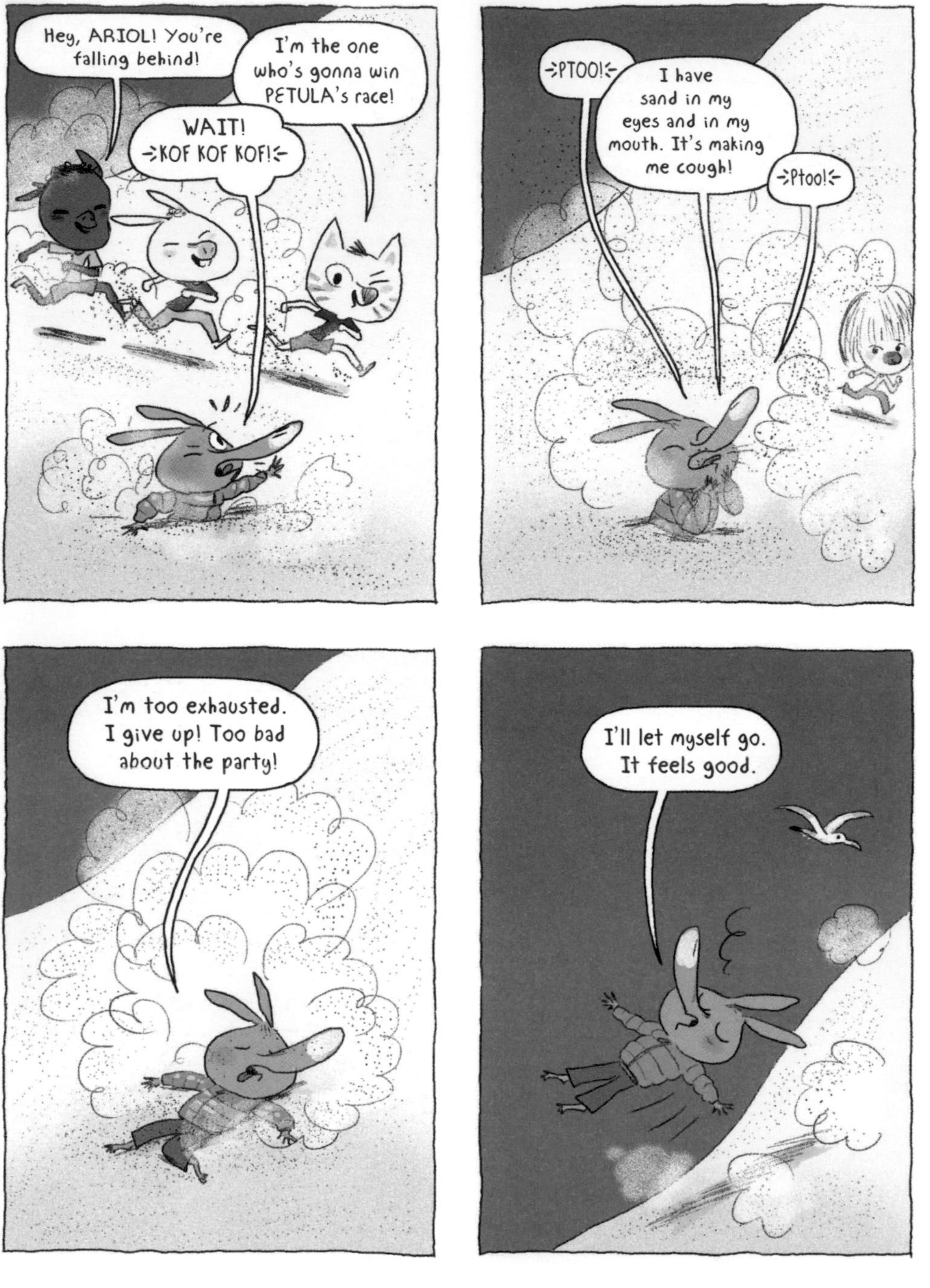
Hey, ARIOL! You're falling behind!
I'm the one who's gonna win PETULA's race!
WAIT!
KOF KOF KOF!
PTOO!
I have sand in my eyes and in my mouth. It's making me cough!
Ptoo!
I'm too exhausted. I give up! Too bad about the party!
I'll let myself go. It feels good.

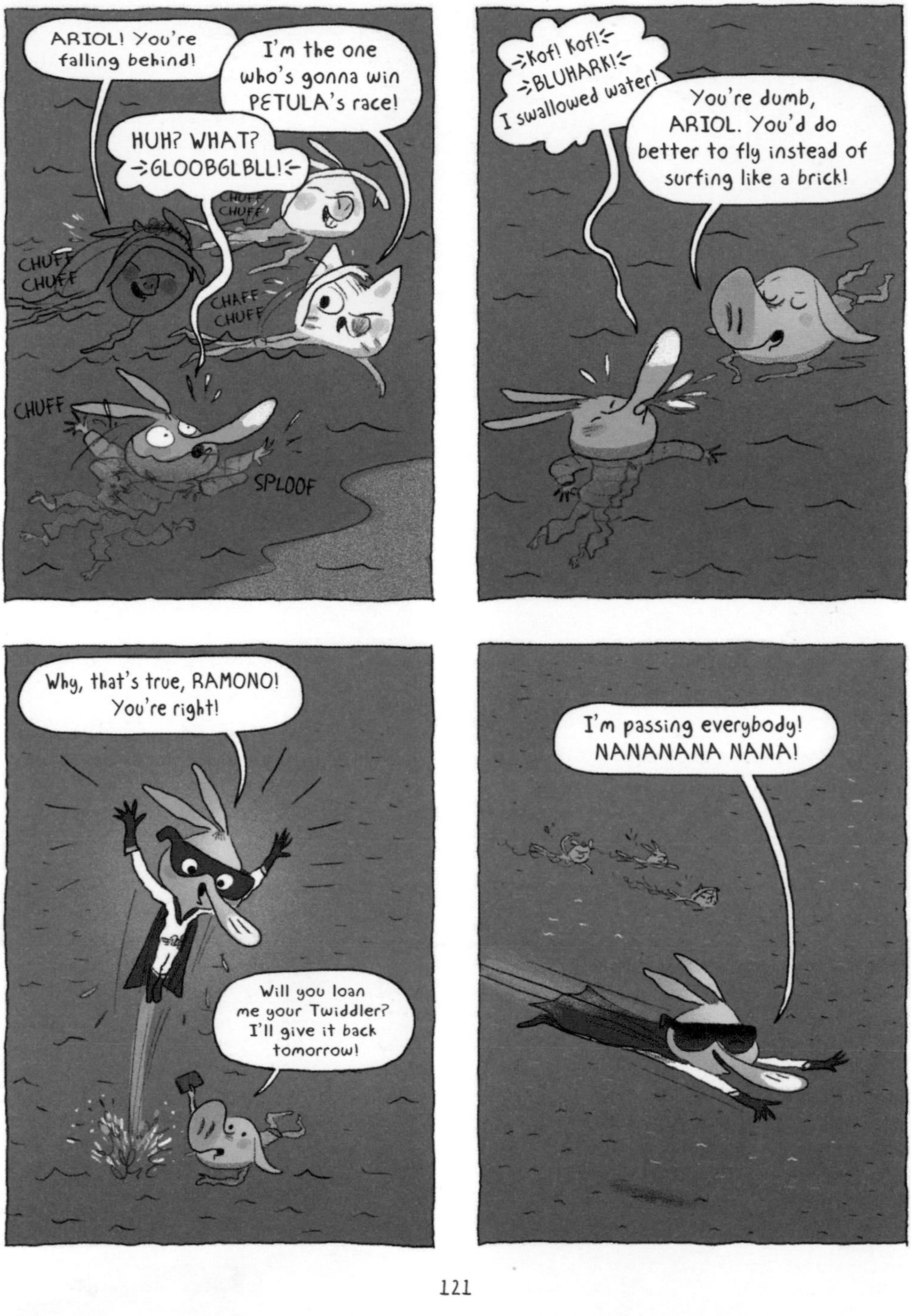
ARIOL! You're falling behind!
I'm the one who's gonna win PETULA's race!
HUH? WHAT? GLOOBGLBLL!
CHUFF CHUFF
CHUFF CHUFF
CHAFF CHUFF
CHUFF
SPLOOF
Kof! Kof! BLUHARK! I swallowed water!
You're dumb, ARIOL. You'd do better to fly instead of surfing like a brick!
Why, that's true, RAMONO! You're right!
Will you loan me your Twiddler? I'll give it back tomorrow!
I'm passing everybody! NANANANA NANA!

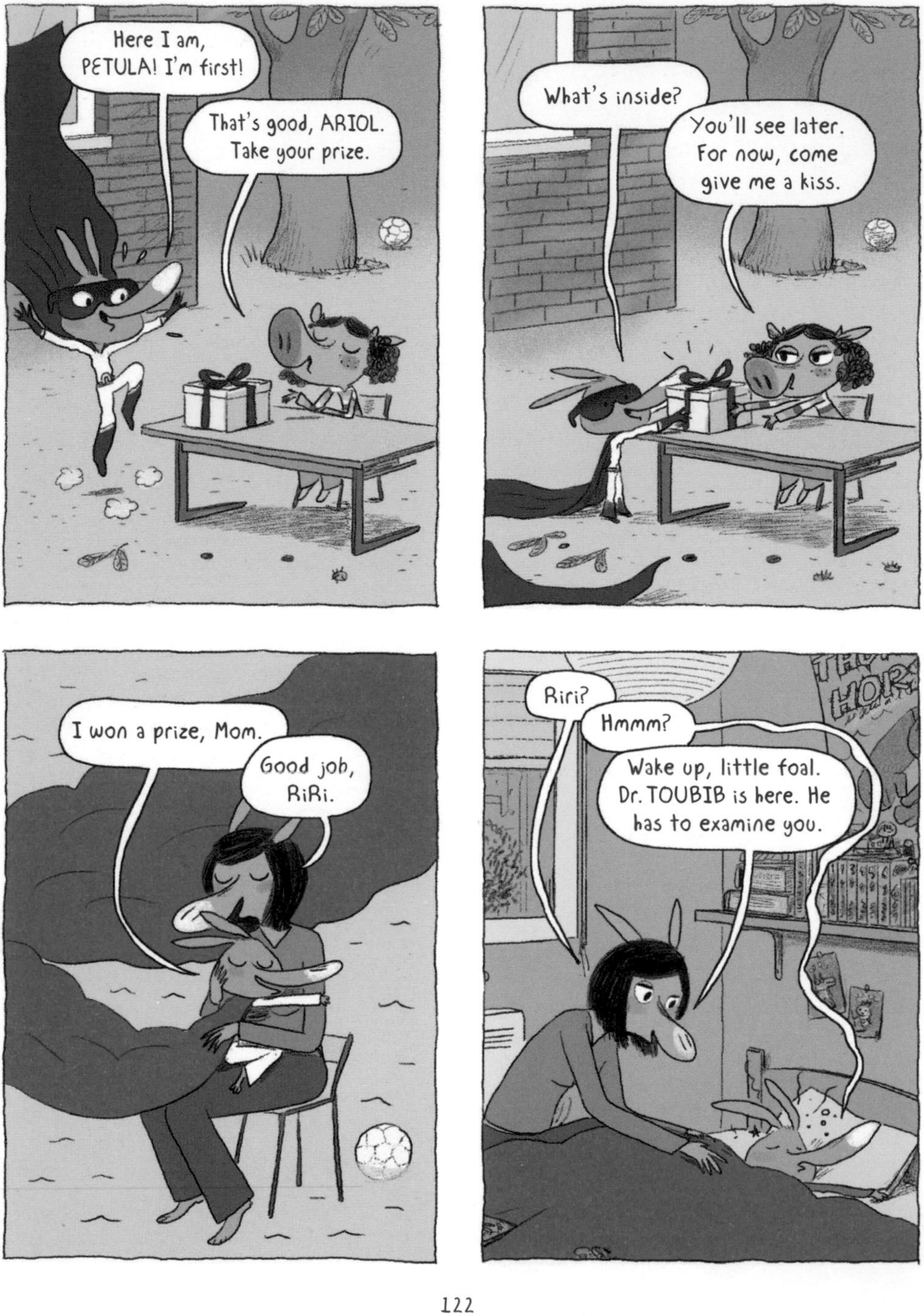
Here I am, PETULA! I'm first!
That's good, ARIOL. Take your prize.
What's inside?
You'll see later. For now, come give me a kiss.
I won a prize, Mom.
Good job, RiRi.
Riri?
Hmmm?
Wake up, little foal. Dr. TOUBIB is here. He has to examine you.

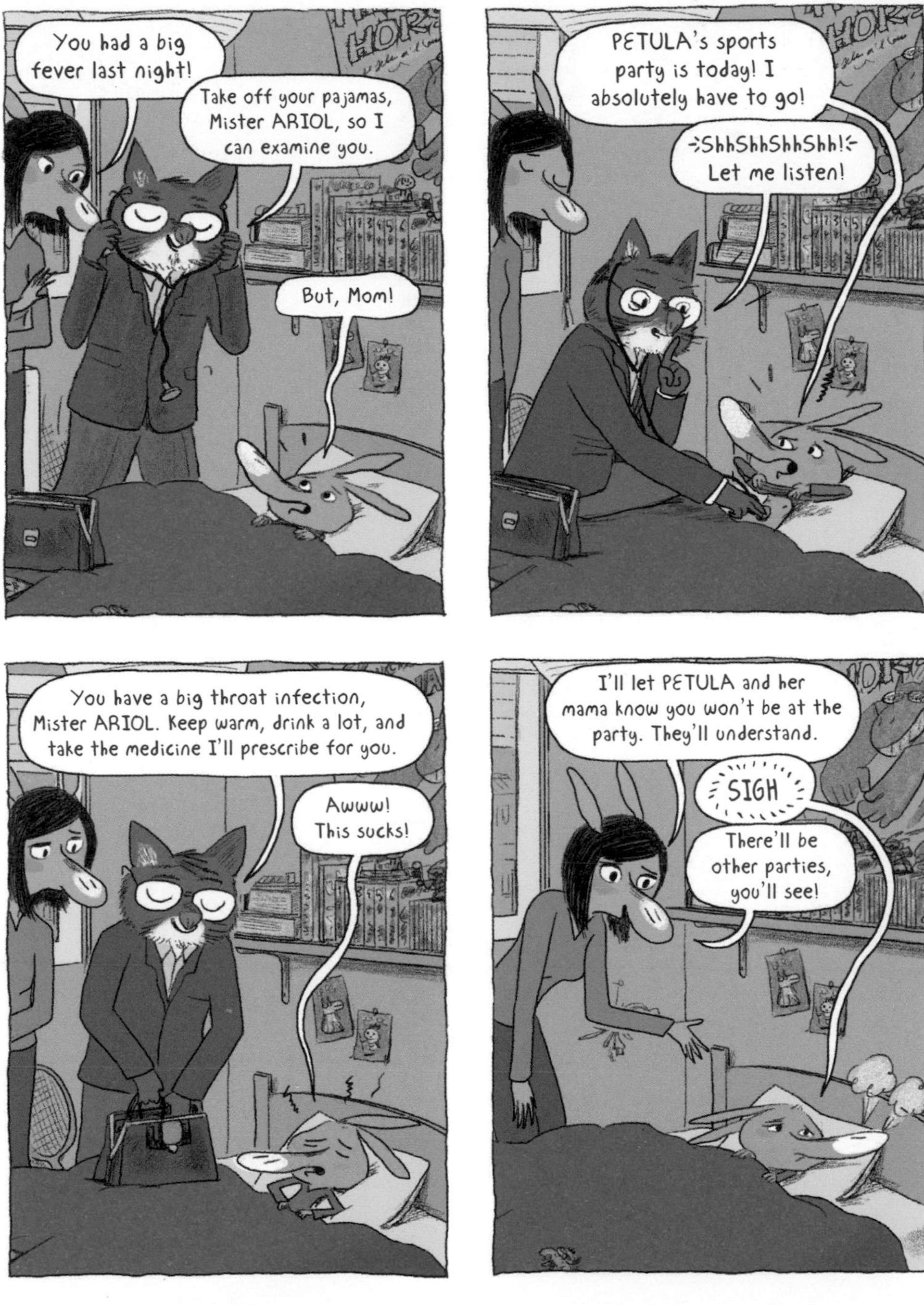
You had a big fever last night!
Take off your pajamas, Mister ARIOL, so I can examine you.
But, Mom!
PETULA's sports party is today! I absolutely have to go!
ShhShhShhShh!
Let me listen!
You have a big throat infection, Mister ARIOL. Keep warm, drink a lot, and take the medicine I'll prescribe for you.
Awww! This sucks!
I'll let PETULA and her mama know you won't be at the party. They'll understand.
SIGH
There'll be other parties, you'll see!

THAT NIGHT...
TOONN-TEENN!
Mrs. CHEWIT and PETULA!
Good evening, Mrs. OATS. We brought a little gift-pack from the party for ARIOL. That way, he won't have missed everything.
There's a piece of a cake, a chocolate Olympic medal, and a little card where Mama told me to write "Get Well Soon."
That's adorable! ARIOL is sleeping for now, because his fever wore him out. But once he wakes up, I'll give him your package, and he'll be very happy!
END

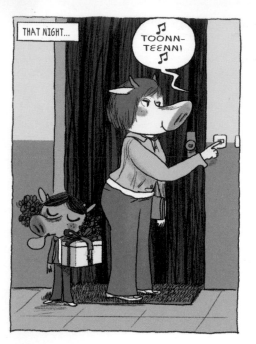

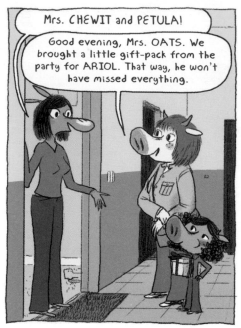

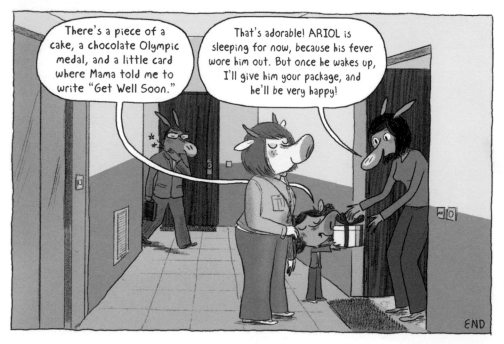

WATCH OUT FOR PAPERCUTZ™

Welcome to the satisfying, slightly sardonic, seventh ARIOL graphic novel, by the lovable team of EMMANUEL GUIBERT and MARC BOUTAVANT, from Papercutz, those constantly squabbling sad sacks dedicated to publishing great graphic novels for all ages. I'm JIM SALICRUP, Editor-in-Chief and nostalgic nabob of positivity. I'm back with some thoughts on this collection's stories and with a fan letter from... an ARIOL fan!

Being a comics editor is the greatest job in the world, if you always wanted to get paid to read comics for a living! Especially working on ARIOL—after all, most of the work has already been done! As you may know, ARIOL is originally created and published in France, and we simply translate and publish the English language edition. I really look forward to each ARIOL graphic novel. They tend to remind me of my own childhood. While skateboards weren't really a thing when I was a kid (yes, I'm that old!), "RAMANO's Skateboard" reminded me of many of my childhood adventures on my bicycle. "Dressed for Winter," evoked thoughts of all the Winter coats I've worn over the years. "Asparagus Jumping" made me remember that my Dad, rather than try to come up with "fun" ways for me to eat my food, was more the "you better eat everything on your plate" kind of dad. "Six-Four-Two" brought back memories of the How-to-Draw books I loved as a child. "RABOUL Passed By," a lovely wistful tale, made me miss my mother. "Mrs. BOURGNE's Money" perfectly captured my own childhood conflicts when finding money. (As an adult, I found an old lady's change purse in a cab, and, yes, I returned it!) "Donkey Salons" brought many barber shop memories crashing back—and yes, I remember wanting one of the STRANGE TALES comics I saw at my barber shop! "Draculiol" brings back my childhood love for the Universal Monsters, and the crippling stage fright I experienced during a fifth grade production of "My Fair Lady" (I was Henry Higgins, but I was too scared to go on stage! Nowadays, you can't get me OFF stage!). "The Majorettes" and "The Grand Finale" (which I was tempted to make the last story in this book) remind me of my dislike of parades (although I was a skating clown in the Macy's Thanksgiving Day parade) and fireworks (I slept through 'em as a baby). And "Petula's Party" and "ARIOL Gets Depressed and Then Things Get Better" take me back to times I've fallen in love and the parties I've missed.

But none of the above should make you think you have to be a dinosaur like me to enjoy ARIOL. Here's a delightful letter we recently received from Nina Cahill that should convince you that ARIOL really is for all ages:

Hello Jim,
I read ARIOL in French here in Paris and now I am reading ARIOL in English which my grandma brought me from NY.
I'm 8 years old.
I think that the translation is very good. My Dad thinks he met you at Marvel Comics when he was my age. You looked at his drawings of Spider-Man. I really love ARIOL!

Thank you,
Nina Cahill

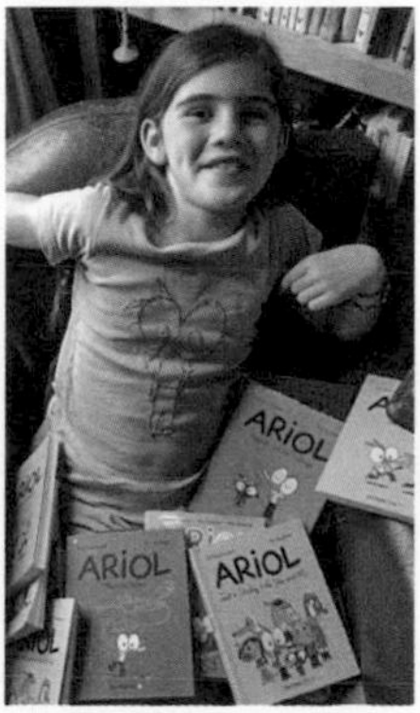
ARiOL
ARiOL
ARiOL

See! I told you I was old! Now the children of the children who used to read the comics I edited years ago are reading the comics I edit now! And I couldn't possibly be happier! Of course, I'm jealous that Nina can read ARIOL in French, while I have to wait for the translations from Joe Johnson! I wish I could speak another language, Nina! Does Smurf count?

Also Nina's grandmother not only brought her the Papercutz editions of ARIOL, she also made her ARIOL pajamas—as you can see in the photo of Nina and her ARIOL collection. Nina, you certainly have a wonderful grandmother, and your dad's pretty cool too! Thanks so much for writing to me—it made my day! I'd love to hear from more ARIOL fans—just send your emails or letters to the addresses listed below.

So until we meet again in ARIOL #8 "The Three Donkeys," don't forget, I'm a donkey just like you!

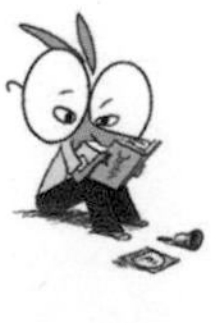

Thanks,
Jim

STAY IN TOUCH!

EMAIL:	salicrup@papercutz.com
WEB:	papercutz.com
TWITTER:	@papercutzgn
FACEBOOK:	PAPERCUTZGRAPHICNOVELS
REGULAR MAIL:	Papercutz, 160 Broadway, Suite 700, East Wing, New York, NY 10038

Other Great Titles From PAPERCUTZ™

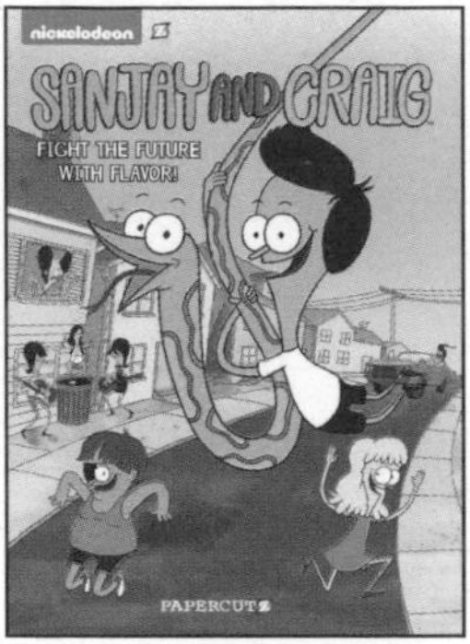
nickelodeon
SANJAY AND CRAIG
FIGHT THE FUTURE WITH FLAVOR!
PAPERCUTZ

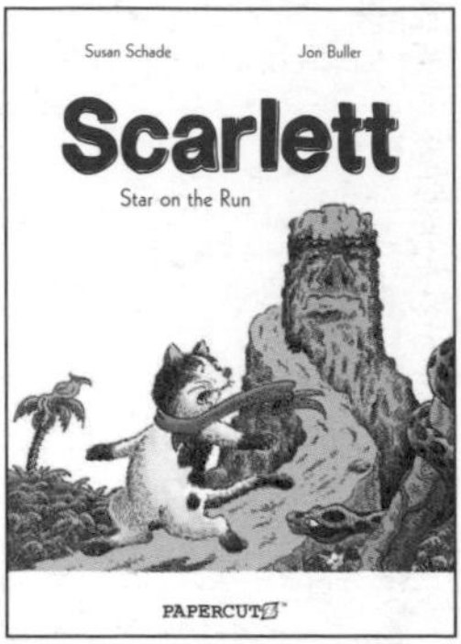
Susan Schade
Jon Buller
Scarlett
Star on the Run
PAPERCUTZ

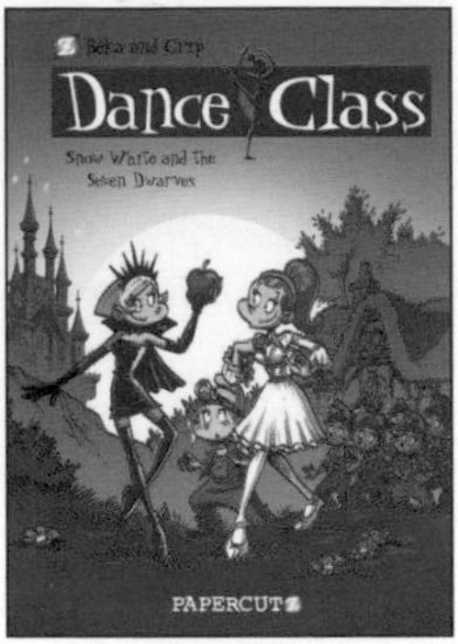
Dance Class
Snow White and the Seven Dwarves
PAPERCUTZ

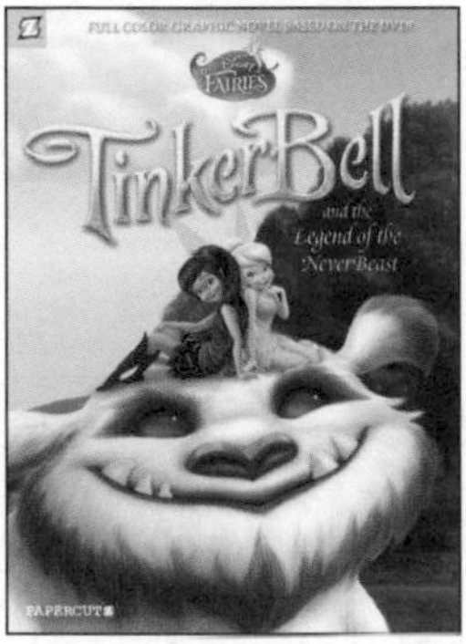
Disney FAIRIES
TinkerBell
and the Legend of the NeverBeast
PAPERCUTZ

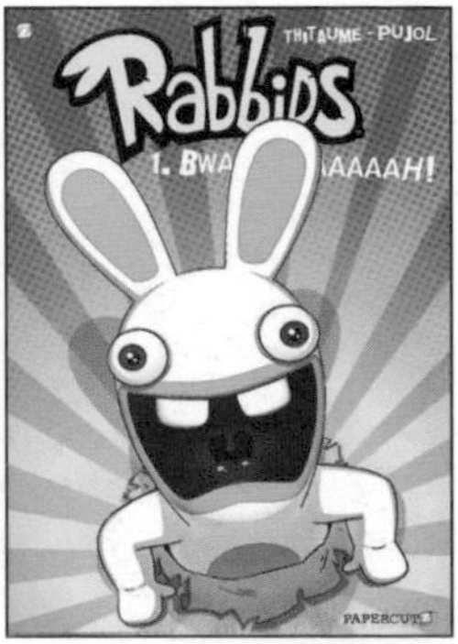
THITAUME - PUJOL
Rabbids
PAPERCUTZ

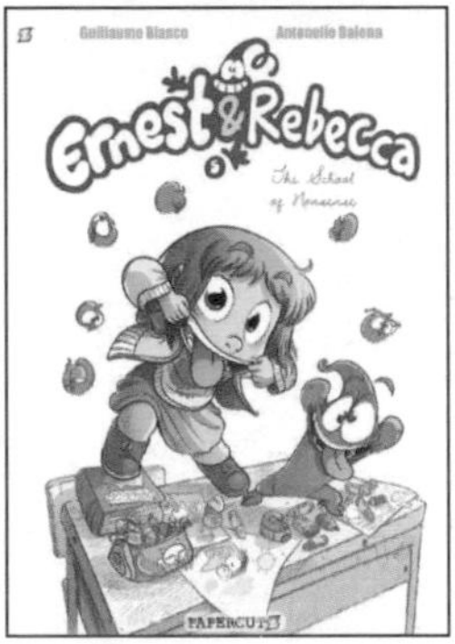
Ernest & Rebecca
PAPERCUTZ

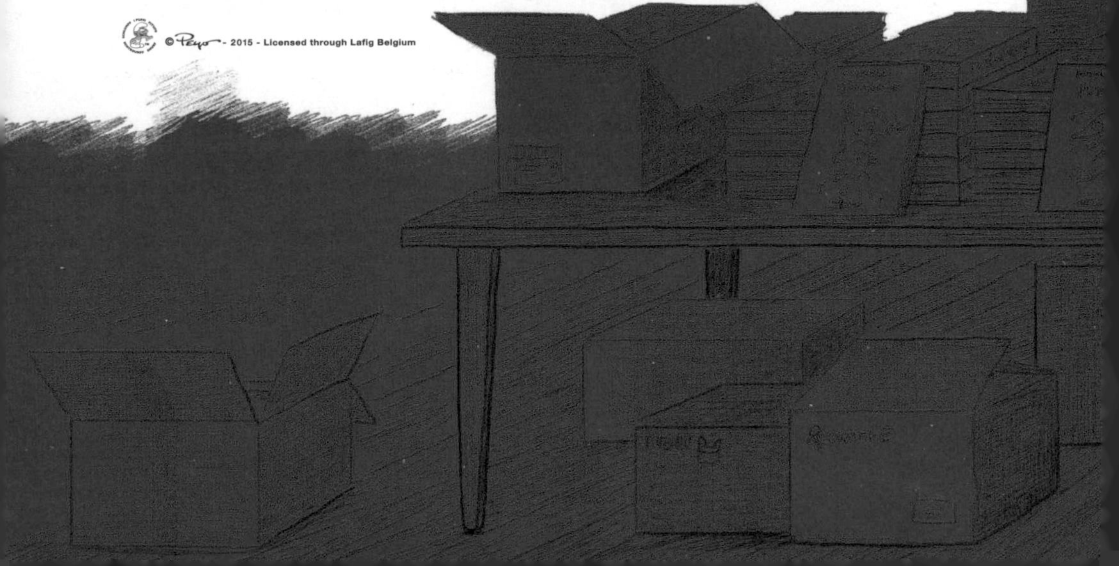

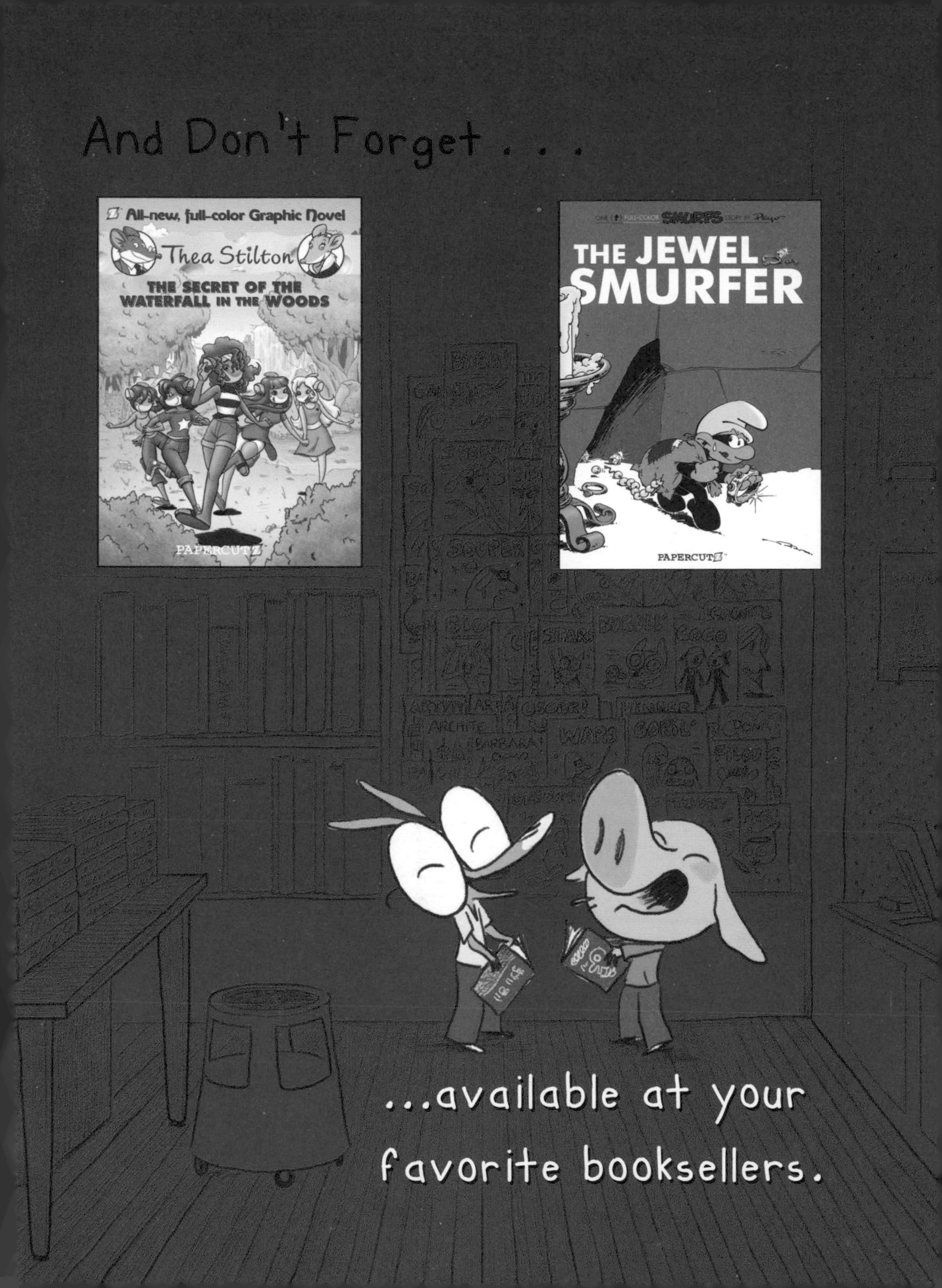
And Don't Forget . . .
All-new, full-color Graphic Novel
Thea Stilton
THE SECRET OF THE WATERFALL IN THE WOODS
PAPERCUTZ
THE JEWEL SMURFER
PAPERCUTZ
...available at your favorite booksellers.

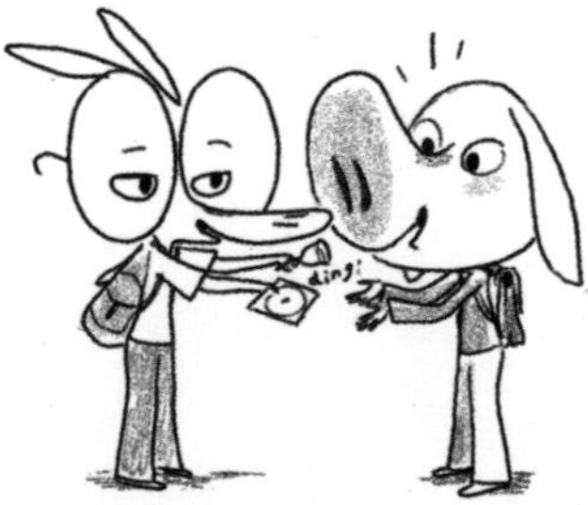
ding!